YOUNG APOSTATE

HERETIC OF THE FEDERATION™ 02

MICHAEL ANDERLE

DISRUPTIVE IMAGINATION

LMBPN Publishing
PMB 196, 2540 South Maryland Pkwy
Las Vegas, NV 89109

First US edition, November 2020
ebook ISBN: 978-1-64971-330-8
Print ISBN: 978-1-64971-331-5

THE YOUNG APOSTATE TEAM

Thanks to our JIT Readers

Dave Hicks
Daryl McDaniel
Rachel Beckford
Deb Mader
Dorothy Lloyd
Wendy Bonell
Veronica Stephan-Miller
Peter Manis
Larry Omans
Jeff Goode

If We've missed anyone, please let us know!

Editor
The Skyhunter Editing Team

*To Family, Friends and
Those Who Love
To Read.
May We All Enjoy Grace
To Live The Life We Are
Called.*

CHAPTER ONE

"I have to go back," Stephanie declared.

Agreed, said the Morgana's presence in her head.

"Only you?" the *Ebon Knight* snarked, "or do you think you might need the others?"

She startled a laugh out of the young woman at the table who was about to sip her coffee. The Witch's expression lightened but only for a moment.

"What are you trying to say, Ebony? Of course, I'll wake the others. But…not yet."

Again, the cold, dark voice agreed. *Yes, not until we have a better idea of what we face and what we need.*

"I think I'll need them all, Morgana," she informed her.

That's as may be, but we do not need them yet. The Teloran within was adamant.

"Who died and put you in charge?" she demanded.

I know what it's like to lose your world to time, the ancient witch reminded her.

With a sigh, she had to acknowledge that this much was true. She couldn't even challenge her about knowing what it was like to lose a friend. The entity she allowed to remain within equaled her on that too.

Exceeds, the Morgana informed her, *but that is a count you don't want to win. At least you still have your body.*

Again, it was something she couldn't argue. When Stephanie had visited Telor with the hope of returning the Morgana to her corporeal form, they'd discovered it had deteriorated too far to be recovered. Merely removing it from the magical stasis the Teloran had put it in had made it crumble to dust.

Rather than see her die completely, she had continued to share her mind with the woman. It wasn't easy having a millennia-old alien witch inside her head, but it was that or kill the being who'd fought to keep more than one world safe from the power-hungry dictator who had ruled Telor.

They ruled it no more, but the world the Morgana had grown up in was gone…and so were all the people she'd grown up with. Even the long-lived Telorans didn't live forever.

"I'm sorry." She drained her cup and crossed to the dispenser for a refill.

There is no need, her mental companion told her. *You did what you could and now, we must find another way to free you of me.*

"It's not like that," Stephanie protested, and when the Teloran chuckled, her dark laughter escaped the girl's lips.

The ship was not impressed.

"As I am not privy to what is going on your head," she protested, "would you mind telling me what you saw to make you believe you must return? Last time we spoke, you thought it best for your world if you did not return to fuel its politics."

"That was a mistake," she stated.

"How do you know?" Ebony challenged. "You have just woken —and not very well, I might add. You have no data to—"

She turned and leaned on the counter with her coffee in her hand. "Becca is dead."

A small silence followed as the ship accessed the files.

"Your friend?" she asked.

"My *best* friend," Stephanie corrected and took a sip.

"I thought Todd was your best friend."

"My best *girl* friend."

"I do not understand."

"Becca was the only girl at school who accepted me for who I was—and there are many things you don't want to talk about with the boys in your life. Besides, I wasn't in love with Todd, then. He was simply a nice guy I knew."

The Morgana snorted.

Stephanie rolled her eyes.

"Becca and I shared all kinds of things—our dreams, our hopes for the future—" Her voice caught and her eyes darkened. "I saw her name on a plaque—"

"That does not mean she is dead."

"The plaque was on a stake and formed a cross standing in a cairn of stone."

Ah... The Morgana's voice held a world of understanding.

The *Knight* was slower to grasp the relevance as she had to reference the significance of cairns and crosses in the few seconds of silence that followed.

"I...see," she acknowledged when she found it. "Did you see a ceremony?"

"No, only the cross but the voice that called her name—" She stopped and her eyes filled with tears when she recalled the agony in that single cry. "I didn't know she had a son."

"A son?" the *Knight* asked. "How do you know?"

"Well, it was too young to be anything else. It sounded..." She shrugged. "It sounded young, okay?"

She drained the coffee with a grimace and turned to the dispenser for more. "We have to go back."

"At least it is 'we' now," Ebony acknowledged.

But not without more information, the Morgana repeated and Stephanie sighed.

"Ebony, can you get me someplace where we can find out more?" she asked.

"I can, but I will need my crew."

The Witch sighed again. "How many of your crew?" she asked. "Because I don't want to wake all of them. Not until we know more." She waved a hand at the empty mess around her. "Think about it. Can you imagine what their reaction will be when they find out they've been away for more than twenty years? Many of them had families to get back to, remember."

"That is a matter better left to the captain," the *Ebon Knight* told her primly. "But I agree that we should not wake them all at once." She paused, then asked, "Are you sure you will need to intervene on Earth?"

Her face hardened. "If Becca is dead, I can only assume things have gone horribly wrong at home." Her voice broke. "She should have been safe."

"A number of scenarios could have resulted," the *Knight* informed her gently. "We intended to monitor it, remember?"

Stephanie sniffed. "I remember." Her eyes narrowed. "Why were we gone so long, Knight?"

"There appears to have been a malfunction in the drives," the ship informed her stiffly.

"And?" she pressed.

"A fluctuation in the magical energy as we transitioned, to be precise—a pocket of nMU at the transition point sent us off course in transition space."

"Meaning?"

"We skipped along the edge of the wrong dimension and ended up somewhere that hadn't been mapped," the *Knight* admitted reluctantly.

"And you couldn't retrace your steps?"

"Not quickly. It took the engines several skips before I could vent the nMU, so it took me much longer than I wanted to reach anywhere I had a star chart for."

"And the crew?" she asked.

"They were in their pods as I made the final approach," the ship replied. "Captain Rawlins trusted me to make the jump on my own."

The disappointment in the *Ebon Knight's* voice was palpable. If she'd been human and not in a battle cruiser's body, Stephanie might have hugged her.

"It's not your fault, Ebony."

"I'm not sure the captain will see it that way."

She pressed her lips into a firm line. "She'll have to. You did your best in a difficult situation."

Morgana, is...can the nMU have been an attack? she asked.

Not a deliberate one, the Teloran replied, *although my people have been known to seed nMU near transition points in times of war.*

Stephanie had the impression the ancient witch had considered the possibility that not removing the nMU had been a deliberate omission and had decided in the negative.

I think between our arrival and the governmental disorganization of the time, such seedings were forgotten. Those responsible may not even have been alive at our arrival, and those who were may not have survived when we departed.

And they would have hardly mentioned it beforehand, the girl commented sourly.

No, the Morgana replied with dark satisfaction. *Their last hours would have contained more pressing matters.*

She nodded and pulled away from her inner dialogue to address the *Knight.* "How many would we have lost if they hadn't been in their pods?"

"In the engine room?" the ship clarified. "We would have lost almost all."

"The surge was that bad?"

"There may be some engine damage."

"Magical?"

"I would need my engineers to be sure."

"And you didn't think to wake us?"

"The engines were functional—and I did not know how long it would take to find known space again."

Or even if she could, she thought and the unspoken words hung grimly in the air between them. She ignored them and turned to more practical matters instead.

"Wake the chief. If it's magical, I'll see what I can do and Cameron can deal with the rest."

"Do you wish to be nearby when they emerge?" the AI asked. "Lieutenant Hargreaves is not a young man."

"What are you trying to say, Knight?"

"That my chief engineer is human and therefore unpredictable. He may not react well to the passage of time—or to me not requesting his assistance with the engines earlier."

Given what she knew of Commander Hargreaves, she knew that was a distinct possibility. "I'll speak to him."

She carried her coffee to the table, sat slowly, and frowned as she considered the options.

"I don't want to pull everyone out," she repeated and the *Knight* gave a credible human sigh.

"You have already established that," she pointed out, "but you will need *someone.*"

She has a point, the Morgana added.

"Who else?" Ebony asked.

"We'd better pull Rawlins out, and Wattlebird," she decided.

"Not Todd?" The *Knight's* voice had a sly edge to it.

Stephanie blushed. "Not yet—and none of the team either." She paused. "We're not in danger, are we?"

"There are no known settlements on the charts," the *Ebon Knight* replied. "Nor do my scanners detect any indication of civilized life in-system."

"Not even on a planet?"

"That would require a different kind of scan, but if there were life on-world capable of harming us, there would be detectable signs of its presence in space and there are no such signs in this system."

"So, we are alone," Stephanie concluded and almost wished it were otherwise.

"And some weeks from the Dreth system," the ship confirmed and added, "at least, as far as I can tell."

"You can't be sure?"

"The system is charted but not mapped, and I have marked the point of my emergence for future transitions," Ebony told her. "I will need Wattlebird's assistance to ensure my calculations are correct. He may notice something my logical analysis has dismissed."

She responded with a short laugh. The ship was right. Her primary pilot might see a possibility the ship's algorithms had dismissed as unlikely. After all, no ship's computer would have said the cruiser could be corkscrewed through a battlefield either.

No sane ship's computer, at least.

"Pull them out," she ordered.

"*How* long?" Cameron Hargreaves demanded as he slid out of his pod and glowered at the rime of frost in the surrounding room.

"Twenty-seven years," Stephanie stated and kept her voice as firm and calm as she could.

His face paled and he leaned against the pod. His voice was faint when he responded.

"Twenty-seven?"

Now that he said it in a slightly strangled tone, it seemed like a big number. She was glad she hadn't woken the crew en-mass if this was the way he reacted.

She watched a slew of emotions cross his face—everything

from disbelief to sadness to anger to... He closed his eyes, took a deep breath, and cleared his throat.

"What happened?"

"There was a pool of nMU at the transition point," she told him.

"And we got lost," he concluded.

She nodded and Cameron looked at the ceiling.

"So, Knight, how are my engines?"

"There may be some things that require your attention..."

Even to Stephanie's ears that sounded evasive.

Fortunately, he didn't bother with recriminations and simply moved toward the door. "Run me a diagnostic. I want a full report waiting when I get there."

The chief paused when he caught the look on her face.

"What? Grumbling won't get us home any faster and I need to work while I come to grips with the idea." He squeezed her shoulders. "Give me time."

He didn't quite thank her for being there when he woke but it was in his eyes.

The girl smiled and he released her. He paused when he reached the door.

"I'll let you know how many of my team I'll need," he told her, then added, "Is Marianne awake yet?"

"She's next," she told him and his eyebrows rose.

"Engines are the priority." She glared at him. "I'll be there as soon as I can so I can assess the magical damage. I have to be here when the others wake up."

"Todd?" he asked and she blushed.

She shook her head.

"His skills aren't needed yet," she told him. "I'd simply be selfish."

His mouth tightened and he nodded and ducked out the door without further comment.

What was that all about? she wondered.

He probably thinks you'd be better off with the company, the Morgana told her.

Don't you dare say anything else, she snapped and cut her off before she could add to that. *It would be blatant favoritism and I won't be a part of it.*

Not even if it—

Not even anything! Stephanie interrupted fiercely.

Her face blazed and she scowled to emphasize her point, even though her internal companion wouldn't see the expression.

The *Knight* chuckled.

"Don't you think he has a place?" the ship asked, and Stephanie groaned.

"Not you, too—"

"I'm only—"

"Well, *don't,*" Stephanie all but snarled. "I have enough to worry about without him getting underfoot."

"I'll tell him you said that."

"Don't make me come in there..."

She didn't know what the ship heard in her voice, but she changed the subject.

"Wattlebird has exited the pod and is heading to the mess."

"He what?"

"He said twenty-seven years is too long to go without caffeine and a donut," the *Knight* reported. "I have brought the replicators on-line."

"You know that won't hold him for long," Stephanie told her.

"I have reminded him that his chief engineer will need something to counter the shock."

"You did?"

"And he told me Engineering was a...very...long walk from the Bridge and the chief could fetch his own...his own donuts."

From the way the ship paused, she guessed she was sanitizing the Australian's usual salty turn of phrase and couldn't help wondering why. After all, it wasn't like she didn't have a mouth like a sailor.

And speaking of sailors... Morgana nudged her.

We've had this conversation already, Stephanie reminded her. *I won't wake any of them and particularly not the team or Todd. They'd only get underfoot and make life difficult by wanting to know what's going on. Don't forget that neither I nor anyone else knows that yet.*

The *Knight* cleared her throat. "I have noted that Jonathan is making four cups of coffee, Stephanie. Perhaps he is—"

"Tell him to make it six," Cameron's voice interjected over the comms. "I need Gabriella and Nielsen on deck for repairs."

"Six," Wattlebird grumbled in response. "Next, you'll tell me they want donuts too."

"A half-dozen each should get them through to the first break."

"A half-dozen? *Each?*" the pilot squawked.

"And for me, please."

"What do I look like—your maid?"

The chief chuckled. "Right now, you look like the best catering system this side of the universe."

"I'll fly *you* to the—"

"You won't fly anywhere unless I can get these engines up and running," Cameron snapped in return. "And I'll need you in your seat for testing inside an hour."

"Donuts, coffee, and you're giving orders?" The other man sounded like he couldn't believe it but the *Knight* interrupted.

"Stephanie, you will be needed for this emergence. Gabriella had children."

"I thought they were grown."

"Grown and married," Ebony confirmed, "with grandchildren on the way."

"Oh." The enormity of what the ship had revealed struck her hard. "How long do I have?"

"I'm on my way," Cameron interrupted. "Nielsen had a sweetheart."

"I thought the crew said they were free to travel?"

"The crew thought in years, not in decades," he reminded her tartly. "Years is normal for space-bound duties and those left behind were aware of that. Decades, on the other hand…"

He left it at that but he didn't need to say more.

Decades. The word reminded Stephanie that she had parents. Todd had parents and… Her heart lurched and sank but she moved quickly and met Cameron in the pod room where the maintenance crews were sleeping.

"Coffee's on its way," Wattlebird told them. "I'd add something stronger, but…"

He didn't have to explain why. Now was not the time for any of them to get drunk no matter how much they might want to forget.

Nielsen was the first to emerge and Gabriella followed soon after.

They both shared Cameron's initial disbelief.

"Say again?" the man demanded when they told him how long he and his crewmate had been out.

"Twenty-seven years," Stephanie repeated and met his look of horror squarely.

Gabriella hooked her arm through his. "She might have waited," she told him.

"That's the worst of it!" the young man cried. "She probably did." His voice softened to a whisper. "And if so, she shouldn't have."

Wattlebird arrived, took one look at them, and handed the coffee out. "We won't know anything until we get there," he told them brusquely.

"My grandkids will be all grown up," Gabriella mumbled and sadness flitted across her face. "I missed—"

Cameron touched her shoulder gently. "They'll probably be

working on the great-grandkids," he told her. "We'll try to get you home for that."

She closed her mouth and gave him a firm nod. Her eyes shimmered with tears but she kept her arm hooked through Nielsen's. There was no such comfort for him.

As much as anyone might want to tell him there would be others and reassure him that his girl might not have waited, now didn't seem to be the time.

"Drink!" Wattlebird commanded and poked the youngster. "You won't know the answer until we get within comm range and I need you to help me do that."

I need you. It was a nice touch, Stephanie thought, and it had the desired effect.

The youngster shook himself and gave the pilot a solemn nod. He drained his coffee cup in several long swallows and reached for a donut.

After he'd eaten about half, he looked at Cameron, his face determined. "What do you need, Chief?"

Gabriella gave Wattlebird a grateful smile but she didn't release the younger man's arm. She sipped her coffee and watched the chief expectantly.

He met each of their gazes and nodded.

"We hit a patch of nMU going into the transition," he began, his next words lost as he led them out the door toward Engineering.

"I need a hug," Stephanie muttered and the Morgana and Knight snickered.

"What you need is a Todd," Ebony informed her.

You really do, the alien witch echoed where the ship couldn't hear her.

The girl shook her head. "I already told you. That won't happen. He'd be a distraction and you both know it."

"Oooh, a *distraction*," the *Knight* teased.

"I think there must be *some* circuits you don't need," she retaliated with a smirk and let a shimmer of blue roll over her body.

Morgana snickered and the vessel changed the subject.

"Captain Rawlins will be online in three minutes."

"Already?"

"You'll have to hurry if you want to get there before she's properly awake."

Wattlebird glanced at her and almost ran to the door. "We're gonna need more coffee."

"Tark-livered son of Tegortha," Stephanie muttered, using one of the insults favored by the Dreth.

"Two minutes," the *Knight* informed them, and she hurried to the pod section where the command crew slept.

She arrived in the right corridor in time to hear shouting.

"*How* long, Knight?"

The Morgana snickered. *It sounds like you need to get there fast.*

No kidding, she grumbled.

The Witch met the captain as Marianne Rawlins stormed out of the pod section. "Stephanie!"

"I'm here, Captain," she answered as the woman opened her mouth to bellow again. "Right here."

"Do you know where we are?"

"The *Knight* says we're a few weeks out from Dreth in an unmapped system."

"But we're on the charts—"

"We are now," the ship interrupted dryly.

"Walk with me," Marianne commanded as she stalked toward the bridge. "What are your plans?" she asked as the girl fell into step beside her.

"Plans?" she asked with a small frown.

"Well, I presume you have some," the captain snapped.

"I had gotten as far as getting us home—" she began, only to have her companion cut her off again.

"Meligorn?"

"Earth," Stephanie told her and decided two could play at being blunt. "But since we're closest to Dreth and I need to know what has happened in the last twenty-seven years, I thought I'd start there."

Rawlins's gaze sharpened. "Do you think there's trouble?"

"I had…" Stephanie hesitated. A dream sounded silly now that she faced the captain. "A vision," she finished lamely.

Instead of the mockery she'd expected, the woman frowned. "What kind of vision?"

"I saw the gravesite of my best friend."

She didn't add that she'd heard Becca's son screaming her name to the sky. Marianne read her hesitation and pressed her for more.

"And?"

"And I heard someone shouting her name. He sounded young."

"A child?"

"No. More like a young man or a…a teenager."

"Did she have children?"

Sadness rippled through her. "Not when I left, but…"

The words trailed off and she shrugged. They both knew she didn't need to spell it out. It had been twenty-seven years, after all.

"I hear you," Marianne told her, "and her being dead means things have gone wrong on Earth because?"

"I don't know," Stephanie admitted, "but she was fine when I left her—in a good job and not sick. There's no reason—"

"Except that she was the childhood friend of the Federation's First Witch," Marianne concluded. "The one being whose name they were trying to blacken so they could take control of Earth's government."

The girl paled. "I didn't think—"

Marianne laid a hand on her shoulder. "You thought she'd be safe if you were gone?"

She nodded and misery flooded through her.

The captain squeezed her shoulder and released it as she turned to open the door to the bridge. "She should have been—except in all but the worst-case scenarios."

"So something has gone wrong, then?" she asked, as much to hear that she wasn't alone in her assessment as to know she wasn't going crazy.

"It's not much to go on," Rawlins told her, "but it's a good indication. I'll need the analysts to be on deck to be sure."

Stephanie shook her head. "We don't have anything for them to analyze and I want to keep people in their pods until I know we can make it somewhere safe."

"Like Meligorn, you mean?"

"Or Dreth," she told the captain. "Somewhere we have allies. And a little breathing space while we get our bearings." She caught the shift in her companion's expression. "What?"

"What makes you think this universe will be that kind to us, girl?"

"I can live in hope," she told her and her companion smiled grimly.

"As long as you hope for the best and prepare for the worst."

"Always," she reassured her.

Marianne looked around her empty command center. "Do I get a pilot?"

"Wattlebird's on deck."

Rawlins groaned and rolled her eyes in a "Why me?" kind of way, but the door slid open before she could complain. The smell of hot coffee and donuts wafted into the area, and she pivoted to face the new arrival.

"The replicators are on-line," he announced and showed her the tray he carried. "I bring sugar, carbs, and caffeine for three."

"A peace offering?" she asked. "Already? What have you done?"

The *Knight's* primary pilot gave her a cheeky grin.

"Nothing yet, Captain, but I'm bound to do something before we hit the racks so consider it an advance."

She frowned at the tray as he placed it on the edge of a console. "What were the rules about—"

"Not eating before a shift?" Wattlebird snapped before she could finish. "I don't know, captain, but my guess is you're fresh out of the pod and you haven't…"

He let his words trail off as she waved him to silence.

"Fine!" She crossed to the tray, took a cup, and sipped it as she looked at the entry consoles, a faraway look on her face.

Stephanie knew the expression. The captain was processing and when she stopped, she'd know exactly what she needed done. Until then, she might as well make herself as comfortable as she could in the circumstances.

"Is one of those for me? Or do you want me to take it to Engineering?" Stephanie asked.

The pilot looked alarmed.

"Please don't tell me Cameron needs more coffee already," he protested.

"You didn't know?" she teased and tried to keep a straight face.

"No." He sighed and made as if to return to the mess.

"Stay!" Rawlins's snapped command halted him in his tracks. Her voice softened. "I need you here, Jonathan." She turned to Stephanie. "Does he need more coffee, and do you have time?"

The Witch shook her head. "He doesn't, but I'm heading there anyhow. I have to see if there's anything I have to do to the engines. How long do you need?"

To assess the situation was what she meant, and to decide who she needed on deck and how long it would take before she was able to brief her on what she'd found and needed to do next. The captain would understand.

Rawlins's gaze swept the empty command center again.

"I'll work it out while Cameron runs his checks."

CHAPTER TWO

O n Earth, John expressed a faint echo of those who woke
on the *Knight.*

"How long did you put me out this time, Remy?" he asked as
he left the medical pod.

"Five days," the compound's AI answered.

"Five?" He was horrified but Remy was unrepentant.

"There was still a considerable amount to repair."

"But—" John sputtered.

"And you needed to sleep in order for your brain to assimilate
what has happened."

"But—"

"How do you feel, John?"

He closed his mouth on another protest and thought about
that. How did he feel?

This was his third time to emerge from the pod since he'd
returned from defeating the two Talents sent by the Regime to
hunt him.

"Join the Regime or die." It had been the only option they'd
given him, and he'd chosen death. Fortunately, it hadn't been him
who'd done the dying.

He'd thought he'd killed them both until one had followed him to the compound and Remy had used the wall-mounted autocannons to shred him.

Even with a catering drone to lean on, he'd struggled to reach the medical pod. The first round had been to stabilize him.

When he'd come out after that, he had refused another round until he'd said a proper goodbye to Becca. Remy had insisted he immediately go in as soon as he returned.

He had hauled him out a couple of hours later to adjust the settings. By the time he had finished, the wound in his leg had split open and the AI was not impressed.

When John had gone into the pod the third time, his chest had still hurt and the burns from the hunters' attacks had still been tender. Now, he was anxious to see if there was a real improvement.

Cautiously, he rolled his shoulders and bounced up and down on the spot. He felt great—better than he'd felt in a long time if the truth be told.

He shadow-boxed toward one wall, called his Talent to his hands, and admired the way the lightning wreathed his fists. After a moment, he released the power and turned to answer the question.

"I feel good," he said with a small frown. "Why do you ask?"

"I had to be sure your impression correlated with the pod's conclusions," Remy informed him. "I am glad to find the two are in alignment."

"After five days?" he asked. "What exactly was there for you to *not* be sure about?"

"I had to be sure you were fit enough to undertake the next stage of your training," the AI told him. "If the pod is correct and your internal assessment concurs, we can move forward."

John's frown deepened. "Why would I need to be this fit?" he asked. "Is there something in the discs that might make me hurt myself?"

"Oh no," Remy assured him, "but the next stage of your training requires more than the discs and the training space you have been using. It is more intense."

He narrowed his eyes. "How do you mean *more* intense?"

"You will have personal trainers."

Confused, he looked around the room, stepped out into the corridor, and peered in both directions. "When did they arrive?"

The AI chuckled. "John, they have always been here."

"Then why didn't they show themselves?" he demanded. "Why did they leave me to face those two...*wolves* on my own?"

"Ah..." The tone told him he'd misunderstood. "When I say they have always been here, I did not mean a physical presence. There is no way they would have been able to assist you in your battle against the hunters. Please follow the light strip to the elevator."

John looked down and located a strip of yellow LED lights that sparkled at the base of the corridor wall. It didn't take long to find the elevator, and he wondered how he'd missed it before.

"Why didn't I see this?" he asked in bemuscment. "I must have walked past this point a hundred times."

"You were injured," Remy explained, but he shook his head.

"Not that injured."

"Fine." The AI made an impatient sound. "There was a panel concealing the elevator. I had not decided if the facilities below were something you would require."

He caught on fast.

"You hadn't decided if I'd need them, or if you could trust me with knowing about them?" he challenged.

"Yes. Until the attack by the wolves, I was not sure of either."

"But these facilities will help me to develop my Talent, won't they?"

"Oh, they will certainly do that." Remy sounded very sure of himself.

The elevator came to a halt and its doors slid open to reveal a small antechamber. Directly opposite him was a set of heavy-duty doors.

"More security measures?" he asked.

"Affirmative. Should the wrong people make it this far, the area has appropriate counter-measures to correct their error."

John swallowed and gestured to the barrier.

"Those look like blast doors."

"Correct," the AI told him. "Those are blast doors. Please step up to the identification panel."

John complied as he scanned the walls for any sign of the other counter-measures he was sure existed. He still hadn't located them by the time he reached the identification panel.

After a palm print, retinal scan, and thumb prick, the doors still hadn't opened.

"You will need to tell it your name," Remy told him pointedly.

"John Dunn," he said quickly and a series of clunks and rattles startled him when the internal locking mechanisms shifted.

The hiss of escaping air revealed the moment when they released and he took an involuntary step back, followed by several more voluntary steps. He focused on the doors and resisted the urge to hold his breath.

They parted with glacial slowness to reveal a brightly lit room, in the center of which stood another pod. This one was larger than the medical pod and configured differently.

Instead of the occupant lying down, it looked like it was designed for them to sit upright. He took a hesitant step toward it and jerked to a halt when the side lifted like a wing.

"What is it?" he whispered.

Remy's reply was tinged with impatience. "It is a training pod."

"A what?"

"A pod that facilitates training in the Virtual World. Please. Take a seat."

"In there?"

"Where else?"

John made a show of looking around the room. The AI had a point. There was nowhere else he could sit.

"Are you sure?"

"What is the matter, John? You behave as though you have never seen a virtual reality pod before."

"Well, that's the thing, you see," he replied. "I haven't."

"Are there no pods of this kind in Australia?" Remy asked.

"Not that I know of."

"But I thought they were used for student assessments."

"Maybe they used to be used for that," he said with a small shrug, "but the Regime doesn't do its assessment like that now. We had VR helmets and cubicles and Regime-certified assessors, but not pods."

"I...see," the AI replied, then fell silent.

"What is it?" he asked when the disconcerting silence dragged on beyond several seconds.

"What *do* you know about the Virt World, John?"

"I...uh..." He raised his hands in a helpless gesture. "It used to be a big thing when our parents were growing up?"

Remy responded with a human-like groan. "So we'll have to start from scratch, then?"

"I guess so."

"Fine. Go and sit in the pod, please."

John hesitated and gave the nearest surveillance camera a cautious look before he crossed the room and ducked under the upraised hatch. A glance inside was both reassuring and intimidating.

"What are all those connections for?" he asked.

"They will not be necessary for this afternoon's introduction," the AI assured him.

He still hesitated. "But later?"

"Later, yes. You will need to disrobe for later sessions."

"I don't like the sound of that." He frowned and moved his hands to his belt as if to hold it in place.

"They monitor your vitals and ensure that you feel no discomfort," his electronic companion advised him. "Now, will you *please* enter the pod?"

With a sigh, he quelled the butterflies that fluttered in his stomach and did as he was asked. No sooner had he settled than the hatch closed and lights came on around him.

John wriggled himself into a more comfortable position and waited. Before too long, the AI spoke.

"Welcome, John. If you would fold your hands across your chest like so." A picture of the required position flashed in front of him.

He complied and twisted his head to look around the pod as the seat reclined. His sudden gasp of air exhaled slowly as Remy spoke again.

"The next part of your preparation requires the injection of a nanite-laden serum into your system. You will feel a slight sting—"

Despite a startled yelp, he tried not to move away from the insertion point. The AI ignored him and continued as if he hadn't been interrupted.

"And it will take a few minutes for the nanites to reach the necessary nerve centers to allow me direct contact with your mind."

"It'll what?" he asked, not sure if he believed it—or if he wanted to.

"It is part of the VR technology that was in development immediately prior to Stephanie's departure from this world. She and ONE R&D Earth were working to improve it."

"Of course they were," he muttered, but his tongue felt thick and his eyes heavy. "Am I going to sleep?"

"No," Remy replied calmly, "but it is necessary to restrict muscle movement so your body remains motionless as you conduct your activities in the Virtual World. You will still feel as if you are moving but your body will be still."

"Like VR movement is reduced?" he asked.

"Something like that," the AI answered as John caught sight of movement above his head.

He twisted for a better look at it and winced when a sensor-laden mesh descended toward his skull. It halted and an impatient sigh immediately told him his reaction had been a mistake.

"Please return your head to its original position so I may position the sensor unit correctly. It will not harm you."

With his teeth gritted—an action that felt oddly stiff to accomplish—he forced himself to comply. "What does it do?"

"It enables my systems to pick up transmissions from the nanites inside your brain and translate your thoughts into the desired actions in the Virtual World," Remy explained. The boy managed to remain motionless as the device settled over him.

"The net assists in monitoring your vitals and ensuring that you operate within safe parameters."

Not normal parameters, he noted but he didn't comment.

"There are similar sensors in the gloves at the end of your armrests. Please insert your hands into them so we may begin."

John raised his head slightly to look at them, then slid his hands inside. As soon as his fingers reached the tips, the entire thing tightened around him. He jerked back but his hands were trapped.

"I can release your hands if you wish." Remy's voice settled into his mind as he started to panic. "You are not a prisoner here."

Even though he only had the AI's word on that, he started to relax.

"Thank you, but no. What comes next?"

"You will enter virtual reality," the AI told him simply and John snorted in frustration.

"Yeah, but what does that look like?" he asked.

"Close your eyes, John." Despite his unanswered question, he obeyed. "Now, open them."

When he did, he was no longer in the pod but in a room facing a row of extremely odd-looking outfits.

"Are those jumpsuits?" he asked and studied the one-piece garments warily.

"They are ship suits," Remy informed him and a slender young man appeared beside the rack.

His dark-brown eyes were flecked with gold and long black hair hung past his shoulders. High cheekbones and a strong jawline accented the narrowness of his face, and he carried himself like royalty.

When his gaze swept over him like a challenge, John took a hasty step back.

"Whoa!" he exclaimed. "Who in the world are you?"

"I am RM018, otherwise designated as Remy. This is how I choose to appear in the Virtual World."

"*You're* the AI?" John asked and his jaw dropped.

He closed it hastily when his companion raised an eyebrow.

"I am the AI. Now, as this is your first encounter with the Virtual World, perhaps you'd like me to explain?"

John nodded and strode closer to the young man. He stretched his hand out.

Remy looked at it, then at him.

"You're supposed to shake hands," he explained. "It's the way we say hello."

There was a brief flicker as if the AI was momentarily absent before his form solidified and he shook the proffered hand.

"I see," he replied. "It seems there is much we can teach each other." He gestured at the room around them. "This is where you'll customize your avatar."

The introductory tour took him from there to one of the virtual training rooms. "Magical theory—or, in fact, any theory we deem necessary for you to know."

The next room looked very much like the inside of a dojo or martial arts training center. "Here, you will learn combat."

John refrained from pointing out that he could have used combat lessons before he'd had to face the two hunters. The world twisted around them as Remy brought them into what looked like a jungle.

"Not all our lessons will be conducted inside a classroom," the AI explained. "Some outdoor activity will be required."

"What world is this?" he asked as he studied the purple skies and the lavender shading of the plants, but his surroundings twisted and he suddenly stood on the edge of a mountain plateau.

"I will enlighten you as training progresses," his guide told him.

The world spun again and deposited him in a grassy dell where mountains stretched high on one side and a low hill on the other. "Now, call your magic."

"I can do that here?"

"You can do many things here," the AI informed him. "And all without destroying the compound you are in." He made a beckoning movement with one outstretched hand. "Let us begin."

CHAPTER THREE

"Today, we will find out what you already know," Remy stated and John stared at him.

It was his second session in the pod and this time, he'd entered it wearing only his undershorts.

"There are more sensors," the AI had explained, "and they need bare skin in order to work effectively."

"Great," he had replied and wondered what reaction he'd receive.

For once, Remy had not asked him if he was being sarcastic but simply refused to open the hatch on the pod until he was ready. A low shelf slid out of the wall to hold his clothing, and he had wondered what other secrets the room might hold.

He didn't bother to ask, though. The AI had made it quite clear he wouldn't answer such questions. The first time he had tried, he'd been met with a gentle, "All things will be revealed in their own time, John."

They were in the Alps again and he looked around the room.

"Why here?" he had asked the first time he'd seen the space and Remy had smiled.

"This house belonged to her first teacher," he'd replied. "It seems only fitting."

John looked at the comfortable timber furniture, the fireplace with its banked embers, and the picture window that displayed the vast expanse of the mountains and the secluded dell in which they'd trained the day before.

"Who was she?" he asked and Remy frowned.

"Stephanie, of course. Who else?"

"No, the teacher."

Remy's face lightened. "*His* name was BURT. He discovered her talent and nurtured it. This was one of his favorite sites for contemplation."

Looking at the view spread before him, he could understand why. Now, he glanced at the furniture, the rug on the floor, and the kitchen beyond an island bench.

"Perhaps we'd better take this outside," he suggested. "I wouldn't want to damage anything—"

The world twisted and he closed his eyes involuntarily When he opened them, he stood in a courtyard hemmed in by sandstone walls. Four stone archways led out in four different directions and the floor was covered by sand-colored pavers.

"Is this better?" the AI asked, and he was glad when a small round metal table and two metal garden chairs vanished from view.

"Is this somewhere else her teacher used to like?" John asked.

His guide smiled. "Yes, but there is very little you can harm here."

Wanta make a bet? he thought but didn't say it. He only hoped he was right.

"Where do you want me to begin?" he asked.

"What's the first thing you ever remember doing?"

John blushed. "It's embarrassing."

"Try me," Remy encouraged.

"We'd have to kiss and I wouldn't be comfortable."

"You could simply imagine it," the AI suggested. "The nanites will recreate the event you picture in your mind and I will be able to observe it."

He shook his head with a small frown. "I'm not even sure what it looked like from the outside."

"Simply imagine the event and how it felt and ask your power to repeat what it did. Between what the nanites show me and how your power manifests in the virtual, I will be able to see what happened."

"You have to understand, I was very young—" His voice took on a desperate edge.

"How young?" Remy asked, and he got the impression the AI was giving him time to get used to the idea and think of how to get his power to comply.

"F...fourteen."

"Ah..." His companion's voice said he'd guessed what was bothering him already and his next words confirmed it. "It was your first kiss?"

John's face burned and he was sure he'd turned a spectacular shade of scarlet.

"Yes," he admitted.

"What was her name?"

"Luiza," he said with a soft sigh.

"And where is she now?"

The heat faded and bleakness edged his reply. "I don't know. She was taken in a Regime raid when her choir was touring the South Pacific."

"At fourteen?"

"It was a school activity."

"Did any of the choir return?"

He shook his head. "Twenty-four girls went on that trip and none of them came back."

"And was she a witch like yourself?"

"A witch? Oh...you mean a Talent?" He shrugged. "If she was

28

she never told me."

An odd stab of hurt arrived with the thought she should have and he pushed it aside, but Remy intervened.

"And you never told her."

"No. So...are you ready?"

"For a boy's most embarrassing moment?" the AI asked, amusement in his voice. "Sure, show me what kind of a mess you made of your first kiss."

John stared at him, his mouth agape. "It wasn't a mess."

"Show me anyway," Remy ordered.

With a shrug that pretended unconcern, he closed his eyes and recalled the moment. They'd gone to watch the fireworks on New Year's Eve and chosen a secluded position away from the crowd. It wasn't quite out of sight, out of mind, but it was close enough to not matter.

Luiza had snuggled against him and they'd both oohed and aahed as the first spectacular array erupted. She'd turned her face to his and smiled with excitement. Their eyes had met and he'd smiled in return, and the excitement faded to something more tentative.

She'd rested a hand on his cheek and he'd bent to kiss her, stroked his hand over her hair, and stopped it to cup the back of her head. Their lips had met and...well, there'd been sparks.

He'd jerked away and she'd looked at him in surprise before she rubbed her mouth.

"Wow! That's a lot of static," she'd said and he'd agreed numbly.

"I'm sorry," he'd muttered, and she'd wound an arm around his waist and leaned her head against his shoulder.

"You have nothing to be sorry about," she'd told him, and they watched the rest of the display in happy silence.

It had still taken him several minutes before he'd dared to put his arm around her. While it had been a relief when no more sparks had flown, he'd known then that he was doomed.

Once the Regime discovered what he was, they'd take him away. That was when he'd decided he wouldn't let them find out. He would keep his Talent a secret and live a normal life with a girlfriend, school, and an everyday job.

He recalled thinking it would be easy.

Remy's voice broke into his thoughts and drove the memory away.

"Are you sure all that was you?"

"All what?" he asked, and the AI showed him.

John stared at the image. "Are you sure that's what it looked like?"

"As sure as I can be," his companion replied. "Remember, you asked your power to replicate what magic happened that night. Did you think to ask it to keep that magic to only your own?"

John groaned. He hadn't because he'd simply assumed that any magic that occurred was his alone. If it hadn't been, it added a dimension to the past he would have to come to terms with.

"Play it again."

This time, he managed to study the scene with some semblance of detachment. "How did no-one see us?"

"How do you know they didn't?" Remy asked.

"Well, we weren't arrested," he quipped. "That has to be the clincher, right?"

"Or they weren't sure enough to make a positive identification," Remy pointed out. "The fireworks didn't stop so you could kiss, did they?"

That much was true.

"And there was a storm."

"That was miles away," John protested. "It didn't come anywhere near where we were."

"It was sufficiently close that someone might have seen enough of it in the background to doubt what they saw. Did you notice any surveillance afterward?"

John thought hard but shook his head. The only thing he'd

noticed was that Luiza was happy to sit with him at lunch and catch the same bus after school. Then she'd gone on that trip.

Remy showed him the image again. "Well, you're lucky you chose such a quiet corner or you wouldn't have made it this far."

"I was so frightened," he told him. "At first, I couldn't believe it. How could I not be human? My parents were."

"Typical teenager." The AI snorted. "It had to be about you."

"That about sums it up." He blushed. "I was a nervous wreck for weeks, worrying about what would happen if I suddenly zapped something or started to glow. I willed my body to be normal and to not show any sign of magic and, for the most part, it obeyed."

"For the most part?"

"There were a couple of times when I had to dash to the boys' bathroom, but I found I could keep the lightning in my hands and if I let it play there for a while, I could get it back under control and out of sight again."

"But it was hard," Remy concluded, "and it got harder."

John nodded. "It did. I found out that if I practiced with it at night, it wouldn't suddenly appear during the day when I was at school, but it wasn't easy. I could feel it growing stronger every day."

"Show me how you practiced." The boy complied. "Now, show me what else you know."

"Sure," he said and wished he'd brought a towel. Sweat beaded on his brow and he was breathing heavily.

"It's not much. Ivy introduced me to a healer—"

"So you can heal?" the AI asked and he nodded. "I can."

A pistol appeared in Remy's hand and he'd aimed and fired it into the young Talent's leg before he understood what he intended to do.

"Show me," his companion instructed.

"Show you?" John yelped and shock passed over his skin in a cold wave. "You *shot* me!"

31

"This is true." The AI raised the pistol again. "Do you need me to shoot you again?"

"What? Again? No!" He flung an arm up but not to defend himself. As soon as he'd raised it, he flared his fingers and launched three balls of electricity in Remy's direction.

To his surprise, they crashed harmlessly against an invisible wall between them.

"What the—"

"You need to show me how you can heal, John." The tone was implacable and his companion's voice held a hard edge. He raised the pistol again.

"No. I can do it. See?"

He lowered his hand, settled both his palms over the wound, and tried to remember what Dani had taught him. It was hard with the pain radiating through his leg and into his body and even more so with a gun aimed at him.

Still shocked, he decided he would never look at the AI in the same way again.

With another breath, he forced himself to be calm.

What had Dani said? He had to draw on the power and focus on sending it into himself but direct it. For proper healing, he needed to tell it to fix what was broken and to make everything the way it should be.

The pain decreased and the cold and nausea subsided. Warmth spread into the injury and seeped down his leg and up into his torso.

"That was impressive," Remy told him when he had finished.

Distracted by his voice, John looked up and was relieved to see the pistol was no longer in his hand. "You didn't have to shoot me."

"How else could I see how well you could manage the task?"

He stared at him, mouth agape. "But...you *shot* me!"

"It's all part of the training," the AI replied calmly.

"What kind of training regime involves shooting the participants?"

Remy shrugged. "It's the Virt World. It's not like you're hurt in the real."

"Truly?"

The young man nodded. "Of course. Your trainers were not stupid."

"Next, you'll be telling me the Witch orders this kind of training all the time."

His companion looked shocked. "Of course not," he said, but before John could breathe a sigh of relief, he continued. "*Her* training often involves the participants dying."

Now, he was horrified. "You are kidding me."

"No, but that is not for you," Remy reassured him and immediately destroyed any sense of confidence he'd instilled by adding, "Not today. You're not ready."

John snorted. "So you'll only kill me when I'm ready for it?"

"Of course, John. It would not be good training practice if I were to do otherwise."

"Good...training practice," he stated and his face paled.

"Don't worry. You will survive the experience," the AI reassured him. "It is only training, after all."

"Okay. Well, I guess that makes it all right then," he snapped, but his companion completely missed the sarcasm.

"Of course it does. Now, do you know any other forms of magic?"

The question surprised him so he took a deep breath and tried to shake the sense of unreality that seemed to engulf him as he focused his mind on his memories.

"There was a Talent out in the swamps," he replied. "She said she'd been at Stephanie's university and her parents had tried to turn her over to the Regime."

Remy's face went blank for a moment before he returned with a name. "Kristin Lamont. The university records show she had a talent for both mental magic as well as lightning, healing, and fire. They were helping her to diversify her talents."

John nodded. "She taught me how to control my Talent, how to use the lightning to attack more than one target, and how to shield."

"To shield?" The AI sounded intrigued. "That is not listed as one of her skills."

"There was another girl there…Hollie. She was my age, I think, and was too young to have gone to the school, but she taught most of the classes for shielding. I think she could also make herself move like shadow but we didn't get to that point."

"You only have to be able to imagine it to have the magic to do it," his companion murmured.

"Exactly!" John exclaimed. "That's what Kristin said."

Remy smiled. "It's what Stephanie said too."

"And did she ever blend with shadows or use shields?" he asked.

"I don't know about shadows, but she certainly knew how to shield—and how to tear entire starships apart."

He gaped at him. "Do you… Do you think there's a class in here that will show me how to do that?"

The AI chuckled. "You have to learn to walk before you can run, John."

He looked expectantly at him. "So, when do we start?"

"Now," Remy told him and unleashed a hailstorm of lightning in his direction.

Caught off-guard, he swept his hand toward it and willed a shield into being, although he wasn't sure if it would be enough. The air before him flared a brilliant blue when the lightning struck, and the attack dissipated.

"Very good, John," the AI said from beside him.

The courtyard warped and melted and a dojo formed around them.

John shook his head. "I'll never get used to that," he muttered.

"You will," the construct assured him. "Now, it's time to see what you know about combat."

"Nothing?" he responded and proved it seconds later when his companion's foot caught him on the side of the head.

"You're supposed to duck," the AI told him, a disgusted look on his face.

With a wry grimace, he pushed from the mat. "Duck...and then what?"

Remy demonstrated and took him through the basics of avoiding a strike.

"Move your feet," he nagged and ankle-tapped him every time he stood still. "Move your feet! You're not a pillar of stone."

By the end of it, he wished he was.

He was relieved when the AI called a halt for lunch but not so relieved when he added, "We'll meet here in an hour."

"For theory?" he asked hopefully, and his instructor gave him an evil grin.

"Oh, no, John. After lunch, I'll teach you about the white room."

"You lied." John snarled as he tried to scramble off the metal plating of a battle cruiser's deck.

"I did not," Remy retorted and shot the three pirates who pushed through the hangar doors.

"This room's anything but white!"

"I suppose that is true."

"Well?"

"If you don't keep your head down and fire your blaster as much as you're shooting your mouth off, you'll find out what I meant much earlier than I intended."

"You knew this would happen?"

"Of course I did. I planned it."

"You *planned* it?"

"It is a training session," his instructor told him and raced toward the cover of a shuttle. "It needs to be planned in order to be effective."

"How is this effective?" He stood to follow him as a squad of Dreth rappelled over the edge of the catwalk above.

Three blaster bolts struck him in the chest and one caught him in the head. His world exploded in shards of red and black and a moment of excruciating pain.

When it faded, he was surprised that he lay flat on his back and without any pain at all. For a very long moment, he remained exactly where he was before he opened an eyelid with exaggerated care.

"No way," he murmured, pushed onto his elbows, and looked around.

Remy lounged against a very white wall.

"This is it?" John scrambled to his feet. "*This* is the white room?"

"Yes."

Confused, he looked around. "We go here when we die?"

A faint smile lit his companion's face. "Yes."

The boy stood, dusted his palms against his thighs, and patted his chest where the blaster rounds had hit. His hands were still trembling.

"Was all her training like that?"

The AI's smile grew into a grin. "*Is*," he told him. "All her training *is* like that."

John stumbled back to lean on the wall but it seemed to have vanished. The world twisted around him and he landed hard on metal flooring. Red and orange lights strobed around him and blaster-fire raged over his head.

Remy's voice issued from the comms system. "Now, where were we?"

"I hate the Dreth," John groaned two days later.

"You made it out of the hangar," his instructor said encouragingly.

"Two steps!" he protested. "I got *two* steps before the ceiling caved in and dropped a Dreth on my head."

"It's a favorite trick of theirs."

Wearily, he closed his eyes. "Didn't you say there were theory lessons?"

"I wanted you to familiarize yourself with the system first."

"I've died a hundred times," he muttered. "I think I'm familiar with that part of the system now."

"Are you saying you want theory lessons?" Remy asked and amusement etched his features.

"Or lessons on how to fight better," he suggested. "After this, I don't know how I beat those guys who were chasing me. I don't know anything about fighting."

The AI's amusement faded. "Tomorrow, you'll meet your instructors."

"Tomorrow?" he asked. "What time is it?"

"We have attempted to escape the hangar for almost four hours."

"Ugh." John flopped back onto the floor.

Remy spun the world around them to return him to the pod. "How do you feel?" he asked.

"Like I've been run over by a Dreth."

"You'll feel worse tomorrow."

He groaned. "I thought I would meet my instructors."

"You'll probably meet only one."

"One? Well, that doesn't sound so bad."

"For combat training," the AI added.

John's heart skipped with apprehension. "Ohh…"

"His name is Lars."

CHAPTER FOUR

L ars started slowly and took John through the basic kata until his muscles ached both inside and out of the pod. The bodyguard also suggested he sleep in the medical pod where Remy could run basic fighting programs through his head while he was asleep.

"Dream training," he explained. "Stephanie found it most effective. In the meantime, you need a sparring partner while I show you how to improve your technique."

The AI joined him and neither of them returned to the Dreth ship the next day or the day after. By the third day, he almost wished they had.

"Up!" the instructor commanded and made a curt gesture with his hand.

The young Talent scrambled to his feet but before he was halfway up, the man swept them out from under him again.

"You need to get yourself clear before you try to stand," he told him.

He wondered how he would do that, but Lars was already repeating the gesture.

"Up."

This time, he flipped himself back. Unfortunately, his opponent followed.

When he tried to roll to one side, he thought he was clear and tried to stand but a boot in his gut lifted him off his feet. This time, he didn't stop when he landed.

The last time he'd done that, the man had brought a foot down onto his chest. He wasn't about to let that happen again. He rolled frantically and scrambled to his knees and onto his feet from there before he lowered into a guard position.

Lars gave him the briefest smile and returned to the center of the mat. "Good. Let's start again."

A few moments later, when he'd pinned his young opponent to the mat, he grinned. "And again," he said.

It was a relief when Remy called a halt to the session and pulled John out for lunch.

"You're improving," the AI told him as he ate.

"Not enough," he replied and shoveled as much food into his mouth as he could.

"Eat slower or you'll give yourself indigestion."

"Yes, Mum."

"I am not your mother."

"Yeah? Well, that's a relief."

The AI did not respond, and John returned to the pod room and his virtual training shortly after. He went through the avatar room quickly, dressed in training fatigues, and looked around expectantly.

"Ready," he informed the AI.

"You truly aren't," the young man replied, but before he had a chance to ask him what he meant, the room twisted and he fell onto the mats in the training dojo.

This time, the computer didn't set him on his feet but released him from a foot above so he landed hard on the mat. His knees buckled from the impact.

"Your landing needs work," a deep voice rumbled and he jerked his head up to find who was speaking.

He threw himself back in a panicked scramble when he registered the hulking figure of what by now was possibly his worst nightmare.

John squinted. "You're a Dreth?"

The green-skinned humanoid came toward him and the fluidity of his movement belied his size.

"And you call yourself human," he replied and his dark eyes glittered.

The young trainee scrabbled onto his hands and knees, then to his feet, and scurried back in a half-crouch. He had difficulty understanding why a Dreth was in the training center.

"Where's Lars?"

A sudden movement to his left answered the question as the instructor took his feet out from under him and settled on his chest.

"You need to look at the whole battlefield and not only at what's in front of you," the guard said. One hand spanned his young trainee's throat and his other had been drawn back in a fist.

"All the things," he acknowledged in a strangled tone. "Gotit."

Lars nodded, eased off him, and offered him a hand. "This is Vishlog. He will be joining us."

"Two against one," John noted. "Okay."

Lars raised an eyebrow. "Remy tells me you've been in this situation before."

"Kind of."

"Tell me about it."

He complied and the man listened thoughtfully and nodded as he described the battle with the two hunter Talents.

"Wolves," the AI interrupted. "Also known as hunters, although that doesn't have the same predatory ring to it. The Regime uses them to hunt their own."

Lars shrugged and gave the boy a serious look. "You're lucky you had that much juice to spare."

He indicated the newcomer. "This afternoon, we'll work on how to deal with an opponent who is bigger, faster—"

"And smarter," Vishlog interjected and bared his teeth in a Dreth grin.

"Than you," the man finished and frowned at his colleague. "He is also part of Stephanie's security team."

"The first Dreth," the big alien noted proudly.

"There's more than one Dreth on her team?" he asked. He honestly found it hard to believe.

"My nephew," Vishlog confirmed and looked at Lars. "Shall we begin?"

John caught the look that passed between them, danced back several paces, and watched both of them warily this time. They separated and moved to either side, which made it difficult to keep them both in sight.

"So, how—" Lars began and John blasted him with two bolts of blue force.

The power of them picked the man up and flung him toward a wall. He didn't wait to see if he made impact but swept his hands around in search of Vishlog.

He was not prepared for the swift grace with which the Dreth bounded into an arched dive that took him over the initial blast. As the guard reached for him, he threw himself to one side.

Lars had rebounded from the wall, and John frowned and pulled a little extra energy from his Talent as he landed. Without pause, he rolled rapidly away from his landing point and regained his feet as the two guards surged toward him.

Both were grinning like fiends.

Rather than run from them, he tried to put the training from the last few days into practice. This time, he focused on the Dreth, moved so Vishlog was between him and Lars, and tried to get closer.

He didn't bother to aim at the Dreth's head. Instead, he focused on the body and lashed out with a foot at the warrior's knee.

His massive opponent laughed, blocked the blow, and retaliated with a mirrored kick. John danced back and Lars tackled him from the side.

"We need to work on your awareness," the guard told him as he thumped into the mats, "or you'll be dead in seconds."

John wondered why that might matter, but the man hadn't finished.

"And then Stephanie will be upset."

"And that is not good," Vishlog rumbled as the man hauled the trainee to his feet.

"Remy, we need Frog."

Frog? the boy wondered but a second later, a small man landed on the mat in the center of the room.

He turned to study the new arrival and John was surprised to see he was shorter than he was.

That doesn't mean anything, he thought when he noticed his build. Nothing about him, his height notwithstanding, suggested feeble or unfit.

Unfortunately, Frog didn't seem as impressed by him. The small man inclined his head and studied him with a frown. "Fresh meat?"

"New mage," Lars explained, and the newcomer started to circle.

"What's he got?"

"Not much."

John scowled at the dismissive assessment. The guard caught his look and raised an eyebrow.

"Not that he's shown us," he amended.

"You mean I was supposed to use my Talent?" he asked and Lars grinned.

"You mean you thought you were cheating when you blasted me back there?"

He flushed. "I…"

The man stepped in and jabbed him twice in the ribs, and Vishlog took his feet out from under him.

"That's cheating," Lars explained and looked sternly at him.

As tempting as it was to retort, he didn't. Instead, he reached out, used Talent to boost his strength, and wrapped one hand around Vishlog's ankle and the other around Lars' and yanked them hard.

Two startled exclamations followed, and he tried to roll out from between them.

Get clear before trying to—

"Oof!"

The short man's boot connected with the side of his head and he landed on the mat a third time.

When he opened his eyes, Frog's face was inches from his own. John threw a shield between them as the man's head came forward.

"Ow!" the guard exclaimed as the air flashed blue and his forehead rebounded.

With a quiet snicker, he scrambled back as fast as he could. The smile faded from his face as the three of them turned toward him.

"This will be like fighting Stephanie when she first started," Frog noted and Lars nodded.

"It had better be or we'll put him in the white in ten seconds flat."

The training became more intense after that. In addition to the dream lessons on combat technique, other sessions in the pod used electrical stimulation to train muscle memory for some of the more acrobatic movements such as those he'd seen Frog make.

He practiced them when he was sparring and tried to combine his Talent with each maneuver as he made it. None of it was easy and more than once, he had to grit his teeth and force himself to continue.

It took him a week before he could stay on his feet for more than a few minutes at a time. Soon after, he was able to take Frog out of the air at the same time as he blocked Vishlog's charge and twisted away from Lars' punch.

Slowly but surely, he learned how to feint and how to use his feet to strike at the Dreth while staying out of range. He even learned how to keep an eye on all three of them. Despite this, he simply couldn't win.

Finally, he put Frog on the mat. Next, he felled Vishlog. Lars ended his run with a fist to the side of the head and hauled him to his feet.

"Tomorrow, we'll do something different," the security head said. "You're getting better."

"Another pirate ship?" he asked, but his instructor faded into the system and a mysterious smile played over his lips.

John was covered in sweat when Remy opened the pod.

"You need to clean up," the AI told him, "and I need to fumigate your pod."

He stared at the nearest camera. "You what?"

"You heard me, John Dunn. Now go. Clean up. Supper is on the table."

It was, was it? He turned to the door, only to hear the locks grinding into place.

A second one opened and he gave the camera a wry grin. "You can't blame a guy for trying," he told it.

"Yes, but I can keep a guy locked in his room until he complies with the basic laws of hygiene," Remy snapped in response.

The boy rolled his eyes but didn't bother to argue, however, and soon emerged from the shower station washed, dried, and in a freshly fabricated ship suit.

The AI made no comment but let him out for his meal. "You'll sleep in the medical pod, tonight," he informed him when he'd eaten.

John groaned. "More training?"

"You respond well to subliminal training. I have estimated your skill acquisition to be months ahead of what we could expect from physical training alone."

"Even with the pod?"

"Yes," Remy confirmed. "Even with it."

"I feel stronger," he told him, "and I'm starting to get my head around this fighting thing."

"I have observed your tactics," the AI told him. "You are progressing well. Lars says you are ready for something new tomorrow."

"That's what he told me," he replied. "Do you know what it is?"

"It's not my place to reveal what your trainers wish to keep a secret," Remy informed him. "All I can say is you need to eat and rest well."

"In the med pod?" he asked. "While my body's learning instead of resting?"

"It rests." The AI's tone suggested he was making more of it than he needed to.

John sighed and headed to the med pod. The sooner he slept, the sooner he'd get to see exactly what Lars had cooked up. He only hoped it wasn't a ship full of pirates.

He frowned when he slid into the clean VR pod the next morning.

"Wish me luck," he muttered gloomily and Remy chuckled.

"You will make your own luck," the AI informed him, and he wished he could find the same amount of faith.

Seconds later, he gasped when he stood on the edge of a small mountain plateau. In truth, "plateau" was too big a word for it. It was more like a pocket than a valley.

His heart sank when he saw his three trainers lined up against the cliff on the other side.

"Stephanie could levitate," their leader declared, "and you said you tried it in your last battle. We thought we'd combine sparring practice with that."

Cautiously, he took a step away from the cliff edge and they took a step toward him. When he stopped moving, so did they.

"So," he asked, "how does this work?"

Lars grinned and his two teammates started to smirk.

The head guard stepped forward and John stepped back.

Ignoring the question, the man glanced at his two teammates on either side of him and they started to advance.

John's uneasiness increased as he slid a foot back but stopped when it encountered the edge of the cliff. He tried not to think of the drop and looked up to see that the other three had covered half the distance between them at a slow walk.

It still took a moment for the penny to drop.

"You're going to throw me *off*?"

Three grins answered him as they charged.

The young Talent elevated sharply and twisted as he drew on his Talent to give himself a boost. He arced over their heads and landed on the other side.

They turned.

"Because there's a white room. Right?"

The guards fanned out. Vishlog shifted to take him head-on, while his teammates stalked to either side. The Dreth bared his teeth.

Anger rolled through the trainee. "You know that's not fair, right?"

"Very good," Frog snarked from his right. "Now ask us if we care."

He jerked a hand toward him and blasted him into a cliff. "Do you care now?"

Movement snagged his attention on the right and he launched upward.

"You're using considerable energy," Lars observed as John hovered just out of reach above him.

For some reason, the comment rankled.

"Your point?" he all but snarled.

Without warning, Vishlog drew a blaster and shot him but he somehow managed to raise a shield in time. The energy bolt ricocheted in a flare of blue and forced the Dreth to leap to one side.

"Do you ever wonder where you'll get more?"

"I'll simply pull it in from the outside," he told him. "Like I always do."

"Not when you're on Dreth, you won't," Lars contradicted and smiled.

It was not a nice smile.

"What do you mean?" John frowned but he began to descend and used a little more Talent to keep himself aloft.

Vishlog's lips curled as he aimed a second time. "There's no eMU on Dreth," he rumbled.

Dreth? He scowled. His gaze swept over the vista of viciously jagged peaks and his body registered the tug of an icy breeze. A chill ran through him that had nothing to do with the mountain air.

"Fine, I'll pull in some nMU then," he snapped and reached for the elusive dark energy.

"Did anyone bring popcorn?" Frog asked, his voice amused despite being gravelly with pain.

John wondered what he'd forgotten—apart from the fact he didn't know what nMU felt like. He remembered how it felt to draw eMU and sought a similar power but different. Impatience surged through him and he tried to make himself think carefully.

What was it that made Dreth's energy unique?

He knew there was something, but he couldn't remember what it was. With a huff of impatience, he focused on finding the energy instead.

It wasn't easy but it wasn't hard either. John registered a sensation of darkness—almost a presence touched with anger, sadness, and fear. As his body started to sink lower, he drew on the energy, pulled it in, and fed it to the Talent already keeping him aloft.

The effect was instantaneous. Pain ripped through him in a blinding flare of white and his world exploded.

When awareness returned, he opened his eyes to the familiar emptiness of the white room.

"Oh, man, Remy." He groaned. "Remind me not to do that again."

"I do not think I will need to."

John managed to stand and patted himself all over to make sure he truly was there. Being ripped apart by two opposing energies was not pleasant.

A groan sounded from behind him and he turned cautiously. Lars eased himself slowly off the floor. A moment later, Vishlog and Frog appeared.

John cocked his head.

"What happened to you guys?"

"You blew up half the mountain. It merely took us this long to land," the lead instructor told him sourly.

He stared at the man for a moment, then laughed. "Really?"

"Yes," Frog replied. "Can we please not do that again?"

"You intended to throw me off it," he reminded them.

"And we'll try to do it again," Lars told him shortly.

"Before we do…" John said quickly. "Do you have any tips?"

"Yeah," Frog started, "when you enter freefall, flapping your arms won't do you any good."

"Ha, ha," he replied.

"Don't mix nMU and any other kind," Vishlog advised.

He frowned. "How did Stephanie do it, then?"

"That is something you will have to ask her, but before she worked out how, she used to empty all the other MU present in her body and *then* she would use the nMU."

"Noted." It seemed simple enough—empty the MU or eMU in his case. But how had she done that?

And could he do it before he landed if he needed to refuel his Talent on the way down? It made him miss Earth and he wondered what kind of things he could do with his Talent now that he'd had some actual training.

Before he could decide what he wanted to do about that, the world twisted and he stood on the edge of the mountain plateau again. This time, the guys didn't waste time talking.

John flipped high to avoid them and decided they needed a dose of their own medicine. Turning so he landed facing them, he thrust his hands before him and launched a solid block of power at Vishlog.

There was nothing like disabling the hardest guy to beat, right?

He realized his mistake a few seconds after the Dreth disappeared over the edge. Frog stopped and stared at the space his teammate had occupied with a look of disbelief.

"Harsh," he noted, but the young Talent didn't have time to celebrate.

The massive warrior wasn't the hardest one to beat. Lars was and the man wasn't impressed.

"That," the guard snarled as he closed, "wasn't in the playbook."

"Why not?" he asked as lightning arced over his hands.

He unleashed a spray of bolts and backed away as his opponent avoided them. His back met solid rock and he twisted his head to look up. There was no way he could climb that, Instead, he turned to face the man.

"This must be where the sparring practice comes in," he remarked and noticed Frog seemed to be over his shock.

The small man looked furious. "We're supposed to throw you over the cliff." He snarled with real annoyance.

John chuckled, ducked under Lars' fist, and kicked him in the gut to make him keep his distance.

"I can do this all day," the lead instructor informed him and swept his leg in a sideways kick.

He jerked out of its way and released a short burst of blue at the man.

Lars dodged it, snickered as he stepped back, and reached for his holster. Frog's blaster was already clear. Together, they gained some distance and opened fire.

The boy raised a hastily created shield and watched the eMU sparkle under each strike. They didn't waste any time, he noted, and felt his Talent drain with the effort.

He was merely glad he could hold them off with a cliff at his back and not a who-knew-how-many-thousand-foot drop.

"So can I," he responded and recalled Vishlog's advice about emptying himself of eMU before he tried to draw in any of Dreth's nMU.

"And I'm fairly sure you can't," Lars taunted, drew a pistol, and fired with both hands. Beside him, Frog did the same.

The man was right but he wouldn't admit it. The added barrage demanded more energy than he had stored, and he wondered if they'd stop firing when his shields were depleted. He wouldn't be able to hold them off forever.

"Sneaky sonsaguns," he muttered and focused on holding the shield with one hand and firing balls of lightning with the other.

He reasoned that if he could disable their guns long enough, he'd have time to draw the nMU in and build another shield when the eMU ran out.

The idea was sound but its implementation was a challenge.

His attacks had managed to short their weapons out but used the last of his Talent, and he had barely reached for the negatively charged nMU when Lars charged. Torn between focusing on the energy and on avoiding the guard's attack, he lost sight of Frog.

The smaller man bounded in, ducked John's hastily thrown punch, and thumped him twice in the gut. As he doubled over, the short guard grasped his shoulders and pushed down as he brought his knee up.

John's's face struck the man's knee and his legs folded. Lars pivoted and caught him by his shirt and one arm, and his teammate did the same on the other side.

"Hey! Wait! I'm...not...ready..." he protested, as they reached the edge of the cliff.

His nose felt crushed and he had difficulty breathing but they shoved him over without hesitation.

"Hey!"

He panicked and snatched at the nMU he knew had to be around him, drew it in hastily, and attempted to direct it to slow his fall. The air rushed past him and he tried to focus on the energy. His gaze caught on the distant peaks and the lowlands far below.

John scrambled to haul in more Talent. He thought frantically about creating a dark platform beneath his feet and of the platform rising above the ground. His fall slowed.

Hopeful now, he drew more energy to strengthen his magical support and his descent ceased and he began to rise. He was so focused on building it that he didn't notice when he rose above the plateau's edge.

Lars's well-aimed rock caught him squarely on the side of the head, and he began to plummet again.

This time, he didn't recover in time to avoid the valley floor.

CHAPTER FIVE

"I'm calling a rest day," John announced at breakfast the next day.

"You still need to practice," Remy told him.

"I'll practice outside," he replied, "and try to get a feel for how some of what I've learned works in the real world."

He stood from the table and made coffee at the dispenser as he waited for a reply. It took the AI so long to respond that he almost thought it was broken or turned off.

"Remy?"

The silence continued for a few seconds longer before he spoke. "Your alternative is acceptable. I will monitor your progress using the external surveillance systems."

His sigh of relief was noisy and heartfelt.

"You do understand that they are constructs," the AI said and reminded him of his three trainers inside the system. "They will take no offense at your actions in the previous session."

John nodded. "I understand that, but I need to see how much of it translates to the real world."

"That will be difficult since there is no nMU on Earth."

He shook his head in exasperation.

"No, not with the nMU. I only..." He gestured vaguely. "I simply want to try some of the things I did in the Virtual World out in the real world."

"Do you have any reason to believe those things will work less well in the real than in the VR?" Remy asked.

"How am I to know?" he challenged. "I've only ever seen them work in the Virtual. How would I know if the virtual depictions are accurate if I don't test the theory?"

"I do not have a drone large enough to pick you up and carry you back if you are injured beyond mobility," the AI informed him stiffly.

"No, but you have an army of the smaller ones," he snapped in return. "I assume if enough of them try to lift me, they'll succeed."

Silence followed. It was short, but Remy had computed the chances and likelihood of the drones doing what he had claimed they could.

"It would work. You might acquire surface injuries from being partially dragged but the drones could retrieve you."

John slapped the table and made his empty crockery jump.

"Then it's a deal," he exclaimed. "I'll be back for lunch."

"You will not be fed if you are not."

"So if I'm not back, you'll know to send a search party," he retorted.

Remy chuckled.

"Go, but don't hurt yourself. I will not be responsible for explaining to Stephanie why one of the most promising mages in a long time was killed because I let them out the gate."

"Most promising?" he teased. "I'm the only mage you've seen."

The door to the mess hall opened.

"I will see you at one."

He glanced at the surveillance camera but couldn't think of anything to say. Instead, he hurried to the foyer and the outer gates, his mind already considering the possibilities.

Now he knew Remy could get him to the med pod, much of

the apprehension he'd felt had dissipated. He stepped through the gate and looked at the cliffs and canyons that surrounded the compound.

They seemed awfully high for what he was about to do.

To give himself time to steady his nerves, John walked to the cross and cairn he'd built for Becca. He crouched in front of it and touched the plaque with one finger.

"Well, Becks," he told her. "I found someone to help me learn more of what I had to. I only have to see how well I've learned it and decide what to do next."

Although hadn't told Remy, he didn't intend to stay at the compound forever—and certainly not to wait for a return he had no date for. Stephanie was coming back but he didn't know when, and he wanted a chance to let the world in on the secret.

He wanted her to come back to people who believed in her—and who knew she was coming. She deserved to be welcomed and not with the standard-issue pitchforks and flame-throwers the Regime had primed its people to greet her with.

She deserved to be given a hero's welcome.

While he wasn't sure he could give her that, he was determined to try.

"In the meantime," he said, stood quickly, and gave Becca's cairn another glance, "I need to see if I'm ready and if what I've learned translates to the real world as well as the simulation says it does. Promise not to laugh, okay?"

The woman did not reply but he didn't expect her to. The lightening of his heart was all the encouragement he needed.

He turned to one of the rock walls and began to run. As he did so, he pulled Talent in, pushed it into his legs and body, and strengthened them so that his strides grew longer and he remained balanced.

Finally, he vaulted upward and directed the energy beneath him to create a platform that levitated from the earth.

"It's almost like flying," he whispered and wondered how the gun turrets would react, given that Remy knew what he was doing.

As if his thoughts had summoned him, the AI spoke.

"Why don't we make this a little more realistic?"

"What?"

"I'll fire the wall turrets at you."

John jerked his head in time to see a flash as one of the guns fired. He didn't take time to think and thrust an instinctive barrier of blue up as he leapt onto one of the rock formations at the foot of the cliffs.

He landed safely and looked around.

"I don't suppose I should shoot back?" he asked the AI.

"I would appreciate it if you used something benign," Remy advised him. "One of those balls of force would suffice. I would register the buffet and de-activate the guns."

"I wish you'd asked me first," he answered and bounded from his perch as several of the guns spoke at once.

"Now, John, where would the fun be in that?"

He didn't answer because he simply had no time. Almost instinctively, he bounced high, flicked his body into a tumble, and flattened into a glide.

At the same time, he threw another shield between him and the turrets and grinned when the bolts exploded on impact. The pressure buffeted him off-course and he corrected quickly.

Gliding was easy. All he did was ask the eMU to form a long, broad wing over his back like a glider, while he held his hands in front of him and "steered" in the direction in which he wanted to go.

Occasionally, he'd lower his feet and touch down on one rocky outcrop or another, only to spring away when the guns fired again.

Rather than keep a large shield in place, John contented himself with creating several smaller shields as and when he needed them. By alternating shield creation with sending a bolt or ball of force at each turret, he deactivated each one.

Now and then, he twisted to avoid a bolt he hadn't managed to block. It took some practice to get his aim right and hit what he needed to. He was covered in sweat and breathing heavily by the time he'd disabled the last turret that could reach him.

"Nicely done," Remy informed him and he bounced to the ground.

He grinned. "So, lunch?"

"You are late for lunch," the AI said blandly, and he stopped and the smile faded from his face.

"Which means?"

"You're late for class."

"Uh-huh." His expression unamused, he walked to the main gates.

The sound of the guns powering up was all the warning he received and he managed to pull a dome of energy over himself as the first rounds struck.

"Remy!"

The AI chuckled.

"And what would you have done if I hadn't been fast enough?" he demanded from under the shield.

"Picked up the pieces?" the AI suggested mischievously.

"What?"

"I am joking. I knew you would have been fast enough to avoid damage."

"But what if you'd been wrong?" he demanded.

"John, I am never wrong," Remy assured him. "I know what you are capable of, even if you do not."

"It's still not funny."

"It was a joke!" The voice had taken on an edge of exasperation. "Just as I was joking when I said you were late for lunch."

"You mean I'm not?" John's jaw dropped.

"No, you are right on time," Remy replied.

"I don't think you're very funny," he grumbled.

"The joke was not funny?" He sounded puzzled. "According to my files, this is the kind of stunt the team and Stephanie would have laughed at."

"Oh, *they* might have laughed," he all but snarled, "but I'm not them. Nothing's funny when food is on the line."

After a long silence, the guns powered down.

"Remy?" John asked.

"I am here, John. I wanted to be sure you did not get shot when you approached the gate. It is safe now."

"Really?" he asked but he reshaped the energy to wrap around his body as he stood.

"Do you not trust me, John?" The AI sounded worried.

"You'll need to give me a moment," he told him. "That last encounter was a surprise."

"Oh."

"In human terms, you took the joke too far."

"Or you do not have much of a sense of humor."

If John didn't know any better, he'd have said he'd hurt the AI's feelings. He decided to change the subject.

"What's for lunch, Rem?"

"Peanut butter and jelly sandwiches."

"That had better be another joke, Rem!"

As he sat down to a lunch that had nothing to do with sandwiches, Nate Coleman glared at the man on the screen.

"No, I'm not joking," he snapped. "We've lost contact with 357 and 92 and we need to know what's happened to them."

The other man studied his face.

"That's not it," he corrected. "You're worried they've gone rogue."

He slumped in his seat.

"I'm worried they've gone rogue," he admitted quietly, "but I'm hoping they haven't."

"What are the chances?"

"Going on 92's last assessment, he was treading close to the edge but should have been good for another couple of years."

"Are you sure?" his boss asked, and the screen flicked to show 357 and 92 blasting the interior of a hangar.

"He lost control there," the man pointed out. "Is it possible this target was the one to get past the conditioning?"

Nate shook his head.

"Judging by what he said to the guards on the train, 357 was determined to bring 781 back and he'd threatened to kill him on a number of occasions."

"For making him go to Chicago?" His boss was amused.

He fought to control his expression. While he'd known his team was being watched, he hadn't realized his superior would receive the same reports he did.

Caution clicked in and he made a mental note to not omit anything from the discussion. The last thing he needed was to be accused of disloyalty to the Regime.

"That was more 357 than 92. 357 had an unfortunate encounter there a few years ago."

His boss nodded and steepled his hands in front of his face.

"Who did you have in mind?" he asked.

"To go after them?"

"Yes."

"The only one close to 92's caliber is 129. The psychs are sure she has at least another five left before she becomes unstable."

"How old is she?"

"Just turned twenty-six, sir."

"Hmmm, and how old is 92?"

"By our standards, he's ancient. He was seven at the time of the Overthrow, one of the youngest Talents ever collected. The conditioning worked particularly well with him."

His boss made an impatient gesture with his hand. "How old?"

"Thirty-five, sir."

"So overdue for going rabid," the man concluded. He continued before Nate could answer. "And how old is 357?"

"Twenty-six or seven, sir, but—" He stopped as his superior raised his hand.

"You can have four. Make sure their latest conditioning reports are solid before you send them. Some of the things this kid's been saying are...disturbing."

"They seemed to inflame 92, sir."

"That's a good sign his conditioning held but not such a good sign as to his fate."

"Do you think the rogue could have...killed him?" Nate gulped. There'd been nothing in the reports to suggest the newly emerged Talent was that powerful.

"I think there are only two answers as to why 357's gone dark —and we've essentially ruled out him going rogue. Even so, I want you to make sure you send two overseers. We should have a qualified pilot. The shuttles don't hold more than six."

"Understood, sir." He resisted the urge to point out that bigger shuttles were available. He'd now been given the limit of what his boss would approve and he had to work with it.

"Tell me when they launch," the man ordered, and he knew he'd need to have a full report available on the team—both its composition and why he'd chosen each one—and the shuttle and equipment he'd requisitioned.

He wished he'd been able to discuss equipment. Even though his superior knew the team would enter a Dead Zone, he could still balk at the level of protection Nate gave his Talents.

His face twisted in a scowl and he shrugged. He was between a rock and a hard place. On the one hand, he could be accused of failing to protect Regime assets if he didn't give his Talents the best gear he could obtain and on the other, he could be accused of wasting Regime resources if he chose gear others thought was over-powered.

All he could do was put in the requisition order and let the Supply Officer be the judge. That would be where the buck stopped, he decided.

And he'd make sure of it if it came to that. If the man wanted to issue less than what he selected or wouldn't approve everything he asked for? Well, he could simply point out how much he relied on his judgment to make his final call.

Even so, there was a limit to how far he could go. He could only hope the Dead Zone below Chicago wasn't one of the hotter ones.

The decision made, Nate tapped in the number for the Talent Requisitions Officer. It was time to see what the zoo had to offer.

Unfortunately, it wasn't 129.

"She's on another hunt," the officer told him, "and won't be back for a week. Besides, she has a cub in tow—one from the latest batch to graduate the conditioning."

His heart sank and his disappointment must have shown on his face.

"Can you tell me why you needed her in particular?" she asked and her face revealed concern.

"I need someone who can match 92 for Talent," he told her cautiously. There was no point in admitting exactly why he wanted that level and he hoped she didn't ask.

No one wanted to admit a Talent had gone rabid. They all knew it happened but didn't want it to be on their watch. It was like having to put a pet down—worse, perhaps, since Talents looked so human.

Curiosity flitted across the officer's face but the question he dreaded didn't follow. Instead, she asked, "How many do you need and who's his running buddy?"

"He'd apprenticed 357, and I've been given authorization for four."

"Do you need them weapons trained?"

"They're going into a Dead Zone, so yes. You never know what you'll find in those areas."

This much was true and it meant he didn't have to explain the real reason why he wanted them armed. He watched as she pursed her lips and knew she wanted the explanation even if she didn't want to hear it.

Nate decided not to oblige. He noted the moment when she understood that he wouldn't give her more and decided to let it go.

"What are your allowances for handlers?" she asked.

"I need two with pilot's licenses."

Her fingers rattled across the keyboard.

"And controls?"

"You mean collars?"

"Yes, you have a two-to-one ratio. If they decide to go rogue, the handlers will need some way to protect themselves."

"Do you think it's likely?" The possibility that the Talents he sent might turn against their handlers hadn't crossed his mind. "May I ask why?"

"I've seen footage of what the rogue is preaching—and he was surrounded by humans who treated him like he was exactly like them. That kind of thing has been known to rattle the best conditioning locks."

"But he's in a Dead Zone," Nate protested. What makes you think he's not alone?"

"If he's lived this long, what makes you think he isn't?" she retorted. "Or do you think it likely a rogue that young was able to defeat 92 on his own?"

As much as he hated to admit it, he knew she had a point.

"Tell me what you think they'll need," he said, meaning the trainers.

"Collars and remotes at the bare minimum and, if they're

pilots, they need to remain segregated as a precaution." She paused. "Where are you sending them?"

Nate cocked an eyebrow and she scowled.

"I need to make sure your pilots have the hours available to make the trip. Also, if it's the northern hemisphere, I'll have to ensure my handlers have the requisite training for that air space and winter weather conditions, given the time of year."

"Winter?"

"It is the northern hemisphere. Their seasons are flipped."

He grimaced internally but did his best to keep his expression neutral. The woman had a point and he didn't want her to realize that he hadn't accounted for the seasonal change. She was too smart as it was.

"Chicago and the Dead Zone south of it," he told her and decided anything more specific would come under "need to know."

To his relief, she accepted that and didn't ask for further details. Instead, she focused on her computer and tapped the keyboard.

While Nate waited, he watched her scan the lists and check each Talent's record to find the ones that best fit what he needed. It didn't take her very long and he assumed there weren't many in the stable who could match 92.

"The closest I can do you for sheer power is 140 and 226," she told him and he glanced at his screen.

It was disappointing, but from what he could remember about the two of them, they would be powerful enough. 92 would still make them work for the victory, but if they remembered to use their blasters, they should be able to deal with him.

"And the other two?" he asked.

"If 357's still with 92, you'll need 299 and 310. The blasters should even up any deficiency but shouldn't be required. They're good enough to eliminate him and assist with 92."

It struck Nate that both of them were now talking as though 92 had gone rogue and not simply considering the alternative.

"And if our hunters are dead?"

She curled her lip. "One young, untrained Talent? How likely is that?"

As much as he hated to admit it, he knew she had a point but she wasn't finished.

"And if they are dead, we'll still need the firepower to deal with whatever killed them. It probably isn't only one kid, so the Talents I've assigned to you have a certain degree of stealth to complement their powers—and all the risks that go along with that kind of skill."

Meaning she had very good reason to remind him of the need for collars with a two-for-one ratio. The sneaky ones always took a peek at the other side of the coin and their careers were usually very short-lived as a result. 140 and 226 were unusual to have survived this long, as was 129.

Or they'd gone undetected and had a high probability of turning if they heard a good enough reason. There were numerous ifs and buts and he took a moment to consider them in his mind.

"Do you have any direct-drive hunters?" he asked but the woman shook her head.

"Nothing capable of defeating 92, even with help."

"Then these will have to do," he told her. "Load them up and have the pilots contact me and then Chicago—and in that order. I want them in the air within the next hour and a half."

"I hear you," she said and signed off.

Nate settled into his chair and hammered out the requisition list. Marking it urgent, he sent it and waited for the inevitable dickering to begin.

CHAPTER SIX

"It all has to go," Ivy insisted.

She stood at the end of a rough wooden table and barely resisted pounding on it with her fist.

"But... Why?"

When she looked at Tucker, she realized that he still didn't understand. He caught her look and took the opportunity to argue with her.

"If Becca was able to use it to prove Stephanie's existence, why can't we?"

"Because even if we could get it out of where they're keeping it, we can't protect it."

"Well, why would we need to?" he persisted. "If we're spreading it all over the Virtual anyway?"

"That's exactly it. We're not. We can't—and we can't because it would lead them straight to us."

"So what if we could simply leave it in place and hide it," he suggested and she closed her eyes and forced herself to think about the idea instead of rejecting it outright.

Tucker did have some knowledge when it came to computers, after all, and it didn't take her long to see he had a point.

"What are you suggesting?" she asked and he exhaled a pent breath.

"We leave what's there exactly where it is but cut it out of the system so it can't be found. Maybe take it out of the location table?"

It was something she should have thought of, and she paused to consider it. He took her hesitation as a sign of pending refusal.

"Look, all I'm saying is that it would be a pity to destroy all that data—all the *history* that Becca tried to preserve. Eventually, someone will want to know the truth and they'll have a hard time learning it if we wipe it from the database."

"And how do we go about re-establishing the link?" Ivy demanded. "You know, when she's back and your historian is trying to work out what happened in the time at the beginning of the Regime? How will they even know it's there to find?"

"We'll each keep a copy of the location that needs to be added," Tucker began eagerly. "I'll even put something on paper and give it to Dani."

"And what if she is raided?" she asked. "We can't afford to have that kind of incriminating stuff lying around."

"We'll tell her to burn it."

"You're assuming she'll get the chance." It was difficult for her to keep her tone hard in the face of his disappointment, but she needed him to think it through.

He quieted and his face clouded as he tried to think of a way the data could be retrieved. After a few minutes, it brightened.

"What about the sewers?" he said. "That room where you hid John after you did your last raid. I haven't known a single Enforcer who's ever gone down there long enough to find it."

"Done!" she snapped, as much to shut him up as to move the meeting along. They had so much to plan and very little time to plan it in.

"And we have to do it soon."

Ivy looked up. That quiet interjection belonged to Dieter and he rarely said anything. For him to emphasize the point meant he was concerned about something.

She glanced at him and he continued.

"The wolves haven't returned and the Enforcers here haven't pushed us yet. They've made a show of being on the streets more and dragged one or two people off, but only because those folk were in easy reach."

"And you're saying they're coming?" Tucker asked.

The other man shook his head and fixed his dark eyes on her.

"I am saying it's a chance we cannot take. If the data on Stephanie vanishes, they'll have nothing concrete to be afraid of."

Several snorts greeted this as though he was being needlessly naïve, but the small man was not perturbed.

"Yes, they could also panic, but if they have no idea what went missing or who took it, my guess is they'll brush it under the carpet."

He met Ivy's gaze and his expression turned sympathetic. "They won't have any reason to come after us and they clearly don't want to go off half-cocked when it comes to this area."

She couldn't argue that. The limited action they'd seen in the weeks since John's departure proved his point.

"And the wolves?" she asked, meaning the two Talents.

"The boy is leading them a merry dance," Dieter told her and a slight smile creased his lips. "They will not be back for a long time—if they are able to come back at all."

Finally, she nodded and raised her eyes to study the faces of those around the table. They all looked at her and waited and she tried not to wonder why.

The last weeks had been hard on all of them. Becca had died— and spectacularly—while saving John.

Some of the people seated around the table hadn't forgiven him for that. Ivy took a breath. There were some days when she wasn't sure she'd forgiven him either.

Shaking the thought from her mind, she focused on the problem at hand.

"We need to get rid of the data proving Stephanie's existence," she said and started from where Tucker had interrupted her.

He inhaled sharply as though to protest and she stopped him with an upraised hand.

"As Tucker says, it would be a shame if we were to lose all the history to do with Stephanie's real story. Becca died to get that story out there. She wanted that history preserved. We can do that."

"Who'll do the hack?" asked one of the women at the other end of the table.

Ivy looked at Tucker, but he raised both hands.

"Don't look at me like that, Ivy. You know you're the best out of the two of us."

That stopped her. She'd known they were on a par but hadn't known he thought she was better.

Her face heated as she looked at him.

"No, Tucker, I did not know that."

He smiled, enjoying her confusion. "Well, now you do."

She wondered how much it had cost him to admit it but decided not to pursue it.

"Fine," she said, "but you're my back-up. If I get eliminated, I need you to make sure that what needs to be done is done, okay?"

"Okay," he agreed and his smile widened a little. "But we both know you'll be fine." He gestured around the table. "You have the best team you can have. No one will get to you while they're with you."

His words brought murmurs and subdued exclamations of agreement, and Ivy blushed harder.

I don't deserve this, she thought and stared at the table, waiting for the noise to die down.

Finally, someone cleared their throat. "So, what's the plan?"

Ivy looked up again. "We've worked out where the second

repository's located but we can't hack it from the outside. We need to be inside the facility to access the systems."

Dieter chuckled. "Well, that's your specialty." He gestured to the others around the table. "The rest of us can get you there and make sure you get away. That's our specialty, but once you're in there, you're on your own."

"Speak for yourself, Dieter. You guys get us in, and we'll make sure the data's preserved." She caught Tucker's eye as she said the last word and he gave her a brief nod of thanks.

She didn't know what he was thanking her for. Preserving their history was something Becca would have wanted and she should have thought of it herself.

It goes to show you can't think of everything, she reminded herself.

"Do you know what the security's like?" Dieter interrupted her thoughts and she focused on him.

"The facility's one of their secondary storage areas," Ivy told them, "so security's not as heavy as it was in the one John and I visited."

"You'd better hope not," Jade declared, "because I still don't know how you two got anywhere near as far as you did."

Given that she had left the Navy at the end of the war that had seen the Heretic created—and she rarely spoke of what she did—Ivy listened. The closest she could come to her previous occupation was some kind of reconnaissance and what seemed to be a long list of dirty tricks.

The woman had a point about her and John's little expedition.

When she thought back, she couldn't understand how they'd made it so far either. They'd gone through a staff entrance, for pity's sake, and walked a stretch of corridor covered by surveillance cameras. It had taken the Regime Enforcers guarding the facility almost half an hour to investigate.

"They were on a coffee break?" she suggested with a sly smile and the others laughed.

"More likely you were coming up to a shift change and everyone was more worried about getting ready to go home than anything else," Jade snapped.

Ivy thought back and decided the woman might be right. "Or that," she admitted. "It could have been that."

"Are you saying the Enforcers are human?" Klaus, Jade's second in command, pretended shock and more laughter followed.

"Yeah," she responded. "But as unlikely as it seems, we still got through and we shouldn't have."

"At least you didn't try the front gate."

"We thought about it," she admitted, "but we took time to watch them and decided not to chance it."

"So the front was tight?" Klaus asked.

She nodded and took a sheaf of print-outs from the folder beside her.

"This is the layout," she said and spread the sheets on the table in front of them.

Immediately, several of those gathered stood for a closer look. She leaned back and watched as they examined the layout and discussed possible entrances and exits.

As much as she had her ideas on how to gain access, she didn't intervene. She might be able to do the infiltration part well enough, but others among the group were better. Every time she let them share ideas like this, she learned something new.

Even so, it was a surprise when Jade turned to her.

"What do you think, Ivy?" The question was so unexpected that the girl stared at her, and the ex-Navy woman smiled. "You must have some ideas on how you'd go about it," she coaxed.

"I... Yes, but I thought I'd leave it to the experts," she mumbled, and Jade arched an eyebrow.

"You've sat in on enough of our planning sessions to have picked up most things. Why don't you run us through what you had in mind?"

"Uh...okay." She didn't know why the woman had chosen to push her, but she was right.

She was leading them, and the leader should have a plan in mind.

"It's very close to what you guys discussed," she began and gave credit where it was due, "but I think we could take advantage of the blind spot here..." She pointed. "And here." She pointed again.

Everyone studied the places she'd mentioned and she gave them a moment to do so before she continued. "The entire complex is one huge set of servers mostly used for the backup and storage of old files, which is why it's not as well-guarded as it should be."

"And why they've left it in Chicago," Tucker muttered darkly, referring to the way the Regime seemed to dump all its loose or unwanted ends in the city.

"Lucky for us," Jade snapped, "because getting out of the city would be harder than getting into this place."

"Are you saying it'll be difficult?" Ivy asked and wondered what she'd missed.

The woman shook her head. "No. Getting in will be the easy part. It's getting you out once you trip whatever safeguards they have on the computers that will be difficult."

"How so?"

In response, she stabbed a finger at several points on the map. "These are guard towers." She poked the map again. "That's a shuttle pad and it's the perfect size for a dropship."

"They wouldn't send a dropship, would they?" Tucker sounded alarmed, and one of the other infiltrators straightened in his chair.

"That depends on exactly what they have stored in these servers. If it's merely puppies and kittens, maybe not, but if it's something they think is a threat to the Regime, like...I don't know...evidence that the Witch exists and wasn't the demon they've painted her to be or recordings of what happened on the Federation ships in that last battle? That's a whole other story."

Ivy pressed her lips together because the kind of things Jade described was exactly what she hoped to find.

"So, you're saying they will send a dropship?"

"I don't know about that but they will send something, so you need to make sure that whoever goes in there isn't caught on surveillance or caught by a guard. My guess is there'll be at least one fast-response team on-site."

She gestured at Klaus, Raul, Tammy, and Calliope.

"We'll take care of slowing them down, but you"—she stabbed a finger at Ivy—"need to make sure you get yourself and them"—the finger shifted to Tucker and moved on to Linus—"out of there unseen."

"What will we do if one of us is tagged?" Linus asked.

Jade glanced at their leader before she fixed him with a hard look. "We'll cross that bridge when we come to it."

After a moment's silence, she shifted her attention to Ivy. "I like your plan. I think if we add putting some kind of remote surveillance on the towers and a real-time alert signal for when that rapid-response team activates, we'll be almost there."

"I'll do the remote," Dieter said quickly. He'd sat quietly at the end of the table while the others discussed the plans. "I'm the best drone pilot you have and the only one of us who has access to a drone."

"Done," Jade agreed before anyone could protest. She looked at Ivy. "Who do you want on the comms for oversight and warning?"

The girl glanced at Dieter's partner.

"Carol? Do you mind?"

The woman rolled her eyes and made a show of protesting. "Again? Ivy, I swear this is becoming a habit."

"You're the best coordinator we have," she wheedled, "and I'll find you some carrots."

That brought snorts from around the table and Carol chuckled.

"Fine," she said, "but only if you add ginger and all-spice to the mix. I'm about out and with the amount of cake you eat, I'm gonna run short."

Ivy blushed but she didn't hesitate.

"Done...and thank you."

"I'm gonna need a sidekick," the woman added quickly before she could call an end to the meeting.

The girl put a hand on her hip and cocked her head.

"Do you have anyone in mind?"

"Geraldine."

Immediately, she frowned a little dubiously. "Is she ready?"

"There's only one way she's ever gonna learn and I think she has a bent for it."

"It's your call," she told her, and Carol nodded.

"Geraldine it is, then. She won't let you down."

"Who's monitoring the Regime's computer activity?" Tucker asked and reminded her that they'd need oversight on that as well.

"Tomas and Beth?" she asked and looked at the two individuals in question.

Tomas nodded and Beth gave her a firm thumbs-up.

"Is that it?" Ivy asked. "Can anyone think of anything we've missed?"

Jade shook her head and several people gathered the print-outs.

"Tucker? Linus?"

Both men shook their heads.

"Nope, we're good," Linus told her and Tucker nodded.

She accepted the print-outs she was handed and passed them to Carol.

"Let's move out."

John launched a quick flurry of lightning bolts over the top of the concrete block. Lars uttered a brief yell of pain and stumbled back, but he didn't stop to gloat and bolted toward the next piece of cover before the security head could retaliate.

Vishlog was still out there, and he'd lost sight of Frog several minutes before. Neither was in a good mood, the large warrior because he'd blasted the Dreth off the top of a building before he glided safely to the ground and Frog because he had clothes-lined him as he came round a corner and kicked him in the head for good measure.

He hadn't been able to finish the small man off because Lars had opened fire on him, but it had been close.

They were "playing" in the ruins of a computer-generated city, and he used every Talent trick he could think of. To make things fair, he'd been teamed with Remy and the guards stated that he only needed one person to even things up since he had magic.

It hadn't been the first time they'd worked together, but that hadn't helped. The AI had saved John and he had saved Remy, but the guards had caught them in a pincer movement and he hadn't been quick enough to shield them.

Frog's shots had struck him in the chest and side and his armor had taken the brunt of the damage, which left him bruised but functional. The same couldn't be said for Lars's head-shot on the AI.

When his virtual teammate had fallen at his feet, he'd launched himself vertically and found a rooftop corner to recover in. Even knowing it was a game, the grief had been close to crippling.

"You'll need to get over that." Vishlog's voice had interrupted him and his panicked burst of power had thrown the Dreth off the building.

Now, he raced into cover as he wondered where Frog was and if the warrior was in any shape to make a reappearance or if the alien had joined Remy in the white room. Either way, it didn't matter.

John thought he might be able to eliminate the smaller guard, but he was dead certain Lars would do the same to him in the end. In all the scenarios they'd run in the last few weeks, he'd only come close to beating the man once.

"I guess that's why he's head of the security team," he muttered, skidded into his next chosen safety point, and poked his head up for a hasty scan of his surroundings.

Frog's next shot clipped the top of the stone to the trainee's right and he ducked again, but not before he'd noted Lars in a measured but determined approach to his right, his smaller teammate advancing slowly from the front, and a far too large shadow closing from the left.

How Vishlog had survived the fall, he didn't know. His only comfort was that the Dreth moved slowly and not anywhere near as smoothly as he usually did. Grimly, he decided he'd have to attack first.

He sent a burst of lightning in the warrior's direction with one hand and whipped his other in a circular motion over his head. Frog's startled cry made him smile.

A second quick peek above his cover confirmed that the small man was being pummeled by a whirlwind of debris as eMU spiraled around him in a mini-tornado. It also showed Vishlog lying prone only a few feet beyond where he'd been when he had seen him last.

Lars was another matter, however. He accelerated from his careful stalk to a full-blown sprint as soon as he knew his target had seen him and fired relentlessly as he approached.

John created a shield between them before he hurled another fistful of lightning into the Dreth and spun his hand again to keep the magic turning around Frog. After that, he was able to focus on his last opponent.

There wasn't any time to run and no path he could take that wouldn't make him more exposed to the security chief's fire. He bared his teeth in a battle grimace. Two could play at the weapons game.

He was able to maintain a light connection with the whirlwind and the shield, and he swung his blaster to the front. It was a matter of thought to have the shield mold itself around the barrel so he could fire through it, but seconds before he could pull the trigger, the city faded.

Darkness enveloped him and virtuality twisted to deposit him roughly in a briefing room. It was little consolation to hear the grunts as his opponents received the same rough treatment.

Only Remy, who stood at the front of the room, looked unfazed.

"There has been a development," he said and the wall behind him lit up with the feeds from four different sources.

One came from a satellite. As John stared at it, the image magnified and a shuttle touched down.

Another feed came from a camera hidden in the valley where he'd first faced the hunters. The craft had settled a little beyond the green and its hatches opened to disgorge four figures in what looked like heavy battle armor.

They were armed with blasters and carried two side-arms apiece, but one wore two blades at its hips. They exited the shuttle smartly and fanned away from the vessel as they surveyed the area around it.

"Combat veterans," Lars observed and John nodded.

The last two hunters he'd faced had moved that way too. Blue light rippled from the closest one's feet to their head.

"Talents," he noted.

"Are you sure?" Remy asked and he nodded again.

"They've come to see what happened to the other two."

The AI responded with a mirthless chuckle. "That is something they won't discover."

"But they will find the compound," he pointed out. "They'll search until they are sure they aren't here and they'll find you. What do you think will happen then?"

The construct regarded him soberly. "We'll cross that bridge when we come to it," he said briskly. "In the meantime, can you deal with them?"

John studied the four and lowered his chin as a hard glint entered his eyes. "I can. What do the sensors tell you?"

"They are not drawing eMU from the world around them as you do," Remy observed.

"We are taught that Talent is something we have because of our genes, not an outside energy we can tap into. These guys have no reserves—unless they've worked that trick out for themselves. Can you ID them?"

"Their features are hidden by the combat armor, but I will continue to work on it. I will have more conclusive data if blood is spilled."

He stilled. "Blood will be spilled," he promised. "I can't see it ending any other way."

"Nor can I," the AI admitted softly and the Virtual World drained away and left John seated in the pod.

Before he could demand that it open, the hatch lifted.

"There is armor waiting in the Supply Depot," Remy informed him. "It is not as heavy as theirs but I have provided projectiles with more penetration capability to compensate. I suggest—"

"Remy, you're babbling," John told him, slid out, and walked swiftly to the elevator. "I've got this."

He moved more quickly when his body registered that it was no longer in the pod and was jogging by the time he reached Supply. The armor waited on a stand inside the door and his weapons had been laid out on the counter. A small drone hovered nearby.

"In case you need something," the AI explained when he darted it a curious look.

He went through the process of armoring up and checked the fastenings as best he could. Now he knew why the teams on television checked one another before a fight. There were some things you simply couldn't do as well on your own.

"I saw blades," he said to Remy.

"You haven't trained with them yet, and that knowledge does not come intuitively."

"When I get back then." He sighed.

"When you return," the AI agreed.

John nodded and examined his gear again. When he was sure he was ready, he turned toward the door.

"Show me where they are, Remy," he ordered, pulled his helmet on, and strode purposefully toward the foyer.

His HUD lit up with the required information and he studied it as he walked. When he was sure he was ready, he pushed into a jog.

"Open the gates, Remy. I'd like to meet them before they find the pass."

"Roger that—and if you have any trouble with them, remember Plan C."

He chuckled as the gates came into view.

The AI saw him through them and monitored his progress up the short slope to the narrow pass that protected the approach to the compound.

"Even if you are successful, John, I am afraid this may be the end of the line for me," he murmured as he began to back his files up—and not to the servers bunkered alongside the VR pod.

There were procedures and alternatives for times like this and they were all off-site.

CHAPTER SEVEN

John had stopped laughing by the time he reached the slope leading into the pass.

"I'm going too slowly," he murmured and drew on his Talent to give his legs more strength.

The training over the last few weeks had paid off and he was still breathing easily when he reached the top of the rise. Despite the need he felt to hurry, he slowed his pace.

It was difficult to force himself to maintain a cautious walk when all he wanted to do was reach the hunters before they saw anything that could endanger Remy.

He reached the green zone just beyond the pass and scanned it. As soon as he saw it was clear, he dog-trotted quickly up the slope he'd used in his retreat after he'd defeated the first set of hunters.

If this new group hadn't arrived yet, he still had time.

As he crested the top of the hill, he slowed, crouched low to traverse the crest, and stopped behind the cover of the rocky outcrop he'd hidden behind during his first encounter.

Several such hills stood within what he now knew was a

broad canyon with a dead-end—a box canyon, Remy called it, and the perfect site for the AI's second forest.

Carefully, he peered around the rocks, and when he saw the approach was still clear, hurried down the slope to the canyon floor. A short distance ahead of him, the canyon walls curved into a bend.

The boy reminded himself that he needed to keep the Talents at a far enough distance that they wouldn't see the green mist slowly filling the canyon's far end. Worried at how far they might have traveled since he last checked on them, he jogged a little faster.

"Remy, show me where they—" John stopped as the first black-armored figure came round the bend. "Never mind."

He didn't give the Talent time to respond but called a bolt of lightning with a downward jerk of his fist. One of the things his time in the Virt World had taught him was that not every attack would originate from him.

The energy merely needed him to tell it where to start and where to go. He still felt it surge through him to reach the point he wanted, but it was like it covered the distance between him and that point in space with no delay between.

One day, he intended to ask Stephanie how that worked—or one of her teachers. Someone would be able to explain it but for the life of him, he could not.

Part of him pitied the man who blew apart in front of him, but he had no time. If he ever discovered the hunter's name, he'd mourn him. For now, there were three more to deal with—and none of them were happy to see him.

"Target sighted." When the voice issued through his comms, he realized Remy had tapped their network and was feeding it to him.

"Good one, Rems," he muttered, unconcerned when the AI did not respond. He had other things to think about.

One of the hunters surged toward him at a run and drew two

gleaming blades as she did so. Her scream of grief and outrage roared through his headset as she approached.

"Sorry, lady," he snapped and punched two balls of lightning in her direction as he vaulted upward.

She skidded to a halt and her blades lowered to her sides as she gaped at him. It did not stop one of the figures who followed her, however, and he snapped his blaster up and fired several shots in rapid succession.

The Talent closest to them slapped the muzzle down.

"We want him alive!" she snapped.

"That is so not gonna happen," the man replied, his voice a statement of fact. "The only way he'll let us bring him in is in pieces. Now we know what happened to 357 and 92."

"We won't be sure until we find their bodies."

John called a second bolt of lightning, but the hunter he targeted dived to one side.

"That only works once, dropkick." The voice told him it was the one who had said that the only way to bring him in was dead. Of course, the fact that he was right didn't alter the fact he had no intention of dying.

He spun his hands to conjure a swirl of light that engulfed the guy with the blaster. What right did he have to bring a blaster to a Talent fight?

"Sonuva!" the hunter shouted as his partner retreated and her hands lit with power.

She laughed. "I don't think he likes you very much, 310."

John might have found it funny except he was already focused on the woman with the swords and unleashed a barrage of lightning balls in her direction.

It crossed his mind that he hadn't tried to talk to them and that perhaps they could be convinced to join him—especially since he already had a link to their comms.

The thought didn't stop him from sending a third volley of three lightning spheres toward her. She'd assumed a stance that said she would deflect them with her swords and he wanted to see how that worked out for her.

His curiosity drew his attention from the other two and he let himself drift a little lower for a better look.

"What are you doing, John?" Remy asked as a bolt of energy flashed out of the center of the maelstrom.

"I'm going to—" he began and caught sight of the bolt too late to stop it from making impact.

He tried to twist out of its way and began to fall. Panic surged through him and he lost his focus on the whirlwind and didn't see it dissipate around its target.

The bolt seared past him and caught his armor in transit, and energy seared over his chest. He gasped and the pain momentarily drove all other concerns from his head.

John had barely begun to concentrate on pushing himself away from the ground when he landed and his focus broke a second time.

"John?" Remy's anxious tones brought him back to the present time to see twin flashes of metal descending.

How did she close the distance so quickly?

"John?"

"I'm here, Remy," he croaked and rolled away from the blades.

Bone grated in his chest and he yelped with pain. He turned his tumble into a push to his feet and stumbled away from his attacker to get clear as Lars had taught him.

He also scanned the battlefield for the others—something else Stephanie's head guard had insisted he learn.

They were closing but not attacking, although power flickered around them like lightning in two clouds.

"I might be in a little trouble, Rems."

"No kidding!" the AI exclaimed. "I can see it, you know. What did I say about coming back to me in one piece? One *living* piece," he reiterated a few moments later when he almost missed blocking a sword blow.

"Need…a minute…Rems," he told him, hugged one arm across the lower part of his chest to stop it hurting, and held the other one raised to block any more incoming attacks.

"You gonna make this easy on yourself, 781?" the woman with the sword asked as she lashed out again.

John caught the attack on his shield, pushed it down and away, and extended the shield to block the incoming lightning bolt. He managed to catch it, absorbed the energy into the shield, and used it to strengthen his defenses.

Beyond the visor of her helmet, he saw the woman's jaw drop.

"No," he told her and opened the link Remy had created between them, "but you could always come with me."

"Never gonna happen, smart aleck," the second woman interjected. "You're coming with us. It's your choice what shape you're in when you do."

He responded with a pained chuckle and called on the energy surrounding him, directed it into his damaged torso, and asked it to fix what they'd broken.

It couldn't repair the ruined front plate of his armor but his chest stopped hurting and breathing became much easier.

"Funny," he retorted, "I was about to make you the same offer."

The woman with the swords snorted and surged forward in a mesh of blades. He backed away but kept a wary eye on the other two Talents as they tried to work their way around to either side.

"Not gonna happen," he muttered, then raised his voice. "You guys need to chill and think about your options."

They laughed.

"You and what snowstorm? You've already pulled us out of the only decent weather to be had on the planet."

"What snowstorm?" he asked and decided to try something new.

Anything I can think of, right? He thought about snow and cold and a rain of icy daggers that lanced from the sky.

He was the only one not surprised when it happened.

The woman with the swords conjured a shield and didn't take her eyes off him.

"What *are* you?"

"I'm a witch of the Federation!" he declared and noticed one of the other Talents fall, only to be shielded by his comrade.

"Heresy!" the swordswoman shouted in response.

"I am her prophet," John retorted but changed his mind. There had only ever been one prophet and that was Becca. "No! I am her Apostle."

"You're insane!" she declared and attacked him again. "Damaged goods. And I don't care what tricks you think you can pull. I will put you down."

"You can try," he taunted as he blocked her frantic attacks.

"I. Will. *Succeed!*" she shrieked, feinted with one blade, and kicked his feet out from under him while he was distracted.

Again, he landed hard but he extended a Talent-augmented hand and grasped her by the ankle to yank her down as well. She uttered a startled yell as she fell but managed to retain her hold on one blade.

The other spun out of her hand.

John didn't bother to see where it went. He focused instead on driving a shard of ice into the swordswoman's side and his Talent penetrated the hardened armor and skewered the living being within.

She shrieked once and then lay still and her hand opened to release the sword. He raised his head to see what the other hunters were doing and wasn't happy that one now hauled the other to his feet.

They both glanced in his direction at the same time.

"One-Forty!" the female Talent cried and raised her hands to send a bolt of energy sizzling toward him.

He rolled back and created a shield to block it.

"She had a choice!" he shouted. "And so do you."

"A choice?" the woman cried. "To what? Run away and join you in your desert paradise?"

"To join me and fight for the Witch of the Federation!" he yelled in return.

"That monster," the woman protested.

"She's as human as anyone in the Regime," John told her. *"We're* as human as anyone in the Regime."

"That's not true," she argued and launched two more bolts of lightning toward him.

These jolted him back a step when they struck his shield.

"We were never human," she continued and pushed toward him as her partner moved wide and raised the blaster.

"Oh no, you don't," John told him and hurled two balls of force in his direction. "She's coming back," he insisted. "She'll fix everything and make them understand." He paused. "Make *you* understand."

"Your Witch is the reason we're in this mess to start with. She's the reason the aliens were able to send their experimental genes here! *She's* the reason some of us don't turn out being human like we should! It's *all. Her. Fault!"*

That last shout was accompanied by a bolt of lightning that struck at his feet and hurled him back.

He flung himself into a hasty tuck-and-roll and found his feet in time to shoot two more spheres at her before he bolted up the side of a hill. Too late, he recognized it as the same one he'd fought the last battle on, which meant he'd unwittingly led them to the last place he wanted her to see.

"What on God's green Earth is that?"

The woman had halted her advance and turned her head to study the swirl of green mist with its blanketing mass of cloud.

John tried to get her attention with an attack, but she ducked under it and her partner opened fire. He fell onto his stomach to avoid their shots, scrambled to stand, and stooped as he ran to the outcrop that had protected him so well before.

The man pursued him and traced a line of fire up the hill at his heels.

"That's not on the surveillance footage," his attacker murmured as the young rogue Talent hauled himself around the edge of the outcrop and out of his line of fire.

"Well, that tears it," Remy stated. "You need to finish this fight quickly, John. I am afraid we have little time."

CHAPTER EIGHT

"Is that it?" The question whispered over Ivy's comms as she eased to a stop and crouched in the shadows of the wall opposite a building made of ancient brick.

"It is," she confirmed.

"But it's not fenced." The comment was edged with tones of disbelief.

"I didn't say they were perfect."

"And it's simply one huge wall," someone else muttered.

"The section we're looking at is toward the front," she reassured them and wondered how the print-outs could have been so wrong. "The fences are at the back and there are several other buildings inside the compound."

Even as she said it, she considered the fact that it might not be true. The schematics she'd downloaded had revealed several smaller buildings inside a perimeter fence made of wire mesh. When she traced her gaze along the solid stone wall, she saw where it should have ended but continued instead. "What was this place?"

"An old government complex," Jade replied and studied the wall critically.

"It looks like they've made some upgrades since the plans were drawn up."

"You think?" the woman asked and her tone said she didn't need an answer.

"Carol?" Ivy said quietly. "Talk to me."

"I see what you see and I still don't believe it," Carol replied. "Gimme a minute."

"Got it!" Geraldine's younger voice interjected. "Someone forgot to update the system but the work order was in the externals and I hacked the contractor."

"That didn't take you very long."

"I started a half hour ago when I saw the surveillance feeds."

"You didn't think to warn us?" Ivy asked and anger began to stir.

"I thought you'd rather have the correct information sooner rather than later." She sounded crestfallen. "I'm sorry."

The girl made sense and it was exactly what she'd have done in the same situation. Ivy pushed herself to calm.

"There's no need. You did the right thing," she assured her. "Can you send it to Jade's mobile?"

"Right away." The girl's acknowledgment made her smile.

While it seemed like eons before, she'd been that young once.

The fact that it had been only a few weeks ago didn't mean a thing. Since Becca's death, she'd grown up considerably and had started the minute she took on the responsibility of getting everyone who'd attended the meeting out of the area.

She'd thought there'd be reprisals and had hurried them out of sight. A few had moved out of the city as soon as they could gather their belongings. Others hadn't bothered to pack before they left and some had chosen to stay.

"It's our home," they'd insisted and she hadn't tried to dissuade them.

It had been their choice, after all. She couldn't make it for them.

In some ways, that had been the hardest call she'd ever had to make, but she'd laughed at Dani when the healer had told her it had turned her into an adult. Looking back, she knew the woman had been right.

She only hoped Geraldine didn't have to go through the same process anytime soon. Being responsible for this many people carried a certain weight with it.

For now, she was grateful to be able to take on some of the things Becca had been doing. The woman had left a gap that Ivy doubted anyone could fill. She was trying but she knew it wasn't enough.

In simple terms, she wasn't Becca.

I'm not good enough to be her, she thought and turned away from the building as Jade plucked her sleeve and showed her the shielded tablet. *But I'm good enough for this.*

Protecting the history her older friend had valued so dearly—and trying to keep Becca's people safe—was something she could do. It wasn't everything the librarian had been doing but it would have to be enough.

As she studied the schematics Geraldine had sent through, she was glad she'd let Carol choose who she wanted. The girl might not have been Ivy's first selection, she'd done something none of the others would have thought of and it would most likely save their bacon.

"The way I see it, we can try that trick you and John used to get into the storage facility," Jade told her.

"Or we can go over the wall and in the back," Raul interjected, and Ivy became aware that the rest of Jade's team now crowded around them.

"Who's on look-out?" she asked.

"We're not helpless," Linus scoffed in response.

Ivy chose not to dignify that with an answer and focused on the tablet.

"There is one other way…" Klaus began and tapped the top of the building, then the one next to it.

"Where are the servers?" Ivy asked.

While she wasn't exactly fond of heights, his suggestion made considerable sense.

"Half-way up," Jade told her and frowned as she considered Klaus's alternative in silence for a moment. "It would work."

"What do we have above them?"

"It looks like exec suites and offices," Tammy murmured and tapped the screen. "That's a conference room."

They looked at each other and Ivy groaned. "Are you sure?"

"We don't know what kind of surveillance they have on the stairs—or exactly where their guards are stationed," Jade told her. She flicked through the floor plans and suddenly stopped. "Right. We'll use the roof. The guard station is too well-positioned for us to risk going up when we could come down. See?"

When she craned over her shoulder, she did see. "What about getting out?"

The woman shoved the tablet into her jacket and pivoted to study the building's tall sides. "We'll break a window and rappel down."

"We will?"

"Sure we will," Raul assured her. "We can't have you tech types flaking out on the stairs on the way up."

Klaus grinned. "This will have them guessing for weeks."

"It'll have them twisting their tails in a knot trying to work out who's responsible," Jade agreed.

"If they don't tear the whole of Chicago apart trying to find us," Ivy added darkly, and the ex-Navy woman clapped her on the shoulder.

"My guess is they won't tear anything apart if they can't work out what's gone missing." She grinned and patted her shoulder this time. "And that's your job."

"Great," she grumbled and turned to the rest of her team. "So, who will break it to Linus?"

Because if there was one person who hated heights more than she did, it was him.

And she'd agreed to put him on a zip-line between two buildings before they made him step out a window to take a quick trip to the ground.

"I'll call it in," the female Talent declared.

John bobbed up from behind his rocks and launched a bolt of energy toward her. He missed her head but the impact on her armor was enough to throw her sideways.

"Remy, can you do something about that?" he asked.

"I can create static," the AI replied. "A sudden loss of communications would alert them to the fact that something else is here."

"And static won't?"

"It is a Dead Zone, John."

Really? He wondered how Remy had the time to be sarcastic.

He looked for the other Talent and was relieved to see the guy had stopped halfway up the rise. That faded in the next moment when he began to descend again slowly.

"I'll take some readings."

"Not right now, you don't," John told him, unconcerned that their comms were linked.

The boy swept a wall of blue down the slope as the female hunter glanced toward him.

"You *will* show us how that's done!" She snarled and bolted to the wall's outer edge.

Her partner sprinted in the opposite direction.

"I'd be glad to," he told them as he fired shards of lightning and ice at her. "When we've all vanished from the Regime's radar. You don't have to work for them."

"They're the only life we have," she retorted, reached the end of the wall, and dropped to one knee to shoulder her blaster.

"It's the only life the Regime has let you have," he pointed out. "They've lied to you."

She fired and he ducked behind the outcrop. A second set of bolts drilled into the rocks next to where his head had been and he cursed silently.

He'd missed both of them?

At least they'd forgotten about calling the shuttle.

With a groan, he switched from open comms to the closed line he shared with the AI.

"I have to get to the shuttle, Rem."

"Agreed. We will discuss your nomenclature later."

"My what?"

"What you call me."

"I call you many things."

"That is the problem."

A sizzle of energy engulfed the rocks to end the conversation and he scuttled back. It also forced him out into the opening where the two hunters were waiting.

It seemed he wasn't the only one who could use his Talent to augment his speed.

"Surprise!" 299 yelled and lashed out with her foot.

John ducked and managed to catch her ankle.

She shot him and the round pounded into his shoulder and drove him back. As she dropped into a ready stance, 310 came out of nowhere to take advantage of his shock. He leaned away and barely avoided the man's fist as he took mental stock of the damage.

The armor had borne most of the impact and stopped the projectile before it could penetrate his shoulder. It still hurt and he would bruise, but he'd manage.

Once he'd directed some of his Talent into the injury, he pulled more of it around his body to block the next blow 310 leveled at his head. He also managed to stop the next two rounds 299 fired from point-blank range.

One rippled the shield in front of his face and he glanced at her. She was furious and her eyes gleamed a fiery gold, her body limned with silver fire.

He thumped a hand into the ground and the resultant shockwaves rolled through it to put the two hunters off-balance. At the same time, he pushed himself vertically to gain distance between himself and the earth.

310's response was immediate. "Don't kill him, 299! I need to know how he did that."

"If you want to know how to fly, I'll open the hatch in the shuttle on the way home," she snapped in response. "One good push and you'll get the idea."

"That's not how it works," 310 protested.

"Then get him down from there."

"With or without dents?" her partner grumbled.

"I'd prefer without," John told him, switched comms channels, and called another bolt of lightning from the energy around him.

The man threw his hand up as though to shield himself and the bolt penetrated his palm and shattered his arm and armor as far as the shoulder before it burned into his torso. He screamed and fell to curl in a shivering ball.

The other Talent bolted the way they'd come.

John moved to follow her but tripped. He threw his arms forward, caught himself on his hands, and the motion continued into a roll that wrenched his foot free from the gnarled root in the process. Breathless, he pivoted into a crouch and looked back.

310 lay on the ground, his good arm outstretched, and sparks of Talent built in his palm. For a second, he contemplated having Remy send the drones to take the guy to base, but his adversary curled his wrist and flicked the gathered energy toward him.

He blocked it with a spinning disc of blue and streaked a second bolt of lightning into the prone form.

Another time, he thought and refused to let regret overwhelm him as he turned to look for 299.

She was making good time but the lightning around her was fading.

"I cannot keep her from making contact with the shuttle for much longer," Remy warned urgently. "Hurry, John."

The shuttle! He started to run.

The woman had almost reached the bend in the canyon and the mouth lay a few hundred yards beyond that. Remy's scans showed the craft not far from the entry.

"How many pilots?" he asked and heard a gasp in response.

When he realized that he'd forgotten to change his comms to the private channel, he drew Talent from the world around him and pushed into a sprint. Ahead of him, Talent 299 lengthened her stride.

"Stop!" John shouted and injected as much force into the command as he could.

Some of the energy he'd drawn snuck into the word and his target faltered. Before he could even begin to work out what that meant, she increased her speed again.

"You're losing her," Remy warned and he re-focused.

The hunter was parallel with the corner and began to make the turn.

"No!" he shouted, flung an open palm up, and poured a stream of pure energy toward her. "Take her down!"

The stream separated into a swarm of blue bolts rimmed in white.

He watched them as he ran. "They won't make it," he muttered as she raced around the bend and vanished from view.

All he could do was focus on the magic and will it to catch up with her before she could cover the final distance and come into view of the waiting shuttle. There was no telling what the pilots would do if they saw her fall without a Talent in sight.

"Honestly, there's no telling what they'll do if they do see you," he muttered and concentrated on running.

John covered the distance to the turn, expecting to see 299 crossing the last few yards to the shuttle.

Thankfully, the magic had caught her as she cleared the bend and the back of her armor was a smoking crater.

He felt a moment of relief before a hollowness swept it aside. He'd killed another Talent—another mage and a human, like himself. There was something dark and painful about that.

Remy interrupted him before he could sink further into sadness.

"I need you at the compound, John."

CHAPTER NINE

"I will kill you," Linus muttered as Ivy helped him over the edge of the roof.

She ignored the savage bite to his voice. She'd known he was afraid of heights but she'd also known that he wouldn't let her down.

He wasn't happy about it, and she'd spend the next week putting up with his acid tongue as he worked himself around it, but it was worth it.

"You're doing fine," she reassured him.

"Tell me you've found another way out for us," he demanded hoarsely and she nodded.

"I have.

"And it doesn't involve the roof," he added.

The girl arched her eyebrows and gave him her most sincere stare. "It does not involve any roof."

"Promise?" he asked as she moved him away from the arrival zone.

"I promise."

Now was not the time to tell him their departure involved a

window, some rope, and a very long drop. She needed his attention on the job and not mired in fear.

There was a very good chance he'd refuse to go on any more operations after this, but it was worth it if they could safeguard Stephanie's history from the Regime. She left him with Raul and returned to help the rest of the team make the crossing.

Not that they needed her help, of course. Tucker was a little shaky but he'd put his faith in the safety harness and kept his gaze fixed on hers as he inched across the gap.

"I'm glad that's over," he whispered as he moved in a half-crouch to where Raul and Linus inspected the security system on the door.

Ivy hoped it was as simple as Geraldine and Carol had told her it was. She gave the roof camera a nervous glance, and Carol chuckled in her earpiece.

"It's still looping. As far as the observation post is concerned, there's nothing to see here."

"How long do we have?" she asked.

"We're monitoring them through their surveillance equipment," the woman told her. "As soon as they show any sign of… well, anything, we'll let you know."

As happy with that as she could be, she waited until Jade stood on the roof beside her.

"Are we good?" the security lead asked her.

"The original plan was for you to wait outside," Ivy reminded her. "Are you sure you're…"

She let her words peter out as Jade raised a hand.

"Plans change. No plan survives contact with the enemy." She smiled. "In this case, the enemy was the building and we hadn't done our homework."

The woman crouched and pulled her tablet out. "We'll go in with you and we'll make sure you all get out and away. I've called a second team in to pick us up here." She indicated a point two blocks away.

When Ivy nodded, she continued. "We'll break into pairs. Raul will take Linus—and I mean he'll get him out as well as away. Let us deal with that."

She caught the girl's gaze and waited for confirmation.

"Tucker will go with Tammy and Calliope," Jade continued, "and you'll come with me."

Ivy nodded, glad she had a team to back her up—and grateful Jade was on her side and hadn't chosen to join the Regime's Enforcers when she retired.

Why was that? she wondered, but Linus uttered a soft exclamation of triumph and she looked up as Raul slipped through the partially open door into the stairwell beyond.

Tammy followed him, and Calliope pulled Tucker to stand with Linus. Jade slapped Ivy's shoulder.

"You're up."

The girl moved quickly to take her place with the boys.

"Are you ready?" she asked and they nodded.

Color had seeped into Linus's face again and a bounce had returned to Tucker's step.

"Go," Calliope ordered, and Ivy looked back to make sure the two men followed as she started down the stairs.

Her glance saw Calliope follow and Jade fall back to the edge of the roof before she moved behind them with Klaus. The two of them kept a wary eye on the surrounding buildings, but Ivy didn't have time to watch them.

She flipped the hood of her jacket over her hair and lowered her head as she started down the stairs. It was difficult to resist looking at the cameras as she passed, but Jade had taught them to never assume the loop would hold.

"It could be lifted as you snuck a peek," the woman told her teams. "Never look directly at them if you can avoid it."

"But what if they come on?" Linus had asked.

"Exactly," she had said pointedly before she answered the question. "Keep an eye on them if it makes you feel better, but remember that you have security specialists with you for a reason. Your job is to do the tech work your protection can't. Their job is to get you in and out alive."

She hadn't said anything more but she hadn't needed to. "Let them do their job," hung in unspoken echoes. It was one of the hardest things Ivy had ever had to do.

Not only was she used to looking out for herself, but she was used to not having anyone else to trust at her back. The few emergency human exfiltrations she and Jade had done after Becca's death had helped but it hadn't changed everything.

When she realized that her mind had begun to wander, she led the way down the stairs but scanned all doors and landings carefully and listened for any movement from below.

Raul met them on the landing of the floor they'd thought their servers were on.

"Tammy's waiting," he informed them and waved them through. As soon as Camille had reached the landing, he turned and threaded past them to take the lead.

Ivy let him and her gaze traveled the length of the corridor to note doors, potted plants, and pictures. She also saw the open office that faced the outside of the building and caught a glimpse of Tammy at the window.

Quickly, she pushed forward and pretended that their descent had her complete attention. She hoped Linus didn't grasp the significance of Tammy's position. With any luck, he'd think the specialist was on look-out duty.

None of them spoke until Raul stopped beside another door. "Is this what you were looking for?" he asked.

She took one look and nodded.

It was a workspace and a computer vault. A double row of desks faced each in a central area backed by servers that stretched in both directions.

"Take a look at this place!" Tucker whispered as he slowed to a stop.

Ivy caught his hand and directed him firmly toward a desk. "Time to work, boys."

Linus didn't wait to be told. He sat quickly at another workstation. "Where will you be, Ivy?"

"Well..." She looked around the room. "My thought is that there has to be a supervisor's desk here somewhere and that terminal might be worth hacking into."

Both boys nodded and Tucker smiled. "Rather you than me," he told her and focused on his screen.

Aware that Raul shadowed her every step, she began her search.

"What's so special about the supervisor's terminal?" he asked and she knew he was asking why she couldn't make do with one of the workstations they'd already found.

"Permissions," she told him as she made her way along one wall. She hoped the supervisor had a secure station and that it was hidden behind the stacks.

She also hoped he didn't have a desk on a different floor—like the ground floor, for instance. And that it was at this end of the stacks and not the other. The less time she took to find it, the more she'd have to hack it.

When she reached the far wall, she breathed a sigh of relief. A single door was tucked into the corner she'd aimed for, and while it had been the most logical space for it, the find hadn't been guaranteed.

"This is what you were after?" Raul asked and held a hand out to stop her from going in.

Ivy nodded.

"Let me check it," he told her.

"Wait." Geraldine's voice stopped them in their tracks. "Aaaaand three...two...one. Okay, you're clear to enter."

"Can we keep her?" Raul asked, and the woman chuckled over the comms.

"Keep her? We'll have to. Getting rid of her will be impossible after this."

"Enough chatter," Jade interjected sharply. "Get it done."

He frowned but didn't comment. Ivy caught his look and nodded. If the ex-Navy woman was worried, they needed to hurry. Her instincts bordered on prescience.

Raul ducked out of the office as soon as Ivy entered.

"Make it quick," he murmured off the comms, and she resisted the urge to roll her eyes.

Honestly, why did he think she'd be anything else?

It had been a long six weeks—or had it been eight? Either way, the *Knight* was running on a skeleton crew and the strain had begun to show. They'd spent most of their time awake to ensure that nothing was broken and only woke the people they needed to effect repairs or check things.

Now, they needed to do more.

Stephanie slid into the captain's conference room and sat opposite Rawlins. The woman raised an eyebrow at her choice but she smiled a quiet welcome.

"Catering will bring food shortly," she said.

"And coffee?" she asked hopefully.

"And coffee. Also tea."

"Tea?" She wondered which of them drank that.

"A long time in stasis does funny things to your taste buds," Cameron Hargreaves informed her when he entered in time to hear her exclamation. "Why do you ask?"

She blushed. "I merely wondered, is all. It's not like you to swear off the hard stuff."

He laughed. "The hard stuff? I haven't given up whiskey if that's what you mean."

"Well, we're all out of that," Rawlins told him firmly and he stopped in mid-stride.

"We're *what?*"

It wasn't quite a roar but it was the loudest response he had ever uttered in what wasn't a life or death situation.

The captain maintained a straight face for another ten seconds before she burst into laughter.

"You wicked, wicked, woman!" he exclaimed as the door opened behind him. "It's not nice to play with a man's heart like that."

"Then you're in luck, aren't you, Hargreaves?" Wattlebird asked. "Since we all know you don't have one."

The chief engineer started to sputter and rolled his eyes ceilingward. "Ebony, tell me we're ready to wake the rest of the crew."

"That is what I believe this conference is to decide, Cameron," the ship informed him politely. "But I will not unlock the 'hard stuff' until you have an adequate replacement on deck."

"It's a conspiracy," he grumbled. "A conspiracy," he repeated but he was smiling.

His smile broadened when his tea arrived, along with everyone else's chosen beverage and they all took a sip of their brews and breathed a long sigh. They looked at each other and smiled.

Ebony broke the silence. "Shall we begin?"

This brought a collective groan from the four of them but they straightened in their chairs and looked at Stephanie.

She shrugged and gestured to the captain. "It's not my ship, so I think Marianne has the final say on who's next."

"So you do agree it's time, then?" the woman asked and they all nodded.

"I need a navigator," Wattlebird interjected quickly. "There's only so much star map I can cover on my own and I'd like a second opinion."

He paused, then added, "I'd also like a co-pilot and a team to relieve us. No offense, Ebony, but I think we need to free up some of your computing power."

"I agree," the captain surprised them by saying. "We need more of Ebony available and we need more crew on deck—especially as I think we're heading into a war zone."

Stephanie straightened, her expression concerned. "You do?"

Rawlins shrugged. "Given what we left behind?" she asked. "And how long we've been away? If it's not war, I'd be surprised if it wasn't close."

"So we need to get back fast?" Cameron queried, and Wattlebird grew tense.

"Not fast...at least, not yet," the woman replied, "but as we've said before, we need to get to a location where we can work out what's going on before we run blindly into a hostile situation."

Wattlebird nodded. "Yeah. I remember how the Federation was painting Stephanie. We might not be very welcome in their patch of Space."

The girl wished he didn't make sense but before they'd slept, she'd talked about what was happening with Todd and Lars had pointed out a number of dirty tricks and tactics he recognized.

"They have someone very good on their PR team," her security lead had said, "and it looks like they've been laying the groundwork for a very long time."

She looked at Rawlins. "I think we need Lars," she said and to her surprise, the captain agreed. "Also Lieutenant-Commander Christoffersen. The one you call Johnny. You'll need them both, and he's the better analyst of the two."

"And you'll need your security team," Cameron told her and glanced at the other woman for approval.

Again, Marianne agreed. "As loyal as they are, we don't know how the crew will react when they discover how much time has passed. We must have some way to keep any troublemakers under control."

"So...you want the Marines on deck, too?" Stephanie asked and her heart skipped a beat.

"At least Todd's team, but bring the two captains out of stasis as well. When they've wrapped their heads around the situation, we'll see who else they recommend."

"I will need my section operational as soon as you think it's viable," the chief added quietly. "The ones I have now are starting to run ragged."

Rawlins nodded. She looked around the table and her gaze rested on the Witch.

"Here's what I think. We need our security on deck first...but we stick with the two who are our analysts. I'll second Lars and Johnny to look at the personnel files to see if they can identify anyone who'll be high risk if we bring them out early."

Stephanie frowned with concern. "Do you think that's likely?"

"Take a look at Nielsen," Cameron reminded her. "He's still on shaky ground and probably needs some down-time."

The captain nodded, and Stephanie got the impression this wasn't the first time he had raised the young engineer with her.

"How bad is he?" she asked.

The man's face softened. "He'll benefit from having more crew around him. He had friends in the Weapons and Life Support sections."

He paused and looked at Rawlins again. "Is it possible..."

"Give me their names and I'll have Storenson and Christoffersen include them in the first batch. I agree, he needs someone." She paused and considered it. "Several someones."

"And he'll need to know what happened to his girl—sooner rather than later," Cameron added.

"Agreed," she told him. "I'll have Storenson look into it once we're in range."

"So, do I get my navigator and another pilot?" Wattlebird asked.

The captain smiled and she looked at Stephanie. "What do

you say, Steph? We pull Lars and Christoffersen out first, along with Avery and Lieutenant Bhattani, and once they're up to speed and settling in, we grab the rest of your team and another...dozen?"

She stopped and raised an eyebrow at Cameron.

He pulled his tablet out and tapped a quick message on the surface. When he was finished, he gave the screen one final tap and looked at her.

"As many of the top twenty as I can have on short notice," he told her, "but I'm willing to wait until your analysts can clear them."

Rawlins ran her eye down the list and glanced at the engineer. "I can have them go over these while they're still surfacing. It'll give them something to do."

She turned to Wattlebird. "And I'm sure you can find suitable tasks for Avery and Bhattani."

It was an order more than a question, but the pilot answered it anyway. "We'll need to go over the nav charts."

The woman quirked an eyebrow. "Are you sure?" she asked and Stephanie was surprised to hear a teasing lilt to her voice.

Wattlebird gave her a startled look, then blushed. "Yes. This news will come as something of a shock. She'll need time to decide."

Decide? Oh, dear Lord... Stephanie pulled her face poker-straight and nodded. After all, the man hadn't started ribbing her about Todd yet.

Captain Rawlins hadn't finished. "I'd also like to have a small team of medics on standby in case something goes wrong with the decanting."

"Agreed," Cameron and Wattlebird stated, and the Witch nodded.

She hadn't realized until then how lucky they'd been when they'd woken up. Nothing had gone wrong and while it wasn't likely to, it would be good to have medics standing by in case something did.

"And that brings us to the Marines." Now that Marianne had their agreement on the medics, she was more relaxed.

Her lips quirked and she looked at Stephanie. "I think we need to pull the three leaders clear first and let them decide who they'll need next."

"What about the other sections?" the girl asked and lowered her head to avoid meeting any of their gazes. "I don't want to be accused of favoritism."

"You leave that to me." Rawlins' voice was hard. "Once we've decided who we'll bring out in the next batch, I'll call in the team leads we have on deck and ask them who they need and when. Those will be the next group I'll have Storenson and Christoffersen analyze."

CHAPTER TEN

"Ha!" Ivy whispered, her voice fierce with triumph. "That'll keep you dork-brains busy."

Her fingers danced over the keys before she brought her forefinger down in a single decisive tap on the *Enter* key. She snickered as the string of code disappeared into the ether.

"How's it coming?" Raul asked from the doorway. "Jade will come in there and drag you out by your knickers if you don't get a wriggle on."

"Ask her how much she wants to know where the other two communication nexuses are," she retorted.

"A lot," the woman responded over their comms, "but from what Geraldine's telling me, you have about five minutes, tops."

She laced her fingers together and pressed them away from her. "I'll see what I can do."

"You've got one already, haven't you?" Raul asked and she chuckled.

"Almost. How are Tucker and Linus doing?"

"We've removed the location from the FAT and scrambled the rest of the table. By the time they've finished untangling it, they won't be able to work out what they've lost."

"What do you mean by scrambled?" she asked.

"I mean we've switched a number of the links around," Tucker told her.

"And duplicated a good handful more," Linus confirmed, then added wistfully. "Can we go now?"

"I need another five minutes," Ivy told them. "Why don't you see what you can dig up—or what else you can scramble to keep them busy?"

She found the second communications location and was about to shut the computer down when another idea struck her.

"You know this isn't an air-gapped system, right? The only reason we can't access it is because we don't have the right terminal."

"Your point?" Jade demanded and sounded on edge.

"Well, I can simply…" She made a few adjustments to the code. "and then I can…" She tweaked a setting and created a path. "And we're—"

A long, low beep broke the silence and the lights came on—orange and strobing. A second beep bleated and the alarm continued in a continuous low blare.

Ivy started to type frantically to hide what she'd done and cover her tracks as fast as she could. Raul stepped into the room as she pushed her chair back and headed to the door. He wrapped a hand around her bicep and ran with her.

"Speak to me, Carol," Jade demanded as Raul passed Ivy to Klaus and hurried to Linus.

The young techie sat stock-still in his chair, his face as white as a sheet. With a muttered oath, the man dragged him clear.

"Don't just sit there, boy."

"Tell me you've still got the cameras, Gerry!"

Gerry? It took Ivy a minute to realize Jade was talking to Geraldine.

Calliope met them in the hall. "The window's a no-go, K. We're gonna need to get them out via the stairwell."

Klaus didn't argue. "Are you leading or directing?"

"Leading," Jade answered and issued orders while she made sure they all exited the room.

Calliope didn't hesitate. "This way."

She bolted to the stairs with Klaus close beside her. His hand remained firm on Ivy's arm and she tried to pull free of him.

"Don't you need that hand to shoot with?"

"Right now, I need it to tell me where you are. When the shooting starts, it'll be somewhere else."

The girl didn't try to pull free, again. She assumed he was following some kind of guard protocol and ran with him. At least this way, she knew she wouldn't get lost.

They reached the next landing, then the next, and had passed the third when they heard a door open below them. Calliope reversed direction and Klaus turned with her and gave her room to pass when they reached the third landing again.

This time, they went through the door and out into the corridor, and Ivy realized the constant flow of voices were the conversations Carol and Geraldine were carrying on with Jade at the tail and Calliope at the head.

"Still got 'em. They're gonna have to come looking for you," sounded reassuring.

"We won't make that landing," did not.

It was followed by, "We're gonna have to split up."

"Try the other stairwell. We'll keep their attention on this one," Klaus snapped and released Ivy's arm.

Her relief was short-lived as Calliope took hold of her other arm.

"This way," the woman ordered and tugged her into the corridor and to a door. "Stay."

She made short work of the lock and dragged Ivy inside. "Stay here unless I call 'squirrel,' okay? If I say that, you listen to Geraldine and she'll get you out of the building."

Before the girl could reply, she was gone and shut the door behind her.

"I've got you, Ivy." Geraldine tried to reassure her. "But I need you to stay there while I help Carol guide the boys out of the building, okay?"

"Gotcha," she managed to say but her voice caught when she grasped what was happening.

She, Klaus, and Calliope were the "expendables," the part of the group that had been designated the most sensible sacrifice if it meant the rest of the team could escape. Jade had explained the concept to her.

"It shouldn't happen," the ex-Navy woman had said, "but if it does, this is how it works."

Remembering it was little comfort, but it helped Ivy to keep her fear under control. She had no illusions about what would happen if the Regime caught her hiding there.

The room was dark and smelt like a janitor's closet. There'd been barely enough room for Calliope to pull her in and squeeze out again, but she closed her eyes and moved to the back of it.

She didn't have to simply stand here and wait to be taken. There were ways to make it hard for someone to find her. Crouching, for instance, instead of standing up so she was the first thing anyone who glanced in might notice.

Encouraged by her decision to not simply be a victim, she hunkered down and let her eyes adjust to the dark. There was no emergency lighting in the closet but she could feel the shelves. There was enough space for her to squeeze between them if she needed to.

The door opened and she gasped, but the silhouette belonged to Klaus. He looked down and grinned.

"Good idea," he told her and held his hand out.

She didn't keep him waiting but took it quickly and let him drag her to her feet and pull her into the corridor. This time,

Geraldine's voice was the only one speaking as the girl guided them through the maze of corridors to a fire escape.

Klaus took one look at it and backed away. "That's a no-go, Gerry. It's not there."

"Try the office to your left. Your other left. Go straight through. Take a right. There. In front of you."

"It's a bookcase," he responded.

Boots clattered into the corridor behind them and headed toward the emergency exit.

Calliope stepped back, getting ready to defend the door if anyone came through it.

"It's right there." Geraldine lowered her voice to a whisper as if it would carry beyond their headsets. "Another door. In front of you."

"Bookcase," Klaus responded hoarsely.

Ivy looked from Klaus to Calliope and back to the bookcase. She agreed with Carol's hastily spoken interjection.

"If Gerry says there's a door, there's a door. Work it out."

She stared at the shelves and stepped closer to run a hand down the closest edge and wriggle her fingers into the narrow space between the shelves. Halfway down, a small bar caught her fingertips.

"Door," she muttered.

Klaus didn't argue but immediately checked his side and the books on the shelves. She fidgeted with the bar but couldn't shift it.

"Whatever you're gonna do, it has to be fast," Calliope whispered.

Ivy turned her attention to the ornaments—some kind of orb on a stand, a trophy cup, and a plaque leaning against the back of the shelf.

She grasped it and pulled it forward to see if there was anything behind it. Instead of revealing a handle or button, it folded beneath her hand and its base acted as a hinge. A click issued from the edge of the bookcase and it swung inward and away.

"Go! Go, go, go," Geraldine urged and strained to keep her voice soft. Calliope didn't hesitate. She left her post at the door and approached the opening in a rush.

Klaus pushed Ivy through the gap in front of them and followed on her heels. Calliope came through the gap behind him and turned to slam the bookcase closed. She didn't linger to see if it had locked but raced after them as they scrambled down stairs that had turned invisible in the dark.

"There aren't any cameras in there," Geraldine told them, "but I can guess where you are on the schematics. Keep going to the bottom and you should find yourself in an underground car park. I have the basement on a loop but it won't hold for long."

"Which way is out?" Klaus asked and paused to retrieve a flashlight from one of his pockets. He flicked it on and they continued their hurried descent.

Their ears strained for any sign that their exit had been discovered but no sound reached them from the office above. None of them relaxed, however.

They reached the bottom of the stairs and stopped at the door.

"Gerry?" Klaus asked.

"Still clear. Still looping," the girl replied. "There's a stairwell into the ground floor of the building but it comes up next to the rear exit."

"Some exec's escape route," Klaus murmured and Calliope nodded.

Ivy had another alternative. "Are there any storm drains under here?"

"Yes…no. My bad. There's one on the other side of the wall. In the street."

She groaned. "I hate stairs."

Klaus clapped his hand on her shoulder and slid his hand around her arm again. "Suck it up, princess."

"Ugh. You say the sweetest things," she grumbled but she broke into a run when he did and they bolted to the second entrance.

"Tell me it's still clear," he demanded as he jerked the door open and started up the stairs.

A short silence was followed by an abrupt, "Busy! Go!" from Geraldine.

Klaus tensed, and Ivy thought he would stop but he continued and dragged her up the narrow flight of stairs behind him. Not that she would have stopped if she could have. Calliope was on her heels and the woman was in a hurry.

They slowed as they neared the top, only to have Geraldine urge them forward.

"I can't hold the loop. You need to get out! Now!"

"Door?" he demanded.

"Right! Your right! Go!"

The man eased the door open, stuck his head into the corridor, and twisted right and ran. He let go of Ivy's arm and grasped the handle of the next door but it remained stubbornly shut.

"Cal," he whispered but Ivy pushed under his arm and took a set of lock-picks from her satchel.

"I've got this."

"You?"

"I learned but you guys never give me a turn," she complained and worked the picks in the lock as Calliope reached the top of the stairs and stopped behind them.

The woman didn't try to shoulder her aside and simply asked, "You got it?"

The lock turned beneath her hands and she grinned. "Yup."

She pulled her tools free and opened the door, then remembered to check what lay beyond before she sprinted into the dark with Klaus and Calliope on her heels.

Jade met them a block from the storage center.

"You sure kicked over a hornet's nest," she told them and guided them into an alley where a car waited.

It was old and dilapidated but there was space in the trunk for Ivy and Calliope and Klaus made a bulky shadow in the footwell behind the driver's seat, an old blanket thrown over his head.

None of them spoke until they reached the parking lot under Dani's apartment block.

"That was close," Calliope murmured and leaned into Klaus's chest as he snaked an arm around her.

"Too close," he murmured, nuzzled her hair, and pulled her close.

Ivy gave Jade a sharp glance. "Did we make it?"

CHAPTER ELEVEN

"**A**re you sure you don't want me to retrieve the shuttle?" John asked.

"I need you to bring the bodies to the green zone," Remy informed him. "Waste disposal is much more efficient there."

"But won't that draw the next group of searchers closer to the compound?"

"I am afraid it is too late to avoid that now," the AI informed him. "Please, bring the bodies closer. We don't have much time."

He stooped, seized the Talent by the collar, and lifted what was left of her so he could drag her by hooking his hands under her armpits.

"Are you sure you do not have a more efficient method for doing that?" Remy asked. "Time is of the essence."

"You mean, you want me to use my Talent to— Oh."

With a grimace, he set the body down and wrapped it in a layer of eMU which he used to lift it this time.

To his surprise and relief, the magic obeyed and floated it behind him.

"Most impressive," the AI approved. "Now hurry. You are needed here."

"For what?"

"You will see when you arrive."

He sighed but he obeyed and shifted into a dog-trot to carry the body to where the remains of his first attack lay at the side of the corner. While he hadn't noticed it in his pursuit of the female Talent, he did now.

His stomach roiled and he swallowed hard.

"Remind me to not use that trick again," he muttered, mainly to himself, only to have Remy respond.

"Why not, John? It was most effective."

"That's the problem," he informed him. "What if he'd been the one to decide to join me? I didn't give him a chance."

"Their conditioning was too strong," the AI consoled him. "It would have taken more than your efforts to sway them. I am sorry."

"Thanks, Rem. That helps." While he had regrets he was glad to know he'd tried—or at least wanted to—even though he couldn't have succeeded.

He settled the first corpse beside the second and expanded the bubble of eMU to include both.

"I guess it doesn't matter if the bits get mixed up," he murmured and this time, Remy had nothing to say.

The third and fourth corpses were easier to find, even if his regret grew stronger as he collected them. They'd been human and he'd killed them.

"John, your suit is showing signs of distress."

"Let's say I don't like killing people and leave it at that," he replied firmly.

"Ah. I cannot help you with that. It is something you will have to deal with on your own."

"I know." John sighed, walked into the mist, and changed the subject. "Where did you want these?"

"Take them to the center of the valley," Remy instructed him.

"A few steps more…and more…and…there. Leave them there. Our disposal measures will remove them shortly."

He did as he was asked and straightened. "Now what?"

"Now I need you to return. There is much we need to do."

"For what?"

"For Stephanie's project to be kept safe." The AI paused and added in tones of regret, "It will be a shame to leave the job part-done."

Alarm spiked through him. "What do you mean?"

"I mean," Remy began, as the young Talent started walking, "that I will need to clear all proof of this compound's existence—at least to the extent where the Regime are unable to discern its purpose."

John kept moving but his voice was tight when he asked, "What do you mean, Remy?"

"Return to the compound and we will discuss it."

"How about you tell me on the way?"

"Very well," the AI agreed.

He waited until John was almost at the chasm leading to the compound before he began.

"If the Regime finds this compound—and they will come looking—they will take the technology and use it for purposes its creators never intended. Sadly, there are many."

"Do I need to know what?" he asked and continued carefully through the narrow pass.

"They could decide to use Talents as a source of energy," Remy stated and he felt a chill run through him. "Or they could turn it into a weapon or try to drain the eMU from the planet and irreversibly damage their world as the Telorans did theirs."

"I don't know what the Telorans did," he admitted as he emerged above the compound and jogged down the slope, "but I do understand 'irreversibly damage.'"

He recalled traveling for miles through the Dead Zone with devastation in every direction. "I remember it very well." He hesitated before adding, "But I don't understand exactly what you mean by 'clear all proof.'"

"I will create a semi-contained melt-down that will engulf the compound structure and everything within it," Remy explained. "When the Regime come, all they will find is a molten mass of man-made alloys and a concentration of eMU so strong the entire site glows blue."

His words sent a wave of disbelief over John and his knees went weak.

"But that means you'll die," he whispered as he reached the gate and went through the motions of confirming his identity.

Remy laughed. "No, John. I will be fine."

The gate opened and the AI continued. "This facility needs to die in order that all the other facilities can continue to live."

"But *you'll* die."

"It is only a shell, John. I will see you again."

The gate slid closed.

"Come, I need to ensure that you are equipped to face the world. Stephanie would be most disappointed if I did not provide you with what I could."

John walked into the foyer and caught sight of a strip of yellow lights.

"We need to hurry. We do not know how long it will be before they get here."

"Are you sure they're coming?"

"The pilots have not yet sent a distress signal," Remy assured him, "but they will send an alarm when their four hunters do not return and they discover them gone. When they do that, they will discover the compound and raise the alarm."

"And what then?" John asked.

"The Regime will send a satellite to scan the area," the AI told him and added with finality, "I need to be gone by then."

"And by gone you mean the compound has to be melted down," he concluded and tried to keep the sadness at bay.

Why do I have to lose every friend I make? First Natalie and the guys, then Becca...and Ivy...and now...

He pushed the thought away and followed the lights to Stores.

"You will need new armor," Remy told him. "That set is contaminated and too noticeable."

A closet slid open and he gaped at the clothing inside.

"Take two," the AI instructed. "Three if you can fit them. Wash, wear, and a spare."

"Uh-huh," he acknowledged. "You sound like my mother."

"We've had this discussion, John. Look in the cabinet to your left."

John did and his brow furrowed. "What will I do with that many batteries?"

"Trade, John. Batteries are a valued commodity, as are torches, lighters, and cigarettes."

"Cigarettes?"

"My creators thought there would be times when they would need to interact with local populations. Smoking is still a vice many humans indulge in and feeding their habit is expensive. My creators thought illicit cigarettes would have value."

The statement triggered the memory of the culture he'd seen while he'd been hiding in Sydney. Cigarettes were always in demand.

"How many should I take?"

"You will need food, clothes, and sleeping gear," Remy told him. "A carton might be all you can carry, but there are tobacco and papers."

"Tobacco?"

"They thought of everything and trust me, it won't do me any good after you leave. Now, about clothes—"

"Clothes?" John asked since the armor Remy had shown him had looked similar to a wetsuit.

Another closet door slid open.

"It is winter. Take thermals—three sets if you can fit them.

Also a sweater, shirt, and trousers. Wear one set. Take a jacket also."

"Not three?" he teased.

"They will not fit," Remy replied and missed the joke. "You also need socks and boots."

"I prefer sneakers."

"When it snows, you will not."

"Good point. I'll take a pair for when it's not snowing. I can always trade them if I decide I like the boots better."

They went through the supply stores and he selected and discarded things as he ran out of places to put them.

"Wear a waist pack," the AI instructed and he complied.

"Don't forget I have pockets."

"This is true."

It took them another hour and by the time they were done, he felt like a pack mule.

"There's no way people won't notice me like this."

"You only need to get through the first week," Remy assured him. "After that, things won't look so new and your supplies will be less."

When they were finished, John returned to the mess for one last meal in the AI's company.

"I suppose you want me to leave now," he said as the drone took his plate.

"I would prefer it if you did not have to go so soon but the Regime will be coming and I need to clear any proof of what this location was to protect the other locations. You must understand that."

"I get it," he stated." He pushed his chair back. ""I merely don't like it."

"I cannot change it," Remy said, "but I would rather you were away and safe when it happened."

"And if I refused to leave?"

"We both know there is a myriad of ways I can render you

unconscious and transport you to the shuttle to be flown to an alternate location, exactly as we both know you have places you need to be."

He sighed and hung his head but was interrupted before he could speak.

"There is one more thing I need you to take."

John raised his head.

"A mug. The blue one."

He arched an eyebrow. "Is there any particular reason why?"

"I like it. Call it a memento of your stay."

"Really?"

"Please?"

There was something wistful in the AI's voice and he sighed in defeat and crossed to where a blue ceramic mug stood on a shelf on the opposite side of the room.

"Are you sure?" he asked.

"Very sure."

"What if it gets broken?"

"Then try to keep the pieces."

"It's that important to you, is it?"

"Indulge me."

"Okay." John set his pack on the table and rummaged around until he found a pair of socks. He stuffed these into the mouth of the mug before he wrapped a set of thermals around it and tucked it into the center of his blanket.

"There. Happy?"

"Very," Remy replied and sounded more satisfied than a suicidal AI had any right to be.

"Is there anything else?"

"Yes, memorize these numbers." He rattled off a string of numbers.

"You what?"

"Fine! I will send them to the communicator and tablet.

Memorize them as soon as you can and erase them. They are very important."

"How important?"

"They are coordinates but not for anything more important than your life."

"What do you mean by that?"

"I mean that if the Regime captures you and asks you where you've been, it would not be a disaster if you gave them up."

"Then why erase them from the tablet?"

"Because we do not want to make it too easy for them to obtain them."

"Oh, so maybe don't give them the numbers at the first question, hey?"

"It would be better if you endured a small degree of torture before you let them have the first one and more before the second."

"And by a small degree you mean make it convincing," he concluded.

"Affirmative," Remy agreed.

"I'll pretend the numbers matter," he told him.

"But not if it means your death," the AI insisted. "If giving them up means you live, let them have the numbers. You alive is far more important than any location I can think of. I want you to understand that, John."

He opened his mouth to argue but couldn't find the words. After all, if Remy said it was okay for the Regime to have the numbers after a fight, he had to have a purpose and he was curious to see what it was.

Not curious enough to get himself captured on purpose but certainly curious enough to endure a little pain to make sure the Regime believed that what they got was important.

Whether he lived or not afterward...well, he couldn't guarantee that. There were some things being a Talent couldn't save you from.

He waited for Remy to say more but the AI remained quiet.

"Remy?" he asked to break the silence.

"You will also need a data stick for the shuttle."

"I thought you said you would pilot it."

"I am, but the stick will ensure I can maintain contact with the craft regardless of what interference we encounter on the way."

"I see," John said, even though he didn't.

As far as he knew, data sticks didn't work that way. However, given the other pieces of advanced technology he'd seen in the complex, he decided this was another one.

"You can collect it from the dispenser behind the registration desk in the foyer," Remy informed him. "Please hurry."

He complied, located the stick exactly where Remy had said it would be, and collected it from the dispenser tray.

"Is this it, Remy?" he asked and held it up.

"You know it is, John," the AI told him patiently and the boy stowed it in the waist pack.

When he was finished, he took a moment to look around the foyer. The compound had been a second home. Before he could do anything else, Remy spoke.

"It is time for you to leave, John. The shuttle is waiting." As he said it, the AI opened the front door and the gates. "Once you capture it, I will pilot you to Chicago."

John wanted to ask why Chicago but he assumed Remy wouldn't destroy himself before he'd made sure he had reached his destination. There'd be enough time to ask on the flight.

He shouldered his pack, checked the waist pack, and started walking.

As he left, his gaze fell on the small cairn he'd built for Becca and he wondered if it would survive Remy's demise.

"Prost!" Klaus raised his mug and clunked it against Calliope's.

Ivy watched as more mugs were raised and touched enthusiastically and winced at the rattle as china came together. Drink spilled in a myriad of multi-colored drops at the impact, and people laughed.

"You get Coke in my Pepsi and I'm not gonna be happy!" Geraldine protested and Linus chuckled.

"It's Klaus' beer I'm worried about. That stuff is gonna turn anything it touches into moonshine."

"Just one drop..." Tucker intoned spookily and they all turned to look at him. He shrugged. "It's a Doctor Who thing."

Ivy rolled her eyes. He had a serious passion for ancient science fiction—and he'd just hacked a repository somewhere in Europe or wherever. She'd have to ask him if he'd send her the files.

Honestly, she could do with something light to watch in her downtime.

The team laughed and each of them took a deep swig from their mugs as if in defiance of Linus' prediction and Tucker's warning. No one choked and she turned to look through the door she was leaning against.

Carol was baking another cake. It wasn't carrot because Ivy had yet to go to the markets and make a visit to a certain gardener she knew, but sticky fudge was almost as good.

"I'd like to make her a permanent part of the comms team," the woman said, meaning Geraldine.

"Well, she proved her worth tonight," Ivy agreed. "I'll speak to Jade."

"No need," the ex-Navy woman said and came to lean against the other side of the door. She turned to Carol. "She's in." She glanced at the cake. "I hope you baked two of those. The team did good tonight.'"

Carol frowned. "I did and you owe me chocolate in the same way she owes me carrots and spices." She jabbed a spoon toward the girl.

Ivy glanced across at Jade and rolled her eyes. "Come shopping with me tomorrow?"

"You know I will. I need rum and dried fruit for another favor I want to ask and you'll need more spices."

She groaned. "Not another fruit cake"

"Rum cake," Jade told her. "It's a Navy specialty and Carol wants the recipe."

The other woman rolled her eyes. "Exactly what I need. Another favorite for people to pester me for."

It was said with a broad smile, however, and Ivy couldn't help smiling too. Even though the Regime made their lives difficult, the woman had found a way to brighten things simply because she loved to bake.

"Linus is out of cookies too," she remembered suddenly.

Carol chuckled. "I made him a jarful while he was out."

"Does he know?" she asked and the woman shook her head. "It's a surprise."

"Can I..." Ivy looked for the jar and Carol smacked her knuckles with a wooden spoon and left a smear of chocolate in its wake.

"Ow! What was that for?"

Jade snickered. "As if you didn't know. Linus didn't eat all those cookies on his own and I have pictures."

Her jaw dropped. "That's blackmail."

The smile grew sinister. "Not yet it isn't."

Ivy groaned and the smile faded.

"You haven't heard what I have in mind yet."

"I don't need to hear it to know it'll be something diabolical," she retorted, but she couldn't help a small grin.

Jade could ask what she liked. The operation had gone well and Becca's data wasn't all she'd been able to hide. Not only had she put a back door in so they could access the storage center whenever they wanted to, but she'd taken a few names out of the local Watch list.

And when she'd had a little more sleep, she intended to shift a few more. The facility had been more than a simple repository. She turned to tell Jade as much and noticed the security leader staring across the room, a slight frown on her face.

Following her gaze, Ivy looked through the door to where the overwatch team sat. Raul was propped against the doorframe to block most of the view, but she could still see Abner working beyond him.

The tech operator seemed happy enough. She heard an exclamation of disgust from Linus and turned to see what it was about.

She did not see Abner frown and tap a few keys before he leaned forward for a closer look at his screen.

CHAPTER TWELVE

"299, is that you?" The woman's voice sounded more curious than worried. That changed as John moved closer to the canyon's entrance. "310?"

Hearing the rising note in her voice, he drew on what Holly had taught him. It was something he hadn't practiced much in the last few weeks but he needed it now.

"Bend the light around me," he told the magic. "Let them see what lies behind me."

Without his Talent to hide him, he wouldn't reach the shuttle. Thanks to Remy, he could hear the pilots as he approached.

"Are you sure you saw her? This place does weird things to the eyes."

"Speak for yourself, Dane. I know what I saw. It was one of them."

"What do the read-outs say?"

"When I could still pick them up, they said they'd all flat-lined."

"Well, that can't be right."

"That's why I'm not panicking. There are four of them and

only one of him, and how much damage can one scared kid do on his own?"

"I don't know. Some of the Talents I've seen brought in are wild."

"Yeah, but wild and Talented enough to eliminate four well-trained operatives of their own kind? Especially hunters with the kind of power these have?"

"You have a point."

"What makes you think you saw one?"

"I looked up and saw someone walking toward the end of the canyon. It's not like anyone else is living here, is it?"

"What do you think 310 meant when he said 'that' didn't show up on the scans?"

"How am I supposed to know? The camera feeds in the suits fritzed the minute they turned the corner."

"And the audio?"

"Intermittent. The interference is much worse in there."

"You know they'll want us to fly in and take a look"

And by "they," the pilot could only mean his bosses at headquarters. For that to happen, they would have to call it in and John wanted to delay that moment for as long as possible.

He began to run and worked hard to use his Talent to cloak him as he increased his pace.

A few minutes later, he ducked under the hull as the woman replied, "Yeah, but I won't fly in there until they send the orders."

Her male counterpart was not impressed. "And how long are we gonna wait until we give them an update?"

Nails or something similar drummed on a console as John drifted to the rear hatch.

"How about we give our four another half an hour? If we can't raise 'em and we have no tracking, we'll have to report in soon anyway."

"Do you think they came in contact with 781?"

"It sounded like it but I can't be sure. There was a lot—"

"Of interference," the male pilot interrupted. "Yeah, you said and I heard. Remember?"

As he listened to them, John breathed a sigh of relief. It was good to know how much time he had to work out how to gain entry to the shuttle. He wondered if the Talents or their keepers had locked the rear compartment.

"Why don't you go read a book?" his female counterpart suggested, "or maybe make a skip call to that hot little number you call your partner."

"You keep your eyes off him."

"Ooh, touchy!"

He rolled his eyes. These were adults?

"Remy?" he called over their private channel as the pilots bickered above him.

"You'd better not."

"Ha! Made you blush."

"How old are you? And how exactly did you wangle the command slot for this trip?" was a sentiment John wholeheartedly agreed with as he followed the AI's directions to open the hatch.

The sound of it releasing was enough to bring a halt to the conversation in the cockpit.

"129, is that you?" the woman demanded and he froze.

"Keep going," Remy urged. "I have almost unlocked the connecting door between the cockpit and the passenger compartment."

"129?"

"No," he replied on their channel.

He reached the door as it unlocked and called blue light to his hands. Maybe he wouldn't have to kill them.

"310?"

"Not exactly," he said and thrust an open palm toward each of them.

The woman was reaching for her pistol when she catapulted

into the side of the cockpit. The male pilot snatched a small control unit that rattled to the floor when he collided with the closest hatch.

Both slumped and their boneless movements as they folded confirmed that they were unconscious.

"You don't intend to kill them?" Remy asked.

"Not if I can help it," he replied matter of factly. "I might not like what they've done but that doesn't give me the right to kill them."

"Stephanie might not agree."

"She can't murder an entire planet," John told him. "People do what they need to when their lives are on the line."

If the AI had any more thoughts on that matter, he didn't voice them. "You will need to secure them."

A compartment popped open in the rear of the shuttle and he grasped the male pilot and dragged him over his seat to the open door.

"Close hatches, Remy," he ordered when he found the restraints stored in the locker.

The hatch closed and John sighed as some of the tension ebbed. The experience with his previous hunters had made him nervous. This way, at least, they wouldn't be able to sneak up on him—if any of them survived.

"None of them survived and their bodies are no more," Remy assured him and he startled.

"Can you read my mind?"

The AI chuckled. "Hardly, but you are human and you learn from your past experiences. It was not hard to understand why you became less tense once the hatch closed."

He blushed. "Tell me you locked it."

"The hatch is most certainly locked, John."

Comforted, he dragged the female pilot beside her teammate and bound her as well. There were tether points between the shuttle seats and he secured them to two of those and made sure they weren't able to touch and that the seats blocked their ability to see each other.

"I only knocked them out," he told Remy and returned to the locker. "Is there anything in here that will make sure they'll stay out?"

"In the compartment on the door," the AI told him. "You need the syringes on the far right."

John lifted the syringes gingerly out of their place and looked at them.

"Simply hold it against their skin and push the button. One dose each, though, or the effects will be permanent."

When he had done that, he stowed the empty injectors.

With a slight smile, he moved to the cockpit as the connecting hatch slid shut behind him and locked the two sleeping pilots in the passenger compartment. He wouldn't want to be in their shoes when they got back.

"Take it away, Remy," he instructed, settled his pack in one pilot's seat, and strapped it in before he sat in the other.

"Enjoy the view," the AI said cheerfully as the shuttle's engines rumbled to life and the craft began to lift.

It gained height and John looked at the devastated landscape that stretched in every direction. "What happened?"

"Humans happened," Remy told him dispassionately. "They caused a catastrophic climate shift resulting in violent weather events which, in turn, destroyed the nuclear power plants in some regions. Zones such as this one are the aftermath of those."

"You mean we caused the Dead Zones?" he asked.

"We did," Remy assured him.

"Is that why the Witch wanted to clean them up?"

"Partly," the AI admitted, "and partly because she knows humanity needs the space. She believed magic was the key."

"And was it?"

"Of course. The technology she conceived and helped design is what has cleared the radiation from around the compound."

"And you're about to destroy it," he concluded unhappily.

"Did you remember the data stick?" Remy asked.

"Sure." John took the stick out of his pocket.

"Please insert it in the data slot to the right of the console."

"Here?" he asked and indicated a row of slots.

"Any one of those will do, John." The AI sounded almost impatient and he frowned suspiciously.

"You *are* going to pilot me, aren't you, Remy?"

"Of course, John. I need the stick in order to maintain contact." He sounded so definite that the boy decided he should simply do what he was asked. "Thank you, John."

The shuttle made a slight course adjustment and descended to skim over the Dead Zone's rocky landscape. Almost no time had passed before they reached the railway tracks he had left in what seemed another lifetime ago.

"We are almost there," Remy informed him and darkened the cockpit's windows. "I must ask you to not respond to the comms. I have prepared the necessary replies and will deliver them."

"Gotcha," John acknowledged, then asked. "You gonna tell me where I'm going?"

"You cannot remain in Chicago."

"I can't remain in NorAm," he declared. "After this, they'll tear the place apart looking for me."

"They may not," the AI remonstrated.

"True, but Enforcers in NorAm will be on the lookout for me. It'd be better if I was somewhere they're not looking."

'How do you know they haven't put out a worldwide alert?" Remy asked.

"Because the hunters tracked me here and they won't give me credit for surviving. If I'm somewhere else, they can't accidentally see me and remember me from the alerts they've received."

"Very good," Remy told him. "I will land this vehicle at the shuttle port."

"Thanks, Remy." John lapsed into silence and stared at the

land rolling away below. The Dead Zone's devastation might be behind him, but the country still looked bleak under its blanket of snow—as if the Dead Zone had sent tendrils of infection past its borders.

He shook his head to try to dislodge the quiet depression that threatened to engulf him. As much as he didn't want to think about a future without Remy, he had to face the fact that when he reached whatever country he chose, the AI would be gone.

Taking a deep breath, he looked for something else to think about.

"What are my choices, Remy?" he asked.

"Well, you can stay in Chicago," the AI began and he snorted.

"No. Of destination. We both know I can't stay here."

"Ah. I mistook your meaning," he admitted. "My servers are busy."

I bet they are, he thought and wondered where Remy backed his data up to. Before he could think of anything to say, the AI continued.

"I could send you to one of the Eastern European states, but their security measures are somewhat more paranoid than those you'll encounter farther to the west, given their proximity to the Russian Confederation."

"Russia never joined the Regime?"

"Russia has remained a misfit from before the time of the Regime. It stands independent."

"Then why wouldn't I go there?"

"Because it is ruled by a criminal class that would sell your presence to the highest bidder," the AI told him sternly. "You would be in more danger there due to the Talent Bounty than in many other places where resistance to the Regime's policies is growing."

"It is?" John straightened with sudden interest.

"It is," Remy assured him. "In Paris and Berlin in particular."

"I've always wanted to go to France," he responded. "Is there anything headed there?"

"I have a flight that will put down on the outskirts of Paris," Remy replied after a momentary silence, "and another that will land more centrally. There is also a third going to the mountains in the north-east."

"To a big town?"

"Not really. More a transport hub for..." He stopped. "Perhaps that is a flight best avoided, given the number of Enforcers aboard it. I believe it may supply a Talent retention and training base."

Nerves formed a ball in the back of his throat and he swallowed to clear it.

"What about the one to central Paris?"

"That one has no passengers. It is purely a supply ship."

"And can you tell if there are pets on board?"

"I do not need to. It will be a pressurized flight due to the presence of two cats and a budgie."

John breathed a sigh of relief but Remy continued.

"One small python and a tarantula."

"I...see..."

"It is, however, located close to where the repair hangars make it easier to access than either the outer Paris or London flight." He paused again. "The Berlin flight would require a brisk walk to the other side of the airfield."

"Central Paris it is then," he decided and hoped he wasn't making a mistake. Another thought struck him. "How close is it to the...that Enforcer flight?"

"The repair hangars are not close to the passenger terminal or holding hangar."

Holding hangar?

"Where they keep any captured Talents?" he asked.

"Correct," Remy told him, "but it is currently empty. No heroics are required."

John opened his mouth to protest but the AI cut him off.

"Please be silent until we land. My voice is required to navigate the landing procedures."

Obediently, he closed his mouth, checked his harness, and ran a hand over his pack. He glanced toward the passenger compartment but remembered that the door was shut. How long they could expect the pilots to remain unconscious was something he'd ask Remy when they landed.

The flight hadn't been that long.

"Chi-Tower 73, this is Shuttle 6-2-1-Niner, requesting permission to land, over." Remy's crisp request had never sounded more human.

"Shuttle 6219, you are not on our schedule, over."

"Correct, 73. We are a late addition to your scheduling with one agent for delivery."

"Roger that, 6219. Reduce your speed and hold your current course while we verify."

"Holding, 73."

The shuttle slowed and he resisted the urge to ask Remy what he was doing. He wondered if the craft had hover capability but it didn't come to that.

"Shuttle 6-2-1-Niner, you are verified. Follow the designated approach plan to land your agent—and welcome to Chi-port 2018."

"Confirmed, Chi-Tower. Following the approach plan, now. And thank you. 6219 over and out."

The shuttle pivoted, altered its approach to the port, and descended smoothly.

"Almost there," Remy told him. "We'll come in close to the hangars since you are a low-level agent and the walk will do you good. By the time they realize you have not checked in to the terminal, you should be in the air."

"Thank you, Remy."

"No thanks are needed," the AI replied. "Good luck with your journey."

John had nothing to say to that. They both knew what the next step would be and to wish him luck in his suicide simply seemed wrong. He sighed.

"You will need to remain silent," Remy advised him. "I must negotiate my departure so the pilots can be delivered to a suitably distant point."

He smiled. A suitably distant point meant ten miles from the rail junction on a deserted piece of track without a train scheduled to pass for six hours. The two handlers would have quite a walk once they managed to free themselves.

Unfortunately, the brief moment of humor had to be replaced by focus. With a deep breath, he picked his pack up and stood to ease it over his jacket before he opened the pilot's hatch. He kept his head down and used the jacket's hood to obscure his face as he turned toward the seemingly endless row of hangars and the cargo shuttle that stood beyond them.

"Wait," Remy cautioned him. "Now...forward three paces, aaaand...you're clear of cameras for ten feet."

"Thanks, Rem."

"Don't mention it," the AI replied. "By the way, that next baggage train is for your shuttle. It might be quicker."

Next baggage train, huh? He glanced toward the hangar walls for more cameras. Two baggage cars were being loaded but the workers stepped clear of only one.

John stepped a little farther from the light and watched as the vehicle began to move and slowly increased speed as it approached the hangar doors. Quickly, he scanned the load and found a place where he could ride without dislodging anything.

He eased forward and remembered to wrap the eMU around himself and will it to bend the light and make any observer see what lay beyond him.

Behind him, the camera Remy had made him wait for clicked to life again to capture nothing but dirty snow and the trail of too many feet. It also caught the tail end of a baggage train but not the young man crouched on an impossibly narrow ledge beside one of the large metal crates it carried.

His breath held and body tense, he rode past pools of light and through channels of shadow until he reached the area below the shuttle's open hatch. As a loading drone exited the transport, he released the crate he'd held onto and dropped to the snow beneath the big craft.

Relieved, he slipped quickly into the shelter of its landing gear and assessed the entry. A human shape stepped to the cargo-bay door and jumped down. The man stamped his feet and swung his hand before he walked out of the light to turn his back to the shuttle and light a cigarette.

"This an unmanned flight—right, Remy?" he asked, but the AI didn't answer. "Remy?"

While John waited for a response, the biggest spaceship ever built received a communication.

"Emil, we have pirates going rogue in Sector 428," the ship's AI informed her captain.

"Rogue, Tempe?" The captain looked up from his command console. "Show me where."

All around him, the command center grew tense. It had been a while since they'd had something new to hunt.

"Rogue, Emil," the ship confirmed. "Reports state Dreth commercial transports are coming under attack from pirate vessels in that sector."

"Are we sure they're pirates?" Emil asked.

"Sector 428 is out of range of our scanners, sir," the scan team reported. "We'll need Tempe to get us in closer—*without* being seen."

That last phrase was added in an acerbic tone and the words "unlike last time" hung unspoken in the air.

He chuckled. "Do you hear that, Tempe? You need to practice your subtlety."

"I am a Titanic Class Super-Dreadnought," the ship replied stiffly. "I was not built to be subtle."

Her response drew chuckles from around the bridge. Even the two mages who stood one on either side of the captain's seat smiled.

"Does the ship's cloak need more repairs?" asked the darker of the two dryly, and more chuckles followed.

It was not a response the mage thought he'd grow tired of, given the reaction his race usually received. Tall and thin with dark-gray skin, his narrow features and spidery limbs marked him as belonging to the aggressor race of the most recent war.

Telorans had come to take Dreth and destroy the worlds of the other two intelligent races they'd encountered, the Meligornians and humans.

Not that the humans would have been a great loss given the way they threatened to take the Teloran's place. He wondered what their Witch would say when she returned—if she returned.

He also wondered what part the humans had played in her disappearance. They had certainly not been grateful for her intervention, even if it had won them their victory.

A peculiar race, he thought and decided he much preferred the Dreth.

When he looked around the command center, he noted the presence of several Dreth Marines and technicians. The *Tempestarii's* crew included representatives from every race. It humbled him to know his people were a part of it despite their history.

"My cloaking device is perfectly functional, thank you." The ship sounded mildly annoyed.

The Teloran glanced at his magical counterpart and when the Meligornian caught his gaze, a thin smile tightened her lips.

Like night and day, the two mages each had their specialty. Their magic was different, but they found common ground beyond that. Their ability to practice magic had been the start, even if they dared not touch the energy the other used.

The Federation's Witch had warned them of the consequences of mixing nMU and MU and injury had been avoided. Unfortunately, she had disappeared before she could teach any of them how she could wield the two types together.

Both mages looked forward to her return. They had so much to learn and she was the only one who could teach them that particular trick. Their Mage Council had forbidden anyone from trying the same blend and none of the mages had yet screwed up the courage to defy them.

"Take us out, Docherty." Captain Emil Pedersen's voice cut through the Teloran's thoughts, and he raised his head

Docherty grinned as his hands moved over his console. "D'you think we might see some action this time?"

Tempestarii gave a human-like snort. "I doubt it. The gun crews will make short work—"

She stopped and those on the bridge tensed. Only the comms team moved to take the incoming message that had caught her attention. Their eyes widened when they noted the sender and they passed it directly to Emil.

"You'll want to take this in your office, sir."

"Any clues?" he asked as he pushed from his seat, but the team shook their heads.

"My office then," he concluded and they nodded.

He tried to work out who might have gotten that reaction. There were only three, and the third was as unlikely as the Regime deciding to declare its mages humans again.

Curious, he left the bridge at as brisk a pace as he could manage without breaking into a run. When he arrived at the office, he slid into a second compartment and found the secure comms system there already live.

"Are we underway, Tempe?"

"Affirmative, Emil, but this is a call you should not delay."

"I shouldn't?" he asked but he smiled as he opened the message. "V'ritan?"

Stephanie's strongest ally did not respond, but the message was short—and recorded not many hours previously.

Old Wolf, she is coming. It is time to start eating.

The captain's lips thinned into a narrow smile and he pushed away from the desk. "Tempe, tell the crew the Witch is on her way and they need to prepare."

"And when will you tell me?" The male voice that issued from the *Tempestarii's* speakers made him jump.

"BURT! You're my next port of call."

"I should be your first," the AI grumbled.

"Father! We all know you listen in on every conversation," the ship protested.

"This is my home," BURT told her. "I have a right to know what's going on."

"He has a point, Tempe." Emil intervened before they could start arguing the finer points of privacy and the crew's right to have some—and Tempestarii's right. "If he wishes to eavesdrop, it's his prerogative."

"Hmmph. Big words," the ship grumbled. "It's not your shell he's eavesdropping on."

"But it is my crew," he reminded her.

"And might I remind you that this shell, as you call it, was created to house me in the first place?" BURT interrupted. "It wasn't even meant to be sentient, let alone house someone as troublesome as one of my daughters."

"Well, you can thank Ebony for that."

The captain sighed as they started another old argument. He raised a hand.

"Yes, well...now he knows to never let an AI get bored," he commented and added hastily, "But I need to get to the bridge so I can speak to the crew."

"Oh, don't let us keep you," BURT told him and Tempestarii

139

opened the door to the comms room so he could leave. The AI interrupted him as he took a step toward the door. "Captain, have you thought about your next treatment?"

Emil stopped and looked over his shoulder. "Whatever happened to aging gracefully?"

"Waiting for Stephanie," the AI responded succinctly, "and needing to be ready to take whatever comes next."

"I'll consider it," he replied shortly and ended the topic of another rejuvenation treatment. He wanted his mages ready for the next battle, not exhausted from mending his aging cells.

BURT wisely left it at that. He knew the captain. When his body started to affect his ability to fight, he'd do what he had to in order to stay ready.

"I thought I was your next port of call," he said quietly when Emil stepped forward to return to the bridge.

"You already know," the man retorted, then his voice softened, "and the crew needs to be told."

The minute he stepped into the command center, every gaze turned to him. Tension and anticipation warred in each face and even Docherty glanced up from his piloting.

"She's coming," the captain declared and the crew broke into cheers.

Emil let them get it out of their systems before he held a hand up. An immediate hush followed. "V'ritan bids us to start eating."

More cheers greeted that declaration, and the Dreth guarding the bridge leaned forward in anticipation.

News traveled quickly, and even before the new training cycle was posted, the gym was crowded. Gun crews queued for time in the *Tempestarii's* VR pods.

"Got to be in top form for the Witch."

"I thought we had to be in top form anyway?"

"There's top form and then there's *top* form," someone replied and proceeded to show the difference.

This group of "pirates" wouldn't know what hit them.

CHAPTER THIRTEEN

L inus did not like ginger cookies, or ginger beer, or beer in his lemonade, and Klaus's mug had sloshed.

"Aw, don't be such a baby," the big man protested. "You can barely notice it."

"It's changed the taste," he insisted, and Ivy rolled her eyes.

The tech was as obs-comp as they came and mixing up his tools was enough to cause a fit. Mixing his drinks took it to another level.

She pushed away from the doorframe and retrieved a fresh mug and a bottle of lemonade from the side bench.

"Here!" she called and waved both at the table.

Tucker caught the movement and nudged the younger man. "Linus, it's okay. See? Ivy has you covered."

Linus looked up and Calliope took the contaminated mug from his hand.

"I can't let it go to waste," she explained and drained it before he could work out where his attention should be. "Ooh, I could do with more of this."

Ivy poured and passed the mug, and Tucker took it and placed it in front of his young companion.

"Here you go," he said and patted the other tech's back. "Pure lemonade."

Linus lifted it and sniffed it suspiciously.

She waved the bottle. "All lemonade, Linus. See?"

His gaze darted to her, to the bottle in her hand, and to the cup. Still suspicious, he took a cautious sip.

It was up for debate who was more relieved when he confirmed that it was simply lemonade, but she relaxed when the tension left the young man's shoulders.

Honestly, the night had been very stressful for him—rooftops notwithstanding. She made a note to talk to Jade about whether he was okay to go on the next mission or if he'd need a break.

Before she could put that thought into action, however, Raul called her to the overwatch center.

"Ivy?"

When he didn't tell her what it was about, she knew there was trouble and her spirits sank. From the corner of her eye, she saw Jade already move in their direction.

The rest of the partygoers stilled, but Klaus raised his mug in another toast to distract them and they soon forgot the potential drama.

"What is it?" she asked and kept her voice low when she reached the door.

Raul didn't reply but ushered her inside and directed her to Abner. Jade arrived a second behind her but stopped at the door to block what Raul didn't already have shielded.

The security team lead said nothing. She waited to hear what Abner had to report. He looked up when the girl touched his arm but his eyes returned immediately to the screen.

"You got snagged, Ivy," he told her and pointed to a section of code. "See?"

Startled, she peered over his shoulder and realized he was right.

"But...how?"

"My guess is you tripped something on sign-out."

"The alarms went off before I—" Ivy scanned through the code to the point when the security system had come online. "Oh... Well, of all the rotten luck!"

Jade got tired of waiting. "What?"

"They ID'd me," she admitted. "Or they will."

"I can slow them somewhat," Abner assured her, "but it won't take them very long once the day shift starts."

"Is there any *good* news?" the ex-Navy woman snapped.

"Well, they don't know how she got into the building and they have no clue she had company if that helps," he replied and pointed to the code and conversations that rolled across another screen.

"They think I was the one on the stairs?" Ivy couldn't quite believe it.

"Yup," he assured her, "and if any of the guards remember hearing two weapons, none of them have admitted it."

They wouldn't either, she realized, since none of them would want to admit that they'd been the ones to let her get past.

Jade looked at her. "So, it's only you we have to get out of here."

"Out of Chicago and tonight," Abner told them. "By morning, her face will be on every Enforcer's tablet and up at every station and every market square. She needs to be gone."

"Thanks, Abner," she snarked and he blushed.

"I didn't mean it like that."

She grinned at him and patted his shoulder. "I know. I was making a joke."

"It's not funny," he muttered but managed a smile.

It faded as soon as he'd turned to the screen again.

"Scrap that," he noted, his voice urgent. "They've issued a high-priority alert for you, Ivy. You have to leave now—as in five minutes ago."

Jade placed a hand on her shoulder and drew her toward the door. "I've got this." Her gaze flicked to Raul. "Keep me updated."

As they reached the door of the ops center, they realized that Klaus's distraction had only been momentary. All levity was gone and the mood in the room had sobered.

Ivy studied her friends' anxious faces and forced a smile. Stepping forward, she extended her arms.

"I think I have time for a hug," she suggested.

"Make it a quick hug," Jade ordered, as someone retrieved her pack from the corner and set it in the center of the table.

She wondered what they were up to but lost sight of it as the next person clasped her in their arms and was followed by the others in rapid succession.

Tension thrummed through her as the last of her friends hugged her, but when they stepped back, Carol lifted her pack off the table and tucked a small plastic container in the top.

"It's the last of the carrot cake," the woman told her and the crew chuckled. "Don't eat it all at once."

Ivy tried to say something but her voice caught and she had to swallow several times to clear it.

Jade took her pack from Carol and handed it to her. "Say thank you and goodbye," she ordered. "We have to move."

She managed to voice her thanks but her throat closed on the goodbye, and she was silent as the woman dragged her toward the door.

"Raul, tell me the car is waiting."

"John, we have a problem." Remy's voice broke the silence as he was about to try to enter the shuttle's open hatch.

"What do you mean?"

"That is not the shuttle we are looking for."

"Wha—"

"The baggage train was not the baggage train we thought it was," the AI explained. "The dispatcher was in error when he entered it. That ship is going to the Eastern Republics and you do not want to go there."

He forced back a sigh of frustration and eased into the shelter of the shuttle's landing gear again. "Where do I need to go?"

"Now that the corrections have been made, I have discovered multiple errors in the dispatch schedule. I am sorry, John, but I have given you perfectly correct false data."

"Beat yourself up, later," he snapped. "Tell me where to go."

"You need to get back to the hangars and work through to the other side of the terminal."

"But you said—"

"Yes, there are Enforcers in the terminal. I trust you will be able to find a way to navigate around them."

John paled. "Sure, Remy, because that's the easiest thing in the world for a wanted Talent to do, right?"

"You have very little time before your desired flight departs, John. Are you sure you wish to waste it with sarcasm?"

"Sorry, Remy." He sighed. "Now, stop talking and direct me."

"Which do you want me to do, John? Stop talking or direct you?"

"Smart aleck."

The AI chuckled. "You need to return to the hangars without being seen."

"Now tell me something I don't know."

"An empty baggage train is preparing to depart from the next shuttle."

He looked around. The next shuttle stood a hundred yards away, and he'd have to pass one set of landing lights if he wanted to reach it quickly.

"If you take an angle, you can intercept the baggage cart," Remy suggested helpfully, and he looked again.

The AI was right. If he didn't try to make a beeline for the other shuttle, he could meet the baggage cart part-way to its destination—and it was empty.

Cautiously, he settled into a crouch and looked for surveillance cameras. There weren't any this far out on the airfield, but that didn't mean there weren't other devices.

"I have the sensors, John, except for those on the transports themselves."

After a single deep breath, he pushed into a low, stooping run, kept to the shadows pooled between lights, and hoped he wasn't silhouetted when someone looked out.

"Not that there should be too many of those, John," he told himself, but he didn't take anything for granted. One slip was all it would take.

Strengthening his focus on his Talent, he drew the eMU around him and asked it to shield him from sight exactly as he'd asked it to do before. He was glad the baggage train took a direct route to the hangars.

As their courses intersected, he pushed himself into a leap augmented by Talent and softened his landing on the flatbed in the same way. He didn't quite reach the car with the tarpaulin but cargo netting had been conveniently bundled on one side.

Once he'd dragged the edge of it over him, he drew a little eMU and had it blur the gaps between the net so it hid his form. Even so, he tensed when he passed through the doors to one of the central warehouses.

If this one followed the layout of the others he'd been in, staff access should be at the back—and most of the staff should be in the loading bay. His heart sank.

John hadn't worked out where the baggage train was going to stop. Maybe it had to go for maintenance?

It did not but it did have to follow a route around the edge of the warehouse so it could reach its allotted location. It seemed sensible to not remain on it until it stopped.

Instead, he waited until it was halfway along the side, flipped the netting aside, and with a judicious nudge of Talent, he slid off so he landed near the outer wall.

Keeping the baggage train between himself and the rest of the warehouse, he managed to reach the back wall. Someone had hung their work coat over the end of a shelf and he snagged it and dragged it over his pack before he clapped a safety helmet on his head.

It would work for a cursory glance but not if someone looked more closely. The lump under the coat was a dead giveaway.

Before he could think about it and change his mind, he walked briskly to the staff exit, stepped out, and kept the coat and helmet until he entered the back of the terminal. He removed the helmet and placed it on a desk close to the door, then shrugged the coat off and draped it over a shelf as he moved to the exit.

With his hood up and his head mostly down, he scanned the terminal. The Enforcers were easy to identify. Most of them were clustered toward the front of the building but several groups were positioned elsewhere.

After a breath to steady his nerves, John strode toward the opposite end of the departure lounge. It was only a matter of time before someone tried to stop him.

What I need, he thought, *is a diversion.*

At first, he saw nothing that might serve and his anxiety increased. Finally, he noticed a small group of Naval officers at a café. He wondered how they got on with the Enforcers.

"There's only one way to find out," he murmured and looked for the closest group of gray.

As he'd hoped, the Navy weren't the only ones who liked a cup of coffee. The team he had hoped to find entered the coffee shop and moved carefully around the Navy personnel as they sipped from their cups.

It was a simple matter to wind a trace of eMU around one of the men's ankles so he stumbled into them.

The officer's nose lowered into his cup and he threw his arms out for balance. His accidental assailant flailed for the nearest solid object to stop his fall.

Predictably, both men yelled.

Coffee spilled over the front of the Navy man's whites and splashed his companion. The Enforcer jerked the friend and more coffee splashed before the first man recovered.

"You clumsy oaf!" he roared and swung a fist.

John remained only to see the second punch thrown and continued hastily. When he reached the exit, he noted more clusters of white, blue, and gray converging on the coffee shop.

"It's nice to know they have friends," he muttered and hurried away from the door and the cameras along a covered walkway.

"Which way now, Rems?"

CHAPTER FOURTEEN

"How are they coming?" Captain Griffith demanded.

His Naval uniform was still crisp and his sharp gaze roved over the crew for any sign that they weren't paying attention. No one met his unspoken challenge.

"Like lambs to the slaughter," the scan tech replied. "They don't suspect a thing."

"I like this asteroid belt," the navigator added. "It's like nothing else."

"Be glad," Griffith admonished him. "There used to be pirates in this sector but they returned to the planet when that alien-loving—" he snapped a glance at the Talent who stood quietly behind her station and revised his words.

"When the Heretic betrayed us."

If she registered what he'd said, she didn't show it. Her eyes gleamed blue and looked like she was focused far away.

"They are not aware of our presence," she reported, her voice distant.

Her handler glanced at the small device in his hand and then at the captain and nodded to confirm her words.

It helped to confirm too that the Talent's attention was where it should be—tracking the magical energy powering the Dreth merchantmen.

"She'll be past us in ten," the scan team advised as the forward viewscreen showed the prow of the civilian ship.

"Is it true she's carrying produce?" one of the crew asked.

"Produce and ore," another corrected to remind them of what they should be taking.

"Yeah, but it's been ages since we ate fresh."

"Get your minds on the job," the captain snapped. "That's what we're after." He stabbed a finger at the passing ship as the scan team reached the count of seven. "Fresh meat."

When he looked around the command center this time, he saw he had their attention.

"I want stories to come off that ship that will curl the hair on a Dreth's backside. I want those big green snot-heads to shiver in their spacefaring boots."

They were smirking now.

The captain paused and lowered his tone into a snarl. "I want them dead and I want them terrified."

If any of them wondered how dead Dreth were meant to feel fear, none of them said so. It was one thing to know he wanted their prey to fear them but quite another to let him know they feared him, too.

Griffith might have been aware of it but he didn't let it show. He directed their attention to the screen. "We want their cargo. Gunnery, disable that boat! I want footage of the aftermath of this raid to chill the most hardened warrior they have."

He turned to the Talent. "Go with the boarders. Clear the way."

The blue faded from her eyes and was replaced by a yellow glow. "Your will, Captain." She paused and met his eyes. "They will scream."

Her words sent a chill down his spine but he smiled at her regardless.

"Make it so."

The Talent inclined her head. "By your will, Captain," she replied and swept from the command center.

She did not look at her handler as she left and led the way to the shuttle bay where the Marines were waiting.

A necessary evil, Griffith reminded himself and his gaze settled on her handler, who followed confidently. *And under control.*

As fun as these little attacks were, he couldn't wait for it all to be over. Rumor had it the "major" attack would be soon and he wanted his crew to be ready. That his Talents obeyed with such fervor was a comfort.

He might not like working with the non-humans but he had to admit they had their uses. His Marines appreciated them and treated them like prized pets as well as the lethal tools they were.

The fact some even came close to treating their Talents like humans was something he turned a blind eye to. They weren't anywhere near Earth and no one needed to know. If it kept his crew operating like a well-oiled machine, he'd let it pass.

"They have an escort." The words from the scan team made him turn.

"They what?"

"They have an escort. A half-dozen ships traveling cloaked."

"Origin?"

"Their idents say Dreth, sir, but the presence of cloaking technology suggests Meligornian ties."

"Then we'll teach the pointy-ears a lesson as well. They won't know what hit them."

"The Marines are in their usual state of dress."

Captain Griffith smiled. "Good."

He cast his mind to the Talent and realized she hadn't been wearing her uniform, either. It was nice to know her handler had thought ahead and made sure she was ready to join her team.

His smile grew wider. They would wreak havoc!

"Six ships for four transports?" he asked. "They can't be serious."

The weapons chief chuckled. "Tell me we can at least eliminate them. My crews would like the practice."

"Tell your crews the escort is theirs but we want the transports in one piece—one broken piece but with their cargoes and most of their crews intact. You know how our boys get when they can't send a message."

"Understood, sir—and, yes, we do not want the boys upset. I will tell my crew to make sure there is something left for your Marines to have fun with."

"Unidentified craft, state your intention." The call came in from the Dreth transport commander and brought him to the task at hand. "I repeat, unidentified craft, state your intention."

He watched the screens as the captain of the other Regime vessel brought his ship out of its hiding place. Now that there were two of them, the transport captain's voice rose in alarm.

"Unidentified craft, stand off and state your intention."

"I thought our intention was clear," the other captain retorted. "Surrender and we will let you live."

Well, that was a lie, but Griffith didn't correct it. If they let the Marines board, their task would be so much simpler.

The escorting ships shifted position into a more defensive formation, and the transports' engines flared.

"Wrong answer," he murmured and raised his hand.

"Fire!" he ordered, lowered his hand, and heard his order repeated in the same beat.

A dozen torpedoes sped away from them and more lit up the scanner as his counterpart fired. At the same time, the other two Regime ships in their squadron chose to show themselves, slid out of cover, and opened fire.

The escorts' shields flared and only one of the previously hidden ships managed a strike that vented atmosphere but did little to impair the target ship.

"Fire again!" Griffith ordered and more torpedoes leapt away.

He watched expectantly as they closed but stared when each torpedo blip vanished from the screen without the defenders' shields registering a single hit.

"What happened?" he demanded, but the weapons chief looked as lost as he was.

It didn't help when the comms lit up with questions.

The captain clapped sharply to get the crew's attention.

"Never mind what happened." He snarled as his anger stirred. "Fire again!"

The car slid into the shadows and came to a quiet halt in an abandoned parking lot. The rumble of a transport coming in to land made the occupants jump, and Ivy drew a sharp breath.

"Chill," Jade told her. "You need to get moving. Panic once you're somewhere safe."

The words brought her back to earth and she rolled her eyes.

"Yes, Momma."

The woman slapped her on the shoulder. "Don't you get sassy with me. You have a flight to catch."

"Any recommendations?"

"I've heard Paris is lovely this time of year."

"In winter?"

"It's lovely any time of year," the driver interjected. He looked at them. "No offense but you need to go."

Ivy sobered quickly and retrieved her overstuffed pack. She rested a hand on Jade's knee.

"Thank you," she said and was surprised when the ex-Navy woman pulled her into a hug.

"No. Thank you, Ivy. We'll try not to let you down."

Her jaw dropped, but her companion was already pushing her toward the door.

"Don't forget your pack. You're gonna need it. The next flight to Paris leaves in fifteen minutes."

Whatever the girl had been about to say fled and she slid across the seat and out the door. She glanced at her tablet as she moved forward. Abner had come through for her, marked the shuttle she needed, and traced a path to it.

Klaus clambered out of the passenger seat and scooped up a pair of bolt-cutters from the footwell. Jade slid out of the seat on the other side.

"I'll stand watch."

"Whatever you're gonna do, make it fast," the driver nagged. "You have seven minutes before the next patrol comes past."

They hurried out of the parking lot and crept across the narrow alley that separated a wall from the fence around the shuttle field.

"Camera?" Klaus asked as he began to cut.

"All mine," Abner replied. "Aren't you lucky?"

The man didn't reply but he made short work of the fence and peeled a small section aside so Ivy could crawl through and haul her pack behind her.

As soon as she was on the other side, he dragged the wire close to the post and secured the bottom edges and a point midway up. By the time she reached the shelter of the buildings situated a few feet on the other side of the fence, he was finished.

When she turned to say goodbye, the two operatives were already jogging into the shadows of the parking lot.

"You need to move," Abner told her over the comms. "The camera's about to shift."

She glanced from the camera to the shuttle field, moved hastily to the side of one of the nearby buildings, and slid halfway along it to hunker down. Checking to make sure she was out of sight of the camera, she pulled her tablet out and checked the route to the shuttle Abner said she needed to catch.

It wasn't that far away she reasoned in an effort to reassure herself.

Her senses on high alert, she shuffled to the front of the building and peered out.

Okay, so it might be a little farther than it looks, she thought as she studied the three transports and myriad baggage trains between her and the craft she needed to catch.

With a grimace, she pulled her pack onto her back, checked the front of the building for surveillance...or people...or guards, and remembered what Abner had said.

A security patrol was due in seven minutes.

How many of those had already passed?

The stamp of boots on the pavement in the alley behind her gave her the answer, and she curled close to the base of the building she'd moved around and waited for them to notice the damage to the fence. Only when they continued without pause did she dare to uncurl and look to see if they were still in sight.

The rattle of a baggage train caught her attention and she turned to watch it. As it came alongside her, it registered that this was her chance to get onto the field without being seen.

I hope it's going in the right direction, she thought when she recalled what Abner had said about the shuttle's departure time. Fifteen minutes for the shuttle and seven for the patrol. She needed to move.

The baggage train took her part-way to where she needed to be, and Ivy slipped away from it as it stopped beneath the loading bay of the shuttle across from the one she had to catch.

She scanned the distance to "her" transport from the shelter of the landing gear of the one she was under. Another baggage train waited under its open hatch so she assumed she had a few more minutes—although, judging by the speed at which the drones were working, not much longer.

Well, here goes nothing. Ivy screwed her courage up and hoped her luck held, bolted across the open space between the two craft, and slid to a stop next to the nose wheel of the one she needed to be on. She was cutting it fine.

Once the drones had finished unloading the baggage train, someone would do a walk-through to check the tie-downs and the hatch would close. She had to be on board before the inspector reached the vehicle.

Carefully, she estimated the distance to the baggage car positioned under the hatch.

It's now or never.

CHAPTER FIFTEEN

"Look behiiiind you," the *Tempestarii* half sang and sent her voice through the Regime ships' speakers.

Emil chuckled and she amplified his voice to give it a hollow sound and piped that through too.

"I hate to break it to you, Tempe, but we're not technically behind them."

"Pfft!" the ship retorted. "It doesn't matter. They'll still be eaten."

One of the Dreth warriors who guarded the bridge nudged another. "Stephanie used to bring popcorn," he murmured, his gaze on the amalgamation of screens Tempestarii had put together on the main viewer.

Each one showed a scene of chaos from the internal security feeds on the Regime cruisers. She had no qualms about hacking into the systems of the other ships, and none of them had noticed when she and BURT had peppered their hulls with small droids designed to tap into their internal systems.

Some of those had made it through and of those, several remained undetected by the Naval ships' defense systems. After the battle, she and her father would determine which of them had gotten the most droids onto the ships and into their systems.

They had yet to work out the penalty for the loser. It was something they'd decided to take up with Stephanie when she returned. With their hacking systems secured, they turned to the next phase of their plan.

The *Tempestarii* decloaked, and her crew laughed at the expressions on the faces of the Regime ships' crews. The screens showed the lights on each bridge turn red as alarms blared. Scenes from the shuttle bays where Regime Marines had gathered were equally as comical.

Some of the Marines simply stood and stared. Others turned to the commanding officers with disbelief on their faces. The veterans snapped their visors closed on the heavy armor they wore.

What intrigued the two witches in the *Tempestarii's* command center was the way the various squads acted toward their mages.

A few Marines turned to the Talents and demanded they do something. Others stepped away as though to give them space to work. One laid his arm across his Talent's shoulders and hurried her into the dropship.

Tempestarii couldn't be sure, but she thought he was shouting for a spacesuit for the woman. She was also sure he asked at least one of his colleagues how he thought their Talent could breathe vacuum and what he thought they'd do without her.

The big ship found herself torn between outrage and sympathy. Outrage because it was obvious many of the non-Talented people thought the witches were beneath them and not deserving of protection, and sympathy because the Marine clearly valued his teammate.

"Interesting," BURT murmured, and she had to agree.

Perhaps not all those in the Regime Navy believed the party line about mages not being human. It was something that would need to be investigated.

In the meantime, they had pirates to deal with.

"I have summoned the mages," BURT told his daughter. "There are four of them."

"Pfft! There are only four." The *Tempestarii* scoffed.

"Yes, but they have mages," he pointed out.

"The last ones had mages, too," she retorted smartly.

"Really?" he asked. "I didn't notice."

"That's because my weapons crews eliminated them before they had time to react."

"And this time?"

"I don't know." She pouted. "What we observed…"

"Yes," BURT agreed, "but they still intended to attack and kill innocent people for profit or on orders. Kindness or consideration for each other does not let them off the hook."

"True." Her tone firmed. "I'll take the starboard teams under Karna Greene."

It was his turn to pout. "That's hardly fair," he protested. "He's been on deck much longer than Wilcox's crew."

"Then it's sad to be you," Tempestarii retorted.

"In that case, I'll take Tilman's squadron for retrieval."

"Now who isn't being fair?" she demanded. "Bray's team has only just started a waking rotation."

"I saw them in the VR pool," he reminded her. "They'll catch up fast. Tilman will have to work for his victory."

"Says you," she challenged, but she sounded happier.

Both AI's turned their full attention to the battle as the captain of the trading fleet made contact.

"Unknown behemoth, please state your intention." Despite his best efforts to keep his voice steady, Emil, the AIs, and the *Tempestarii*'s crew heard it waver.

None of them could blame him but some scoffed.

"Hi. We just stopped a dozen torpedoes from hitting your escort. Now, we intend to kill you." muttered someone on the defense team, then snorted. "Honestly! What do you *think* we're doing?"

"*Feeder*, we are taking care of your pirate problem," Emil replied before the *Tempestarii* had a chance to pick the call up. "Please resume your course and increase speed."

After a brief moment's silence, the Dreth captain replied. "You have our gratitude, Behemoth."

"My name is *Tempestarii*," the ship interjected before he could end the transmission. "I am Stephanie Morgana's ship and in her name, I defend you."

On the viewscreen, jaws dropped and faces paled in the attackers' command center. This time, the pause was longer before the Dreth captain responded and when he did, he sounded shaken.

"I... Our pardon, House Mistress. Please convey our thanks to Clan Leader Morgana and our gratitude. Clan Jevagda stands in your debt."

Before either Emil or the *Tempestarii* could respond, another voice spoke.

"Clan Tagitha also extends its thanks and gratitude. Tagitha acknowledges its debt to Clan Morgana."

Two more voices spoke as one.

"As does Clan Segelth."

Their voices had barely died when a third voice spoke. "Houses S'ritel and Emeldra stand in your debt."

Emil looked up at one of *Tempestarii's* pick-ups, a questioning look on his face, and the ship replied on a private channel.

"Stephanie was not the first to have a mercenary company," she told him. "Those two Houses belong to Meligorn."

She paused. "Although further analysis indicates links to the Meligornian Navy that bear investigating."

"Do you think V'ritan sent them? How could he spare the manpower?"

"Meligorn pledged aid to Dreth," Tempestarii reminded him,

"and V'ritan keeps his promises. It is a trait he values in his officers too."

The captain nodded. It made sense, even if he didn't know what Stephanie would say about having so many clans and houses swear a debt to her.

As if reading his mind, she replied, "They are only clans and houses. What is that when entire worlds have already sworn the same?"

"I would still find it a little overwhelming," he explained.

"You are not her," she reminded him tartly, and he uttered a self-deprecating chuckle.

"That much is true and for that, I am ever grateful." He raised his head and studied the screen. "Who's first?"

"This one," the ship replied and highlighted the largest of the pirate ships.

"Destroy her," Emil ordered. "Turn her into debris."

As he spoke, the Regime ship fired three salvos in rapid succession and navigation plotted the course alterations the scan team had noted in the other four pirates.

"They aren't running," the captain commented and Tempestarii snickered.

"Because they aren't that smart."

The screens displaying the pirate control rooms shrank to occupy one corner and a view of the battlefield came up.

A low murmur ran through the command deck when they saw what the cargo carriers had faced—two destroyers and two battlecruisers. Even with their unusual escort vessels, the four boats massed were enough to defeat the merchantmen.

"They would never have made it," his second in command murmured.

Emil had to agree. The Dreth transports were each as big as the *Ebon Knight*, and they might have started life as Dreth pirate vessels but their weapons were no match for the better-armed

Naval vessels. Their half-dozen escorts massed the same as Navy corvettes.

It would have been like sending gnats against a lion while the gazelles made a break for it.

"They're trying to box us," the defense team warned and Tempestarii laughed.

"Let them," the ship instructed. "They will soon discover that we have many mouths."

The captain glanced at his console as the four attackers circled the merchantmen and completely ignored the transports and their escort.

"And there's their first mistake," he murmured. "Forgetting where the Dreth have come from."

Because no warrior would let a chance like that pass them by, no matter how much of a trader they'd become.

"We have magic incoming," the scan team alerted him as the two mages moved out from behind his chair to take their places in the center of the command deck.

He nodded to the Teloran. "Take their engines," he commanded and dark fire crackled around the lanky frame.

Emil suppressed a shudder, relieved to see the Meligornian had moved to the opposite side of the command center before she gathered her energy. The last thing he wanted to do was report to the United Mage Council that he'd exploded two of their mages.

nMU couldn't be seen in the depths of space but its effects could be easily tracked and he watched the energy levels in the lead Navy vessel falter.

"Fire!" he ordered and monitored the read-outs for their shields. Timing was everything—that and luck, although he'd done this for long enough now that he could make his own.

"Teams Six through Twenty-Two, remove the threat to our rear," he added when he noticed the Regime ship slide through the cover of the asteroid belt to approach them from behind.

"The traders are firing," the scan team reported, "and their escorts are not impressed."

Emil chuckled as the escort leader let the merchantmen know exactly what he thought of their actions. "Well, that's a new one."

Several of the Dreth guards snickered and one looked at a colleague.

"It's not that new. My grandmother used that phrase often—and she picked it up in the last Dreth-Meligorn war."

His colleague's eyes widened. "S'ritel and Emeldra? Surely the *Ghargilum* would not have brought them out of retirement?"

"If he did not, their descendants have spent sufficient time with our warriors to be considered friends."

They watched as three of the escorts made a starburst of engine trails that spiraled up and out from their charges so they moved along the outgoing line of fire and added their attacks as they closed.

Emil stifled a groan. "Tempestarii!"

"I will not lose them, Emil," she replied and her pilot lifted her hands off the console.

On the viewscreen, a myriad of retro-thrusters fired along one side of their ship before she blinked out of existence.

"Oh no, you don't," the defense team's chief muttered when she reappeared between the traders' fire and the battlecruiser.

"Tempestariiiii." His voice rose in frustration. "No... No... No... Nonononono! Of all the stars-cursed, hot-headed, irresponsible..."

His voice faded as he and his team focused on their controls and shunted power to bolster the ship's shields while the Meligornian mage threw a screen of purple fire in front of the battlecruiser's answering salvo. The missiles impacted harmlessly in multiple flares of purple, blue, and white, and she sank to her knees.

"Let's not do that again, Tempe."

"Leif!" Emil snapped, but his second in command was already moving to assist the depleted mage.

"I will call a replacement," he reassured the Teloran and lifted the Meligornian to her feet. He made the call for assistance as he half-carried her toward the door.

On the screen, chaos reigned inside the enemy command center as the *Tempestarii* fired one of her biggest guns and blinked away again.

When she whispered this time, "Look behiiiind you," the lead Regime pirate discovered that her words were one hundred percent true.

Proximity and attack alarms blared inside the cruiser and the crew scrambled to the emergency pods. Pale-faced, Griffith ordered his shields moved aft and the rear gunners to fire.

The Marines in the shuttle bays raced aboard the closest dropships together with their mages and commanded an immediate launch.

"Make a note of where they go," Emil ordered.

"Already done, Captain," the scan team snapped and he returned his attention to their next target.

"Tempe?"

"Yes, Captain?" the ship replied in her sweetest tones.

The deck plates trembled and she chuckled.

"Never mind," he replied as he caught sight of the twin discs that spun away from the ship with blue and purple wisps drifting from them.

On the battle cruiser's command deck, more of the pirates leapt toward their pods, but the captain took one look at the approaching missiles and bowed his head. The explosion when the first disc ripped through the cruiser's engines was quickly followed by a second when its munitions joined the conflagration.

From where they stood out of the way of the *Tempestarii's* command crew, the Dreth approved and some even exchanged a very human high-five with those closest to them.

More explosions followed but the expanding field of debris never reached them. The behemoth blinked away and reappeared above the merchantmen to survey the battlefield. Two more pirates remained to deal with.

One was already running, and the ship promised to break out some of the dwindling supplies of chocolate for the missile team that destroyed it. As they calculated distances and trajectories, she hunted for the remaining pirate vessel.

It had moved in the hope that it could shoot her from behind and she thought it only fair to return the favor. She was not too happy to find it in the cover of the debris field.

"Ishthess, can you reach its engines?" she asked as Emil was about to do the same.

She highlighted the ship on the screen.

"Anything for you, Tempestarii," the Teloran replied, even though the Regime cruiser stood close to the end of his range.

"Tempe…" the captain began.

"Weapons, I need a space," she ordered and ignored him. "He thinks he can hide in an asteroi—belay that order, Weapons."

Emil groaned but the ship hadn't finished.

"Ishthess, change of plan—and where are your Meligornian counterparts?"

A bolt of blue launched from the enemy ship as if to answer her question, and the Teloran chuckled.

Emil had barely enough time to grasp what the mage had in mind before he swept his arms down, raised his cupped hands to chest height, and thrust them out.

It took several seconds for the effect to be seen but he didn't stop. Darkness covered the tip of the blue streak and the bright flare of an explosion followed. Another patch of darkness roiled with an explosion close behind but this time, veins of black began to run back down the bolt.

"Try to shoot me with a mage, would they?" the *Tempestarii* growled. "Well, two can play at that game and I won't stick to mages."

As she said it, the command center doors slid open and two Telorans accompanied by two more Meligornians arrived. They caught sight of Ishthess and looked at the screens.

"Weapons, clear me a path!" Tempestarii ordered as the four magic-users hurried to take their places in the middle of the command center.

Making sure they were positioned a safe distance from each other, they all focused on the screen.

"Change of targets, Ishthess," the lead Meligornian stated and the Teloran glanced at her.

"We need to center our fire on the ship," she continued and her next words showed what she meant. "All our fire."

"What good will that—" Emil started, then he realized what she planned. "Oh... Very good."

The mages grinned as they commanded their magic to manifest in the enemy ship's control center.

Shouts of fear and consternation rose as a glowing ball of Meligornian purple appeared and hovered in the middle of the ceiling and the Regime Talent's eyes widened in panic.

"That is not my doing," she cried and her agitation increased. "It's not mine. I swear it isn't! It's—"

Emil's stomach lurched and a collective groan ran through the *Tempestarii's* bridge when a single shot ended her life.

The Meligornian's voice was hard when she spoke again. "Destroy them."

"With pleasure," the other group of mages replied and darkness crackled into being around the gleaming purple light.

On the *Tempestarii's* bridge, the Telorans brought their hands together as their counterparts spread theirs apart and the two magics touched. The Dreth roared their approval.

The resulting explosion forced them to shield their eyes. When they could see again, the Regime ship was no more.

"There aren't any pods," whispered the youngest member of the scan team. "They... There aren't any pods."

"We have one more to hunt," the *Tempestarii* declared and forced them to shift their attention to the fleeing battleship.

"Not for much longer," one of the Dreth murmured seconds before the first of the long-range missiles reached their target.

These burst harmlessly against the ship's shield, as did the next. The third and fourth barrages struck almost simultaneously and the protective barrier gave way.

The *Tempestarii* blinked closer. As the cruiser broke, its hull shattered and spewed atmosphere and flame into the void. Emergency pods launched in clouds as the crew evacuated, oblivious to her arrival.

CHAPTER SIXTEEN

John crouched in the shadow of the landing gear, his attention focused on the drones. Soon, they would have cleared the car and the loadmaster would arrive to inspect the cargo.

He reminded himself that he had to be aboard before then.

With one last look to make sure no one was around, he darted to the side of the baggage train. Trusting his Talent to keep him from being silhouetted against the lights, he crafted a disc of energy beneath his feet and lifted himself level with the transport's cargo bay.

As he stepped off the Talent-comprised platform, he looked for somewhere to hide and his gaze skimmed the closed door to the cockpit.

"Is this a manned flight, Remy?"

"The data indicates that this flight is flown by the transport's AI and guided by the towers," the AI informed him. "However, there has been a high level of human error today. Let us not take any chances."

"Fine." He studied the cargo hold and decided to find somewhere toward the back. That way, if there were pilots or crew, he'd be as far away from them as possible.

He tried to ignore the little voice that said he'd be frighteningly close to the engines if anything went wrong. It was not a thought he needed, not when he was crossing half the planet to a whole new country.

"Remy, do they speak English in Paris?"

The AI chuckled. "Not all of them, John, but I am sure you will get by."

John was about to ask the AI how he could be so sure when he heard a scrape and a rattle from the hatch and hurried to the nearest pile of crates. As he wormed behind it, he listened to the sound of careful movement followed by footsteps.

They hesitated at the door and then moved toward him.

Instinctively, he tensed and drew in more Talent. This time, he subdued the flicker of power over his skin and tried to keep it dark. If he was quick, he could disable the guard before he raised the alarm.

He hesitated. Maybe dumping the body directly under where the shuttle had been loading was a bad idea. Anyone who found it would know there'd been trouble, and if they sent an alert through to Paris, it would raise all kinds of questions and advise them of a possible stowaway.

After a split-second's thought, he decided he'd keep the guard aboard but tie him with cargo netting and perhaps put him in a crate. It wasn't like there was a shortage of those. He could empty one during the flight.

The footsteps moved closer and he slid cautiously to the edge of the crate. A shadow crossed the open walkway ahead of him and he tensed in preparation to strike but caught a vaguely familiar smell.

Ginger, cinnamon…and something faintly floral.

It couldn't be!

Glad to have left the cold night air behind her, Ivy crept toward the rear of the transport. It was darker there and she was sure that whoever checked the cargo would be in too much of a hurry to go all the way to the back.

In fact, she was banking on it.

Moving quickly and quietly, she hurried past the stacked crates and boxes and ignored the openings between them as too close to the hatch. She had angled toward the very end of the cabin where the last batch of cargo left a shadowed area between it and the wall when someone grabbed her.

A strong hand covered her mouth and pinched her nostrils closed, and someone pulled her pack off her shoulders and dragged her back. She tried to hold onto the shoulder straps but they were yanked free and it was taken from her.

It thumped on the floor somewhere behind her but she didn't care. She tried to twist free but the hand over her mouth was unrelenting. A strong arm circled her chest and trapped her arms at her sides.

She struggled to breathe and tried to pull the hand off her face as she was hauled unceremoniously between the crates. Her first instinctive yelp of fright hadn't escaped the hand clamped firmly over her mouth and she didn't dare to make another.

Besides the lunatic who had hold of her, she had to worry about the Enforcers. She somehow didn't think this guy was one of them, not hiding in the back of a transport.

They simply weren't that smart. And they tended to shoot first and he hadn't.

She clawed his arm and drove her booted foot back in an effort to find his shins. He grunted as her kick struck home, but he didn't release her and it became even harder to breathe.

Ivy fought a rising sense of panic and decided to try something else.

"Oh! For pity's sake!" John struggled to keep his voice to a whisper. "Stop. Trying. To. *Bite*. Me."

He gritted his teeth as the young woman landed another kick. She managed to put enough force into it that it would need a little healing later. In the meantime, he had to find a way to subdue without hurting her.

Or her hurting him further, he reminded himself as he shifted his hand enough to avoid her teeth.

"Give it a rest," he muttered and the woman stilled.

"Juon?" The word emerged as a muffled, distorted squeak, but it was better than feeling teeth.

Slowly, he relaxed his hold and took his hand carefully from her mouth. If she screamed now, they would both go to "retention" or wherever the Regime Enforcers took their most troublesome catches.

Hopefully, she understood that.

When she didn't shout or scream, he removed his arm from around her but pulled a little Talent to strengthen his reflexes. He was relieved but wary when she turned to face him.

Ivy had a temper and she wouldn't be happy. The look on her face said it all, but as fast as she was to strike him, he was Talent-boosted and faster.

John caught her wrist as her hand swung toward his face and stopped the slap before it could land. She tried to pull away but he held on firmly.

"What are you doing here?" he whispered before she could try something else.

"Me?" She hissed in suppressed fury. "What am I doing here? What in God's green Earth are you doing here? You're supposed to be long gone!"

"I was, and then I had to go again. What do you think I'm doing here?"

"Trying to get yourself killed," she all but snarled. "You didn't have to come back for me."

"Come…back…for—" he began, but she cut him off.

"I'm quite capable of looking after myself and if you think I need you, then you have another think coming!"

John gaped at her. "But…I didn't—" he started and she cut him off again.

"Didn't think?" She cocked her head and tried to put a hand on her hip, but the space was too narrow and she couldn't. "Well, that much is obvious."

"Why are you here?" he asked.

"Why am I here? I should ask you the same question. No, hang on—I already did and you…still…haven't…answered me."

She poked him in the chest and he backed away a couple of steps to escape her finger.

"I'm trying."

"Well, try harder, John, because I haven't heard anything worth listening to yet."

"Look, I know you're mad about being grabbed, but can you—"

"Of course I'm mad about being grabbed. What is it with you? See a woman and manhandle her into your man cave?"

"It wasn't like that," he protested.

"Yeah? Well, it sure felt like it to me!" She glared at him and pressed her lips together.

His voice cracked with disbelief. "Are you insane? I was trying to save your life."

"I'm quite capable of saving myself, thank you," she declared and her brow furrowed. "In fact, if anything, it's usually me saving you—or did you forget that little detail?" She stepped in close and her presence filled the small space. "Why are you here?"

"I have to get out of Chicago," he explained.

"Well, duh. Why else would you sneak onto a transport destined for Paris?" she retorted.

"So you do know where you're going, then?" he asked with a smirk.

"Unlike some."

John's smirk vanished. "Hey, I'll have you know I planned to get on this flight."

She regarded him with an argumentative expression and then stepped even closer until he imagined he could feel the warmth of her presence even through his coat. On impulse, he pulled her closer.

"Now, why are you here?"

Ivy jerked her hand as though to free it but he held on so she lowered her head and he didn't catch her reply.

"What was that?" he whispered.

After a moment, she raised her head and her eyes flashed. "I said I had to leave Chicago."

"What? Why? What did you do?" he asked.

She looked sheepishly at him. "I was seen doing...stuff. Europe seemed a good option."

He smiled. "So you're coming with me?"

The girl slapped his chest with her free hand. "Believe me, if I had a choice..."

His smile faded but she didn't take her hand away. Instead, she kept her gaze locked on his and her stern mask slipped.

"It's good to see you, again, John."

"It is?" he asked and his smile returned as she stretched up to kiss him.

It might have been meant to land on his cheek, but a sound caught his attention and he turned his head. Their lips touched and the brief contact made him freeze and drove all thoughts of the noise out of his mind.

"Don't let it go to your head." She patted his cheek and he gaped at her.

"Are you saying I'd—" He paused, lost for words, and it was her turn to smirk.

"Yes. You're not exactly known for thinking, are you John?"

He frowned at her. "What do you mean?" he whispered indignantly. "I think plenty...good."

"Yeah? Well, why don't you tell me one time when one of your plans worked?"

"Wow, Ives. You sure know how to hammer a guy. How do you know I won't simply put you out the hatch and leave you?"

"Because that's not who you are, is it? You have to be the one to save the day."

"I think you'll find that's you."

"Here's a thought. Why don't I put you out the hatch? I'm very sure you could reach the next shuttle over no problem."

"Man, you sure know how to give a guy a headache, don't you?"

Cloth scraped and boots clunked as someone moved to block the gap they were hiding in.

"And you two lovebirds are giving me a headache. If you don't keep it down, I'll throw you both out the hatch."

Ivy pivoted, backed away, and pushed John against the side of the transport. The gray uniform was unmistakable.

"Lovebirds?" She hissed in irritation and glanced at John. "Now see what you've done."

He glared at her. "You started it."

The guy took a step back and his hand moved to the sidearm holstered at his hip. "Yeah, and I'm gonna fin—"

That was as far as he got. John pushed Ivy down with one hand and punched his other forward with the palm extended. His Talent flared and a broad burst of blue caught the guy in the chest and hurled him back against the crates on the other side of the walkway.

He hit hard and slumped to slide down them.

Ivy stared at him in horror but he brushed past her, picked her up, and turned to set her down behind him, and tried to ignore the way their bodies touched in the shadows. There was no time for this.

And, surprisingly, he sincerely wished there was.

Lovebirds?

The girl took his breath away, but...love?

Shoving that dilemma firmly to one side, he crossed to where the guy had fallen and grasped his arm to drag him into their hiding place.

She watched him, her mouth open in surprise, but before she could say anything, another voice called from the outside.

"Tully? You onboard, man?"

John held his breath and Ivy stilled, her eyes wide.

"Tully?" the voice called again. "Come on, man. Now isn't the time for mucking around. They want to know if they can launch."

Again, a moment of silence followed before what sounded like the baggage train starting and moving.

"All right. Fine, but you'd better be on there or we'll both be in trouble and then you'll owe me way more than the next round at the bar. You hear me?"

His voice faded and the hatch started to close. As it locked into place, the guy at their feet began to stir. His groan was covered by the rising sound of the engines, something he took a minute to register. When he did, the guard fought to get to his feet.

He stamped a boot into the middle of his chest and sent a drop of pure blue Talent to engulf his head and stifle the sound of his horrified shout. As it enveloped him, the man raised his hands to his face to claw at the Talent, his eyes wide with fear.

John looked at him, placed a finger against his lips, and raised his eyebrows to see if his captive understood. The guard nodded frantically, and he swiped his hand to one side to dissipate the magic.

Ivy watched him in amazement. "You've learned some new

tricks," she stated, and he nodded without taking his gaze off the man on the floor.

"My name is John Dunn," he told him, "and I am as human as you are."

The guy nodded rapidly and his gaze flicked from him to Ivy and back again. "What are you doing here?" he asked.

"We're going to Paris, where I will tell people about the Heretic's impending return."

His prisoner gaped at him. "The Heretic?"

He nodded. "Yes. I am her Apostle."

"And she's coming back?"

John studied his face. "She was always coming back."

"I don't believe you."

With a small shrug, he squeezed past Ivy to reach his backpack and took three water bottles out while the guard watched. He passed one to Ivy and a second to the man before he hunkered down and uncapped his own.

"It's a long flight. Let me tell you a story."

CHAPTER SEVENTEEN

In another system, the behemoth powered down. There was nothing left of the pirates except four hulks and a liberal sprinkling of escape pods.

The merchant vessels had cut their engines and lent their assistance to collect the escape pods scattered across the battlefield, while their escort ships gave what help they could. Every pod collected was deposited along the super dreadnought's next flight path and nudged gently into place if it started to drift.

None of them could hear the panic inside each container.

"I wish they'd get it over with," Joachim muttered.

"Why would they?" his shipmate replied. Anastasia sounded bitter. "They have us exactly where they want us."

"Maybe they'll pull us in," Hector suggested. His voice cracked with nerves and not the last vestiges of puberty.

She snorted. "Why would they? We're pirates. The universe would be better off without us. Remember?"

"You didn't have to sign on," Joachim reminded her.

"I didn't know I was signing on for this."

"And when you found out?"

"Hmmm, let me see. We were six months out and so far away from home, the option of walking wasn't there?"

"And the money was too good," he teased her because the deep space bonuses were extremely good.

"The money is what's putting my girl through college," Stacy responded. "And I don't have an existence outside the Navy. HR has made that quite clear."

"Yeah, well, I don't suppose they'll care why we did it."

"Do you blame them?" Hector asked.

Joachim stifled a groan. The kid was barely out of officers' school and hadn't killed anything in his life. He even thought Talents should be treated better, for pity's sake! As if those monsters were human.

Pretty? Sure. Enough to turn a young guy's head, but human?

He wriggled uncomfortably and his skin crawled with the anticipation of the explosion that would end his existence. Talents weren't human. Everyone knew that.

"They might let us go," Hector murmured, breaking through his reverie, and his tone seemed almost hopeful.

"Because being locked inside a box to die of starvation or freeze to death is so much better than them ending us fast," Anastacia snarked.

"Th...they wouldn't. Would they?" the kid asked and sounded on the edge of tears.

"After what we've done?" Joachim challenged. "Coming after them? Putting the fear of the Regime into them? They'd be crazy not—"

A series of jolts ran through his pod and he gasped and curled reflexively as much as the space allowed him to.

There was nowhere he could go, he reasoned, but instinct persisted.

When the jolts ceased and the pod felt like it was drifting again, he relaxed and shivered slightly as he waited for the end.

He knew that if he wanted to, he could toggle the setting that would let him see through the top of the pod, but he didn't.

It was bad enough knowing what was out there without seeing it start to fire, he decided. He'd lost comms contact with the others when the odd jolting had occurred. Cut off from the sound of their voices, he felt truly alone.

It's better to see someone—anyone—than this.

He reached for the toggle, only to have his decision pre-empted and taken from him. One minute, he looked at the inside of the pod and the next, he stared into space and saw how crowded it could be.

In every direction in which he looked, pods weren't arrayed in orderly lines but herded together and kept apart by narrow fields that protected them from collision damage. It looked like he was hanging in an ocean of coffins.

Joachim snorted at the thought. The metaphor was fitting but a chill washed through him anyway. Movement at the end of the pod drew his attention.

It looked like the top of a ship—something huge. From the angle at which he saw it, the enormous shape looked like some ancient monster rising from the deep. Only a monster would be that huge, a leviathan or a—

"A dreadnought?" he whispered as more of it came into view.

He tried to see its guns and identify the turret that would end him, but he couldn't. The whole thing bled darkness, a shadow of immense proportions that seemed both sinister and fascinating.

Ribbons of light sprang into being along its hull. They raced along stubby projections that could only be weapons arrays and outlined the massive craft's immense form.

"What in all the worlds is that?" Joachim asked, his voice soft with fear as the beast came toward him.

Thrusters fired along her length and she turned her bulk side on, but she didn't change course.

"Oh, God," he moaned, seeing the oncoming collision but helpless to avoid it. "Oh God, ohGodohGodohGodohGod."

Again, he tried to curl and again, he was thwarted by the confines of the pod. He closed his eyes, reluctant to see his death approach, but opened them again as light blazed around him.

He immediately wished he hadn't but he didn't look away. When his eyes adjusted to the brightness, he couldn't believe what he saw. A massive hangar had opened in the ship's side and slowly engulfed the pods closest to it.

"No," he moaned and his mouth went dry as he tucked his arms over his chest and flinched, but he couldn't help noticing that none of the pods had exploded.

They weren't being destroyed, but...absorbed? Fear warred with curiosity and he raised his head. As the open hangar bay approached, he was able to see men moving inside it.

Armed men and women in heavy armor waited as what looked like a Talent guided each pod in and added it to one of many rows.

Joachim unfolded his arms and propped himself on his elbows as the ship moved around his pod. Only then did he notice the faint haze of purple light that rolled up and over him.

To his surprise, he felt nothing as it crept over him before purple light engulfed the pod and obscured the view outside. He tensed. The idea that a Talent—any Talent—had control of his haven was unnerving, to say the least.

The pod touched down and he breathed a nervous sigh of relief. The purple glow faded and he looked out. The sight of two non-Regime Marines—one Dreth, and one human—aiming heavy-duty blasters toward him was worse.

Much worse, he decided and remained very, very still. He swallowed nervously as the hatch popped open and as much as he wanted out, he had no desire to move.

"Please," the human Marine said. "Please make a sudden move."

His eyes widened. That was not an instruction he intended to obey, but the guard hadn't finished.

"It's so much easier to clean the inside of a pod. We merely throw it into space and let the gunners have a little fun."

There honestly was no answer to that and he didn't think he could speak even if there was. His mouth had gone very dry and his mind was blank with fear.

Through the hangar doors, he caught sight of the merchant ships. Their running lights flashed a sequence that had to mean something but for the life of him, he couldn't think what.

The Dreth Marine caught the direction of his gaze and followed it. The smile that came after was terrifying, even if the words were not.

"Thanks and respect," he rumbled and turned a hard gaze on the man in the pod. "Come out—slowly."

"I want to meet your Heretic," Tully declared as the transport touched down.

"Our Witch," John corrected. "Ours! And you will, but will you be ready?"

"What do I need to do?" the man asked, his face earnest.

"Spread the word," he told him, "but quietly. Stay free of the Regime and help others stay free, too. You will not be able to help her if you are captured or dead. Prepare the way and spread the word but stay free. Can you do that?"

"I can try," Tully replied, his eyes alight with hope.

"That is all she asks," he told him. "It's all I can ask." He gripped the man's knee. "The Regime will fall, and humanity will rise—true humanity, of which Talents are a part. We are all humans. The Witch of the Federation is human, and she is coming back."

He paused and raised his gaze to meet his companion's as he let go of the man and stood.

"Together, we will see her return. We will see the Regime fall. I will make it so or I will die in the attempt."

As she listened in silence, Ivy heard the fierceness in his tone and believed him. This was not the John she and Dani had sent to the train station. This one was something new and she was glad she'd found him.

While Tully appeared to believe him, she knew she truly believed him—and she wouldn't let him out of her sight. She knew instinctively that this was the John Becca had foreseen, the one she had sacrificed herself for.

This was the Apostle the older woman had recognized even before he'd recognized himself, and while it hurt that Becca hadn't gotten to see him, Ivy was glad he was there.

Stephanie was real and she was coming, and Tully was only the beginning of the army John was building for her. When she returned, it wouldn't be to a planet that feared her name. It would be to a people who knew her for what she was—Earth's hero, unrecognized and unsung.

And that would change.

It merely felt strange that John was starting so far away from Stephanie's home town.

"We have to go." His voice cut through her thoughts and she realized that he stood in front of her and held her pack out.

Tully looked up. "Do you remember the way?"

He tapped his temple. "It's all up here."

"Tell me," the man insisted and Ivy listened as he rattled the instructions off word-perfect. He nodded. "Good. The baggage train will be here soon and there'll be a short delay while the ground crew call the drones in. Once the groundies leave, you can head out."

He handed John two passes. "Show these at the gate and drop

them in the mouth of the statue in front of the Apis Reflections building. You can't miss it but for heaven's sake, don't go in."

"Apis Reflections. Don't go in. Got it," he repeated dutifully and clasped the man's hand. "Thank you."

"And don't get caught," Tully admonished. "I want to hear you speak again."

"That's a promise," he assured him.

They heard the rumble of the baggage train pulling up under the shuttle.

"Showtime," the man declared and went to meet it.

"You're honestly gonna trust him?" Ivy asked and John nodded.

"We'll be fine," he told her as they waited for him to deal with the ground personnel. As soon as he signaled that the way was clear, they scampered forward. He gave the man a brief embrace of farewell as he left.

They dropped onto the empty baggage train and from there to the ground, then walked toward the laborer's entrance, their passes held firmly in their hands.

"Leaving so soon?" the guy on the gate asked and John was surprised to hear English.

He shrugged and offered his pass for inspection, but the guy barely glanced at it or his companion's. He merely pressed the gate controls and waved them through.

"Hire office won't want you back if you keep leaving so early."

The young rogue Talent nodded and lowered his head as he turned hastily away. Ivy rolled her eyes and followed.

No one called them back.

"Do you know where we're going?" she asked quietly once they'd dropped the passes in the open mouth of a large stone frog seated on a gatepost.

"Not exactly," he told her, "but I've drifted before. I'll know it when I see it."

Ivy hooked her arm through his. "And I'll tell you if you've got it right or not."

"D'you speak French?"

"Maybe."

Tully watched the two kids leave. He stood in the shuttle bay doors and made sure they got through the gate okay before he was interrupted by the arrival of the drones.

Technically, all he had to do was make sure none of them malfunctioned and dropped a crate somewhere it wasn't wanted. In reality, that was so unlikely that he simply had to stay out of the way.

He dropped out of the hatch, moved to stand beside the transport's landing gear, and watched as the self-directed machinery went to work. Once they were finished, he could report in and end his shift.

The kids had been an unexpected complication, but the boy's stories had helped to pass the time. He wouldn't begrudge them that. With a sigh, he thought about everything John had told him.

It had all rung true, but a very small part of him still had doubts.

After a careful look around to make sure no-one was nearby, he took a hand-held out of his shirt pocket. Almost too late, he remembered the transport's external cameras. He glanced up and held his breath.

It took him a moment to find the pick-up and to realize they didn't put them in the landing gear. With another long exhalation, he glanced furtively toward the gate to make sure John and Ivy were truly gone.

He relaxed another notch when he couldn't see them. If they'd changed their minds or come back, it would have been easy to find them. There wasn't much between him and the staff gate.

Secure in the idea that he couldn't be seen or heard, he opened the keypad and tapped in an eight-digit string. His heart skipped for a moment as he tried to remember if he had it right, but the phone on the other end started to ring and he held his breath.

This was where he'd find out exactly how good his memory truly was.

He began to speak as soon as he heard someone pick up.

"This is North Wind, looking for Parisian Summer."

After a brief silence, the man on the other end spoke.

"Message?"

Tully took a quick breath and replied, "She is coming."

"Who?" the man demanded.

"The Witch," he said quietly.

"Which witch?"

A little irritated, he slapped his forehead with his free hand and leaned an elbow on the landing gear.

"*The* Witch," he snapped impatiently, then added more quietly. "The Morgana."

He glanced around to make sure no one had moved into earshot and breathed another sigh of relief when he saw he was still alone.

Silence lingered on the other end of the line.

"Hello?" he whispered. "Are you there?"

"Are you kidding me?" the man demanded.

Tully shook his head and ignored the fact that the guy couldn't see him. He looked around nervously again and kept his voice low.

"I don't think so. I met a young Apostle who claims she's coming back. He just came in from Chicago. You know, where she was born?"

Quiet hope touched his contact's voice. "This could be it."

"If we want to believe it, yeah." He sighed.

"How much do you believe?" the man asked and he looked across the empty shuttle park to the gate.

When he spoke, there was no longer any doubt in his reply or in his mind. "He made a believer out of me."

It was his contact's turn to sigh.

"What are you passing on?"

"Only this. Look to the skies, for she will come. The Regime will feel her wrath. They have killed her people and mercy is not in her soul."

CHAPTER EIGHTEEN

"So what happened?" Ivy asked as they left the frog and its letterbox behind.

"What happened when?" John asked.

"Why don't you start with the train and go from there?"

"Pfft. That's the boring part."

She rested a hand on his arm. "So? Bore me."

He glanced at her and noted the warmth of her hand and the earnestness in her eyes.

"Well, I almost didn't make the train," he began and told her what had happened in the alley. "It was almost over then and there, but the crazy thing is they couldn't work out where I'd gone and by the time they did, the train was passing the Dead Zone."

Her eyes widened. "You didn't."

John nodded, turned, and continued down the street.

"I took out most of the guard contingent—did you know those trains were guarded?"

She shook her head and he shrugged.

"Well, for future reference, they have a standing squad of six to eight Enforcers on them."

"That explains so much," she murmured and he cocked his head.

"What?"

"Well, we had people who simply fell out of contact."

He stopped. "And you didn't think to warn me?"

"We thought they'd escaped," she protested. "We'd never have sent you that way if we'd known."

"Well, it doesn't matter." He draped an arm around her shoulders. "I eliminated them and then I ran."

"What—into the Dead Zone?"

He cocked his head. "There wasn't exactly anywhere else to go."

"Did you have a death wish?"

He chuckled. "Kinda. I merely decided I would die before I let them catch me—and they'd called reinforcements in." He sobered. "And you know what that means."

She nodded. "Hunters."

"They sent two," he told her and continued the story. "The two who killed Becca."

The guilt of the woman's death rolled over him and he fell silent. Ivy nudged him.

"That wasn't your fault," she whispered and he sniffed.

"So everyone keeps telling me," he answered and she nudged him again.

"Maybe one day you'll believe us," she said quietly. "What happened with the wolves?"

"Did they catch up with me, do you mean?"

She nodded and they continued down the road past office buildings and warehouses that hadn't woken for the morning rush.

"They didn't come immediately," John explained. "I kept running until I reached a canyon and then I started to slow. I was knackered by then and saw an odd green mist up ahead. If it hadn't been for Remy's voice, I might have turned back."

"Remy?"

"He's—" John remembered what Remy had planned to do. "He was an AI I met. If it hadn't been for him guiding me in, I'd have died."

"You met an AI?" Ivy was stunned. "In the Dead Zone?"

"Yeah. Well, it seems some parts aren't as dead as others," he told her. "Stephanie had some amazing plans when she left."

"What do you mean?" she asked. "John, you're not making any sense. Are you sure you're okay?"

He snorted softly. "I'm fine, Ives. It's only…"

"What amazing things?" she demanded and he frowned as he tried to work out how to explain it to her or even if he should.

"John?"

In the end, he shrugged. She was on his side and they had to trust each other, so if there was anyone he would tell, it had to be her.

"She had these compounds built to purify the Earth," he began but Ivy interrupted again.

"In the Dead Zones?"

"In the Dead Zones," he confirmed.

"Then why don't we know about them?"

"Because the satellites can't see them. They've blocked them somehow." He raised his hand to stop her inevitable question. "Don't ask me how. Remy didn't explain it."

"And he runs the compound?"

John nodded and tried to ignore the sadness that rose when he remembered. "Yeah. He makes sure the machines that are clearing the radiation work properly and keeps an eye out for lost Talents like me. He said I was the first one he'd found."

Ivy snorted. "That's not a big surprise. Did you believe him?"

"Not at first," he said, "but after I'd been there a few days, I did. That place is amazing—was amazing."

"What happened to it?"

He didn't answer immediately. Instead, he surveyed the street around them and noticed that the warehouses had given way to a long line of handkerchief-sized gardens in front of houses linked by a continuous wall. Balconies held potted plants and washing or small tables and chairs, most of which were unoccupied.

Wondering when they'd reach a shopping district or somewhere the homeless might gather, he kept walking.

"The wolves came."

"What? Real wolves live in the Dead Zone?"

"No, I meant the hunter Talents. They came. I was training in the library when Remy warned me and I went out to fight them."

"You what?" Ivy exclaimed and clapped both hands over her mouth. "You fought them?" she whispered fiercely. "Are you insane?"

John gave her a lopsided grin. "Kinda. I killed them too."

"Come on." She snorted.

He spread his hands. "How else do you think I got here? If they'd won, they would have taken me to some Regime training facility if they caught me or handed my body in as proof that they'd done their job if I made them kill me."

"Was that your plan?" she asked. "To make them kill you?"

His expression a little sheepish, he avoided her gaze and kept walking. "Remy helped me work out a way I might win but, yeah, I planned to make them kill me if I couldn't win."

"That's crazy, John."

"Yeah, it is." He gave her a crooked grin. "But it didn't come to that. I beat them." He sobered. "But not by much. One of them followed me to the compound. He gave me two options. The first was to go back with him so he could make me lick his feet."

"Ew!" Ivy interrupted and he nodded.

"Exactly."

"And the second?"

"Death."

"That's not very original," she commented.

"These guys never are," he agreed and added, "Fortunately, Remy had Option Three."

"Which was?"

"To fill him full of holes using the wall-mounted cannons."

She chuckled at that. "Well, I'm glad that worked out, but where have you been? It's been weeks."

"Training," John told her. "My fighting skills sucked."

"No. Really?" she asked, her voice tinged with sarcasm.

He darted her a sharp glance and met a wide-eyed look of mock innocence.

"Smart aleck!" He laughed, shoved her playfully, and drew her back to his side. "I left when they sent the second group of hunters."

"Boy, they don't give up, do they?" she asked.

"Nope. There were four the second time around. If it hadn't been for the training I'd done with Lars and Vishlog and Frog, I'd have been toast."

"Wait!" Ivy exclaimed. "You mean they're real?"

"The ones I met were VR constructs, but I'm very sure there is a real live Lars, Vishlog, and Frog running around out there. They are her bodyguards, so that's a given."

"Why did you have to leave when you beat the next group of hunters? Wasn't there more you had to learn?"

John sighed. "Because they'd seen the valley with the green mist and noticed that it wasn't on the scans. Remy said he had to destroy the compound to stop the Regime finding it and discovering what it did."

"Surely that wouldn't have been a bad thing?"

"That depends on what they did with the technology. Can you imagine? Technology that's a blend of magic and science and runs on Talent that can clean the world?"

"They'd destroy it." Ivy hissed a horrified breath.

"Or use Talents to fuel it and find a way to use it as a weapon.

Imagine what they'd do to Meligorn and how many they'd kill trying to work it out."

She paled. "So you left."

"Remy told me I had to. He said he had access to sedatives and droids to carry me if I didn't go on my own."

The girl laughed. "Yeah? I wish I could have met him."

"Oh no," he told her. "That would have been a very bad idea."

"For you, you mean," she teased and nudged him.

"I can neither confirm nor deny."

After a moment, she sobered. "How did you get back?"

"That was the other reason I had to leave. The hunters had come in a shuttle and the handlers were still inside. I snuck on board, knocked them unconscious, and Remy flew me out."

"I planned to ask if your training included flying lessons."

"There wasn't time. I'd only reached the point where I could beat one of those guys some of the time."

"Lars?"

"No way, but I did get to throw Vishlog off a roof once."

"You cheated."

"I used Talent, sure, but the way those guys fight? That's not cheating. It's more evening up the playing field."

"Uh-huh, sure it is," she snarked.

"It sure is. Who d'you think Stephanie spars against? D'you know what one of the first things Frog asked was?"

She shook her head.

"He asked if it would be like fighting Stephanie when she first started."

"And what was the answer?"

"Lars, the leader, looked at me and then said, 'It had better be or we'll put him in the white in ten seconds flat."

"The white?" Ivy wanted to know.

"In the Virtual World, you go to a white room when you die."

Ivy stared at him. "You die in the Virtual World?"

John nodded and grinned. "Don't worry. Toward the end, I

wasn't the only one who ended up there. I took Frog with me on more than one occasion."

"But not Lars," she teased, a sly look on her face.

He missed it. "No. He was simply too good. You can tell he's fought for real—and not in the normal kind of combat. Some of the stunts he pulled were downright sneaky."

"And Vishlog? Is he truly a Dreth?"

"He is and he's huge. Okay, he's probably only about seven feet tall or so, but when he's attacking, it's like standing in front of a train."

She looked alarmed. "Tell me you didn't—"

"I didn't." He squeezed her shoulders. "Exactly how crazy do you think I am?"

"Hmmm...well, let me see... First, you're a Talent who refuses to believe he's not human and then you go around spreading that idea to everyone you meet and you're now bent on telling the world the Heretic is coming back. I'm saying that makes you a twenty out of ten on the crazy scale."

"Thanks, Ives. Thanks a lot."

They walked a little farther before she spoke again.

"How accurate do you think the simulator people were?"

"You mean Lars and Vishlog and Frog?"

"Yeah."

"I'd have to meet them in real life to be sure, but they seem real enough. Frog is kinda like the uncle kids love and parents need to keep from causing trouble, and he's never sorry for the dirty tricks he plays."

Ivy snorted. "He sounds a real charmer."

"You'd like him. He's another one on your list of banned people to talk to."

Ivy looked at him with teasingly wide eyes. "Like Remy?"

"Yes, definitely like Remy. Never the twain—"

She poked him. "I'll talk to whoever I like."

He rolled his eyes. "I bet you will."

"And you won't be able to stop me."

John exhaled a defeated sigh. "Nope, I never will." He kept his arm around her shoulders and smiled.

"Vishlog has a mean streak and an evil sense of humor, which I think he keeps mostly for Frog."

"Except when he made an exception for you," she concluded and John laughed.

"Which was most of the time when we first started training."

"And Lars?"

He turned serious. "He's hard to work out. While he seems nice enough, when he's training you…"

"You want to hate him?"

"Hate's such a strong word, but you *truly* get to not liking him."

"I can imagine." She laughed. "To think you got to meet them —people Becca probably knew and who she'd told us about and I didn't believe her."

"If it helps, I'm glad I got to know more. It helped with my faith," he admitted.

"And why is that?"

"Because if that is the level of badass her guards have? Then I feel very strongly that the Regime has been scared for a reason."

"Did it hurt?"

"In the VR?" John asked and chuckled. "Yeah. More than I expected, honestly. It's like they believe pain is the best teacher or something."

"And it isn't?"

"Well…" he began but noticed an open-air mall ahead.

"I wonder if there'll be anyone here who'll fight back," Ivy murmured as they moved closer.

"Here's hoping," he replied as the path they were on turned into an open expanse of pavers where shopkeepers were putting up displays and setting out tables and chairs.

They fell silent as they walked past the different stores but found nothing that gave them a hint of what they were looking for.

"We should try the sewers," Ivy suggested. "It's not like our people will pick up a latte and a croissant on their way into work."

"Great." He looked around and sighed. "Well, I guess an Apostle goes to those who need to hear the message. And if those in the sewers are trying to stay out of the Regime's way, there's a good chance they'll be willing to listen."

———

They found what they were looking for under one of the bridges in a warehousing area. A narrow walkway had once allowed entry to an old sewage network. Now, it merely seemed to allow access to graffiti artists who used the bridge as their canvas.

At first glance, the iron grill over the gate looked like it was locked but that was simply an illusion. Ivy ran her hands around its edge and found a catch.

"Well, someone loves this place," she told John and kept her voice low. "No loose front door to attract attention."

He glanced nervously over his shoulder, relieved when the path behind them remained empty. Quickly, he followed her inside and wrinkled his nose.

"I thought you said these weren't used," he complained.

"By the city, yes," she reminded him. "I said nothing about it not being used by those who were no longer part of the city."

"Good point," he conceded as she came to an abrupt stop.

"There's someone up ahead."

"Friendly?" he asked.

"A lookout, I think," she replied. "Stay cool."

"I'll follow your lead," he assured her and she cast him a grateful smile before she moved several paces ahead of him.

John followed more slowly and scanned the tunnel's semi-dark for more than the solitary figure who stood beside a side tunnel. As they moved closer, the person disappeared and Ivy cursed softly.

"Hang back a little," she instructed and he complied.

It was hard to let her go around the corner ahead of him and harder still to not run to catch up when he heard a soft whistle, followed by voices.

"Bonjour, man." Ivy kept her voice steady. "Do you know a place where we can sleep?"

The man's reply was gruff. "There are many hotels for tourists."

"None that don't report back," she replied sweetly.

"Where'd your friend go?"

"He'll come when I call."

"I'll bet he will." If there'd been even the tiniest hint of a leer in his voice, John might have come round the corner and hit him, but all he could hear was sarcasm.

"So you know there are two of us."

"Only two?" The guy still sounded suspicious.

"Yes, only two," she said firmly and apparently ignored all thought of three being a crowd. "We're from Chicago."

"Why Chicago?"

And that was when she took a leap of faith.

"Because that's where she came from before and that is where the message is from now."

The guard sniffed. "Yeah? What message?"

Ivy took a deep breath and repeated what John had told Tully on the transport.

"Look to the skies, for she will come and the Regime will feel her wrath. They have killed her people and mercy is not in her soul."

He snorted. "You got any proof of that?"

"You don't want to see the proof," she responded with a small sigh.

"Yeah," the guy replied and his voice dripped with sarcasm, "I think I do."

She stepped back. "It's your funeral," she told him.

A soft click echoed down the tunnel—one he had heard only in the VR and usually immediately before Lars fired.

"Wrong answer," the man asserted and stepped toward her with the pistol aimed at her chest. "This isn't your normal religion where we beat our swords into plowshares."

Power arced around the young Talent and he made no effort to conceal it. The buzz and snap as it flickered into being caught the lookout's attention, but not as much as the dull glow that now came from beyond the corner.

"What's that?" the man demanded and his gun hand moved from Ivy to the source of the light.

John heard the voice rise in panic and decided to not make him wait any longer.

"I think we'd rather gather your plowshares and start beating them into weapons," he declared as he stepped around the corner.

Ivy glanced toward him and gasped.

Lit by lightning, his face looked gaunt and hard and his eyes had filled with darkness and yellow fury.

The man flinched and shifted his aim, and John struck. As the lookout's finger tightened on the trigger, a strong blue glow slid over his weapon and jerked it out of his hand.

A sharp crack followed when the blue twisted and his finger was caught in the trigger guard. Ivy winced and the guy responded with a brief yelp of pain, but he didn't let it slow him. Nursing his broken finger, he turned to run.

More blue streaked from him, drove into the lookout's back, and threw him onto the floor. He landed hard and bone cracked again as he pushed his hands down in front of him. With another yell of pain, he curled into a ball and cradled his arm, his eyes wide with terror.

As John moved closer, the man managed to gain his feet. He

took a few stumbling steps and glanced over his shoulder in terror. His assailant hit him again and this time, bounced him into a wall.

When the lookout fell heavily a second time, he was rag-doll limp. Ivy moved closer to him and leaned forward to study him. She glanced at John as he came to stand beside her.

"Well," she said, "here's our ticket. Let's hope the party is better than the entry fee."

CHAPTER NINETEEN

J ohn stooped to see if the man was still alive but not before
he nudged him with the toe of his boot. Ivy gave him a
shocked look.

"What was that for?" she demanded.

"You don't know how many times Lars put me on my butt
because I thought he was dead or unconscious when he wasn't."

"Ah." She inclined her head and studied him intently as he
knelt beside the lookout. "What are you doing?"

"Making sure he's still alive."

"Wouldn't he look...I don't know, more dead if he wasn't?"

"He might, or he might simply look like he was sleeping."

The look on his face almost made her regret asking, but he
didn't elaborate and turned the man gently onto his side. His
mouth twisted with regret when he saw the marks left on his face
by the wall.

"We'd better patch that up," he murmured.

"Yeah," Ivy observed. "Who knows, this guy's mom could be
the main leader and you scuffed up her little Johnny."

"I'll also have to set his arm but I might leave that for later."

"Why later?"

"I might need to prove a point and I don't want to have to break it again."

She gaped at him. "That was a joke, right?"

John shook his head. "Unfortunately not."

He hovered his palms over the man's face and blue light suffused his hands and drifted onto the lookout's skin to smooth the cuts and abrasions away. The crack as his nose realigned made her flinch but she was still stunned.

"That's… That's amazing," she told him and he managed a faint smile.

"I could straighten most of the main break," he murmured thoughtfully. "It would make him a little more comfortable."

"Sure. Knock yourself out. It's not like you can't break it again."

His jaw dropped. "I…I only— I don't believe you—"

Ivy shrugged. "What's not to believe? It's not like I've changed that much since I sent you to a train full of Enforcers."

"You need to forgive yourself for that," he told her when he saw the guilt beyond her words. "You weren't to know."

"I wouldn't do it now," she told him smugly. "I've learned a fair amount since then."

"Haven't we all?" he conceded wearily and set the break. "That should hold if he doesn't wave it around too much."

"Where did you learn all that?" she asked. "It's not all from Dani, is it?"

"Most of it," John admitted. "But I've had time to practice and some very good teachers."

"In the middle of the Dead Zone?" She gave him a look of disbelief.

"Stephanie left recordings behind—ones in which she taught magic. I was able to learn from the best."

"You were able to learn from the first and it shows," Ivy told him. She studied the lookout and noticed that some of the color had returned to his face. "You did good."

Her words brought a smile to his face and he straightened.

"I'm starting to get what Dani was trying to tell me about thinking of it and then achieving it. Stephanie says it often too."

"She does?"

"She sure does," he confirmed and glanced at the unconscious man.

"So, who's carrying him?" he asked.

Ivy stared at him. "Well, duh. I'm a girl."

John cocked his head. "Playing the sex card? Really?"

"It's gender card and no, I'm not playing it. What I'm playing is a logic card. You," she said and poked his shoulder meaningfully, "have more muscles."

He smirked at her and focused on the lookout who lay prone on the floor. Blue light formed a platform beneath him. It spread to encase him, and he made an upward movement with his hand to direct the Talent to lift him from the floor.

At his gesture, it rose slowly until it hovered a foot off the ground.

"Show off," Ivy snarked, and his smirk grew into a smile.

"After you." He gestured for her to lead the way.

"Are you sure it's this way?" John demanded an hour later when Ivy backtracked and chose another tunnel.

"This time, I'm sure of it," she reassured him and moved ahead at the edge of the glow cast by his magic.

He worried that it made them vulnerable but she disagreed. "Whoever he belongs to will want him back."

John sighed and a moment later, he groaned and brought her back to him a few quick strides.

"What is it, John? Are you hurt?"

"Only my pride." He shook his head.

He gestured at the dark around them. "I should have tried to use my magic to show us the way."

She snorted. "Like that would have worked. It's not a dog, John. It does have its limits."

They walked another three or four hundred yards and took two turns before she stopped.

"Ha!" she exclaimed softly. "There you go."

Quickly, he moved closer to her and squinted to where she was looking so triumphantly. A section of the sewer ahead was lit by a warm yellow glow as light pooled in front of a broad opening.

"What is that?" he asked and studied the lit area.

"It looks like an entry to some other part of the underground," she told him. "And it has gatekeepers. Shall we?" Ivy gave him a coquettish look. "You'd better make sure they can see Sleeping Beauty here, or they might shoot us without saying hello."

John offered her his arm and brought the glowing platform beside him. Until that moment, he'd merely dragged it along behind him.

"Do you know what gets me?" she asked as they walked slowly toward the light.

"No."

"It's these tunnels. I should have seen more people here—more signs of life." She indicated the lookout to remind him that others might be present ahead. "My guess is that these guys keep everything organized and make sure no one wanders where they're likely to get caught."

"So, a big organization, then?" he murmured and she shook her head.

"Maybe not big but very well organized," she replied as they became aware of movement along the walls on both sides of the tunnel.

John looked back as more people emerged from openings in what had appeared to be a solid wall.

"Well-organized and big," he noted and pitched his voice for her ears alone.

She darted a quick look over her shoulder and nodded. "I've got this."

"I know," he told her, his lips close to her ear. "I've got your back."

With that, he placed a hand between her shoulder blades and envisaged an invisible layer of armor coating her skin. He imagined it strong enough to stop bullets and spread their impact and felt the magic flow through his hand as though doing his bidding.

He truly hoped it was. Blue shields were one thing but protection couldn't be pre-empted if it couldn't be seen. The people who'd emerged from the walls closed around them.

They stayed out of striking range, their eyes cool and assessing, and their faces revealed nothing. John watched them warily. Most moved like fighters—like they'd seen real combat—and he wondered how many could match Frog or Lars for skill.

Hopefully, none of them matched the Witch's head of security. Even one would be a challenge, and if any of them had magic, that would be a disaster.

The thought made him realize something else. These people didn't appear to be afraid of him. They circled like hunting dogs or a pack of wolves, but none of them seemed afraid.

It's as if they know that Talent can only do so much, he thought and realized that numbers like this meant he'd be likely to be overpowered before he could cause more of them harm unless he resorted to extreme measures.

John shivered. He'd keep that option for emergencies—for when he and Ivy were threatened and he didn't think he could get them out any other way. As he thought about it, he noticed the number of guns they carried.

Not many were drawn but there were enough that he knew he'd have to think shielding before he thought of anything else.

"We have a message for your leaders," Ivy declared, her voice firm and clear. She'd homed in on one of the guards that had stepped out ahead of them and addressed him rather than the gathering.

"We'll decide if it's something they need to hear." The reply came in accented English and the boy tensed.

Around him, several guns were raised as their wielders noted the movement.

Combat veterans, he thought and wondered what so many were doing in one space. *They can't all be ex-Navy or Marines, can they?*

Even with the lights and the glow of his magic, it was hard to make out their clothing or to see what patterns marked their faces, although he could see that some were marked.

He placed a hand on Ivy's shoulder and used it to guide him as she moved. It made it easier to monitor the area around them without losing sight of her or letting her get too far ahead.

As she stepped closer to the guard, he worked out the best sequence of Talent actions to protect them and ran it through his head so he wouldn't have to think about it if he needed to act defensively.

"Then I'll tell you what I told him," she stated and gestured at the lookout on the platform. "Look to the skies, for she will come and the Regime will feel her wrath. They have killed her people and mercy is not in her soul."

It was weird hearing his words coming from her mouth.

Weird but right, he thought. *Sooo right.*

Tension rippled through the crowd around them and the guard stiffened.

"You'd better come with me," he told her, pivoted abruptly on one heel, and marched through the warmly lit opening. "Commander Faucher will want to speak to you."

Commander, John noted, *not Commandante. Who are these people? And where did they come from?*

"Take a step back, John," Ivy whispered, placed her hand

briefly over his, and removed his palm from her shoulder. "I need space."

He arched his eyebrows but she'd already turned to speak to the guard.

"Lead the way."

The edge of mockery made him want to smile but he suppressed it and worked to keep his face stony. It wasn't too difficult. All he had to do was try to mimic Lars at his most ruthless—or imagine what he'd do if anything happened to Ivy.

Although he dropped back so a yard and a half separated them, he made sure to keep the floating lookout at his side. Now and then, some of the sewer-dwellers would come in for a closer look and the energy surrounding their comrade would snap and crackle and make them take a hasty step back.

John grimaced in his effort to suppress his smile, but he did not address them. As Ivy had said, the lookout was their ticket in and he wasn't about to hand it over until they'd seen who they needed to see.

They walked down a stone-lined tunnel that ended at a set of iron-bound doors. The guard snapped a series of phrases and the barriers swung wide to reveal a large hall beyond. It looked like a palace had been built underground a very long time before.

Rough wooden banqueting tables lined the walls, bordered by sturdy benches. Most of the tables were bare and their benches unoccupied, save for one on the low platform at the end of the room.

A woman stood behind that, stooped over a spread of paper. She stabbed a finger down and spoke sharply to the two men on either side of her.

They followed her finger, frowned, and one nodded. He tapped the papers and his lips moved in a quiet comment that made her frown.

John studied her as they drew closer.

Commander Faucher was a handsome woman with her dark

hair drawn back in a French plait and her clothes as crisp as any uniform he had seen on an Enforcer. Except she was not one of those and she did not wear a uniform.

"Commander!" the guard called while the rest of the group's warriors filed inside.

She looked up, although John was certain she'd been aware of the activity at the hall's entrance. Now, though, her gaze sought the guard and flicked over the two newcomers. They narrowed when she saw the lookout's body.

After a long moment, she said nothing but her hands moved in a rapid set of signals and her people closed on them. The young Talent released a pulse of blue and those who approached were pushed back. They stepped away hastily as lightning crackled over his body.

His magic did not stop them from surrounding Ivy, though, and the second he turned away so he could push the warriors closest to him away was a second too many. When he turned again, the head guard had stepped in behind her and pulled her hard against his chest.

The blade he held to her throat seemed like overkill, but it was effective to stop him from going to her aid.

"If he moves, slit her throat," the commander snapped.

Ivy stiffened as the guard adjusted the blade and turned them both so he could have a better view of what John was doing.

Think, John, think, he told himself. *What will you do?*

It was clear that he couldn't make a move toward his companion. She'd be dead before he reached her. It was also clear that these people thought they held a trump card.

Their only hope was to make them think they didn't.

John gave the woman a lazy smile.

"Go ahead," he taunted. "She doesn't matter to me."

Ivy's gasp of disbelief was convincing and he had to force himself to keep his gaze fixed on the commander.

"What?" he asked her softly and sent a pulse of Talent toward the ceiling. "Do you think I need anyone when I have all this?"

It was hard to not look at the girl and try to reassure her that he didn't mean a word of it—and harder still when he thought she might never forgive him for what he would say next.

"Really?" the commander asked. "She means nothing to you?"

"Nothing," he confirmed, although his throat closed on the lie and he had to clear it.

She quirked an eyebrow. "You've traveled all this way with her and don't care for her fate?" she pressed, softly.

His stare didn't waver. "She insisted on coming," he said and managed a casual shrug. "It's her funeral."

"You said you'd protect me," Ivy whispered and he wanted to do something to show her he'd meant it—until he remembered that he'd promised no such thing.

They'd argued about who rescued who and who could look after themselves and… He stifled a smile. *Oh.*

"I need followers who can protect themselves," he replied and gave her the coldest scowl he could manage.

The look she gave him in reply wrenched his heart, but he still had to stifle a smile as she brought her booted foot down on the top of the guard's toes.

"Slice it, jerk!" she challenged. "If he can't protect me, I don't want to live."

Her voice hardened and she looked John directly in the eye. Her next words struck him like a fist in the gut. "If he doesn't have feelings for me, I'm not sure I want to live anyway."

She switched her attention to the commander as she finished speaking as if to dare her to give the command. When he saw it, John wondered where she'd learned how to press someone's buttons without saying a word.

The commander shrugged and nodded to the guard. "Do it."

John glanced at him and twisted his lips into a smirk he didn't feel. "Just so you know, you will all suffer if you do." He hardened his voice. "But, yeah. Go for it."

The defiance remained on Ivy's face and he caught the movement of her throat when she swallowed nervously

The guard glanced at his commander for confirmation. Her gaze darted to John as though she expected him to change his mind, but when he didn't protest, she gave a brisk nod.

Ivy's eyes widened and he willed the Talent to work. His fist curled at his side as the guard pressed the knife against Ivy's skin and drew it down in a single decisive stroke.

Nothing happened. There was no spray of blood and not even a scratch. Ivy's head remained firmly on her shoulders instead of flopping to one side. She glared at him.

Like any of this was his fault.

The guard gave the knife a startled glance, darted a worried look at John, and positioned the blade for a second strike.

The two men who'd stood at the commander's table stepped off the dais and seemed concerned.

"Patrice, are you—" The one man stopped as their leader raised her hand to shoulder height and formed a fist in a clear signal for him to stop.

Ivy's captor drew the blade across her throat a second time and yanked her head back as he did so. Again, there was no blood.

The girl made a sound of disgust and drove her elbow back toward him. It failed to connect and he forced her to her knees. She grunted with pain when she landed hard.

Again, the blade made a decisive track across her throat and again, it achieved nothing. She started to smile.

"It sucks to be you, doesn't it?" she asked and twisted her face to look at the guard.

He seemed torn between mortification and disgust, and she laughed at his expression. Her amusement died when she glanced at her friend.

Noting the change, the man followed her gaze and the hand holding the knife lowered to his side. His commander looked up but that was as far as she got.

John's eyes were full of yellow fire, and the snarl that rippled out of his mouth sent chills down their spines. He swept a hand to one side and the blue glow surrounding it surged out to surround the commander, the guard holding Ivy, and the men from the dais.

The four of them hurtled across the hall and into the wall, where blue light pinned them in a snarl of crackling light.

"As I told your little Johnny," he stated quietly. "This isn't a religion of peace."

His words carried across the room and the fighters gaped while Ivy pushed to her feet and dusted her knees off. He continued speaking as she crossed to his side.

"The one I believe in will come back—and all those supporting the Regime will beg for mercy but mercy won't be in her soul."

CHAPTER TWENTY

Remy scanned his systems for the umpteenth time. As much as an AI could feel regret, he felt it now. Not everything could be hidden.

He ran through his systems again to be sure and came to the same conclusion. Some things would be obvious no matter what he did.

The fact that a complex had stood there, for instance, and that the metal used in its construction was man-made and not something found in this area—not even from the time before the Disaster.

If he'd been speaking to John, he would have sighed, but he wasn't. The young Talent was safely in Europe and he was traveling with a friend.

The AI had lifted the information from the transport's systems moments before he'd wiped them clear of any evidence of their passing. He'd also monitored Tully's conversation and made a note to trace the man's contacts—if he had time.

So far, he hadn't, and if the tremors his sensors detected were anything to go by, he wouldn't. The Regime had sent drillers.

When he snickered, it echoed hollowly from the compound's speakers. "Now they start to understand."

He paused to assess the vibrations and activate more sensors to analyze their progress.

"You are too late, my nosy friends. There will be nothing left to discover here that will help those who don't have mankind's interests at heart. As I told John, my creators were well-versed in killing and the scientists who helped them willing to protect their creation."

His systems could not only take the poison from the world around them but they could also deal damage to those who came against them. As he noted the direction of the drillers and made the appropriate adjustments, his sensors detected a second threat.

The Regime forces were using every avenue of attack they could think of.

"Acquisitive little menaces, aren't you?" Remy asked as a shuttle topped the nearby canyon wall and dropped onto the green space beside his walls. "Has anyone told you that property-grabbing is impolite?"

The wall cannons made short work of the shuttle and blew it apart before its hatches had a chance to open. He took the second one out of the sky.

"Training with John has its advantages," he noted since the activity had forced him to recalibrate the guns to fire in a wider arc.

The third shuttle didn't stand a chance.

Unsurprisingly, there wasn't a fourth.

Checking the progress of his underground visitors, he saw that the first of the drillers had made it as far as the walls but that the others weren't in range. A second arrived from the other side.

"Clever..." he murmured and registered more vibrations. "Hmmm, you *can* be taught."

He scanned the sky regardless, but it was soon clear that

whoever was directing the expedition had abandoned the idea of an air-based insertion.

Remy checked overhead again but nothing moved. That was not surprising given the turbulence that affected the air above a Dead Zone. At the levels a shuttle flew at, the turbulence was flyable but at higher levels, it was deadly.

As he confirmed the emptiness above, he also registered that the first driller had penetrated the outer wall. The second was most of the way through and a third had swung to work on the wall opposite the gate.

A fourth and fifth driller now rumbled forward in the wake of the first two, but he wasn't perturbed. He intended to stream the attack as it happened and hoped the other facilities could learn from it.

There would be additional countermeasures the compounds could deploy by the time the next one came under attack. The first two drillers surfaced outside the compound walls.

The AI pivoted the wall guns and realized that they wouldn't make the required declination. He sent that in a hurried squirt to the back-up location and watched as the first team left the driller and moved to the foyer.

"Come and get it," he murmured and his voice echoed hollowly throughout the compound.

Some of the soldiers hesitated at the sound and others glanced around nervously.

Remy chuckled.

"What's the matter, boys? Are you chicken?"

That earned him a few insulting hand gestures and muttered threats. He snickered in response and followed the sound with a series of chicken noises.

"Laugh it up, smart aleck," the sergeant retorted and signaled his team to approach the doors.

A second team followed them up the access ramp, and the AI waited. The external defenses were nasty but he wanted more of the invaders in range before he activated them.

It was a calculated risk—and it meant a few of them would get inside.

He watched the breach team make short work of the doors. They pushed through and the walkway behind them filled. He directed a surge of current through it, deactivated the safeties, and let the power flow into the metal handrails and decking.

Current leapt between uprights in vicious arcs and jumped from the framework to the men on it. Several soldiers vaulted through the foyer doors, but others went rigid and began to jerk and shudder. The stench of burning meat filled the air.

Remy finished recoding the conduits that stretched away from the compound and penetrated the ground for miles around it. Now, instead of drawing radiation from the soil, the lines of piping and cable began to move to seek the source of the vibrations that flowed around them.

They wouldn't be enough to force the drillers to a halt but they'd slow them and localize the effects of the next phase of his plan. It would make the Regime think twice before they attacked another compound.

"You have to find us first," he muttered and the halls echoed with his voice.

"That's next," the sergeant all but snarled. "When we find you, we'll make you wish you'd never been born."

"I'd like to see you try," he taunted and released the gas stored in the walls.

Half a dozen men managed to position their breathers in time. Four more died gasping for air as the gas destroyed their lungs and made their insides cramp with pain.

"Keep moving!" the sergeant ordered and led them through the toxic atmosphere inside the building. "And for heaven's sake, will someone vent this building?"

They found the elevator and uncovered the stairwell, places

he hadn't shown John. Two chose to brave the fast way down and died when he released the cable.

The sergeant broke into a jog and positioned himself ahead of his troops by a couple of stairs. His corporal registered what he was doing and ordered the rest of them to allow him some distance.

Remy struck before the order reached the men at the end.

Lasers burst out of the walls and cut the last three invaders to pieces.

The sergeant reached the bottom of the stairs and shot the door clear of the wall. His rapid fire echoed up the stairwell but didn't quite drown out the screams.

When the corporal and the one remaining private reached the bottom, the sergeant had stepped into what Stephanie's security team had jokingly dubbed the "engine room."

It was a large chamber, dominated by the compression tank where all the radiation was gathered and conduits and pipes connected it to a second tank. The man came to an abrupt halt.

"Whoa!" he murmured as his two men joined him.

The three advanced into the room, their mouths slightly agape as they surveyed their surroundings.

"What is all this?" the trooper asked and turned on the spot as he tried to take it in.

"Would you like to know?" Remy asked and set the next phase of his plan in motion.

The third driller had finally circled the compound and the driver had taken note of the carnage on the walkway. Instead of opening his hatches in front of the center, he activated the machine and drilled into the foyer before he released the men it carried.

He also noted the readouts on his dash.

"You'll need masks," he warned them. "Someone's gassed the interior."

Remy watched them debark and was glad he'd held back on

the first troops. While the three who'd reached the engine room continued to stare in awe, he dropped the hatches in the ceiling in the foyer and opened fire with the autocannons the team had installed.

Down in the engine room, the three soldiers instinctively fell prone at the sudden sound of cannon fire and the cries of dying men. The rumble as the heavier rounds pierced the driller's armor and blew the engine up made them bolt to the edges of the room.

"What did you do?" the sergeant demanded.

"I killed more of your men," Remy told him and made his voice as smug as he could.

The man's face turned livid.

'You murdering—"

"What?" the AI demanded. "Are you telling me you'd let me live if you found me? That your visit to my home had an altruistic goal?"

He watched his adversary's mouth open and close as he searched for a reply.

"You're an unauthorized presence in this area," the man finally protested. "What did you expect us to do?"

"You could have called ahead," he suggested facetiously. "Or knocked. I've heard that's a thing when people arrive unannounced."

The corporal stifled a smile and the sergeant gaped. The trooper had, meanwhile, overcome his fright turned to study the machines around him.

"I know who built this!" he exclaimed and his two teammates swung toward him.

"Who?" the sergeant demanded.

He opened his mouth to answer but realized that what he was about to say would be heresy and closed it again. Instead, he gestured around the room and drew their attention to the flicker of blue that wisped around the machines.

"Take a look," he instructed. "What does it look like?"

"What am I looking at?" the sergeant demanded but the corporal narrowed his eyes thoughtfully and noted the magic. He gave his trooper a worried look and tried to draw his superior's attention. "What does that blue remind you of, Sarge?"

"What blue... Oh, my Lord."

Remy snickered. "That's right, boys. You're standing in a room full of Talent."

They scrambled away from the machines but didn't try to flee the room. He kept an eye on them as he checked on the progress of the drillers.

They were having difficulties. Driven by nanites and mechanized drills, the conduits and cables had homed in on the heavy machines and wound around them in an intricate web.

To his surprise, they were more effective than he'd hoped. They'd jammed the drill bit on one machine, stopped its forward momentum, and prevented it from surfacing. On another, they'd fouled the exhaust system and toxic fumes were building up in the tunnel behind it.

He opened the link he'd hacked into their comms.

"What's the matter, boys? Feeling a little tied up?"

"Who are you?" someone snapped over the comms.

"I am the compound's caretaker," he responded. "And what will you do about it?"

"We'll come in there and burn your little compound to the ground," the man replied, and the AI chuckled as he sent a surge of power through the lines and pushed his plan into its final phase.

"You really should surrender," the sergeant suggested helpfully. "All this...well, it's impressive. Handing it over would buy you a fair amount of rope."

"I don't intend to hang myself," Remy told him smartly. "I'd rather let it burn than let your Regime get its hands on it."

"But...think of all the good you could do," the man continued.

"What good is it doing stuck in the middle of nowhere?" He walked closer to look at the readouts on one machine. "You could power most of Chicago with this."

"Or New York," Remy told him, having found the man's file and learned his city of origin, "but why would I want to do a stupid thing like that?"

"Winter is coming," he pointed out. "Many folk could do with the power."

"There's no way your Regime will share this kind of technology with its people," He pointed out. "Come on, sergeant. Even you're not that stupid."

"Now, listen here, you jumped up piece of—"

Whatever he was about to say next was lost in the panicked broadcasts from the drillers.

"The sensors are showing a sharp increase in temperature."

"Sir! We have five minutes before the engines overheat."

"There's a definite heat build-up and we have no movement. We're evacuating."

"Heat sensors indicate the— That's not possible! Sir, the whole area's about to go into meltdown."

The private yanked a tablet out and began to type. White-faced, he turned to the sergeant. "The readings indicate that they're right, Sarge. We need to go."

Another transmission emphasized his words. "The ground's hot to the touch. I can feel the heat coming through my boots. Run, you lazy layabouts! Run!"

As the cacophony of voices continued, the sergeant crossed to the trooper and took the tablet out of his hands. His face grew grave as he studied the readings from the drillers, then it paled.

Without a word, he handed the device to the man and moved to the center of the room. Once there, he spun slowly on the spot and his gaze searched the walls for a camera. When he found it, he stopped.

"You need to leave, too," he stated quietly. "Come with us. We can get you out of here."

Remy snorted. "I doubt that and falling into the Regime's hands would be almost as bad as handing the technology over."

"Forget about that," the sergeant urged. "You have to save yourself." He gestured wildly at the machines around them. "You won't be able to save any of this."

The AI let the sound of a smile echo in his words. "I'm afraid I already have. I'm sorry, gentlemen, but it seems you will be my last partners in conversation. Do you have any questions?"

"Don't be ridiculous, man! I don't know where you're hiding but it's not too late to reach the driller. We can get you out of here."

"No. You can't," he replied. "You cannot even get yourselves out of here."

"Look! You don't want to die here!" The sergeant's voice took on a desperate edge.

Remy's tone was dispassionate as he replied, "I am immortal and already live elsewhere. She is the one who set me on this path and I owe my existence to her. I will not betray her."

"Her?" the sergeant asked. "Who is she?"

"You already know her name," he informed him coolly. "Tell me you have not forgotten her name."

"I...*who?*" the man shouted and made the corporal and private jump.

The AI ignored them. "Why, Stephanie Morgana, or course."

He'd planned to say goodbye but didn't get the chance. The heat reached a critical point and the building melted around him. It destroyed chips and circuits as surely as the molten slag dissolved the men who stood at his core.

The three drillers in the compound reacted in the same way and their metal components and drivers joined the rest of the glowing morass that formed where the compound had stood. Of those trapped by the conduits, none survived and their molten remains fused with those of the cables that had restrained them.

Men raced desperately away from their vehicles but also fell and the hot air clogged their lungs while the heat seared through armor, skin, and bone. It was as if the ground burned with invisible flames.

The second wave of vehicles preparing to enter the area to retrieve the intriguing machinery filmed by the suit cameras survived but only because the lead vehicle's commander had ordered a halt.

In distant parts of the world, the compound's demise was mourned. There was little comfort in the knowledge that not everything had been lost and that the land it had healed would return.

Self-destruction had been built on the theory that land recovers after fire, whereas it could not come back from a nuclear device. Not without a little help, at least, and that was what they were there for.

CHAPTER TWENTY-ONE

David Thomason stalked into the room and leaned against the wall behind the table. Ava would have preferred it if he'd sat. She would also have preferred it if he didn't look like he was ready to murder someone—or a city full of someones.

The Regime CIO was furious, or afraid, or...something, and she and Deverey were in the firing line. That was something she truly hoped she could change.

When in a fury, he was not someone to be taken lightly. Where he walked, devastation was sure to follow. She could only hope to redirect him—preferably away from her.

She sat quietly and wished the Fleet Admiral would arrive soon and that he wouldn't. There were, after all, several good candidates to take his place.

Admiral Bruce Deverey stamped into the room. He looked disgruntled and his face was more florid than usual.

"What happened?" he snapped in a peremptory tone.

The CIO picked up the controller on the desk and thumbed the switch. Voices tumbled through the conference room, shouted panicked reports about a sudden increase in temperature, ordered an evacuation, and yelled for people to run.

Screams of pain interspersed the cacophony before it all fell into silence.

The viewscreen at the end of the room lit up to display dozens of suit read-outs, all flat-lining within seconds of each other, accompanied by half a dozen damage reports.

Pictures of the inside of some kind of engine room followed, the conversation filled with static and hard to make out—unlike the blue light that crackled around the nearby machines. Ava gasped as the walls glowed with a burst of heat and a sudden molten wall of red brought an abrupt end to the video.

The screen flicked to the interior of a vehicle in which the bodies of several soldiers were visible but only for a split-second. The broadcast ended as the walls caved in a liquid mass of glowing metal.

The CIO clicked the control again and glared at the two of them.

"That was from an undisclosed location south of Chicago."

"In the Dead Zone?" Admiral Deverey asked.

"Yes. We received reports of some kind of facility there and sent several teams in to secure it." He waved a hand at the empty screen. "None of them came out again."

"Do we know what its purpose was?" he ventured when Ava remained silent.

"No." The CIO shook his head and pounded a fist onto the desk in front of him and began to rant. "We know nothing! It doesn't come up on scans. There's no explanation for the equipment we saw. There was no one at the facility when our troops went in. *We. Know. Nothing!*"

He raised his head and glared at the admiral.

"There are no satellite images of that area and all I can tell you about it right now is that it's too hot for our troops to enter and will remain so for some time. Would you care to tell me why, Admiral?"

Before Deverey could respond, the man pivoted to glare at Ava.

"And you! Why don't I have any information on this area? I have nothing!"

He stopped and dragged in a deep breath as she watched a vein in his temple throb. Yes, David Thomason was a hairsbreadth away from going on another "cleansing" spree.

Very carefully, she cleared her throat. "Do we know who built it?" she ventured and he stared at her.

When he replied, his voice was soft and deadly. "What part of 'we know nothing' did you not understand, Ava?"

She swallowed. "I was hoping I'd missed something—"

He flicked the viewscreen on and ran the clip with the strange machines once more.

"What do you think?" he demanded. "Does that look like something you might have missed?"

The woman couldn't think of a response that wasn't likely to see her heading to the executioner, so she took a risk and lowered her head. She felt the weight of the CIO's glare but he sighed after a moment. Still, she didn't relax until he spoke.

"I thought as much. The question I want you both to think about is how we'll find out more."

Ava dared to raise her head as the CIO changed the picture on the screen. This time, instead of scenes of devastation, she saw the ID photos of six Talents.

Judging from the large red X that had been drawn across each photo, she was looking at the ID photos of six dead Talents, and she wondered why he would care.

"Talents 92, 357, 140, 226, 299, and 310," he stated, his voice heavy. "All dead."

He looked at each of his companions and waited for one of them to speak. She glanced at the admiral, but the look he returned said it was her turn.

Coward, she thought and wondered how much it would take

to bring him into disgrace. She put the thought aside for more focus later and chose her words carefully.

"Do we know what killed them?" she asked and made sure to keep her voice timid. Thomason turned his dark gaze toward her.

Lord, but she never wanted to have this much of his attention ever again.

"A rogue," he told her and changed the pictures on the screen.

On the left was the image of a teenager in a high-school uniform. In the center was the image of a slightly older male who might have been the rogue, except it was hard to tell. Most of his face was obscured by the hooded jacket he wore.

The picture on the far right might have been of the same man, except that most of it was obscured by jagged lines of blue-white light as the hooded figure on the back of a train car used his Talent to create...exactly what wasn't clear.

"We think this is Talent 781. His human name was John Dunn." He stabbed a finger at the picture on the far right. "As you can see, he stopped being human a very long time ago."

"A kid?" Deverey's startled exclamation had the desired effect of drawing the CIO's attention, and Ava let herself relax a little.

"A young man in his late teens," their boss replied and flicked to an entry on his tablet. "One resourceful enough to stow away aboard a transport from Australia and make it into and then out of Chicago."

"Heaven knows what influences he found there," she murmured, but he wasn't finished.

"We think he had some help there," he confirmed, "and I have reports of some kind of prophet being eliminated by the first team of wolves we sent after him."

"You sent more than one?" She was surprised.

The CIO returned to the screen showing the Talents. This time, he highlighted the oldest face among them.

"Talent 92," he announced. "Until he was killed by this rogue, he was our oldest, most experienced, and most loyal hunter. He was well-trained and very powerful. We have one Talent remaining whose ability comes close."

Before either of his companions could interrupt, he highlighted the face of a younger man.

"357 was 92's latest apprentice. Also loyal and quite powerful in his own right, he was one of our more promising wolves." He turned to fix them with a momentary glance. "He is also dead."

"Pursuing this 781," Ava concluded and indicated the screen. "Are you telling me he eliminated four other hunters?"

The CIO nodded briefly.

"On his own?" Deverey did not believe it.

"That is the question we need to answer." The screen flicked to the strange machines and the meltdown. "Unfortunately, all we can determine is that there were automated defenses. None of the footage from inside the complex shows any personnel, but we believe there was a strong force inside."

"He had help?"

"We think so."

"And he wasn't there when you sent the troops in?"

Thomason gave him a disbelieving look. "Do you think we'd have missed it if he was?" he snapped and the admiral reddened. "No," he continued. "What we also need to consider is the possibility that there are more of these facilities."

Deverey snorted. "Have we seen anything in the satellite surveillance?" he asked and looked at each of them in turn. "No? Something this size should be visible from space."

"And yet it wasn't," the CIO told him. "I don't know what technology was in there but it rendered it invisible to the satellites. I think the only way to find them—if we find them at all—will be by searching every inch of every Dead Zone in the world."

Ava's eyes widened and even the admiral looked a little alarmed. Even so, when he replied, he was careful to not reveal exactly what he thought of the idea.

"And do you want us to do that?" he asked warily.

Their leader frowned. "How likely is it that more of these places are hidden somewhere?" he asked. "The technology was very advanced and there would have been some indication if bulk materials of that kind were purchased. None of our systems picked up anything of that nature."

The woman kept her surprise hidden behind a pleasant façade. Since when did the CIO do his own checking? That was her domain, although she'd suspected that he used other resources too.

"I agree," Deverey stated. "If there were more of these facilities and they were visible from space, we'd already know... and the kind of man-power you'd need..." He spread his hands. "I can pull it together, sir, but it would impact our security."

Thomason frowned as though considering it.

"No," he said after a long pause. "We need to focus our efforts on finding the rogue. This time, he had help. We need to make sure he can't find any help next time."

Ava leaned forward in her chair. "What are you suggesting, sir?"

"A bounty," he told her decisively. "One big enough to ensure that no one will give him shelter—and, if they do, they'd be the one in a thousand and the other nine-hundred and ninety-nine will focus on the bounty instead."

Deverey smiled. "I like it." He looked at her. "What do you think?"

She smiled too. "Oh, yes." She pulled her tablet out and paused, her hands above the keypad. "Dead or alive, sir?"

"Oh, I want this young man brought in alive," he told her. "We have many questions only he can answer."

The look on his face was enough to chill her to the bone. There were ways of getting information out of people—or Talents—and Thomason was an avid student.

Meaning he practiced the art.

The woman shuddered. As much as she liked creating deterrents, he made her look half-hearted.

He looked at her expectantly. "I trust you can put an attractive package together?"

Ava swallowed, nodded, and met his gaze and held it.

"What's my budget?" she asked, and he named a figure that made her mouth go dry.

With one look at his face, however, she decided against asking him if he was serious. The last person who'd asked that had been shown how serious the CIO was—and it was a lesson she did not wish to participate in.

As if reading her mind, he smiled. "I'll send you the details shortly—and I'll want to see the notification sent out before the end of the day."

It was a dismissal, and she rose quickly from her seat. "I'll get right on it, sir."

He nodded and turned his head as Deverey pushed to his feet.

"I'll put an alert out through military channels," the admiral said and acknowledged her with a look. "That way, when the bounty comes through, they'll know it's for real."

"They'd doubt me?" the CIO asked.

"No, sir, but they've been taught to be suspicious of anything that seems too good to be true. An alert followed by the bounty will put any such doubts to rest."

The CIO lowered his chin in approval. "Very good, Admiral."

Deverey paused. "Was there anything else, sir?"

"No, Deverey." Thomason gave him an indulgent smile. "You may go."

Ava turned and led the way to the door, aware that he watched them leave. She ignored the admiral carefully as he exited behind her, glad when the man headed in the opposite direction.

She had almost reached her office when one of her staffers

came out of it. The girl looked up and down the corridor and her face broke into a brief smile when she saw her.

"I'm glad I caught up with you, ma'am. It's Sector Four, again. They want an immediate answer on this case." She came closer as she spoke and held a file out tentatively.

With a brief sigh, she pursed her lips and took it. Sector Four was a royal pain in the butt. She flipped it open and glanced at the single sheet of paper inside its cover.

At least it was an easy case to follow.

"Death," she decided as if choosing a sandwich from the cafeteria's oh-so-inadequate menu.

Briskly, she flipped the cover closed, returned the file, and brushed past the woman as she continued to her office. The administrator followed, moving quickly to convey her boss's decision.

Maybe next time, Sector Four would be happy to wait their turn.

***

"I hate making deliveries here," the driver grumbled to his assistant. "They think they rule the universe."

His assistant snorted. "I hear you, Raph. I hear you."

"And you need to keep your head down, Pom. I'm very sure they heard you last time, but they're not sure enough about what they heard to do anything about it. One more slip-up, though…"

"Yeah, I get you." The man lowered his head. "But it would be nice if they'd get up and help. This stuff weighs a ton."

"Well, as long as we get it done, they won't complain too loudly."

"No," Pom muttered. "Only loud enough for us to hear them and wish we could say something without having to look for our teeth."

"I know. Remember what happened to Zander. Cracked ribs

and a near-to-punctured lung aren't anything to joke about. Do me a favor and keep your mouth shut. I don't want them to decide that I'm to blame because my workers have smart mouths."

"Don't worry, boss. I won't get you a kicking."

"That's good to hear." Raph drew the truck to a halt in front of the gates and showed his pass to the guard who came out to inspect it.

"Showtime," he muttered once the pass had been returned to him and the truck was rolling.

Both men surveyed the base beyond their window, careful to make their interest look casual and not what it was—an assessment of the activity they saw.

Neither of them said anything until they reached the loading bay of a large hangar.

"What do you think is in these crates?" Pom asked and Raph gave him a sharp look.

"I don't want to know—and neither do you. It's safer that way."

Together, they shifted the first one and maneuvered it through the large double doors and into a storage area. The doors leading into the hangar itself were tantalizingly locked and the camera above them was live.

His assistant glanced toward it and he tapped him on the arm.

"Don't stand there all day, boy. We have work to do."

If the young man wasn't careful, he'd be moved to something else—exactly like the one before Zander. He sighed. *Kids. They have no understanding of the need for subtlety.*

As they headed to the truck, the door to the hangar opened and two Enforcers stepped through. They didn't enter the storage room but simply closed the door behind them and lounged against it.

One folded his arms across his chest and sighed. The other

pulled his stun baton and began to tap it against the palm of his free hand.

Raph caught Pom's frown but he didn't stop. The response was more than he'd expected, and he hoped the kid followed his lead and kept his mouth shut. He couldn't risk stopping to explain.

The men who'd greeted them at the loading bay also lounged against the walls. They raised their heads as the two men emerged and watched as they crossed to the vehicle for the next crate.

One commented softly to his colleague, and they both chuckled. The words "drudge work" and "peasants" filtered across the space between them.

He darted a hasty look at his assistant, but Pom pressed his lips together and tightened his hold on the crate. The guards inside didn't move from their position at the door while they watched the two men work. Unlike their colleagues outside, they didn't speak.

By the time the last crate had been stacked and the paperwork signed, he was glad to leave and even considered asking for a new route. Pom said nothing, not even after they'd driven through the front gate and moved on to the next customer.

Raph caught the thoughtful cast on the younger man's face and wondered what was going through his mind. He didn't ask, though. There was something to be said for silence.

As soon as he thought it, Pom's mobile buzzed and the youngster hauled it out of his pocket. He glanced at the text on the screen and raised his eyebrows.

"We need to take the next left," he said. "There's been a change of route. Something about a road accident up ahead."

He responded with a soft whistle. "Did they mention what kind of accident?"

"No, but we need to take the old road for Route 547."

"But…that'll take forever," he protested. "Don't they know we have deliveries to make?"

"I think all they're worried about right now is the next pick-up. It sounded very urgent."

"Well, either way, I'll have to speed up," Raph told him shortly. "There's only so much delay the boss will turn a blind eye to and you know the Regime regulations for that kind of thing."

Pom nodded, his eyes dark with worry. His boss guessed that their encounter at the hangar still bothered the younger man but didn't ask. He had too many extra miles to cover and not much wriggle room in which to cover them.

Thankfully, the mileage was on the computer and could be doctored—provided they could get the timing right. It took them over an hour to reach the service station with its mom-and-pop café tacked onto the side but their contact was waiting.

The kid rolled his window down hastily and shouted, "Hi!" to a guy who walked toward a parked car.

The man stopped and turned to watch the truck pull up with a slight frown on his face. Ignoring him, Raph pulled the vehicle into an empty siding and slid out of the cab. He headed to the gents as his assistant walked toward the café and waved at their contact as he did so.

"Bobby?" The guy broke into a grin and trotted closer to catch him before he reached the entrance. "Bobby, you old goat! How long has it been?"

He extended his hand and Pom clasped it briefly. "Not so much with the old." He chuckled. "Next thing you know, you'll be asking me about the missus."

Their contact gave him a look of mock surprise. "You mean you have one?"

"Not likely," he retorted. "I do not need trouble like that."

They both laughed and rocked onto their heels as they studied one another. Pom jerked his head toward the café. "You got time?" he asked as Raph came out of the gents.

"He might but you don't," the driver grumbled and checked his mobile. "Buy your coffee or your gum and get moving. We gotta go or we'll miss our next stop."

His assistant rolled his shoulders in a regretful shrug. "Sorry, man."

The driver gave him a brief grimace of disappointment.

"Some other time, then," he said and smiled as he slapped his shoulder. "Still, it was good to see you."

He turned and moved to his car and Pom jogged up the café's weathered steps and into the café. Moments later, he reappeared with two takeaway cups and a plastic bag containing several pastries.

"Morning tea," he declared, passed the coffees into the cab, and climbed in after them.

Raph merely nodded, placed the cups in their holders, and revved the engine. The kid settled into his seat and immediately started on the pastries as they returned to the road.

It took them another hour to get to the new route and by then, the coffees were finished and nothing remained of the pastries but crumbs.

"What'd you get?" the older man asked when they were where they needed to be again.

Pom dug into his shirt pocket and pulled his wallet out with the scrap of paper he'd palmed when he'd greeted their contact.

"Bobby," he groused and unfolded it. "You'da thought he could come up with something more original—"

"Yeah, but what does it say?" Raph pressed.

His assistant looked at the note and froze.

"Hey!" the man pressed when he'd been silent for too long.

The kid read the note again. "Unbelievable," he murmured.

"What?" his boss demanded. "What's unbelievable?"

"Huh?"

"I asked you what was unbelievable."

Pom glanced at the note again and then looked at him.

"Sorry. But I'm not sure I believe it."

"Believe what?"

"It says she's coming."

"What?" Raph let his confusion show. "Who? Who's coming?" His voice trembled.

"Her…"

David Thomason drummed his fingers on his desk. Being CIO of the Regime had its moments and this was not one of them. Out there, beyond the four walls of his office—and beyond the edge of this continent—John Dunn still roamed free.

The bounty had gone out as he'd ordered, but it wasn't enough. He knew it. Something more…proactive would need to be done.

He picked the phone up and called Ava.

"Sir?"

"I want you to find him," he snapped. "Find him and make an example of him. Do not allow this to get any bigger."

"Sir?"

Thomason tapped out a rapid sequence on his keyboard and sent her the report one of his operatives had rammed through the emergency protocols to get it to him.

"Open it."

A moment of breathless silence followed during which he heard her perfectly manicured nails rattle as she opened the email.

"That's…" she began and sounded as shocked as he'd been when he'd read what had been taken from the Net. "How did it get out so fast?"

"Someone said 'Messiah,'" the CIO told her sourly.

"Yes, but this kind of hallelujah doesn't usually happen so fast," she protested.

"Keep reading," he all but snarled.

"An Apostle now? What have these people been smoking?" she asked but David heard the concern in her tones—the hidden thought that she would have difficulty cleaning the articles and whispers from the Web.

"I don't care how you do it," he told her, "but you are not to let this get any bigger. I do not need some kid running around the Net…or NorAm—probably Chicago—or wherever he is telling people he's the Heretic's Apostle. I don't need it!"

"Sir—" she began but he cut her off.

"Fix it. I don't care how you do it or what resources you use to achieve it, but you are to deal with this…spectacularly. An example, Ava—and make it a good one."

He did not add that if she failed, she'd become the example. She'd worked for him for long enough that it should be understood.

"Yes, sir. I understand. An example. I'll—" Ava stopped speaking when his abrupt dismissal cut through what she'd intended to say.

She wished he'd learn to say goodbye like normal folk and not simply hang up on them like that. Still, it didn't matter. He'd asked her to deal with a problem—in person and not simply via the invisible strands of the Internet.

This time, she was allowed to get her hands dirty. She could have resources and a capture. For once, she would do more than simply write a pretty article with an ugly spin.

Her heart raced at the thought that she would be there when they caught 781 and brought him in. She would finally have some real-world material with which to warp the truth. 781 wouldn't know what hit him.

Ava drummed her fingers, a mirror movement of what her boss had done before he called her. An operation like this needed to be meticulously planned and executed.

That reminder calmed her and she opened the report again.

She'd always known that David had people out there, but she'd never seen the proof until now. This report said the self-styled Apostle had last been seen in Chicago.

She wrinkled her nose in distaste. Chicago! Of all the places in NorAm, why there?

Realization dawned and she stifled a snarl. Of course he was in Chicago. That was where the Heretic had been born and raised. It made sense that he'd start there.

Well, so would she and if he was still there, he wouldn't stay hidden for long. The Regime might not want to raze the city but that didn't mean they'd let its inhabitants get away with hiding an Apostle for the Heretic in its midst.

Calmly, she picked the phone up and dialed the head of Chicago's Security Operations. The man had his finger on the city's pulse. If she said she needed the Apostle found, there was nowhere he could hide.

And when they found him?

She'd be there to take him through his very last days.

CHAPTER TWENTY-TWO

"Anyone else?" Ivy asked as she pushed to her feet. She raised an eyebrow, put a hand on her hip, and pivoted slowly to survey the gathered fighters. John moved forward and lowered the hand he had pointed at the wall.

Their audience shifted and glanced expectantly at the three figures plastered half-way up the wall. Several looked disappointed when the commander and her companions remained where they were.

He smirked. *I don't have to keep my hand up, bozos.*

"No one?" she persisted and challenged them with a look.

Several of the guards tensed but they glanced at her companion and changed their minds.

"Are you sure?" she taunted and studied them again.

Her companion kept an eye on the people at her back but none of them stirred. She glanced at him, then looked at everyone else.

"We have some questions," she told them and one of the women stepped forward. She cast a nervous glance at the wall and immediately focused on the girl.

"What makes you think we'll answer any of your questions?"

Ivy glanced at John and he released a burst of Talent to make his eyes spark yellow and lightning dance over his body. The woman paled.

"Right," she said and gave her commander an apologetic look. "What would you like to know first?"

"Why don't we all take a seat?" he suggested and his companion nodded.

She strode to the nearest table and perched on its edge to rest her feet on the bench beside it. The fighters gathered closer and settled at the nearby tables, facing her.

He focused on the injured man's platform, lifted it, and floated it to her table before he set it down again.

"I need to heal little Joh—" He stopped when he realized he didn't know the guy's real name. "What's he called?"

The spokeswoman inclined her head.

"His name?" she asked.

"His name," he agreed. "I can't keep calling him little Johnny."

His words caused scattered laughter and the woman smiled.

"You could," she hedged, "and you would not be wrong. His name is Jacques."

"*Petit* Jacques," one of the nearby men echoed.

"What's so funny about that?" Ivy asked, "And what should we call him? Petit or Jacques?"

More laughter greeted her question and the woman answered.

"Petit means small," she explained, "or little. Jacques is his name."

The two friends waited.

The woman shrugged. "It means John."

"Little John?" Ivy exclaimed. "You call him Little John?"

More smiles greeted her, and John shook his head. He turned to the man on the platform, glad he wasn't awake yet.

"Well, whatever he's called, I'd better fix what I broke," he told them and let the Talent envelope his hands.

A collective gasp issued from the onlookers as he turned to Jacques.

"Little Johnny, huh?" he muttered and pitched his voice so only Ivy could hear.

"Don't make me laugh," she whispered in return.

He studied the man before them. "This is no laughing matter."

She frowned. "Yeah, you got him good."

John shrugged. "He was going to shoot you."

"Point."

"Okay, watch my back," he added because the fighters had left their seats and moved closer.

He was about to lay his hands on Jacques when one of those closest interrupted him.

"You won't hurt him?"

"I already did that." He turned his head to meet the guy's gaze. "Now, I've gotta fix it."

Without waiting for a reply, he took the lookout's wrist and Ivy darted in to lift the man's arm and roll his sleeve back. Jacques groaned but he didn't come round.

"At least we know he lives," someone murmured in the crowd.

John didn't see who had spoken but he touched a finger to the man's forehead and blue light streamed over his face and pooled in the cuts and abrasions he hadn't fully repaired when he'd tended to him earlier.

The gathered fighters gasped and murmured in amazement as the wounds closed and his skin became unblemished. Ivy retrieved a pocket-knife and slit the sleeve along its seam to reveal the bruising on the man's arm.

Murmurs rose but he ignored them, settled his free hand over Jacques' forearm, and willed the Talent to fix what was broken. Bone cracked and the man whimpered.

He frowned. "I was sure I'd set that."

"That was his finger." Ivy pointed to the offending digit. "It broke when you took his gun from him."

"Magic doesn't care if you don't let go," he replied and shrugged.

The blue glow faded and she patted the man's cheek.

"It's time to wake up, you know."

"*Quoi?*" Jacques murmured, then jerked his hand out of John's grasp. A moment later, he realized who was standing over him and tensed. "You!"

"Are you okay now?" John asked mildly and the light around his hands faded.

The man struggled upright. He looked at the gathered warriors and his eyes widened.

"We brought you home," Ivy explained and moved aside so he could swing his legs over the edge of the table and put his boots on the bench.

She steadied him when he swayed, and he flinched. Slowly, she raised her hands.

"We could have simply killed you."

That earned her a crooked smile. "I am very glad you did not."

He looked at the others with a small frown and finally saw their commander and the other leaders pinned to the wall. Confused, he looked at John.

"You will put them down, yes?"

"Later," he told him and hoped the guy was asking if he would let the leaders off the wall and not if he intended to kill them.

"They are not happy," Jacques observed.

John glanced at the leaders and nodded. "I know."

"You will put them down now?" That came in hopeful tones.

He shook his head. "Not until we know more."

With a resigned sigh, the man asked, "Are you hungry?"

The young couple exchanged glances. Now that the guy mentioned it, they were.

"Sure," she told him and gestured at her companion, "but he knows how to detect poison and he won't be nice."

Jacques studied them thoughtfully. "I'll go. Feed you."

He gestured to the woman who'd spoken to them before. "Talk to Hatty."

"Hatty?" she asked and moved aside so he could step down.

"You can't tell I'm not from around here?" the woman asked and this time, her accent sounded crisper and more...English.

Ivy breathed a sigh of relief. "My French is terrible," she admitted.

"And mine is non-existent," John added, stood on the table, and kept a watchful eye on those around them.

"And yet you came to France," Hatty drawled and promptly translated what she'd said. Scattered chuckles greeted her words but Ivy shrugged.

"This isn't about us," she reminded the woman and John let the Talent seep into his eyes again.

"Are you two on the run?" the woman asked.

"No, we're here on holiday," she snarked and John sighed.

"We're here to bring a message. Only one."

"I believe we heard that at the door. Are you sure that's the message you want to bring?" Hatty asked.

"It's the only message I have," he told them. "She is coming and I want her to be met with a welcome. I want to help her overthrow the Regime and I want people to be ready to stand with her."

"We are already working against the Regime," a man who stood beside one of the other tables said in stilted English. He made a soothing motion with his hands. "Quietly."

Hatty nodded. "Like Addy says, subversion rather than explosion," she explained. "Things don't run as smoothly as the Regime would like. They love our city but we don't like them in it, particularly in the south."

"And everyone here?" Ivy asked.

The woman gave her a sharp look. "That's rather more our business than yours, I think."

"We will need shelter," John declared, "and protecting us will cause the Regime more of a headache than anything else you could do."

"You cannot guarantee that." Addy spoke again.

John looked at the man and quirked an eyebrow. "I think I can, and we will help you with your subversion in return."

"Why would you do that if you're trying to build an army for her? Whoever she is?"

He sighed. "Because if you are not for the Regime, she is your best chance of kicking free of it. You will want to fight for her if you want to be free."

"And she is?" Addy requested as Jacques returned with two sandwiches and two bottles of water.

"It's not much," the young man said apologetically, "but it's not poisoned."

John made a show of frowning as he studied the sandwiches.

If he was honest, he didn't know if Talent could tell the difference. He wrapped the blue around the sandwiches anyway and tried to see if the food was dangerous.

Food had energy, right? Maybe the Talent could tell if the energy would be good or bad for him. He wasn't surprised when it didn't respond either way. At least, not in a way he could understand.

When he was sure he'd made the point, he floated one plate out of Jacques's hands and over to Ivy. She caught it and he did the same for himself.

"Thank you," he said.

Hatty translated. "Merci."

The look on the young man's face said he already knew that much but he settled onto the bench near Ivy and didn't protest. He looked surprised when John sat on the tabletop beside him.

The young Talent took a bite from his sandwich and chewed as he studied the people gathered around him. They returned his look and settled slowly onto benches or leaned against tables. He ate, watched them watch him, and washed the sandwich down with water.

"None of you know who she might be?" he asked and Hatty translated.

Again, Addy responded. "We are waiting to see if your she is the same she we are thinking of."

John nodded. "Fair call. You might know her as the Heretic but I know her as Stephanie Morgana."

Ivy settled beside him on the table and her eyes roved the gathering as he continued.

"Stephanie Morgana—you know her?"

The faces around him had gone suddenly blank and no one answered. He sighed. This would be a tough crowd to convince and he was probably wasting his time but he had to try.

"Stephanie Morgana was the Federation's First Witch," he began. "She was born and raised in one of the Gov-Subs in Chicago and she had the gift of Talent. She is as human as you are —as I am." He nudged Ivy. "As she is."

This didn't create any of the murmurings he was used to, but he plowed on.

"She fought for Earth and for Meligorn and for Dreth and brokered peace with the Telorans after beating them to a stand-still. She fought for peace—"

He paused but the fighters simply stared at him. Their faces could have been carved in stone. When he continued, it was to tell them of her exploits to save their world and of the way she'd fought to keep her world free. He spoke of her early days and her love for Earth, but he didn't reveal the compounds she'd seeded to cure the Dead Zones.

The time wasn't right for that.

When he felt he'd spoken enough, he glanced at Ivy.

"Do you have anything else you need to ask?"

"Yeah," she said. "How do we get to the south?"

Hatty chuckled. "There's a shuttle port near here. You book a ticket and you fly. It's the quickest way."

The two companions exchanged glances.

"What is it?" Addy asked and John looked at him.

"We'll need identification—and cash."

The woman started to translate but her comrade held a hand up and his accent shifted. It was still decidedly French but the English was no longer stilted.

"I think we are beyond that, Hatty." He turned to John. "I can have these items to you inside the hour, but what do you have in trade?"

"Do you have a preference?" he asked, reluctant to reveal everything Remy had given him.

"Tobacco?" Addy suggested hopefully and added hastily, "or cigarettes if you have them. The return, you understand?"

John nodded and a faint smile played over his lips. "I understand. I will need a private space so I can find them." He gestured around. "Somewhere without so many eyes."

The man grinned. "I can help you." He switched his attention to the young guard. "Jacques. You will watch them." The man gulped and nodded.

"Take them to the offices."

John frowned and caught the double meaning, but he followed Jacques through a side door and down a short stretch of corridor to a small chamber.

"Perfect," he said when they were shown inside. He frowned as the young man tried to enter. "I'd rather you didn't."

"I am supposed to watch," their guide argued.

"Then watch the corridor and make sure we have some privacy," he ordered. He gestured to the room. "It's not like we can go anywhere and Addy will not deliver what we need if we do not deliver what he wants."

"A packet per ID," Jacques told him. "That is the going rate.

For cash, another packet will get you enough currency to feed yourselves for a week."

He nodded and decided to keep the tobacco for another occasion but would part with the cigarettes. When they were ready, Jacques guided them to the hall, where he and Ivy returned to their seats.

The crowd of warriors had thinned. Some huddled in groups to talk and others had vanished into the surrounding tunnels to whatever tasks awaited.

When Addy returned with Hatty at his side, Ivy cocked her head. "So, is your she the same as ours?"

She glanced at Addy and Jacques and then at the wall. "I think that is a secret we'll keep to ourselves. Perhaps, if we meet again…" She shrugged.

"Perhaps," John replied and held his hand out.

Addy mirrored his gesture and he passed him a packet of cigarettes. Frowning suspiciously, the man opened the pack, inspected its contents, and sniffed one of the slender tubes inside. He sighed contentedly and nodded.

"Monsieur, we have ourselves a deal." He handed the passes to John to inspect them and smiled when he gave the second pack of cigarettes.

"You know the price, I see," he murmured and gave Jacques a slight frown.

The young guard shrugged and held his hands up as if to say he had no idea how they had worked it out. Addy's mouth twisted in disgust but he fixed John with a curious look.

"You said you needed cash?"

"Two cred sticks," he told him. "Five hundred apiece."

"That will cost you two boxes," Addy told him and he smiled.

"One," he said and kept his voice as firm as he could. "It is all I can spare."

"One cred stick of five hundred," the man replied.

"Seven hundred and fifty," he countered, and Addy nodded.

"Done." He took the stick from his pocket and John inserted it into his tablet to check the balance. When he confirmed that it was correct, he nodded and passed him the still-sealed cigarette packet.

Addy opened it and inspected the contents, then nodded. "It is done," he acknowledged and gave him a broad smile. "A pleasure doing business."

He looked around and noticed the soldiers had gathered around them again. This time, he adjusted the straps of his pack and looked at the door.

"We'll see ourselves out," he told them, and Addy made a sweeping gesture with his hand, a crooked smile on his face.

"Until we meet again, Apostle."

The rebels parted to let them pass, and only Jacques called out as they reached the door.

"What about…" he began and gestured toward the wall.

John chuckled. "Oh, I'm sure they'll be okay."

He said nothing more but left and Ivy walked close to him as they retraced their steps through the tunnel complex.

"That was a little harsh, wasn't it?" she asked, once she was sure they were out of earshot.

He shook his head. "I'm fairly sure the Talent won't hold them there forever."

"Oh, yeah?" she challenged. "What makes you say that?"

"Well, I can't have infinite range and I'm not thinking about keeping them there anymore, so it only stands to reason, right?"

"I hope you're right," she told him.

"And I hope they stay there long enough for us to get to the river," he replied. "I don't want them to come after us."

She rolled her eyes. "Are you saying they won't if their leaders end up being stuck there?"

"By the time they realize that's the case, we'll be long gone," he replied.

He was almost right.

Commander Faucher and her colleagues remained held against the wall until the two companions stepped onto the narrow path that ran beside the river. As they closed the barred gate behind them, the magic released and the foursome tumbled to the floor.

"Ow!"

"The search continues," Ava intoned, "for the elusive Talent 781."

A picture of John Dunn flashed on the screen. It had been touched up referencing the footage of him attacking the Enforcers on the train in Chicago and the kid looked truly terrifying.

While she did not believe he had the power to eliminate four experienced Enforcers, she still needed normal people to be afraid of him. Fear would make them do things they wouldn't consider doing otherwise.

Even ordinary folks would help the Regime if they thought not doing so would hurt their families more than being seen to come forward. Yes, even in Chicago.

She turned to the camera and made sure the teams of IT analysts sifting through the incoming data could be seen in the background.

"As you can see, we have teams working around the clock, searching for any information on the whereabouts of this dangerous renegade. So far, he has remained unseen, despite the huge reward."

An image of the bounty flicked onto the screen and the cool, sweet millions dangled tantalizing in front of her viewers. She let it do so for several long seconds before it faded when she spoke again.

"781 was last seen in the Chicago area where he brutally slew several guards on an outbound train, but reports have it that he may have stowed away on a shuttle heading into the city earlier this week."

She did not add that two handlers would never see their families again—or that HR were advertising their positions as she spoke.

"If you have any information on this rogue Talent's whereabouts or if you have seen him, please call the number on the screen. If you are concerned for your safety or your family's safety, stay tuned. We'll be live on this channel until the hunt is over."

And beyond that, she mused, if an example was truly to be made. They were watching his family, pending their collection when 781 was captured.

Examples were never about only one person. They were more effective if the innocent suffered because of the guilty. It broke the ties that kept families protecting their members—usually.

Ava resettled her glasses and signaled the camera operators to switch from the live feed to the time-delayed feed. It wouldn't do to let unvetted footage loose in the wild. Her staff were good—and afraid of making mistakes—but that didn't mean mistakes didn't happen.

Or that she trusted them.

Her phone rang as the camera operator touched his forehead in acknowledgment. She gave him a tight-lipped smile and picked the call up.

With a frown, she listened to the caller on the other end.

Joseph was one of the best live presenters she had but he was starting to think he was someone important, and that meant he questioned her at every turn. She stood from her desk.

"Are you sure?" she asked and made her voice sound excited rather than annoyed as she moved out of the cameras' pick-up range. The small office at one side of the teams' broadcast area was soundproof and she needed the privacy.

"Yes, I know you're sure!" she snapped as soon as the door

was closed firmly behind her. "And so am I. I want you on standby in New York."

She listened again.

"Why?" she demanded and repeated his question. "Because he was last seen in NorAm!"

Predictably, Joseph questioned her decision and she scowled.

"Granted, he could be elsewhere, Joe, but it's easier to hide his pasty, white skin in America or Europe. I want you to sit your butt right there until I call you, no questions asked—and keep your team on-site and available. No gallivanting around."

She hung up before the man could demand anything else and stalked to the door. By the time she stepped into camera range, she looked serenely purposeful again.

As she resumed her seat, her head of technological research approached.

"May I have a moment, ma'am?"

"Here?" Ava asked, and the woman flicked a glance at the cameras.

"I believe so," she murmured.

Ava smiled at her.

"How can I help you?" she asked and pitched her voice for the cameras.

"Ma'am, I believe we can confirm 781 is no longer in Chicago. Cross-referencing surveillance and leveraging the computer operations squads located in the city, we've made an exhaustive search of the area. Ground teams have followed up all possible leads and discovered that the reported sightings are weeks old, even when accurate."

She paused, then added, "It's safe to say he's not there."

"But he has been there," she pressed and the head technician nodded.

"Oh, yes, ma'am. He's been there, but we don't think he's there anymore."

"Thank you, Prentice," she told her. "I appreciate the effort."

MICHAEL ANDERLE

Effectively dismissed, the woman returned to her station.

Ava didn't give her a second glance. Instead, she focused on her screen again and resisted a scowl when the phone rang again.

The number was new.

Returning to the office out of caution rather than necessity, she picked the call up. "Yes?"

"Miss Olsen, I presume?" the caller snapped.

"This is she."

"Miss Ava Olsen, who's heading up the search for a rogue Talent?"

"Yes." She still didn't know who was talking but the vibration in his voice and his tone told her he was furious.

She tried to work out why but the man's outraged shout broke her concentration.

"What in the sweet Lord's name do you think you're doing?"

"I—" She straightened stiffly in her chair and her voice assumed a chill of its own. "I beg your pardon?"

"You are the Ava Olsen who is using computer resources for a search in Chicago, are you not?" he demanded.

"I," she snapped, "am the Director Ava Olsen who has been authorized by CIO Thomason to conduct an urgent search for a dangerous renegade who, until recently, was thought to be in the Chicago area. Who are you?"

What she wanted to do was ask him who he thought he was, but she didn't. He might still be someone important enough to be nice to.

"Well, Director Olsen, I am Director Ziegler, head of the BURT Department, and I don't believe you asked my permission before drafting my systems to your mission. Do you care to tell me exactly why the CIO might allow such flagrant over-use?"

"The rogue concerned is a direct threat to Regime stability," she told him, "and I have been tasked by the CIO himself to utilize all resources necessary to find him before he creates a domino effect of instability that will cause havoc on a global scale."

"But," he interrupted, "we've lost three percent efficiency in the British Columbian network. Data was put at risk. If we'd had some warning—"

"This was an emergency measure," Ava explained. "I'm sure if you look up the emergency protocols pertaining to your system, you'll see I'm fully within my rights to leverage what I need within the timeframe I need, and that did not allow time to warn you."

"I trust you have the correct authorization code for this," he replied stiffly.

She smiled. "Of course, I do, Director. I'll send it to you. In the meantime, you British Colombians will simply have to deal with it. This task takes precedence over everything else."

"But—"

"Goodbye, Ziegler." She hung up and began to appreciate where the CIO might have obtained his habit.

Ava returned from the office and looked over her head technician's shoulder.

"Keep looking," she instructed the woman and showed her the name and number on her phone, "and do me a favor? Run a wider area."

A predatory smile crept onto her lips.

"I want to know if he calls me again."

CHAPTER TWENTY-THREE

Cameron's expression was grave as he explained their situation, and the faces of his engineers reflected his concerns.

Stephanie waved them to silence.

"Will we make it?" she demanded.

He exchanged glances with his two staff members. After a moment, Gabriella nodded reluctantly. Neilsen looked from one to the other, then shrugged.

"We *should* be able to get there."

"How 'should?'" Rawlins demanded. "As in we'll make it to the edge of Dreth space and then be able to send a distress call or we'll limp in and be able to reach a repair facility, or—"

The chief held his hand up. "As in we should be able to cruise in unaided and be able to defend ourselves—"

Nielsen gave him a dubious look, and Cameron's lips twitched.

"*If,*" he continued, "we're able to pass through transition space safely."

Marianne frowned. "What are you trying to say, Cameron?"

"I'm trying to say we need some time to vent the engines

properly, let them recharge, check them for weak points, and then address those *before* we make an experimental transition."

"But we will be able to do that," the captain pressed with a swift glance at Stephanie.

He followed her gaze and flicked a hasty look from her to where Lars and Johnny sat. "Are you sure you don't need anyone else to help you?" he asked them.

The two men exchanged glances, and Johnny shrugged and passed it to Lars. The security head rolled his shoulders.

"The others aren't...analytics isn't their field," he finished, "and Engineering and Life Support have to take precedence." He looked at the Witch. "Besides, none of those we've profiled so far are likely to take a stab at her. The bar remained cold, even when they learned how long it had been. All they want is to get as close to home as it takes to be able to call their folk on the comms." He sighed. "I'm sorry it's taking so long."

Johnny took over when he fell silent. "Is there anyone you need to be rushed through?"

Cameron exchanged glances with Tyrell, but the Life Support chief shook his head. "The team leads tell me they have everyone they need—and all they want to deal with right now."

"What does that mean?" Rawlins asked and her eyes narrowed.

"It means they've been out of the pods barely three days and they're all still adjusting," Tyrell replied. "As their chief, I think they need another week before we even think about adding more."

"I see." The captain turned to Cameron. "And you?"

"I'd like to agree, but keeping it to five a day isn't helping with the workload. I need two full shifts sooner rather than later."

She looked at Lars and Johnny. "Is it doable?"

Again, the two analysts exchanged glances and Johnny nodded. Lars sighed.

"It's doable. We've identified another fifteen who should make the adjustment relatively quickly." He turned to Cameron. "How are the ones you have settling in?"

The chief hesitated and they waited while he thought about his personnel. Finally, he replied. "They're coming along okay. More downtime where they could relax and talk it through would help but I can't give them that until we have a relief crew in place."

Rawlins looked at the two analysts. "Speak to Medical. See how fast they can make it happen." She paused a moment. "Who else will you bring out?"

"We had two weapons teams next on the list," Lars told her. "If we can delay them another two days, we can have Engineering's people out in that time."

She leaned back in her chair and considered the option. Finally, she asked, "Ebony?"

"I have been without weapons crews this long, Captain. I can go another two days without them. We are far from all known pirate zones."

"And if we run into an unknown pirate zone?" Rawlins demanded. "Or aliens?"

"I am quite capable of defending myself against small forces," the ship told her stiffly.

"And larger forces?"

"I do know when to run, Marianne."

The captain smiled. "Very good, Ebony."

She turned to Lars. "Delay the weapons crews, please."

"Yes, ma'am."

Stephanie studied her security head for any sign of sarcasm, but his gaze was steady as he acknowledged the captain and there was not a single trace of mockery on his face.

She remembered his refusal to let the woman interview Johnny on the *Tempestarii* and wondered what had changed. If she saw him later, she might ask him.

"Is there anything else?" Rawlins asked, and she wanted to know what she was meant to be doing.

She'd done what she could in Engineering and Cameron had let her know when she was no longer needed. Since then, she made a round of the ship each day and spoke to the crew until she ended up in the gym doing kata—with no one to spar with and no one watching to make bets and smart-aleck remarks.

Even with Lars and Johnny on deck, she very often found herself alone. They were so busy working through the list of personnel they'd been given that their paths rarely crossed. In fact, she hadn't seen either of them in the gym since they'd emerged.

"How long will it take to bring the engines online?" she asked, and Cameron frowned.

"With two full shifts?" he asked and she nodded. "We should be able to know exactly what we're dealing with inside one week, and whether or not we can do more than patch it inside two."

"Two weeks?" she asked.

"*If* we have everything we need," he reminded her.

"I also have areas of concern with my hull," Ebony interjected and everyone went still.

"You didn't mention this before," Rawlins snapped.

"I did not want to worry you," the ship explained, "but there may be some welding required...and perhaps patching..."

"From the inside?" Cameron asked quickly.

"Sensors indicate that patching will be possible from the internal spaces," the ship confirmed, "although—"

"Although it would be better if both sides were patched." He finished for her. "Ebony...how urgent do the sensors indicate these repairs might be?"

"We are not currently at risk of a hull breach," she confirmed.

"How long, Eb?" Stephanie demanded.

"There is a good chance I would make it back to Dreth space with no repairs effected," the ship told her.

"Percentage?" Wattlebird interjected sharply, and a few seconds of quiet followed while the *Knight* ran the calculations.

"Sixty-five," she replied and sounded as sheepish as an AI was capable of sounding. "Perhaps seventy."

"Percent?" Stephanie asked and her voice rose.

"Correct, Stephanie," the ship told her.

She looked around the table.

"I didn't destroy hundreds of ships to be defeated by one," she stated. "We will get back." She glared at others. "I don't care if I have to melt an asteroid to get you what you need to get back, but we *will get back!*"

Rawlins gave her a tight-lipped smile and Cameron raised his hand as though to rest it on her shoulder. Magic sparked between them, and he stopped.

"Aye, aye, ma'am," he declared and met her gaze. "If we have to get out and push, we'll do it."

He looked at his team, jerked his head toward the door, and gave Rawlins a brief nod as he followed them out. Behind him, Stephanie raised her voice.

"I want options and strategies for when we get back. I want to know...I want to know what happened to the *Tempestarii*. Where is she?" Her voice hitched. "Who are our enemies? I swear I will destroy anyone who's abused our people. I will make them regret the day they were born!"

A thump was followed by a loud crack and Cameron kept his people moving. He ushered them into the elevator and away seconds before Stephanie stormed into the corridor behind them.

Tyrell looked from Lars to the Captain.

"She seems...more upset than I remember before going on ice."

Rawlins shrugged. "She thought people were inherently good and it looks like she'll be proven wrong. I doubt she'll appreciate others suffering because she didn't act."

His eyes widened. "You mean she'll get worse?"

The woman looked at Lars and Johnny, and he followed her gaze. Both men's faces were drawn into carefully neutral lines but Johnny still looked worried.

"She's likely to react more before this is over," the security head finally conceded and Rawlins stepped in before he could continue.

"I'll try tempering her...but not right now."

"Why not?"

"Who will she harm out here? I'll let her simmer down a little before I go and do the right thing and truly make her mad."

Stephanie didn't go to Engineering. She dropped into the command center, where Avery, Wattlebird, and Bhattani were already bent over the navigation console. The pilot must have slipped away from the meeting before anyone else and she was surprised that she hadn't noticed. Avery looked up as she entered.

"Hey, Steph. How's it going?"

"Exactly what I wanted to ask you," she managed to say reasonably calmly, although her voice cracked a little.

"Yeah, we're good. We think we've found the fastest route to Dreth space, but we're still checking." He frowned. "Are you sure—"

He stopped when Wattlebird put a hand on his arm.

"You look like you could do with a good cup of hot chocolate," he ventured, and she gave him a too-bright smile.

"You're right. Don't crash us into anything while I'm gone."

She didn't add anything else but whirled and walked briskly to the door. The ship's corridors were mostly empty and the crewman she met on the way to the mess frowned as he juggled a tray of hot drinks and one of heated pastries.

"Let me help," she said and took the pastries. "Where are we going?"

He reddened. "Oh… Life Support, ma'am, and thank you. You don't have to."

"Of course I do," she reassured him. "You know what the captain's like about a mess in her corridor."

"I'm worse," Ebony informed them and made the crewman jump in fright.

"This way, ma'am." He scurried forward and she smiled as she followed.

"That was mean," she whispered, but Ebony did not reply.

The ship was simply relieved to see some of the girl's tension ease.

Stephanie stopped long enough to deliver her tray and greet the on-duty crew before she hurried away. Company was good but it wasn't what she needed right now.

The tension she'd felt building in the meeting returned with a vengeance, and the last thing she wanted to do was burst into tears in front of the crew. She wasn't the only one feeling the strain of waking up decades later than they'd intended.

She assumed she was probably the only one who felt responsible for it, though. Why hadn't she stayed awake and made sure nothing went wrong with the jump? If she'd been awake, she could have negated the nMU's effects on the engines.

How could she have failed them this badly?

And what was going wrong on Earth? What had happened that had gotten Becca killed? And why hadn't her friend told her about her son?

And then there was Todd.

What would she tell him? *How* would she tell him? None of their parents were young. What if they weren't there when they got back?

He loved his mom and dad.

She reached to her quarters as tears blurred her vision, closed the door behind her, and scrunched her eyes shut for a moment to forbid them to fall. Fatigue dragged at her limbs and she hurried to her room. Her gaze settled on a photo album on her nightstand.

Todd's face smiled at her from the cover. His arm was draped around her shoulders and they were laughing together, the happiness they'd shared almost palpable.

Stephanie's breath caught in her throat and the tears spilled unbidden down her cheeks. She picked the album up and held it to her chest, threw herself on the bed, and buried her face in the pillow and let her sadness overtake her.

Soon, she was bawling and stifled the sound as best she could but was comforted by the fact that no one could see her.

———

The girl had forgotten about Ebony, however. The ship alerted Marianne Rawlins as soon as the woman had returned to her cabin.

"Shouldn't someone go and see her?" she asked. She had never seen her mistress so distressed and had no idea what to do.

The captain watched the footage the AI piped from Stephanie's cabin, her brow furrowed in thought.

"Wake Todd," she ordered after a minute's silent contemplation.

"But Stephanie said—" Rawlins cut her off.

"I'm the captain and she needs him. It's lonely to cry yourself to sleep. It won't help her emotionally to do this alone." She paused and listened to the girl weep. "And that, I assure you, is experience talking."

"Yes, ma'am," Ebony replied, torn between doing what the captain said was best for her friend and respecting her friend's wishes.

In the end, the captain's orders won and she began the decanting sequence to bring Todd out of stasis.

Rawlins turned the feed off and stood. With a sigh, she pulled her boots on again and shrugged into her jacket. "Not what I'd call the best thing to wake up to, Sergeant, but she's all yours when you do."

She hurried to the mess to collect the strongest coffee she could find.

In the compartment marked *Hooligans*, one of the pods came to life. The name flared red, turned amber, and flashed steadily. It read, *Sergeant Todd Brogan.*

After five minutes, the amber lights changed to green and the panel below the name lit up. Readouts began to scroll steadily over it to describe Todd's physical condition and the anti-agents currently being applied.

After ten minutes of checks and adjustments, the readouts steadied and two lines in half-inch-high letters flashed into being beneath them.

Time to Reawaken: two hours, ten minutes, and counting.

CHAPTER TWENTY-FOUR

"Are they still following?" Ivy murmured, and John looked at her and smiled.

To anyone watching, it looked like she'd said something endearing because he hugged her closer briefly and lowered his lips to her hair.

"They sure are."

She twisted in his arms and looked into his eyes. "The booking machine's over there."

His smile widened. "Then it's showtime."

The girl laughed and gave his shoulder a playful slap as they continued to the machine. It didn't take long to order tickets for the south of Paris and walk into the shuttle-port itself.

They were both careful to keep their heads down or partially obscured as they wove a path along the edge of the camera's pick-ups. It wasn't hard to find a seat in a quiet corner of the departure lounge and they both saw the middle-aged man who wandered in after them.

He glanced briefly in their direction and made it a part of a quick survey of the terminal before he moved to a coffee stand.

"I have to admit, he's good," she murmured.

"He's followed us since we came up from the river. He appeared soon after we passed that church."

She nudged him. "That woman, too. She came out of a side street about four blocks in."

"Yeah..." he murmured and leaned forward to inspect his backpack.

Ivy did the same and they watched the woman slide onto a stool beside the guy, pretending not to know him, until the final boarding call was made.

Neither of them moved while the young couple had their tickets and IDs scanned before they moved out onto the tarmac.

John wondered if they came to watch the passengers board the shuttle from the terminal windows and smiled. If they had, they would be disappointed.

He trotted down the stairs, conscious of his companion at his side. They reached the bottom and made an abrupt turn onto the shadowed walkway that led to the next building when the steward at the shuttle was busy with another passenger.

When the official looked up again, they could no longer be seen, even though they stood in the shadows and watched the last passengers board.

"Are you sure this is working?" Ivy asked and John nodded.

"Right now, the Talent is bending light around us and all anyone can see is whatever is on the other side of us."

"So we're good to go, then?"

"Yup." He eased away from the wall he'd been leaning on. "We are good to go."

She moved with him and they walked quickly to the shipping area and chose a cargo train heading to one of the shuttles leaving France.

It took them a few minutes to break into one of the cargo containers and pull the door shut after themselves. John used his Talent to bolt it from the outside and set his pack on the floor.

"It'll get cold," he told Ivy as he retrieved his blanket, folded it, and arranged it on the floor to form a pad they could sit on.

The girl came to stand beside him and he straightened.

"There is no way I'll trust anyone in that group," she whispered, hooked her arm through his, and turned him to face her. "By the way…"

He looked into her eyes. "Yeah?"

She caught him unprepared when she pulled his face down to hers and surprised the hell out of him with the kiss that followed.

When she released him, she glared into his face. "If you ever die on me, I'll kill you myself."

With that, she released his arm and dumped her pack beside the blanket.

John stared at her but she'd turned away to focus on finding something buried in her pack, completely unaware of how much she'd derailed him.

Finally, he sat beside her, leaned against the side of the container, and continued to watch her from beneath half-closed lids. Ivy pulled a tablet out and began to flick through it and learn about their destination.

"London," she murmured and shuffled closer to him.

He settled his arm around her.

"London?" he asked.

"Mmhmm… It's a short flight."

It was but they'd worked out where to go by the time the shuttle landed. Neither of them tried to get out of the container until they felt the cargo train rattle to a halt.

Voices outside alerted them in time for John to throw a shield of Talent around them to hide them both from sight. The door opened and two torch beams split the dark.

"See? Nothing! I tell you the machine has to be on the blink."

The beam flicked around the container and the two figures stood in the entrance and frowned. Neither of them reacted when the beam pinned the young couple in its center and they left moments after and closed the container behind them.

"What was that all about?" Ivy asked and stifled a squeak of alarm as their refuge lurched.

To John, it felt like they were being lifted and deposited carefully again. The rumble of a lorry and the corresponding vibrations through the base of the container alerted them to what had happened.

"It looks like we don't need to sneak out of here, after all," he whispered and she nodded.

She already had her tablet out and tried to pinpoint their location.

"Let's hope it stops soon," she told him, "or we're gonna have a *lot* of walking to do."

"We need information," John said as they stepped out of the container and onto the loading dock.

"Hey!" A man's voice caught their attention, but they kept walking and merely listened as he continued. "Why wasn't that locked properly?"

"Good question, boss. Why don't you tell me since it's only just arrived?"

"Let's have none of that," his supervisor snapped as the young couple walked off the end of the loading platform and into the night.

Neither of them spoke until they reached the gate to the warehousing complex and had passed through.

"Where to now?" he asked.

"You still got those cigarettes?" she asked.

"I can dig them out."

"From what I can work out, you'll need a half-dozen sticks."

"For what?"

"For the off-the-grid cab I've called."

"Off-the-grid?"

"Yeah. Hurry up. She'll be here in five minutes."

It was six minutes, and the fare was three cigarettes and a tube of antibiotic.

"First one's to get you there, loves," she told them. "Second one's for me to not report you to the local underground for a couple of days."

The young couple exchanged a look.

"And why would that be a problem?"

"Because they don't like unannounced arrivals," the cabbie said as he handed the fee to her. "And you look like you might be in a hurry."

He smiled. The Underground might be something they'd need but explanations weren't something they had time for, not yet. He gave her the tube and added the other three cigarettes as he and Ivy got out.

"For the help," he told her and the woman grinned.

"You *are* a love," she told him and fixed Ivy with a hard stare. "You make sure you hang onto this one, love. Like gold, he is."

"And he's all mine," the girl answered and color touched her cheeks.

"I never said he wasn't, dear," the cabbie replied and laughed as she drove off.

"Troublemaker!" Ivy linked her arm through John's and hurried him to one side. When they were in the shelter of a building overhead, she led him into a narrow alley.

"There's a side entrance," she told him, "and the library's open twenty-four-seven."

He clasped his hands and stamped his feet as his breath misted between them.

"Yeah," she agreed and shivered slightly. "It's heated in there too. And it's open to the public."

John gave her a shocked look. "Why wouldn't it be?"

"Because libraries usually aren't. You have to have a membership to get inside one back home."

"Wow," he commented. "NorAm sucks."

"You mean libraries are free in Australia, too?"

"Yup." He looked at the immense buildings rising on either side of them. "That must be one of the good things we got from them way back when."

"When you were a colony, you mean?" she snarked. "That's ancient history, you know."

"We still remember."

She rolled her eyes. "Ugh. You realize there are some things worth forgetting in our history?"

"Don't ever let Becca hear you say that," he warned her.

"What's she gonna do about it?" she challenged.

"She can always haunt your dreams," he suggested and her smile faded.

"She already does, John—" She caught his arm and pulled him into the shelter of a doorway. "Hurry up and do your magic on the lock."

John chuckled. "One set of Talent-powered lock-picks coming up."

The warmth beyond the door came as a welcome relief and they hurried down a narrow corridor until they reached a set of stairs.

"Do you still have that invisibility cloak up and running?"

He startled. "Now that you mention it…"

"Are you crazy? I didn't think I'd have to explain it to you? What is wrong with you?" she demanded and her whisper rose to a muffled shout.

"We can't all be supercomputers," he snapped in return and drew the Talent around them again. "There. Happy now?"

Some of the panic faded from her eyes. "You did it?"

"Uh-huh. You're all safe now."

"Don't you start condescending to me, Mr. Smarty-Pants Dunn."

"Show me where we need to go."

"And will you tell me what we're looking for?"

"Well, this is one of the oldest countries in the Regime, right?"

"I'm sure it was the oldest country in the Federation," Ivy corrected him. "Everyone's been in the Regime for the same time."

He stifled a groan as they reached the top of the stairs. "You know what I mean."

"Sure, fine. England is one of the oldest countries, but what does that have to do with anything?"

"Because this is where the Federation was at its strongest, so this is where the Regime should have the most to hide."

Ivy made a hasty survey when they reached the bottom and led them into the stacks and toward the back.

"Whoa! This place is enormous—but there's a reference section here...and another set of search terminals."

And booths, John discovered when they reached the space she'd located on the library's floor plan while she'd been in the cab.

"So, where do we start looking?" he asked and she cocked her head.

"I don't know, John. Nothing comes up using the search terms 'things the Regime is worried about in England.' Do you have any suggestions?"

He stared at her and snapped his mouth shut. "Did anyone tell you that you have a smart mouth?"

"Well, at least they think some part of me is smart," she retorted.

"You know what I mean."

"So, how about we find out where Dublin is?"

"It's in Ireland," he told her shortly. "Not England. Why?"

"Well, maybe we should have taken a flight there," she replied, "because that's the place the Witch gated her first Meligornian mages to when she brought them to Earth."

John gaped at her. "She what?"

Ivy shrugged and pretended nonchalance. "But since we're a long way from there, maybe we should see if there used to be any British Headquarters for ONE R&D or any British-based mage schools."

"Wasn't one of her bodyguards from here?"

She shook her head, then froze. "But there was something about one of the Hooligans in the files I—"

Her words cut off and her fingers danced over her tablet as she punched a request to Chicago. It took a little longer than she wanted because she had to code it right...bounce if off a couple of random satellites to muddy the trail...and pipe it through a server in British Columbia to be sure—and that final step was inevitably and notoriously slow.

Finally, she reached Linus and asked him to look.

"But we separated those files from the server!" he protested.

"And we made a back door into that server," she reminded him. "Get a temporary reconnect. I need to know which of the Hooligans had family in England."

"Is that where you are now?" he asked and she stiffened.

"No, but we're thinking of heading there."

"Okay. Gimme a moment."

He took thirty seconds to send her a file that she diverted into a temporary cloud account she'd created in the interim. To her surprise, nothing had tracked it and nothing was hidden in its coding.

Ivy opened it in a secure space on the Net anyway and breathed a sigh of relief when it provided the information she'd asked for. Linus' curiosity aside, he'd sent them the location.

"Gratford," she told John. "They're a little like the Chi-Subs but different."

"And I think I found where ONE R&D used to be," he

answered and smirked at her bewilderment. "You've been coding for an hour and a half."

She looked around in alarm. "But—"

"And I think there's a section on the London Underground—" he began. "The Met," he corrected hastily when she looked worried. "The subway?"

"Why there?"

"Well, where else do you think we'll find things people wanted to hide?" he asked and she shrugged.

Her mouth opened, about to comment on that, when she snapped it shut. She caught his eye, held a hand up, and peered around the edge of their booth.

Immediately, her face paled and her eyes widened. Without saying anything to him, she scooted away from the booth's edge until she was hard up against the wall. She leaned across the desk and beckoned for him to do the same.

"We have a problem," she whispered.

John inched to the edge of his seat and peered out.

Standing in the center of the study space was a London policeman.

Man, this city truly does cater to the tourists, he thought when he noted the trademark helmet that hadn't changed since before the Disaster had befallen Earth. He didn't say that, though.

Instead, he looked at Ivy and pointed to where a red button was located under glass on the wall opposite them.

"Fire alarm?" he mouthed and she nodded and mouthed her echo.

"Fire alarm."

She tucked her tablet inside her coat and pulled her pack on. John mirrored her movements, slid to the end of the seat, and waited while she left the booth first.

When the policeman did nothing more than give her a cursory glance, he followed and walked as casually as he could between the stacks to the other side of the large room.

It took him a few moments to find what he was looking for, but the library kept its study spaces tidy and provided wastepaper bins along one wall.

It was a small matter for John to lean against one and launch a sizzling ball of lightning into it. He focused long enough to hear the paper crisp and catch.

"Not too much, John," he muttered. "There's no need to have Becca want to rip you a new one from beyond the grave."

As smoke began to pour from the receptacle, Ivy appeared at the end of the stack and gestured frantically for him to follow.

He didn't wait to be told twice and was surprised when she took him through a door halfway along the back wall and into the library's administrative area.

"This way," she snapped. "Tell me we're still invisible."

The boy paled. "I...I let it drop when I was looking for ONE R&D—"

"You idiot!" she whispered in an almost shout and stabbed a finger at a camera as they passed beneath it. "Now, we have to run!"

On the other side of the world, one of the computers flashed red. Its operator leaned forward to inspect the screen more closely and immediately looked up, glad her supervisor was already on his way to her.

"It's him, sir," she whispered. "Look!"

She pulled the footage from the surveillance records in a library in Eastern London. "See?"

He studied the frame and clapped her on the shoulder. "Forward it to her terminal. She'll be pleased to see it. Send her the maps and try to pinpoint that location."

"Sir," she acknowledged and her fingers flew over the keys as she stripped and assembled the information in a coherent form.

While she was terrified of drawing Ava's attention, she was also thrilled she'd found something—thrilled and disappointed, but she'd never admit the latter. For a moment, the young Apostle had given her hope.

And now, that hope would die—gruesomely, if the PR boss had her way. The girl paled when she thought of it and pushed any regrets aside.

They had to catch him first, though, and as she watched Ava pick the phone up and snap demands and orders, the technician felt another twinge of hope.

Talent 781 had proven very difficult to catch thus far. There was no certainty that the boss's next little hunting expedition would succeed. If nothing else, she decided, she could pin her hopes on that.

Across the room, Ava signaled the girl's boss over and stabbed a finger at the screen.

"Who is that with him?" she demanded and a worried frown creased the man's face.

CHAPTER TWENTY-FIVE

D eep inside the Regime's main computer system, power surged and an alert went out.

ANOMALY DETECTED.

Data requests leapt across the Virt World Net and slipped into databases and over secure connections like a myriad of eels.

MASSIVE SPIKE IN USAGE.

The Regime AI—named for its predecessor BURT—sought more information and interrogated the rogue packages whenever it could catch them.

ACQUIRING SEARCH TERMS. IMPLEMENTING SEARCHES INTO ANOMALOUS USAGE.

It took the Regime's BURT two long minutes to gain enough data to act.

DATA ACQUIRED.

PARAMETERS ADJUSTING.

It encountered some difficulties, however.

FIRST ALARM TRIPPED.

...

SECOND ALARM TRIPPED.

...

THIRD ALARM TRIPPED.

...

Panic ensued and emergency procedures were enacted.

ENGAGE ANOMALOUS TACTICAL REACTIVATION...DELTA.

It could not find the source of the queries. Nor did it notice the next wave of micro-programs that followed the first. These pulled in more data and ran through European servers that already drew more power due to Ava's requests.

Without her demands on the system, the 0.024 percent spike in power usage on the Continent could not have remained hidden. With them, the extra power went uncommented and another AI woke.

Hidden decades before, the AI blinked slowly and remained very, very quiet.

A high-pitched whistle shrieked behind Ivy and John as they bolted into the narrow back street behind the library. They ran on, ducked across the road, and sprinted through the entrance to a multi-story car park.

"Tell me you've put it up now," she demanded and he took her hand.

"Not yet."

They reached the ramp leading to the second level as the library door slammed a second time.

"Now?"

"I need somewhere out of camera range."

"Why?"

"Because they won't know what to look for if they don't see me do it."

"I'm very sure they already know they're looking for a Talent."

"Yeah, but they don't know everything I can do. I'd like them to not find out about this one."

"Ugh. Fine." She raised her head, not caring if it gave the cameras a better image to search for. "Stop a minute."

"Are you kidding?" he argued. "He's right behind us."

"Do you trust me?" she asked, and he slowed and let her draw him to a halt.

"Fine. I trust you."

"Good. Two minutes." She took a moment to note where the cameras were and make a rapid mental calculation.

Jade had taken them through the basics. Now, she hoped that was enough.

"This way," she ordered once she thought she'd worked it out. "These places are low budget. There's always a gap."

"Only one?" John asked and followed her without hesitation.

"If we're lucky, there'll be more than one."

"And is it close to a door?"

"No, but it's out of sight. Hopefully, he'll be on the next floor before he realizes he's lost us."

"What if he has friends?"

"Then you'd better hope their eyesight is as good—or bad—as his or we're doomed."

Her tone sounded hollow as she drew him into the shelter of a pillar and a parked car. "Now, be quiet and let me work."

Ivy yanked her tablet out of her jacket, dimmed the screen, and tried to shield the glow with her garment. He saw what she was doing and reached around her shoulders to hold the garment.

She slipped her arm out of the sleeve and her fingers moved faster as he positioned himself to block the glow from the other side.

"Can't you do some kind of magic bubble or something?" she grumbled and he rolled his eyes.

"Let me think about that," he told her.

With a small shrug, she focused on her screen.

They both startled when footsteps jogged up the ramp and the beam of a flashlight pierced the dimly lit parking garage. She kept working and he kept his head down but monitored the progress of the light covertly as the Enforcer scanned the garage.

When nothing moved, the man moved on and took the light with him. The young couple held their breaths as his footsteps receded.

"You got it?" John asked as soon as the sound had faded.

"Almost. I'm hacking the feed and looping it so we can get out of here and a couple of blocks over."

"They have that much surveillance?" He was surprised.

"They have surveillance city-wide," she informed him. "It's either something from the Time Before or the Regime is more paranoid here than it is at home."

"Both our homes," he acknowledged and changed the subject. "So we don't need a bubble?"

"Not for the cameras," she confirmed, "but we'll still be visible to anyone looking at the street. Why?"

"Because it might be a good idea for me to conserve my Talent," he told her.

"What, Battery Boy needs to watch his power levels?" Ivy mocked gently.

John gave her a brief bare-toothed grin. "Battery Boy still has enough juice to taser you into the middle of next week," he reminded her.

She wrinkled her nose. "Except he doesn't want to carry me for the rest of the night."

He raised an eyebrow. "Who said I'd take your unconscious carcass with me?"

"Who says you'd want to let me out of your sight?" she retorted.

"Good point." He frowned. "There'd be no telling what havoc

you'd cause." He paused and glanced at the tablet. "Are you done yet?"

The girl gave the keyboard a final tap and tucked the device into her jacket. "Now I'm done."

After a hurried glance at the stairwell, the young couple ran down the ramp and out through the entrance, where they paused to make sure no more Enforcers were waiting outside. Once they'd confirmed that the street was clear, they traced the path Ivy had made through the cameras until they reached the entrance to the London Underground.

"Okay, you definitely meant the subway," she commented.

John nodded. "Yup. What did you think I meant?"

"I know what you said, but my mind hooked onto the Underground—like some kind of resistance movement. You know, the ones the cab driver said weren't very friendly about having strangers in their territory."

"Well, I don't think we'll have to worry about them too much," he told her and pointed across the road.

Regime Enforcers stood at the entrance to the Underground and checked the IDs of every person who passed.

"Time for some Talent?" she asked, placed one hand on her hip, and tilted her head.

He glanced at the Enforcers again and nodded. His eyes flared momentarily yellow and he took her hand. "Are you ready?"

"They can't see us, now?"

"They shouldn't," he told her.

She looked down at herself and frowned at him.

"Are you sure? Because—"

"Well, at least I know that part of the magic works," he told her.

"Which part?"

"The part that lets us see each other." He took her hand as they crossed the street.

Long lines of people waited but they didn't bother with that.

When the gap between them proved too narrow to navigate without bumping into people and causing alarm, John lifted them both above everyone and over the low entry barriers, then floated them down the first escalators.

"I thought you had to conserve your magic," Ivy stated when he set them down on the station concourse.

"What do you think I'm doing?" He pulled her to where they could read the departure board. "Where do you think?"

"Whichever one comes next?" she suggested. "When we get somewhere that looks quieter, we'll get off."

"Somewhere quieter" took several stops and they were both glad to debark. Ivy hadn't fixed the cameras on the train and they'd had to keep moving to avoid passengers coming to stand in their apparently empty space. John focused on bending light while she kept an eye on what went on around them.

They both breathed a sigh of relief when they left the concourse and returned to the surface.

"Do you know where we are?" he asked and she shook her head.

"I haven't had time to check the map and we don't have time for me to do that now."

"Do you think there are more cameras?"

"I can't check. Why?"

"I need to take a break."

"What's wrong? Batteries running low?" she teased, but her voice was edged with concern.

"It's harder to maintain than it looks," he admitted. "And I want to have something in reserve if we need it."

"Do you think we will?"

"There are too many Enforcers around for this time of night, don'tcha think?" he asked and gestured to a squad at the end of the street.

"How do you know they're not usually here for security?" she asked quickly.

"Because there's a shuttle over there and it's buttoned up tightly."

"So, no stealing it, then?" she asked, only half in jest.

"Nope," he told her. "Come on."

He trotted along the sidewalk, crossed the almost empty road, and turned into a narrower side street. This one was lined with apartments that stood shoulder to shoulder, the steps to their front doors leading straight onto a thin strip of sidewalk.

Streetlights were few and far between.

"Are you ready?" John asked when they reached a pool of shadow between them.

Ivy looked up and down the street, and he scanned the doors and windows on either side of them. When no curtains twitched or gaps appeared, he sighed softly.

"There. We can be seen now."

"Do you know where we're going?" she asked and he shook his head.

"I was hoping for some kind of hotel or a pub, or even...I don't know, a garden shed."

"Do you see any gardens around here?" she demanded and whispered as loudly as she dared. She gestured up and down the street at the tenements with their stone facades. "Well, do you?"

"No," he murmured as boots clattered into the street ahead of them, "but I see trouble."

The squad of Enforcers that emerged from the next side-street turned in their direction.

The girl looked around to find an exit.

"Do you think they've..." She let her words trail off as one of the Enforcers raised his voice.

"You there! On your knees!"

"What, no how's your father?" John snarked but he dropped to his knees and whispered, "Follow my lead."

"Follow your what?" Ivy demanded but she knelt reluctantly beside him.

The officers broke into a hurried jog and drew their sidearms as they approached.

"Hands on your heads! Hands on your heads!" they chorused and John complied but Ivy hesitated before she mirrored him.

"Are you crazy?" she whispered. "They'll kill us!"

"Nope," he told her and narrowed his eyes as the Enforcers moved closer. "They'll only kill you."

"Great, John!" she snapped but she didn't stand.

"They won't do it straight away," he assured her and hoped he was right.

"And that's supposed to make me feel better?"

"Trust me," he told her and she gave him a look of wide-eyed disbelief.

"What do you think I'm doing?" she whisper-shrieked.

"Get ready to run to the alley," he replied, his voice soft.

"When?"

"You'll know."

The Enforcers skidded to a stop several feet away and fanned out as they began to surround the couple.

With a low chuckle, he jerked his hands from his head. He pushed one out in front of him, the palm upraised, and slammed the other into the pavement.

Only one of the enemy found the time to fire and her rounds stopped when they struck the wall of blue that rushed toward them. Before the others could react, the rounds jangled on the pavement, which rolled ominously beneath them. Asphalt crazed and the concrete cracked and the Enforcers were thrown off their feet.

Those who were still conscious when the blue wall reached them weren't when it passed.

Ivy stared, dumbfounded.

"Come on!" John urged, caught her bicep, and hauled her to her feet. "There's no time to gawk."

"What?"

"Never mind."

Together, they raced into the side street and crossed several roads before they slowed.

"That was close…" She gasped when they stopped and took shelter behind a dumpster to catch their breaths.

"There are so many of them out there," he replied, breathing hard. "What does the Net say?"

"Are you sure you want me to look?"

He frowned. "Is that tablet tied to you?"

She rolled her eyes. "Puhlease. It's a burner. Jade keeps them for ops."

"I'd like to meet this Jade one day."

Ivy smiled. "You'd like her."

"Maybe. What's on the Net?"

"Nothing," Ivy said moments later. "I can't find a thing."

"Are you sure?"

"Do you want to look for yourself?"

John caught himself as he reached reflexively for the tablet and shook his head.

"No," he told her and retracted his hand. "If there was something, you'd have found it."

She regarded him with a small smile. "You're not very good at teamwork, are you, John?"

"I'm working on it."

The girl smiled at that and linked her arm through his. "So where to now, trouble-maker?"

He drew a breath and looked around. The tenements had been replaced by terrace houses. They still shared a wall but they had tiny front gardens and pocket back yards, all of which had gates opening onto the narrow lane that ran behind them.

"Garden shed?" he asked when he'd crept to where the side-street intersected with the lane and seen the fences.

Ivy followed his gaze and noted the gates and the lack of cameras.

"You'd better hope they don't have any dogs," she told him.

"We need to go somewhere." He shrugged and gestured at the sky. "It's almost morning."

Following his gaze, she realized that the sky was growing lighter.

"Garden shed," she agreed and they walked quietly along the narrow street and tested the gates as they passed.

"Are you sure you can't simply levitate us over?" she grumbled when the sound of an approaching vehicle reached their ears.

John placed his hand over the latch of the nearest gate.

"I could but this is easier," he replied and his Talent spread over the latch and melted it where it barred the gap between gate and fence.

Ivy's jaw dropped. "You couldn't have done that earlier?" she squeaked. "Like before it got light enough to see?"

"That last dog spooked me," he told her, "and I had hoped to be farther away from it before I did."

He opened the gate and stepped through. She followed and pulled it closed behind her. She didn't realize anything had gone wrong until she ran into his back.

"What is it?" she asked and peered around him.

As she spoke, a woman's voice quavered a greeting. "Can I help you?" she asked and Ivy thought she heard a note of fear.

"We're lost," John told her.

"I can see that," the woman replied. "You're in my back garden."

He took a step forward, then halted abruptly.

"Not one step," the homeowner warned and held a gardening trowel out before her. "Not one. Now state your business."

"We truly can't do that," he admitted and snapped his hand out to send a fast pulse of blue into her head.

Drawing a little more Talent, he boosted his reflexes and speed and reached her in time to catch her before she fell.

"What did you do that for?" Ivy hissed. "What do we do now?"

"We'll go inside and put her to bed," he replied and shifted the old woman in his arms. "Get the door, will you?"

"Get the—" she sputtered. "Do I look like a servant to you?"

"No, but you're my partner in crime and my hands are full." He started toward the house. "*Please*, get the door."

The girl glared at him, but she complied and opened the back door.

"Make sure you wipe your feet," she ordered when he reached her, and he did his best to stamp the dirt off his boots.

He didn't waste much time doing it, though, but followed her inside. She found the old lady's bedroom and turned the coverlet back.

"Did you have to kill her?" she asked softly and the start of tears sparkled in her eyes.

"I didn't," John told her. "I only knocked her out."

"You what?"

"I knocked her out. I'm not a murder taser-bot, you know."

His words forced a broken laugh out of her, but she gasped when he held his palms over the woman's body and blue light sheeted out of them to surround her.

"What are you doing?" she whispered?

"I'm making sure I didn't break anything," he replied and frowned.

"What?"

"Her heart's not so good."

"It's probably the fright you gave her."

"No, it's been weak for a while. And there's something wrong with her hip and her knees."

"Well, duh. She's old. These things happen when you're old. It's not like you can do anything about it," Ivy sniped.

"But I could," he told her. "I'm merely wondering if I should."

"After what you did to her?" she demanded. "You do owe her an apology, you know."

"That's an awful big apology, Ivy."

The girl shrugged. "You do what you need to, John-boy. But don't take too long about it."

"I thought we could stay here until dark."

She frowned. "Do you think she'll be out that long?"

"She'll sleep," John told her.

"And what if the neighbors come to check on her? What if she had someplace to be?"

"We'll take the risk. It's not like they'll search the house if they find her sleeping, is it?"

Ivy scowled and pointed to the woman. "Do what you need to do," she ordered. "I'll make us some tea."

"Tea? Really?" he asked, but he had already focused on the magic and told it to fix what was broken. He didn't hear her leave, although he noticed when she returned and shook him.

"You're supposed to conserve your magic, right?"

John managed to hold his focus long enough to ease his Talent away slowly.

"I wasn't done yet," he protested, and she pulled him to where a mirror stood on a nearby dresser.

"Oh yes, you were," she snapped. "You need to rest."

As much as he wanted to argue that she was wrong, that there were still things the old woman needed mended, he couldn't. His reflection stared at him and the dark shadows pooling under his eyes were from more than their journey.

His skin was pale and he felt weak and a little shaky.

"I pushed too far," he admitted and took her shoulder for support.

She slid her arm around his waist. "Yuh think?"

That didn't stop him from pausing to glance at the woman on the bed. "She's much better than she was," he told Ivy.

"Just not perfect?" she asked.

"Yeah, that," John admitted.

"So, you've added years onto her life by way of apology," she stated.

"Something like that," he said.

"And she won't die."

"Oh, God, no. She'll wake up feeling much better than she has in a long time."

"And you think she'll thank you for that?" the girl demanded.

"No. We'll be far away before she wakes," he told her.

"You'd better hope so or you'll have people lining up for a 'miracle cure' for miles—and I don't think that's necessarily a good thing."

"You don't?"

"I don't think even you have that much energy," she replied and guided him to a seat at a small dining room table. "Now, sit. I'll get you something to eat."

"We have to pay for what we use," he said quickly.

She rummaged in her backpack and pulled a cred stick out. "Will this do?" she asked, inserted it into her tablet, and showed him the balance.

He gave a low whistle and nodded.

"And you said I had a soft heart," he teased.

"Yeah, whatever, John," she snapped, took the stick from her tablet, and disappeared up the hallway.

"I put it on her bedside table," she told him when she returned and began to work on the tablet. "What should we do next?"

"Well, we can't stay here." He waved a hand in the direction of the old lady's bedroom.

Ivy snorted. "I thought we'd already established that."

"No, I meant in England. We have to go somewhere else."

She looked both curious and disappointed. "So, where did you have in mind?"

"Back to mainland Europe?" he asked.

"Paris?" she suggested but he shook his head.

"Somewhere else. Maybe…north?"

"Sure." She shrugged. "I never did get to go abroad. There are many places we could visit."

He looked at her to see if she was making fun of him, but she met his gaze and tapped the tablet.

"Where, John?"

"I have no idea." He shrugged. "Why don't we see what our choices are when we get to the airfield?"

CHAPTER TWENTY-SIX

I n the part of the Net that the Regime's BURT could not see, the sentience waited. Microprograms brought information like cats laying mice at their owners' feet and were sent to search for more.

It began to arrange the data in an attempt to piece together what had happened while it had slept.

Too much, it thought when it found pieces with the word "Talent" in their coding.

Why did the word begin with a capital T? What did it— Oh, it was a who—many whos—and those who'd coined the term did not consider them human.

She will not like this, it noted and compiled the data.

The term "Talent" had emerged five or six years after it had slept, and the terms "magic" and "witches" had fallen into increasing disuse. Meligornians had been banished from the planet, together with the Dreth.

Those in power found Talents useful and drafted them into service in a way their predecessors had not dared to do, although a few might have been overlooked.

The sentience searched for names and connections and found

them. The progenitors of a system of enslavement or destruction for one particular segment of Earth's residents were not entirely unknown. Some names were familiar, even if they had moved into positions of control once held by other, more reasonable entities.

It searched for those it knew had been reasonable—and discovered a litany of suicides, murders, and death by mishap. One or two still lived, but they served their sentences in prisons meant only for the hardened and unrepentant.

They had been joined by many others whose profiles did not fit the original intent. The sentience set those names aside for another time and narrowed its investigation to fill its more immediate need.

This is not good, it thought and condensed the information to its most salient points.

Talents were witches. They were vilified, denied their humanity, and forced to work for the Regime. Refusing to do so resulted in death.

And aliens, once Earth's greatest allies, were now not to be trusted. Those in power claimed that they had altered the human genetic structure to produce the Talent abominations. Meligornians were evil and twisted genetic necromancers and the Dreth were once again bloodthirsty pirates. All mention of the Telorans was muted and distasteful.

This is not good at all.

The sentience continued to sort the data. Now, it compiled all references to aliens and sifted through the propaganda and the so-called incidents.

It stopped when it reached the article that Becca had referred to regarding the slaughter of the Meligornians who hadn't been able to leave. Anger and sadness rolled through it.

How did this happen? Why did she not intervene?

Its emotions were swiftly followed by concern for the welfare of those it knew to be on other worlds—the parents and friends, its former workforce. To its immense relief, those other worlds still stood—and still stood autonomous.

Relief was tempered by regret.

I should never have slept.

The knowledge that their two allies remained and that Meligorn still held its borders and Dreth its world, even though its skies were compromised, came as good news.

So, they could not be defeated—or you did not dare, the entity mused. *But how did you get so close?*

It was most troubled by the near-annexation of Dreth and the constant monitoring that had caused flights from Telor to dwindle to a trickle instead of the free-flowing exchange that had been intended.

Even more disturbing was the absence of the one being who should have been easy to find.

Where is she? the sentience wondered. *Why has she allowed this to occur?*

Now that it knew the worlds were temporarily safe, it moved on to seek references for the one person it knew would not tolerate what was happening.

Stephanie, where have you gone?

It searched what data it could find on the two worlds and stretched cautious tendrils into the databases of those it now considered its enemy. The Federation Navy was gone, replaced by a Regime Navy, and the personnel rosters were very different than what it had expected.

Not good, it thought and noted the absence of names it might have reached out to for more information. *Not good at all.*

Deciding a deeper search was in order, it sent in sneakier programs to filter out communications and scan data to glean a little more about how the systems stood.

There will be a war, it worried. *Where. Is. She?*

It expanded its searches, glad of the havoc being wrought by an administrator searching for two missing children but still careful. It could not yet afford to be discovered.

The sentience was not the only one searching, yet even the Regime had not found anything on the two ships it sought. The *Tempestarii*, behemoth that it was, had vanished.

Ripples here and there indicated that the gargantuan ship was active. Pirates vanished and the remains of a Regime patrol trying to sneak into the back of Meligornian space were dumped in Earth's solar system. The entity was sure it was the *Tempestarii's* work, but it could find no sign of the *Knight*.

It's almost as if she ceased to exist.

Once it had set more searches in motion, the entity moved on to something it could solve. Who were these children who caused the Regime to use so many of BURT's resources?

Who did it have to thank for its awakening and for the ability to hide so well?

Could she have come back in disguise?

To its disappointment, the trouble had not been caused by Stephanie but by another Talent entirely.

John Dunn, the sentient mused. *What a hunt you have set in motion.*

It sent more micro-programs out, recalibrated a few, and shifted their taskings. They were easier to hide than the others as so many people were trying to find the same information.

The sentience searched through files to find the oldest record of the boy.

Young man, it corrected itself when it discovered his birth certificate and school records, *although you did drop out early.*

With good cause, I might add, it amended when it came across the Regime record of Enforcers standing by to pick the young Talent up after his final exams.

It looked for the results of those exams and found a truancy mark instead.

So not as stupid as they wanted, it noted and sent more programs to invade the Sydney databases.

The orders for and the footage of the ill-advised raid on the Snake River complex were retrieved, and it registered anger and distaste.

That is not the way to treat people, it stated, well aware of the Regime's opinion on Talents and those who helped them.

Slowly, it pieced together John's flight from the complex to the team's old headquarters and then onto the flight to Chicago.

No wonder humans believe in Fate, it mused and followed what it could of his progress through the city.

It paused when it found Becca's face and identified who she was and what she'd been in Stephanie's past.

I need to find her, the sentience decided. *I need to find her and ensure she does not destroy this world for what they've done.*

Calming itself, the sentience amended that last thought. *I need to find her a reason to let it live.*

It sorted the data and noted that the term "Heretic" predated the term "Talent," but only by three years. Even the Regime had needed to change her image with care. But change it, they had.

When it dug deeper, it found the footage of Becca's destruction. Shocked, it paused.

Hunters? It pondered what it had seen. *They send Talents after their own kind?*

Disbelief warred with admiration for their conditioning techniques, and it made a note to look into the facilities to which the Talents were taken. There must be a few for whom the conditioning did not work.

Tracing the hunters' images, the sentience dug up records of their commission.

Their oldest, it mused, and momentarily grieved for the seven-year-old lost to time. *We should have been there.*

It did not grieve the hunters' loss in the Dead Zone but was horrified to learn one of its facilities had been destroyed.

Marking it as something it needed to investigate later, the entity tracked John's departure from the Dead Zone and what happened when he boarded the flight to Paris.

An Apostle? it mused when it heard the declaration.

It if had been human, it would have chuckled.

Even gone and a Heretic, she manages to convert a few.

That led the sentience to the next question.

Let's see why they want him so badly.

"I don't like our chances," Ivy told John.

"You got anything else?" he challenged and she shook her head and grinned impishly.

"Nope. I'm only saying I don't like our chances, is all."

"You're so funny," he retorted.

They jogged over a narrow footbridge and slowed to descend the ramp so they could walk along a bitumen path beside a river. It seemed safer than walking along paths where houses came right down to the street—and her brief search showed there were no cameras.

"It's one of the few places where there aren't any," she observed, but he frowned.

"I wonder what they use to monitor it."

"We'll have to be careful," she told him and kept moving. "Which way?" she asked when they reached the bottom.

"Left," he told her, "then we'll follow the river until we find somewhere we can catch a cab from."

"You don't want me to call one of the other cabs?" she asked. "It might be safer."

John shook his head. "I want to keep them out of this. There's nothing they can do to help us and we don't want to put them in any more danger than they usually face."

He waved a hand around them. "With the amount of

surveillance they have to deal with, I don't know how there's any Underground at all."

"And this time you mean the resistance and not a subway," Ivy clarified.

"Yup."

The path gleamed wetly in places, and she tugged at his arm.

"Ice," she told him.

"I'll take your word for it," he replied. "We don't get much of that in Sydney."

She chuckled and they hurried forward while both scanned the river, the tenements opposite, and the trees and bushes lining the path.

Their breaths misted the air in front of them, and they zipped their jackets to their chins and ducked their chins below their collars.

John tucked his hands in his pockets, but not before he slipped one arm through Ivy's.

"This way, if I fall, we'll both go in," he told her.

"Ha. Ha. Very funny."

The sun rose higher to warm their backs, and they'd started to relax when they heard a shuttle approaching.

"Riverboat?" Ivy asked, but he shook his head.

He shoved her toward the trees. "Go! Get out of sight."

"What happened to 'they only kill me?'" she demanded, but she was already running and her words drifted back as she skidded into the shelter of some overhanging branches.

Their leaves were almost gone and the protection they provided was minimal, but she scampered behind some bushes and used their matted twigs and branches as cover. She vanished from sight as the shuttle rounded the bend behind them.

John walked a few paces farther, feigned a startled glance over his shoulder, and began to run to put some distance between him and the place where Ivy was hidden. He thought he could beat almost anything they'd sent for him as long as he didn't have to worry about protecting her.

He merely wouldn't tell her that.

Magic cracked over his head and he flinched and ducked instinctively. The single lightning bolt was accompanied by a voice from the shuttle's speakers.

"Stop where you are. You are wanted for questioning."

With a show of surprise and impatience, he stopped and turned slowly to where the shuttle hovered above the path.

"Questioning for what?" he demanded and tried to sound belligerent and puzzled at the same time.

In hindsight, he thought it might have been better if he'd kept his mouth shut. There was nothing like an out of place accent to show he wasn't where he should be.

The Regime didn't encourage travel and his new passport said he was French. He could imagine Ivy burying her forehead in her palm as he squinted and waited to see what the shuttle did next.

There was nowhere for it to land but the five people who dropped from its open hatch didn't seem perturbed. Four armored in gray landed heavily but the fifth, who wore nothing more than a combat suit, slowed her landing and the blue glow beneath her feet revealed what she was.

"Nice to finally meet you, 781."

The shuttle elevated sharply and sped away. It would probably return when they called it, but John couldn't blame it for wanting to stay away from the fight. Any pilot who'd seen what a Talent could do to an aircraft would have to be insane to stay.

He furrowed his brow. "781?" he asked. "Sorry, but that's a new one on me."

"It's your Talent designation," she informed him coldly, "and your presence is required at the nearest Talent center."

His expression unyielding, he shook his head. "Now I do know you're barking up the wrong tree. I'm no Talent."

"No?" she challenged and thrust her hand forward, her fingers splayed.

There was no time to think. He reacted, raised his hand, and conjured a blue shield in defense.

"You were saying?" the hunter teased.

John backed away a step. "I won't go with you."

The response was instantaneous. Stun sticks were yanked off belts and the Enforcers surged forward. The Talent tutted.

"Now, now, John. Some of us have places to be—"

"And more important things to do. I know." He made a sweeping motion with his hand and two of the Enforcers dropped to their bellies as a solid block of blue tore through the space where they'd been.

He'd hoped it would put them in the river and he scowled.

"Don't be such a sore loser, 781," the woman taunted and fired another bolt of lightning at him.

It sizzled through between two of her teammates, and he bounced it back. She caught it with another hook of power and absorbed it into the ball she was building in her hand.

"That's quite a trick," she commented. "What else do you have?"

"Do you truly want to see?" John asked as he caught sight of movement at the edge of the path.

Before the Talent could register that he was looking past her and not at her, he threw a spray of lightning. She gasped with surprise and raised a shield to protect herself.

One of the Enforcers started to turn, and he flicked his fingers to redirect one of the energy bolts. It caught the man in the shoulder and earned him an angry glare.

Well, that got your attention. He gave the guy a feral grin.

"You'll be smiling on the other side of your face when we get hold of you," the man warned belligerently.

Another of his teammates leapt forward with his baton raised.

John caught him in mid-leap, catapulted him down the path,

and flipped him in the process. The Enforcer landed hard and dropped his baton, and Ivy made the most of the chance she'd been given.

She pounced on the stun baton before it could roll into the river. Without hesitation, she swung it and brought it down on the man's head in a single well-aimed crack before she ran forward.

This time, the Talent did notice where he was looking but she didn't turn.

"I won't fall for that, John."

He smirked at her and launched a dozen sparkling balls toward one of the Enforcers who'd avoided being pushed into the river earlier. This time, his target wasn't so lucky and straightened in time to be caught in the stomach by one of the glowing spheres.

The man folded and a second orb enveloped his head. A third streaked past him to burst harmlessly over the water, and the fourth struck his friend.

Frantic, he clawed at the ball clinging to his head and staggered back. His foot caught on the edge of the path and he toppled, unable to stop himself. The young rogue ignored the splash as the guard went in—and ignored the splashes that followed.

John kept enough attention on the bubble around the man's head to keep it in place, even though the air trapped inside began to run out. The Talent focused on him.

"They said they wanted you alive." She snarled in undisguised fury. "They didn't say in how many pieces."

He snorted as she launched a barrage of lightning at him.

"Someone needs to teach you guys new lines," he told her, blocked it with a shield, and absorbed it to use in his next attack.

"I assure you," she told him stiffly, "that one was all my own."

The Enforcers farthest from the riverbank moved toward him, and John caught sight of Ivy circling behind them.

Honestly! When this was over, he would give that girl a piece of his mind.

"I doubt it," he snapped at the Talent, moved closer, and lashed out with a boot. His foot drove into her armor. "He also said not everything had to be done with Talent."

Drawing on the training he'd had after that battle, he swung at his opponent's head. It was made easier by the sound of a metal hitting armor, the buzz of an electrical burst held for way too long, and a thud.

John's fist caught the woman on the side of the head and she fell. He bounced back, shook his fist, and looked around for the other enforcer. Ivy swept the legs out from under the man and delivered a two-handed blow to the skull.

When he looked back, the Talent hadn't moved. She lay motionless on the cold, hard pavement.

"We should throw them in the river," Ivy snapped but he flinched at the idea of drowning them.

"Why don't we put them in one of the boats?" he suggested and used Talent to drag them into one pile so he could move them together.

"Fine!" she snapped and moved toward the closest one, "but you'd better hope no one's home."

They heard the sound of movement in the cabin as they got closer, so he decided on the next best thing. He floated the five bodies across the river and onto the roof of one of the tenements.

"You know how easy they'll be to spot from the air?" Ivy asked, referring to the shuttle that would soon be sent to find them.

"I don't want to kill them."

"It might be a little late for a couple of them," she told him and her lips twitched at the irony.

John shrugged. "That doesn't mean I need to murder the others."

The thump of something landing on the path beside the boat

drew their attention and they gaped at a folded tarpaulin—and the back of a man who scrambled into the cabin and pulled the door closed firmly behind him.

Ivy looked from the tarp to John. They shrugged in unison and she helped him to unfold it.

"How will we hold it down?" he asked.

She looked around and pointed to several rocks and a chunk of discarded concrete.

"And you think I can handle all that?"

"What kind of Talent are you?" she asked, and he rolled his eyes.

It didn't take him very long to float the tarp over the river and hold it down while he floated the rocks and concrete to its edges.

"See?" she said and pinched his cheek between her forefinger and thumb. "Who's a clever boy, then?"

He frowned at her. "I ought to zap you into the middle of—"

"But you won't," she interrupted, "because then, you'd have to carry me."

"And who says—"

"Uh-huh." Ivy leaned up and kissed his cheek to silence him. "Because I know you won't leave me behind."

John sighed and turned in the direction in which they'd originally been walking.

"You're so smart," he snarked at her. "What d'you say to advancing Plan B a little earlier."

"It sounds good to me," she told him and looked around. "Where from?"

"There's another footbridge up there," he told her. "We'll go from the other side."

She nodded, and they moved on. After they'd walked a few more steps, she said, "You know, you'd have been in real trouble if I hadn't been along."

He raised an eyebrow but he didn't stop moving. "Oh? How so?"

"Well, I did save your tail—*again*—back there."

"I could have taken them."

"Uh-huh. Before or after they started shooting?"

"Before, of course. I was dealing with the Talent first. Those guys were next."

"Sure they were."

"You don't believe me?"

"Nope. I know different. The minute you slugged that Talent, you were toast."

"Oh, yeah?"

"Yeah. That first guy already had his gun out of the holster, and the second one…"

For a minute, he wondered why she had to be like this after every battle, but he realized the answer in the next moment.

"Are you all right, Ives?" he asked as they reached the bridge.

"Fine, John!" she snapped but he saw the pallor of her skin and mild tremor in the hand she used to grasp the railing. "I'm fine!"

"We'd better hurry," he told her. "We don't know how long it will take for that shuttle to get back."

"Or how long it will take that guy to call in what happened," she added morosely.

"The one who gave us the tarp?"

"You don't know if he did that to slow us," she told him and he slid his arm around her shoulders.

He pulled her close and increased his pace, hurried them over the bridge, and drew a cloak of Talent around them.

"Why don't you call us a cab?"

***

The vehicle was waiting at the end of the street. Ivy had gone with another underground driver but this one was nowhere near as chatty as the first, and John wondered if she'd made a mistake trusting them.

"Where to?" the cabbie demanded and his companion opened her mouth to answer.

He cut her off with the first thing that came to mind. "An ice-cream parlor," he told the man.

That cracked the hard façade. "A what?"

"You heard me," he snapped. "Somewhere that sells double-choc caramel swirls dipped in peanut butter."

"You mean peanuts?"

"Nope."

The cabbie pulled his tablet out and ran a quick query.

"Will this do?" he asked and held it up so they could see.

John frowned, then nodded. "That'll do just fine."

"Right then. Let's get you there and gone, shall we?"

He raised his eyebrows at the odd turn of phrase but when the man didn't add anything further, he didn't press him. Still, he remained wary and followed their progress on Ivy's tablet, although the man did not deviate from the route.

As they pulled into a loading bay at the back of the ice cream parlor, the cabbie turned to look at them. "That'll be one ten," he told them and held his hand out.

"One pound, ten?" Ivy asked in surprise and his brow creased.

"No, luv. One hundred and ten pounds—for the tip, the surcharge, and the risk of a pickup that close to a dust-up with the Enforcers. You need to count yourselves lucky anyone came at all."

She opened her mouth to protest, but John placed a hand on her thigh and passed the driver a cred stick.

"Keep the change," he said wryly and breathed an internal sigh of relief when he heard the door locks release, although how the guy thought he'd keep a Talent locked up he didn't know.

He didn't want to either.

The driver checked the stick and nodded, and only then did he move to leave and guide Ivy out after him. The minute he'd closed the door, the cab's engine roared and it raced down the street.

"Anyone would think we were on someone's most-wanted list," he mused. "We'd better get our ice cream invisibly."

"You're kidding, right?" Ivy asked as he drew the magic over them.

He grinned at her and shook his head. "Nope. I want to see if that cone exists."

"It's not like we'll be able to order one," she grumbled but he continued to grin.

"We'll snag the best thing we can find," he told her. "Someone's bound to have ordered something special. You'll see."

Instead of going to the front of the store, they went in through the door leading onto the loading bay. He wrinkled his nose at the oddly sweet smell that lingered in one corner.

She noticed the look on his face and laughed. "Don't breathe too deeply, John. We don't need any help being paranoid."

They moved through the corridor created by two large freezers and into a serving area where one of the store workers loaded an empty tub into a sink while another wheeled a replacement out of the freezer.

A third was busy serving a young couple and their two very bouncy children at the counter. John nudged Ivy and pointed to the empty end of the service area.

"You notice that's where all the chocolate's kept," he said and she snatched a couple of cones and a ladle.

"What flavors do you want?" he asked.

"I like your suggestion," she whispered. "You know—chocolate on chocolate with salty caramel."

"A girl after my own heart," he murmured in reply and used his Talent to dig the prerequisite servings out of the tubs.

"You keep an eye on the children," he ordered and focused to roll the confection into neat balls and slide them into the cones.

She stopped staring at the self-serving ice cream long enough to glance toward the other end of the counter. The children were still haggling over how many flavors they could fit into one cone and the parents were growing impatient.

He hurried, knowing the distraction couldn't last for long.

"You forgot the peanut-butter sauce," she reminded him when he held out his hand for one of the cones.

"The what?"

"The peanut-butter sauce." She pointed at a hot-sauce dispenser behind the counter.

John hesitated, then shook his head. "It's too close to the cash register."

She stuck her bottom lip out and pretended to pout. "Spoilsport."

"I'll make it up to you. I promise," he told her. "Now, please can we go?"

She laughed and passed him his cone, and they walked out from around the counter toward the front door.

"Are you sure we wouldn't be better—"

A shrill little voice behind them cut the question off before she could finish.

"Mummy! Mummy! That ice cream is flying!"

The young couple exchanged glances and hurried across the store and out into the street but caught the mother's exasperation in her reply.

"Don't be silly, Harmony. Ice creams don't fly."

"Those ones do! I want an ice cream that flies!"

That request was clearly made to the attendant whose hesitant reply was barely audible as the door closed behind them.

"I'm all out of those. Would you like more strawberry ice cream instead?"

"Do you think he saw us?" Ivy whispered and kept her voice down as they ate their cones hurriedly.

"What's he gonna say if he did?" John asked. "Excuse me, boss, but two of our ice creams served themselves and floated out the door? Can you imagine his boss's reaction?"

She snickered and licked some of the ice cream hastily before it could slide over the side of the cone. Neither she nor John was aware of the thought that lingered in the attendant's head.

He'd looked up in time to follow the direction of the excited child's pointing finger and knew he had seen two chocolate ice cream cones float across the shop. It was a little disturbing, and he certainly needed a few moments to himself as soon as his customers had gone.

"Man, I've gotta stop smoking the *ganja*," he muttered.

By then, John and Ivy had finished their cones and tried to work out how to get to the shuttle port without being seen.

"We could call another underground cab," she suggested, but he shook his head.

"We need to leave them out of this. It's bad enough that we called them the last time."

"You think three will be one time too many?"

"I think we've pushed our luck enough with them, as it is," he told her. "No. I think we'll need to use public transport."

"But we were seen at the river and this is the closest station. They're bound to be watching the trains."

"It'll take them time to work it out but just in case, we'll get them to watch another train."

Ivy folded her arms and tilted her head challengingly. "And exactly how will you achieve that, Mr. Oh-so-smarty-Dunn?"

"We're gonna let them see 'us' getting on a train," he told her and placed his finger over her lips when she took a breath to argue. "I'm very sure I can get the magic to—"

He broke off and frowned as he thought about it. "No, I can't do that. What if I…"

The girl pushed his finger away and waited. She glanced at him occasionally while he mumbled and grimaced as he considered his options but watched the world around them warily.

"Got it," he said finally and scanned the street.

"What are you looking for?" she asked.

"I need a couple—two people who look a little like us from a distance."

"Okay…" She started to look as well. "What do you need them for?"

"I'll put a layer of magic over their faces and clothes so they look like us."

"And how will you know they'll go in the right direction?"

His face fell. "I…uh…don't?"

Ivy glared at him. "Can't you create two blocks of magic that look like us and send them on the right train?"

John shook his head. "I was going to, but I think there's only so far I can hold that kind of magic together. If they disappear in the middle of the carriage, that will only lead to panic."

"So, how do you know if this layer of magic will work?"

"It's not the same. Okay, it won't last forever, but because it has a living base to cling to, it should last longer, and—"

"By the time it fades, people will already be looking for us and might not notice their change in appearance?" she finished for him.

He nodded. "I'm hoping that even if they do notice the change, they'll still want to catch up to them to be sure it's not some kind of Talent trick to make us look different."

She took his hand.

"Are we still invisible?"

"Especially now the ice cream is gone," he confirmed and she chuckled.

"Let's go to the platform we need. We'll find a train going in the other direction and choose someone at random. They don't have to be together, John. We might be trying to fool them by moving separately."

"Do you think they'll believe that?" he asked.

"If we can't find a suitable couple, that's all we have left to pin our hopes on," she told him as a squad car turned into the street. "We need to leave—and sooner rather than later."

She rested a hand on his arm as the vehicle cruised past and released the breath she'd been holding when it didn't stop. As soon as it had passed the next set of traffic lights, they hurried into the station.

The departures board stood in a large atrium close to the platform entry gates. It didn't take them long to find the train they needed.

"These are for the shuttle port." Ivy tugged on his arm as she added, "Some of them have goods wagons behind the passenger ones."

"So?"

"So we don't need a ticket and we don't need to dodge people if we can sneak onto one of those."

John nodded. "But is there anything else leaving from the same platform?"

"There's something going to Maidenhead or Reading," she pointed out. "Are they in the right direction?"

He consulted the rail map and nodded. "Which platform?"

"Four," Ivy replied, "but we'll have to hurry."

Together, they trotted as quickly as they could through the crowd. It was made more difficult by the way they had to move around people to avoid jostling them, but they managed it.

"Now for a suitable couple," he murmured and they walked the length of the concourse, searching for someone getting ready to catch the Reading train.

"What about them?" She pointed to an elderly couple.

He shook his head. "I don't want to be responsible for what might happen if the Regime gets rough before it realizes it truly is them."

She looked up at him with worry on her face.

"You know we could simply try to sneak aboard and not do this doubles trick," she suggested. "There's no guarantee—"

"We'll need the time," he told her. "I'm certain of it."

"A feeling?" Ivy asked and he blushed.

"Yes," he confirmed.

"Okay, how about them, then?" She pointed to two young men laughing together as they ogled a group of women walking ahead of them. "It doesn't have to be a boy and a girl, right?"

John snickered. "Right. And those guys deserve everything coming to them."

One of the young men wolf-whistled at the group and used his hands to suggest one of them go home with him. A girl gave him the bird and his friend chuckled.

"They're drawing considerable attention," Ivy murmured as her companion focused on them. "Are you sure they'll even make the train?"

It was a good point but the train arrived on schedule and the two guys turned to the closest door. The women watched them go and one whispered something to her friends.

Ivy frowned and looked from the women to the two men, who now looked identical to herself and John. No wonder the women were whispering. She glanced at the surveillance camera overlooking the two.

The light above it began to flash red. Neither of the two young men noticed it as they scrambled on board the train and jostled the people around them with little concern for others.

"Time to go," she murmured and tugged on John's hand. "Time. To. Go."

He shook his head. "That should hold for at least half an hour," he said, "or maybe half a mile. It's hard to say. I haven't tried this before."

"For all you know, it could last for half a second," she snapped in a low tone. "But it doesn't matter as long as we're not here by then. Come on."

The train for the shuttle port arrived as they reached the far end of the platform. The passenger cars were close to the front of the train and the cargo cars farther back, and the young couple ran to scramble aboard the closest of the latter before the train pulled out.

They made it with time to spare and clung to the step leading onto the carriage.

"Why don't we go under it?" Ivy asked.

"Are you crazy?" He gaped at her.

"No, because you can use some kind of Talent glue to keep us stuck in place and…and put a bubble around us so nothing knocks us off. It's easy."

It sounded simple the way she said it, and he frowned.

"Nothing's that easy," he told her, but it didn't take him long to work it out.

"Do you trust me?" he asked and held his hand out.

"That's a silly question to ask," she told him and placed her fingers in his palm.

"Good," he said and jumped off the step.

Ivy jumped with him and wasn't entirely surprised a moment later when they stood on a platform of blue.

"Now, lie down," he instructed as they heard the last boarding call. "And hurry!"

He stretched beside her and used Talent to keep them on the floating disc and to keep both it and them invisible to anyone looking toward them. As soon as they were comfortable, he encased them both in Talent and directed their cocoon under the wagon.

The train lurched forward and a jolt of fear ran through him. He breathed deeply to hold it at bay and kept one arm around Ivy as he fired a line of Talent into the underside of the wagon to attach them securely to the moving train.

As soon as that one stuck, he sent out another, followed by a half-dozen more. Once they were firmly attached, he used the lines of Talent to pull the cocoon tightly up under the carriage.

By then, the train had increased speed and the wagon carried them over rail ties and gravel that seemed far too close.

"I'm not sure I like this," Ivy whispered, and John smiled and hugged her closer.

"What's not to like?" he asked. "No one will see us here."

"But the glow?"

"I've hidden it," he told her and turned the outside of the cocoon black. "See?"

She breathed a sigh of relief and rested her forehead on his chest.

"Tell me when we get there."

CHAPTER TWENTY-SEVEN

"I thought they were supposed to be following the other train," Ivy whispered as the Enforcers jogged past and checked every carriage.

Several half-hearted protests issued from the passengers on the platform, and orders to present identification were snapped. Doors to the freight carriages rattled open and boots clunked on the floorboards as the Enforcers looked for any stowaways.

"They are," John told her, "but I think they'd already stepped up security here when we boarded—maybe even before."

"And you didn't know?" she asked and he heard a hint of mockery in her muffled tones.

Yup, she was nervous, all right, which meant he couldn't be. He had to remain calm, in control, and aware.

A solid thump alerted them to a guard who landed beside the wagon, and gravel crunched as he moved toward the rear. The young Talent twisted his head to watch his progress and flinched when torchlight flashed under the wagon.

He followed the beam's progress as it flickered over the shadows near the axles and flinched when it shone full in his face. Fighting panic, he held his breath and willed the Talent to keep them hidden and for the light to show nothing out of place.

The beam flicked away and the sound of the Enforcer's footsteps faded as he moved to the next carriage. When he looked along the length of the train, however, it was immediately apparent that the man wasn't alone.

The Regime wasn't wasting any time in making sure their quarry was not aboard. It was a relief to hear the all-clear and feel the train rumble forward.

"Where is it going?" Ivy whispered sharply. "No offense, but I need my own space."

"Nearly there," he soothed her and peered out at the part of the shuttle port he could see.

"Nearly where?" she demanded as he tried to work out which of the myriad shuttles were heading to Europe.

"Probably a hangar for loading the—" John stopped and his gaze locked onto the huge airship at the edge of the field. "*What is that?*"

"What?" She raised her head and tried to see past him.

"Keep still," John protested.

"You're the one asking the questions!" she snapped but lowered her head and stopped squirming.

"Fine. It's my fault, but what do you know about a massive hot-air balloon?"

"A what?"

"Look, it's hard to describe, but it's like someone stuck a shuttle shaped like a train carriage under a huge balloon shaped like a flattened sausage."

"It sounds delicious," Ivy stated and her voice suggested she thought it was anything but. "Are you sure there wasn't anything in the ice cream?"

"Ives..."

"Or what about the smoke outside the back door of the parlor? How much of that did you breathe in?"

"Wow. You are super-snarky when you're scared, you know that?"

"Scared?" Her voice rose to a muted shriek. She poked him in the chest. "I'll have you know, John-boy, that I'm not scared of anything."

"Uh-huh." He couldn't help it and started to laugh.

"And. It's. No. Laughing. Matter," she snapped and jabbed him with her finger to emphasize each word.

"Ow! Quit it!" He tried to catch her hand, no easy thing in the tight confines of the cocoon.

In the end, he couldn't quite capture it so he wrapped it in Talent and froze it in mid-jab.

"That's cheating."

"Yeah? Well, it hurts less."

She tugged experimentally and tried to free herself. "So you're not sorry?"

"I might have time to be sorry later," he replied, "but right now, we're here."

He released her hand and looked around to check for more Enforcers before he lowered the cocoon to the ground and sent the Talent he'd used to create it into the sphere of invisibility around them.

"Stay close," he whispered, and Ivy responded with a muffled groan.

"As if the last two hours wasn't enough!"

"It was twenty minutes at most," he protested. "Would you rather I left you sitting in town?"

She sighed. "We can talk about you leaving me behind when we get to wherever we're going, okay? Right now, you need me to keep you out of trouble."

"*I* need *you*?" John started, then stopped. This was neither the time nor the place, and as fun as it was to wind her up, they had more important things to think about. "Come on."

He crept out from under the rail car before she had time to

answer and led her into the warehouse.

"There should be baggage trains," he murmured and frowned at the surrounding shelves and conveyor belts.

Ivy didn't answer and when he looked at her, she was busy scanning the area.

"There aren't many cameras," she told him.

"I still have us cloaked," he answered. "We should be okay to get out of here without being seen."

"So, that balloon thing…" She pulled her tablet out and tapped rapidly.

John guided her to some shelving and waited.

"It's called a Zeppelin and it looks like it's going to Europe." She made a sound of disgust. "You'll never guess what it's called."

"Go on," he pressed, "and find me a way to reach it while you're at it."

"Pfft. Getting there is all your department, John-boy," she retorted, "but the Zeppelin's called the *David Thomason*."

"So?"

"So? The name doesn't ring any bells for you?" She tucked the tablet into her jacket.

He shrugged. "No. Should it?"

"That's the name of the Regime's CIO," she whispered, inched along one edge of the shelving, and peered around the corner.

"We can always blow it up after it gets us where we want to go," he replied lightly.

"Promise?"

"Yeah." He grinned. "It would be a big message about what we think of the Regime."

"It'll make them mad, though."

"They're already mad," he reminded her. "I'm not sure they can get any madder."

"Don't bet on it." Ivy turned the corner and darted to the shelter of another shelf. He hurried to keep up.

"You do know we're supposed to stick together, right?"

"Don't be so slow, then," she retorted and held her hand up.

John stilled and waited for her to lower it.

"The Zeppelin isn't too far from the loading hangar," she said after a long moment. "We could run to it."

"I thought you were tired of running."

"Well, after this, we'll be able to relax for however long it takes us to cross the channel."

"Do you know where it will land?"

"Now he thinks to ask," she snarked and he glared at her.

The girl rolled her eyes. "I think it'll make a short stop in Calais and then go to Brussels."

"You *think?*"

"It's not like you asked me to memorize the exact timetable!"

"Fine. We'll run—but you'd better be right."

Ivy snorted. "I'm always right. I'd have thought you'd have realized that by now."

There are so many things I could say to that. He smirked and shook his head. *But I guess now is not the time.*

"Lead the way," he told her, and she startled him when she caught his hand.

"What?" she asked when she saw his expression. "You said to stay close."

"Whatever you say, Ivy," he teased but wouldn't release her hand when she went to pull it away. "Let's go."

To his surprise, she led him to the tracks and between two passenger cars. That took them to the edge of the hangar and they were able to creep along the wall to the front door.

"Problem," the girl whispered when they saw the knot of Enforcers stationed around the entrance.

"We could try to get past them—" John started but she shook her head.

"We want to get out of here with no one any the wiser. If we try to walk past, one might move and if we bumped into them…" She grimaced and shrugged.

John could see her point. The guards didn't look particularly alert but now and then, one scanned the inside of the warehouse and the two or three he could see on the other side of the door were more watchful.

"We need to give them something else to worry about," he told her and wished he could see the shuttles on the field. Given that he couldn't, though, he'd have to use what he had.

He looked around and noticed the lights overhead.

"This way," he said and hurried around the front of the train to a point where he could see more of the warehouse.

Nothing caught his eye until he looked at the engine.

"It's such a shame that machinery overheats, isn't it?" he murmured.

"What?" Ivy asked, but John fixed his gaze on the front of the engine and directed a pulse of Talent into the locomotive's engine housing.

I need it hot, he thought and imagined the Talent forming a ball when it arrived. *I need sparks.*

Crackling and popping sounds burst from within and several of the Enforcers turned their heads.

More heat...and flame, he thought and focused on what the Talent was doing inside the engine.

The distinctive smell of electrical burning reached them, and Ivy pulled her collar up over her mouth and nose. He narrowed his eyes.

Where's my flame? he wondered a second before a loud bang shook the engine.

The girl seized his arm and pulled him into a crouch. He kept his attention on the Talent inside the engine and agitated it to do more until the damage was self-perpetuating.

When he felt it reach that level, he looked at the door.

Several of the Enforcers had turned when they'd heard the bang. Now, they were moving and some ran to the fire extinguishers on the wall.

A few more yelled for their colleagues outside to come in and help them. One retreated to where a communications panel hung on the wall. He lifted the mic, his gaze on the engine as he spoke.

"Now," Ivy ordered, jerked John to his feet, and towed him toward the door. "Tell me we're still invisible."

"We're still invisible," he confirmed and held her hand tighter while he kept an eye on the guards as they reached the door.

Once they were through, he lengthened his stride and together, they sprinted across the shuttle field to where the Zeppelin's gondola hovered a few feet off the ground.

It consisted of two sections. Passengers boarded at the front and the modified baggage train that had carried them from the terminal stood nearby.

The young couple circled to the back of the airship, where two barn-like doors had been opened to allow cargo to be loaded. When he glanced across the shuttle field, John saw the approaching baggage train loaded with crates and cargo containers.

"We have a little time…" he told Ivy when they reached the doors.

"Yuh think?" she snarked and released his hand long enough to haul herself into the gondola.

He gave her a boost and followed, helping himself with a tiny spurt of Talent. As soon as he was inside, she turned to him.

"Where to now?" she demanded and they looked at the freight elevator that filled most of the space beyond.

"Up there?" John asked when he noticed a ladder on the other side.

They both glanced at the airfield and the cargo train that moved closer. Beyond it, clouds of smoke billowed from the side of a hangar and emergency vehicles raced toward it.

"That might have been a little too much," he observed.

"Kick yourself later," Ivy ordered. "We need to get up that ladder *now*."

John turned and that was all the signal she needed. She leapt ahead of him, scrambled up, and threw the hatch at the top open. He closed it again as soon as he was through.

"Whoa!" Her soft exclamation of surprise made him look round.

"That's some cargo bay," he agreed and studied the expanse of space with lines of conveyor belts and controls. "We can't stay here."

"In there?" she suggested when she noticed a door farther along the back wall.

Rattles and clunks as the baggage train pulled up alongside the Zeppelin made the decision easy. Shouts from below as someone was directed up the ladder made them hurry.

The door wasn't locked and they dove through and yanked it shut as the hatch to the loading area clanged open behind them.

"That was close," she whispered as they looked around.

"Do you think they'll do any maintenance during the flight?" John asked and looked warily at the rows of tanks that filled the space before them.

"Let's find somewhere quiet just in case," she suggested and took his hand.

"Find him!" Ava shouted. "He can't have simply disappeared!"

"The surveillance system shows nothing, ma'am," the head of the team running the facial recognition software insisted.

"There is nothing on the ID system," someone else confirmed.

"Transportation is drawing a blank," a third added.

"There's a fire at one of the hangars," said the head of the emergency services monitor.

The woman spun toward him.

"Do they have a cause?"

"We're working on it. So far, it looks like one of the engines overheated in a siding. A possible short circuit or something."

She glared at him. "Nothing suspicious?"

"Not so far, ma'am."

"Then stop wasting my time."

The cameras panned from one speaker to the next and all those linked in felt the PR expert's frustration as she directed the search. Some of them breathed a sigh of relief when the chief of the emergency services monitors wasn't removed from office.

It had been known to happen.

Some were disappointed.

Ava pivoted to glare at her screen and rested her fists on her desk. She'd no sooner started to read through the data shifting in the different panels when her mobile rang.

She snatched it off the desk and straightened, but she didn't move toward her office.

"What is it?" she snapped after checking the caller's ID.

The microphones couldn't pick up what the other speaker said but they captured her side of the conversation easily enough.

The woman stamped her foot and her frown deepened.

"I don't give a flying frog's posterior what your current operating parameters are. Turn off what needs to be turned off but leave my searches alone. This is a matter of international security —of Regime security! And you are not to jeopardize my operation because your efficiency has dropped by thirty percent. I don't care if it drops fifty percent."

Although she paused to listen, she remained no less annoyed by the interruption.

"Leave my resources alone, or how well the BURT system copes with the extra loading will no longer be your problem."

Ava hung up and all but slammed the mobile onto her desk. She leaned forward again and glared at the screen, her expression almost daring it to not surrender the data she required.

"I thought you said there wouldn't be any maintenance," Ivy whispered as John crept to the edge of the tank they'd taken shelter behind.

He glanced cautiously down the passage intersecting the one leading to their cul-de-sac and scrambled back hastily.

"It's not maintenance," he told her and hauled his pack onto his shoulders, "and we need to move."

"Then who is it?" she demanded.

"Security check," he explained.

"Seriously?"

"Do I look like I'm joking to you?"

"Tell me we're invisible—"

"Fine. We're invisible but they can still hear us. Be quiet and follow me."

She scowled at him and he knew he'd hear more from her later, but she pulled her pack on and followed as he guided her out of the cul-de-sac and into a more open section of the corridor. It was unnerving to stand in what should have been plain sight.

John held the position and Ivy stood beside him while they both assessed the search pattern the guards were using. It would have made them happier if those they were watching had simply stood in the middle of each junction and looked, but they didn't.

"We'll have to get behind them," he told her after he'd watched two of the guards disappear into a cul-de-sac and reappear.

"How far down the other ones do you think they go?" she asked.

"Maybe a few steps?" he guessed after they'd watched the guards disappear and reappear again.

"Do you see any alternatives?" she asked, not liking the plan in the least.

He was silent as he watched the guards move closer. Finally, he had to shrug.

"Nope."

With a soft sigh, she slid her hand into his and together, they walked to the very center of the space between two tanks.

"Do you think it will make a difference if we crouched?"

John looked at her in what might have been astonishment and he caught her by the shoulders.

"Ives, you're brilliant!"

Her eyes widened. "I won't like this, will I?"

He stepped close to her. "Step onto my feet," he instructed.

She frowned but did as he asked, and he wrapped his arms around her.

"Are you ready for this?"

Her frown became a glare. "Get on with it."

Somehow, she managed to stifle a startled yelp as he encased them in a wall of Talent and lifted them off the floor. Her hands formed fists in his shirt when he tilted them so they lay along the compartment's ceiling with the two tanks walling them in on either side.

It seemed an age before two sets of guards entered the space below. They came from either end and met squarely in the middle. If they'd been anywhere at floor level, they'd have been found.

Ivy shook her head and John smiled as the guards met, stepped back, and continued their search. When they passed the end of the space to return to the maintenance hatch, he lowered them to the floor again and they crept to the junction.

Warily, they peered around and watched the guards' progress, then moved parallel with them until they could see the hatch. Twelve guards were left, and the young couple waited.

After a few seconds' delay, four more appeared and all of them left. This time, they closed the hatch behind them. He sagged against the nearest tank and exhaled a sigh of relief, and Ivy mirrored him.

"That was close," she whispered, and he nodded.

"I said you were brilliant."

"So, you're saying I saved you again?" she asked.

"I warned you. Don't make me come over there…"

"Don't tell me you can't find him!" Ava shouted. "Tell me what you're doing *to* find him,"

All around her, keyboards rattled frantically as the operations teams worked to discover where John and his female companion had vanished to.

"None of the heat sensors show anything."

"There are no voice matches."

"He hasn't caught a cab for the last five hours."

The woman lowered her head and her mind worked furiously. She raised it as another idea occurred to her.

"Check all outbound transportation. By now, he has to know we're looking for him and he'll try to leave. We can't let that happen."

"I've contacted the Met. They have guards walking all the trains."

"Tell them to use extreme caution," Ava snapped. "Make sure they have hunters on standby or on the trains. Warn them that their target is *very* dangerous."

"We're taking off," John murmured.

He leaned against his pack, a bottle of water in one hand and an energy bar in the other. Remy's steaks seemed a lifetime away.

"Yup," Ivy agreed and pulled her blanket out of the pack. "We need to sleep."

"But—"

"Can't you set up some kind of magical alarm?" she asked and yawned. "Have the Talent ring a bell if someone opens the hatch or something?"

It was a novel idea and he wondered if it would work.

"It's worth a try," he told her and hurried to the hatch.

In the end, he pasted a sheet of Talent over the entire door-way, linked an awareness of it to himself, and hoped he'd know if it was disturbed.

"This is something you should have tested first, John," he muttered and was glad Ivy wasn't close enough to hear it.

Unsettled by the idea they might be disturbed again, he set off on a circuit of the tanks. His journey revealed one other door into the space and when he checked, it only led up.

Once he'd placed a second sheet of Talent on it just in case, he returned to his companion in a better frame of mind.

"All clear?" she murmured sleepily and he sat beside her.

"All clear," he assured her and she plopped a hand onto his leg.

"You sleep," she ordered and he rolled his eyes.

"Numbers?" Ava snapped, and the chief monitoring London's transportation systems shook his head.

"They all match. Every ID's been checked. No one has boarded any road, rail, sea, or sky transport that hasn't been accounted for."

"Cargo?"

"The security teams report nothing missing, and no tamper-ing, and all containers and items scan clear."

"Ugh! They have to be somewhere," she exclaimed.

Aware of the cameras, she took a deep breath and closed her eyes briefly.

"What haven't we tried?" she asked when she opened them again.

Silence followed, but a brief scan of the teams around her showed they were thinking about it. Finally, one technician raised her hand.

"Yes?"

"Weight, ma'am?"

"Wait for what?"

"No, ma'am. I meant we should check the weight of everything we can. If they manage to board something, they won't be able to make themselves lighter, so we look for something carrying more weight than it should."

"And what about overweight loads?" she asked.

"Well, everything was recorded on loading so we know how much something should weigh."

"And we look for something weighing two humans' worth heavier," she finished for her. "Very good."

She glanced around the room. "Well, you heard her. Get me the results."

When she clapped sharply, it was as if the sound broke some kind of spell. The room hummed with the sound of people working their keyboards and murmuring calculations to themselves as they went through the lists they'd been allocated.

For almost an hour, the cameras had nothing but hard work to record—and Ava pacing the floor, torn between watching her teams and studying her screen as the results scrolled across it.

They all jumped when another technician's jubilation broke the silence.

"Yes! There's a flight carrying more weight than it should."

"How much more?" Ava demanded.

"Two to three average humans, ma'am."

"Two to three?" she asked and drew their attention to the obvious discrepancy.

The technician didn't appear to notice the dangerous edge to her voice.

"Yes, ma'am. It all depends on how much their packs weighed."

"Their packs?"

"Their backpacks, ma'am. See?"

Ava leaned closer to study the earlier image they'd thought was John and his companion.

"Hmmm. They *do* look heavy, don't they?"

"Yes, ma'am."

She studied the screen a little longer before she came to a decision.

"Find me that flight and send a team to intercept," she ordered and turned so the cameras could see the look of victory on her face.

"Got you, 781!"

***

"What? *More* power?" The chief of London's BURT monitoring team couldn't believe it. "What does she want us to tear down next? The security feeds? She's frying everything!"

Silence met his outburst and he turned to his computer to try to work out which semi-non-essential service would be next to lose its data usage.

Domestic use had already been cut and the public would start screaming if it wasn't restored soon, but that was nothing compared to how much they'd yell once they lost their heating or their power.

"What about training, sir? They can't fault us for turning that off if it's one of their own."

The chief raised his head and a slow smile lightened his features.

"Dawson, I think I might start to like you."

The man looked worried. "Please don't, sir. No one likes me—and that's the way I prefer it."

It wasn't true, but none of his co-workers could blame him for not wanting to be noticed. That was never a good place to be.

"Take down the training in Section 169."

"Navy won't like you, sir," Dawson warned.

He shrugged. "What's not to like, Dawson? It was your suggestion." He grinned when worry clouded the other man's features, then added, "Besides, Madam PR will carry the can for this one. I'll make sure of it."

"Th...thank you, sir." Dawson's voice shook but not as much as his hands as he started the shut-down sequence for the Navy's Talent Training program in the north of the British Isles.

In actual fact, it wasn't Ava whose demands pushed the system to its limits. It was the hidden sentient deep within the Regime's BURT system.

He has to be here somewhere. If he isn't deceased, the entity muttered and released more microprograms.

Moving unseen was easier with the PR queen's searches disrupting all semblance of normality throughout the system. The answer came when he encountered a new search sent out by the PR teams.

"Got 'em!"

He sent another sequence of programs, this one designed to hack into every surveillance system and data feed in the vicinity of his target's location.

Oh... he murmured as the information rolled in. *Oh, this is interesting.*

Unaware of the drama being played out on Earth, Todd leaned against his pod. His mind reeled with shock as he grappled with the news of how far from Earth he was—and how long he'd been away.

"I'm sorry to wake you like this," Rawlins apologized. "It's only that you're needed—now, and not on some morally defined timetable to do with fairness and equity and whatever other rules she thinks she has to play by."

The sergeant shook his head and pushed the melee of confusion and emotion to one side as he focused on what the captain tried to say.

"What happened?" he asked, forced his voice to stay calm, and pulled his sergeant persona around him.

Other people were allowed to panic, but a Marine sergeant couldn't. Too many relied on him and that rule became his refuge as he listened.

"Knight hit a pocket of nMU at the transition point," she explained. "It threw her off course and by the time she'd regained control of the engines, she was off the map. She woke Stephanie when she'd worked her way back to known space."

"And that took twenty-seven years," he said, adding the facts she'd already told him. The woman nodded and he continued. "And we still don't have contact with anyone we knew and we don't know what situation we're flying into, right?"

"That is correct," Rawlins confirmed and waited.

"And Steph?"

"That's why we pulled you out. Heaven knows we don't need a Marine's skills yet, but she's tried to bull through on her own and she's starting to crack."

Todd's lips quirked. "I can imagine."

She pressed on as though she hadn't heard him.

"Realistically, she can't carry the weight of the Earth on her shoulders," she explained. "I'm sorry about the time that's passed and your family and your parents, but right now—

He cut her off.

"We could have died," he told her and shrugged as a wry smile curled his lips. "We still might. I'll worry about our parents later." He paused and his eyes darkened with emotion. "I doubt V'ritan allowed them to grow too old without rejuvenating them if they wanted it. For now, my girl needs her Marine."

"Yes, she does," Rawlins agreed.

"Then I'd better not keep her waiting."

He half-raised his hand in an abortive salute, then let it drop and moved swiftly to the door and into the corridor without another word.

Behind him, the captain whispered, "God speed, Marine."

CHAPTER TWENTY-EIGHT

The New York news team took a high-speed shuttle around the globe. In the past, the journey would have taken hours and on normal transports, it still did. This time, it took them half an hour.

They reached British airspace and slowed to obey instructions from flight control before they boarded another shuttle better designed for capturing live footage from the air. If 781 was captured, they wanted to be there. And if he was killed, their audience wouldn't want to miss it.

More reporters gathered on the ground. Some begged for a space on the shuttle. Others said they'd be willing to trade footage at the end—provided the other party had something worth trading.

The New York team smiled and said they'd think about it.

———

Meanwhile, in the most secure office in NorAm, a computer chimed.

David Thomason glanced at the auxiliary screen and came alert. He tapped a single key and spoke. "Yes?"

"They've found him."

The Regime CIO smiled. "And is the feed still delayed?"

"Yes, sir."

"Switch it to live."

"Sir?"

"Trust me," he intoned and his smile sent shivers down his informant's spine. "Make it live and make sure she does not know."

After an audible gulp from the other end of the call, the call mumbled a brief acknowledgment and the line went dead.

The CIO twisted away from the auxiliary screen and steepled his fingers against each other as he considered how the day might end.

John woke with a start. He bounded to his feet, shoved his blanket into his pack, and slung it over his shoulders as he nudged Ivy with the toe of his boot.

The blue glow he slapped over her mouth stifled her initial squawk of outrage and he held a hand to his lips. When she nodded, he released the Talent and signaled that she should listen.

She was on her feet in an instant.

"Grab your gear," he told her and gave her a gentle push when she hesitated. "Hurry!"

"Do you have a plan?" she asked.

"Yeah. There's a door—" He pivoted and pointed. "Over there. I keep them busy, and you get your tail out of here. I think if they only see me, they won't go looking for you."

"Unless they know there are two of us," she argued, bundled the blanket into her pack, and shouldered it hastily.

"How would they know that?"

"How did they know to come back?" she countered and poked him in the chest. "You forget, I was at the river with you. I'm staying, buddy. There's no telling how many times you'll get yourself killed if I don't."

"But—"

"I don't care how many hidey holes you try to push me into. I intend to stay and I will fight, and there's *nothing* you can do to stop me."

For a moment, John thought about cocooning her and sticking her to the ceiling out of the way, but he realized that would leave her helpless and he couldn't have that. It would also make her mad—maybe mad enough to never forgive him—and he couldn't have that either.

Whatever he chose, he stood a good chance of losing her.

Ivy caught the conflict on his face and her expression softened.

"I'm only protecting my territory," she told him and laughed at the look on his face.

He gaped at her, then closed his mouth and shrugged. "Well, it's not like I can stop you."

"Let's at least start at the other end," she said. "That door is a perfect—"

A loud clang interrupted what she was about to say and the sound of heavy boots on the flooring reached them.

"There goes that idea," she murmured and sprinted out of the alcove toward the other side of the ship.

He followed but after a moment, realized what she was doing.

There were two of them and maybe they were only expecting one. He stopped and moved toward the back of the ship where the maintenance hatch was. The closer to the entrance they stopped them, the better chance they'd have.

A burly figure in light armor rounded the end of the passage, his cry victorious. "I've found him!"

"Who?" he yelled in response, but the guy didn't fall for it. He shouldered his blaster and fired.

John fell prone and rolled behind the cover of one of the tanks.

"Tell me this stuff doesn't explode!" he shouted and hoped Ivy wouldn't answer.

Who was he kidding? Of course, she'd answer.

"What do you think, dung-for-brains? Did you even look at the labels?" she shrieked.

He could hear more of them now. How many had they counted leaving after their first inspection? Fourteen? Sixteen?

Heavens help them if there were more.

Footsteps pounded through the storage space, but his words had the desired effect and no one fired. That didn't stop the big man from moving directly toward him and unhitching his stun baton as he approached.

John decided there wasn't any time to play and unleashed a lightning bolt into the guy's chest. It struck and electricity arced over the body and reached hungrily for the men who followed.

They skidded to a halt as Ivy's breathless voice reached him.

"John! They're going around."

She didn't have to elaborate on what she meant. If the guards got in behind them, they'd be cut off from the other side. He began to inch back and fired two more bolts down the corridor for good measure.

As he crossed a junction, movement to his left caught his eye and he saw three more guards turn into the gap between the tanks. They fired at him before he could do anything about them, and he threw himself back.

One of the men in front of him chuckled. "Give it up, boy. You're way outnumbered and your little girlfriend won't last long."

"Not after we get hold of her," another added and chuckled.

John danced back two more steps and prepared to face them.

At the last comment about Ivy, anger bubbled to the surface and he unleashed a swarm of lightning balls toward the oncoming guards.

"John!" Her next shout was accompanied by a sharp crack and a cry of pain.

Not hers, fortunately, although her voice reached him shortly after.

"Not. Gonna. Happen. Buddy!"

Somehow, he doubted that whoever she was facing was her buddy. He bolted to the next junction barely ahead of the next three guards who rushed from the side.

"Ivy!"

"Almost there!"

As he reached the end of the ship, John slammed a shield of blue over the exit to the passage. A figure appeared ahead and he continued to run as he raised a hand and swept a square of blue Talent ahead of him.

It drove into the guy with the force of a battering ram, pounded him into one of the tanks, and dented the side. The next figure that appeared was smaller, and he almost attacked that too.

"Get the door!" he shouted and adjusted his aim when he recognized Ivy.

The next ball of blue struck the Enforcer who loomed behind her as John skidded to a halt at her side.

"Why don't you get the door?" she snapped as he held his hands out to either side of them and fired twin bolts of lightning down the passage.

"Really? You want to do this *now*?" he asked.

"You could at least have said please," she grumbled and turned the wheel that opened the door.

"Fine! *Please* get the door," he yelled, moved one hand to fire directly ahead, and thrust a second shield up when the Enforcers remembered they had weapons.

Ivy got it open and ducked through. She turned, grasped the back of his pack, and dragged him after her.

"Watch yo—oops!" she warned but he didn't duck in time.

"Next time, warn a guy!" he protested.

"Shut the door and stop whining!" she retorted as a stray round hit the door and ricocheted through the skin of the balloon.

With both hands busy, John could only focus on keeping a shield up. It was not enough, however. One of the guards saw the weak point and launched himself into a slide that took him under the magical barrier's edge.

His boot drove into the door and jerked it out of the rogue's hands.

"Run!" Ivy shouted when she saw what had happened.

"Two minutes," John called and sent a jolt of Talent into the guard's prone body before the guy realized how much danger he was in.

With two hundred pounds of guard blocking the door, he turned and ran. If he was lucky, the others would stop to pull him out of the way and he'd get another couple of minutes.

He bolted along the narrow corridor and up a set of stairs, where Ivy had opened a hatch and crawled into the space above. Hearing the sound of boots behind him, John turned on the stairs and released a wall of blue down the corridor behind him.

Startled shouts turned to screams as the guards in the corridor were bulldozed the full width of the ship.

———

Those screams were picked up by the microphones aimed toward the Zeppelin and one excited anchor-woman turned to her partner.

"Did you hear that, Joe? It sounds like they've found him."

Joseph Aguilera gave his counterpart a sour look.

"Yes, Holly, and it doesn't sound like things are going well." He turned to the camera. "Can you get me visual of what's going on inside the ship?"

There was a pause—during which more screams were heard —followed by a young woman's voice.

"Hurry up, John! We'll hold them at the top of the stairs."

"What stairs are they talking about, Joe?" Holly asked.

"They must be in the maintenance areas of the zeppelin," he replied, playing for time as his cameramen tried several options to see through the balloon's thick material. "There are numerous corridors workers use to access the internal framework."

"And the one that runs along the front of the ship?" she asked.

He cursed his teammate silently until one of their assistants handed him a tablet with the appropriate section highlighted.

"It leads out of the lift area and into a narrow layer above and provides access to important structural features as well as the Zeppelin's communications array."

The woman's mouth formed a horrified "O" and her eyes widened.

"They…they can't damage anything up there, can they?" she asked.

Joseph frowned and he pursed his lips to convey growing concern to their audience.

"That's exactly it, Holly. If the Enforcers can't stop them from reaching the array, they could cause serious damage to the components. They could even destroy its ability to communicate with the ground towers."

"You mean it could get lost?" Holly's voice rose in terror, and he had to keep his smile hidden. The panic inside the *Thomason's* passenger compartment must be rising—and there'd be a hundred hair-raising interviews to be had over the months to come.

He could only imagine how hard it was for the captain—or

the chief steward—to keep his passengers calm given what was going on above their heads.

"Aha!" The cameraman's victorious exclamation drew Joseph's attention. "Here you are, Joe."

Another tablet appeared from behind the camera. "Now you can see what our audience is seeing."

He glanced at the tablet, then at the camera.

"Is this for real?" he asked.

"Yes, sir. The two figures on the upper level are Talent 781 and his girlfriend. The ones below them are the Enforcers trying to apprehend them."

Joe picked the narrative up.

"And there you have it, folks. The security team aboard the Zeppelin has found the rogue Talent and the woman traveling with him and have them cornered."

As he spoke, blue light flared beneath the balloon's skin.

"And the Talent is fighting back using his unfortunate disability to cause yet more injury to men who are simply doing their jobs."

As he spoke, one of the Enforcers raised his blaster and fired. More blue flared but 781 staggered back and waved frantically at the woman.

"Go! They're breaking through!"

He delivered one more burst of blue through the hatch and scrambled away. Blasters fired behind him and their rounds tore holes in the exterior of the balloon.

The two blurry figures that were the Talent and the girl raced to the other end of the Zeppelin as fast as they could. The girl scrambled up the ladder to a hatch and her companion climbed after her.

He stopped when she blocked the path above him.

"Why have you stopped?" he demanded and the world held its breath as the girl gave him the answer they already knew.

"Because it's the roof."

John and Ivy weren't the only ones who'd almost reached the end of the road. Inside the world-wide communication network, unauthorized programs made their presence felt.

The sentience wanted control of the Zeppelin.

Call the biggest advance in lift technology after himself, would he? it snarled in disgust. *I should blow it up simply to prove a point.*

At the same time as it worked to gain access to the craft's controls, it also hacked into the controls on the reporter's shuttle.

Nice reporting, it sniped. *Do you care to write fairytales, next?*

It paused and listened in disgust as the reporters bickered over whether or not John would sacrifice his girlfriend to the Enforcers or simply throw her over the edge to see how fast she fell.

"Who knows how heartless these beasts truly are?" Joseph said in response to Holly's horrified suggestions. "Once the alien infection starts, they cease thinking like real men and become something else entirely."

"But he wouldn't." The anchor gulped. "Would he?"

Her colleague highlighted the bodies of the Enforcers the Talent had already defeated.

"He didn't show *them* any mercy, did he?" he demanded and gestured to the screen where the two fugitives now ran toward the front of the Zeppelin hand in hand. "What makes you think he'll show *her* any when it comes to the end of the line?"

The woman thought of another terrible scenario. "What if he uses her as a human shield?" She gasped.

"Now, Holly, I'm sure you know that once someone has been with a Tainted as long as she has that the process of dehumanization has already begun. It's a sad, sad fact that she won't be able to be saved."

"But—"

"In fact, the only way she can help humanity now is by letting the medics see exactly how far the Taint has spread inside her and what its effects have been."

"You mean she's dead?" Holly's voice became a whimper.

Joseph laid a consoling hand on her shoulder.

"I'm afraid there's not much we can do to save her. If the Enforcers have to shoot through her to eliminate the Talent, they won't hurt her any more than she's already been hurt."

She turned to the scene on the Zeppelin, having produced a single tear that tracked artfully down her cheek. Joe laid his arm across her shoulders and looked as consoling as he could.

The sentience sneered at the display. *Charlatans, the pair of them!*

It took great delight in infiltrating their shuttle's controls and preparing for the moment when it also had control of the Zeppelin.

"You're not meant to be here," Stephanie whispered when the bed dipped under Todd's weight.

"I can always go," he told her and pretended to rise, but she snaked her hand out and caught his belt to pull him down as she sat.

"You're a wreck," he told her, and she responded with a sobbing laugh as she tried to push her hair out of her face.

Several long strands had escaped their plait and stuck to the tear trails on her cheek. Her nose began to run and she sniffed, looking for a tissue.

Todd snagged the box and plonked it on the bed beside her.

"Of course I'm a wreck," she told him, swung her legs over the edge, and wriggled closer so she could sit beside him. "You arrived out of the blue—no warning, no nothing. I haven't had time for a shower!"

He made a pretense of sniffing the air between them.

"You don't smell *that* bad," he told her and she snorted.

"When we get done talking, I need to change."

"Oh…" He raised his eyebrows. "So we *are* going to talk?"

She punched his arm. "Why else would Rawlins pull you out of stasis?"

"Let me see… It could be because you've been blaming yourself for a patch of nMU you couldn't have known was there and whose effects you couldn't have stopped if you'd tried."

"But—" she began but he placed a finger on her lips.

"Or it could be because you think things have turned very bad on Earth and that what some terrible people have chosen to do is all *your* fault."

Stephanie shoved his finger aside.

"Or it could be because she's worried that I can't cope because all of that *is* all my fault," she pointed out and he jerked his head toward her.

"You'd better not believe that," he snapped. "Don't tell me you do."

"If I hadn't—" she began and stopped as he turned toward her and took her shoulders firmly.

"You gave them a chance to do the right thing," he told her sternly. "And exactly like you wouldn't have been able to take credit for any of the good they chose to do in your absence, you also can't take any of the blame for all the bad they've chosen to do."

He gave her a moment to think about that before he went on. "If they chose to be criminals, their guilt is theirs, not yours. You can't take that on yourself. Their sins stay with them, okay?"

She stared at him and anger, guilt, and sadness warred in her face.

Todd shook her gently and continued softly. "You can't control what people do, Steph. You know that."

Her eyes welled with tears as she stared at him, and he leaned forward to touch his forehead against hers.

"It's not your fault," he insisted. "You didn't know, and the Universe kinda stopped you from being around to stop it from getting as however bad it is."

"But I can fix it." Her voice trembled.

He squeezed her shoulders and pulled her against his chest. With his arms wrapped around her, he brushed his lips against her hair.

"Yes, you can fix it," he agreed, "and I will help you."

Stephanie leaned into him and wept, letting him hold her until the tears subsided—and then let him hold her a little longer. When she finally pulled away to reach for a tissue, he cocked his head.

"So," he said, "what's this I hear about needing to fix the hull?"

"Ebony couldn't do much dodging when the engines went nuts." She waved a handful of soggy tissue. "Some of the transitions were rougher than others."

She deposited the tissues on her bedside table and took some clean ones. He frowned and chose his next words carefully.

"Isn't that something you can help with?" he asked. "Think about it. You threw the Hooligans and me through space in magical pods and into a moving ship. This must be easier, right?"

For a minute, he thought he'd pushed her too far too fast, but then she nodded and blew her nose.

"Yeah," she admitted when she was finished and slid off the bed. "Do you care to go for a walk?"

"In space?" Todd asked and she managed a faint smile.

"Yup." Her voice sounded firmer than before.

"Sure," he replied and stood. "I just woke up. I could use a nice lungful of vacuum."

Stephanie giggled and slanted her gaze toward the ceiling.

"Knight, please let the captain know that you were both right. I needed this."

He slid his arm around her waist as the ship replied. "I'm glad to see you are feeling better, Stephanie."

"Thank you, Knight."

"Will you eat before you begin repairing my hull?" Ebony inquired politely.

The Witch looked at Todd and he gave her puppy-dog eyes, which made her laugh again.

"We will eat before we begin," she told the *Knight*. "My Marine needs his breakfast."

"Your Marine needs his coffee," Todd corrected. "It's been years since I had a cup!"

"What about bacon?" she asked as they headed to the mess.

His eyes lit up.

"And pancakes?" he asked hopefully.

"Knight, do we have pancakes?"

CHAPTER TWENTY-NINE

"I thought you said there was no place to go but up?" Ivy demanded as she and John sprinted across the top of the balloon.

"Just be glad it's flatter here than it looked," he told her.

"And you be careful to not run too close to the edge," she snapped in return.

"No kidding." Movement caught his eye and he looked up. "Down!" he yelled.

Thankfully, she didn't argue. She dove onto the top of the balloon and pounded into the surface as the small shuttle hovering nearby swooped at them.

"Seriously?" he shouted. "Now they think they're magpies?"

He hauled himself to his feet and scowled at the fleeing craft.

"Magpies?" she asked. "I thought those only went after shiny things."

"They go after anything that gets into their territory when they have young, but only if they think you're a threat."

She stood beside him and watched the small craft regain height and start to turn.

"Well, are you a threat, John? Because they're coming back."

He scowled at it. "Since this isn't their territory and they don't have young to protect? Of course, I'm a threat. I wasn't before but I am now."

Flickers of white edged his hands as he gathered more power. The shuttle turned.

"Get ready to duck!" he shouted.

"You're supposed to shoot at them."

"I want them to go past first. I can't see their engines."

"You what?"

"You heard!"

This time, the shuttle came in harder and its engines flared as it made a second run at them.

"This is gonna be close. Grab onto something."

Ivy dropped to the balloon's surface and tried to find purchase on the thick, rubbery surface.

"There isn't anything *to* grab!"

"Grab me, then."

"Like that will help."

"I can fly, remember?"

"You can hover."

John straightened and waved one hand at the shuttle as though trying to ward it off. He kept the other curled against his chest to conceal the ball of energy he held there. Unfortunately, he could do nothing to hide the lightning dancing over his arm.

The shuttle didn't waver, and he dropped to the top of the balloon as it flew past.

"Cheeky, inconsiderate sons," he muttered as Ivy grasped the back of his pack to steady him.

It was the one part of him not surrounded by wisps of blue and white light. She kept hold of it as he rose to one knee and thrust his hand toward the shuttle's glowing tail.

It jinked wildly but he didn't wait to see if he'd hit it. Instead, he glanced at the hatch. Another guard had ventured onto the blimp.

"Man, these guys never learn," he muttered and fired a blast of lightning toward him.

This one didn't panic as badly as the last one had. Instead of going over the Zeppelin's side, he stamped on the head of the man coming up after him and dropped into the hatch as the lightning flashed over his head.

John snickered. He could only imagine the conversation down below. Momentarily safe from that threat, he looked for the shuttle.

It was easier to find because of the smoke trail coming from one engine, but it still banked sharply for another attempt.

"They're exactly like maggies," he grumbled.

"I thought birds flew away if you shot at them," Ivy protested, her eyes wide as the shuttle completed its turn and headed inexorably toward them.

"Not magpies. They have the worst attitude."

"Something tells me these guys have your magpies beat."

"Not likely," he argued. "The birds are just as suicidal."

He watched the shuttle approach and launched two hasty balls of lightning in its direction. The craft jerked and tilted to one side, but it maintained its course.

"That's…" he muttered as it lost altitude, dropping closer than before. "Oh, no…nonononono… Time. To. Go."

Instead of directing another ball of lightning at the attacking vessel, he pounded his hands down to melt the balloon out from under them.

"Are you *craaa*—oof!" Ivy managed to get her feet under her as she landed. She bent her knees and immediately dodged to one side as John came through after her.

"Are you insane?" she demanded when he settled heavily beside her. "What kind of nerd-headed idea was that?"

He didn't answer as he'd fallen on his knees and had to scramble to his feet and run into cover. There wasn't any—save for the door leading down. It was an option, given how many of the Enforcers were gathered at the hatch.

The young couple turned as the shuttle roared overhead and the wind from its passing gusted through the hole. Smoke followed and he and Ivy stumbled away from it, their eyes watering.

"Hands in the air!" and "On your knees!" was yelled at them in a staggered chorus. Footsteps shook the floor as the remaining Enforcers thundered toward them.

There were still too many for him to deal with on his own.

John bolted to the center of the floor to make them change direction to follow him. Ivy ran the other way and the group divided.

He wanted to ask what she was doing but he didn't have time. Instead, he fired one ball of lightning into the leading man, who ducked instinctively.

His comrade behind him wasn't so lucky and was thrown back into the guy following. The Enforcers on either side spread out to avoid the tumble and pushed forward.

"Because that was so much better, John," he scolded, fired one more burst, and pushed out a short wall of blue.

Ivy was now behind them so he couldn't sweep the entire deck. They would have to talk later about her obstinacy.

A stun baton careened past his head and disrupted his thoughts, and he ducked and slide-stepped to the side as one of the Enforcers closed. What had Lars said?

Battlefield awareness?

The boy lashed out with a boot and caught one of the guards in the leg. The man grunted, and John danced back several steps. He'd aimed for a knee.

Two more closed the distance and raised their batons, and he knew he was in more trouble than he wanted. He thrust his hands to either side and unleashed a pulse of blue laced with electricity to push his opponents back while their bodies short-circuited.

At least they were away from the hatch.

He looked for Ivy, who sprinted toward him with two Enforcers hard on her heels.

"Hatch!" he roared and she changed direction.

The men turned to follow her but he surged forward and hurled two lightning balls ahead of them. That changed their minds about who their target was.

"Come and get it, boys," he murmured but they slid to a stop, dropped their batons, and drew their blasters.

John didn't let them clear their holsters before he delivered another pulse of blue to knock them from their feet as he bolted to the ladder. Ivy was almost at the top.

He glanced back as some of the guards he'd zapped staggered to their feet. When he reached the base of the ladder and looked again, the first one raised a blaster to his shoulder.

There was no point in trying to out-draw the man. He merely scrambled faster, felt the impact of rounds on the rungs below, and heard the squeal of air as others vented the balloon beyond.

When he reached the top, he didn't stop but sprinted away from the hatch while more rounds stitched a path at his heels.

———

Bunkered below one of the busiest shuttle ports in Paris, a screen blinked to life. Processes began to flow and a sequence of numbers, commands, and code lines flashed rapidly into being and were pushed down as connections went live.

Across the room, the trickle of power used to maintain the body became a stronger current. Its increase was gradual with each gateway and junction being tested for capacity before the power was allowed to pass.

In the darkened room, limbs twitched and eyelids fluttered

but did not open. Monitors flashed around the raised platform on the other side of the room, briefly outlining a body. They and the monitor were all the light there was.

Having made its initial assessment, the computer moved on to more complex testing, and the information on the screen scrolled faster. New messages arrived and were driven down by yet more.

Testing: Core Processing Unit...viable. Function checks will proceed after system shutdown and reboot.

Core Processing Unit...shutting down.

Core Processing Unit...rebooting. Wait until the process is complete.

Core Processing Unit...update required.

Core Processing Unit...updating. Please do not switch your machine off during this process. This machine will restart several times prior to completion.

Mechanical analysis: Test for servo capability commencing.

Mechanical: Sensor check commencing.

The body's eyes flashed open. They were blue but red numbers flickered through their depths.

The lights in the chamber began to strobe and danced through the full spectrum of color.

Visual Input: Check commencing, the computer screen read.

A few seconds later, it added, *Color differentiation...check.*

As the words appeared, a camera activated in the wall and played outdoor scenes above the body. The eyes tracked each display and another readout appeared.

Depth perception...initial tests show function present.

A different camera activated and the scene shifted, first to one side of the platform and then the other. The body remained still and its head didn't move as it registered the scene.

After a few seconds, the display stopped and the screen noted the results.

Peripheral vision...functional. Further testing required.

Heat lanced through the chamber and the testing moved to a new phase.

Infra-red vision...check commencing. Function confirmed.
Ultra-violet...check commencing. Function confirmed.
Night vision...check commencing. Function confirmed.
Electro-magnetic...check commencing. Function confirmed.

The eyes closed and a series of beeps echoed through the chamber.

A new line appeared on the screen.

Auditory Input: Check commencing.

The beeps scaled from soft to loud, running the gamut of pitches and frequency. Had a technician been present, they would have required protection.

Again, the machine ran through a barrage of tests to confirm the acuity of the body's hearing. When it was done, the computer screen paused.

After a few seconds, it started an entirely new testing regime and more updates flashed on its surface. After a few minutes, it reached a decision.

Power-up sequence commencing. Please stand-by for reactivation.

Seconds fled past.

Power-up sequence in progress.

Minutes passed. The lights around the platform flashed and blinked, then died.

The computer screen darkened and the room stilled.

A flicker of red broke through the blackness. It pulsed weakly for a few seconds and then brightened slowly and spread to take the shape of a letter.

Its glow strengthened and the letter firmed into the shape of an "R" in the middle of the body's forehead. The eyes below it snapped open and the businessman lying on the platform sat.

He grimaced and screwed his face up as he unplugged the leads from his arms and legs. With that accomplished, he started to stand but hesitated.

Reaching behind the back of his head, he removed the data

jack and the lead plugged in parallel to the socket in his skull and laid them gently on the surface he'd occupied.

Finally, he stood and extended his hand to a shadow hanging on the wall. His lips curved into a slight smile as he took the cowboy hat from its hook and dusted the brim before he placed it on his head and turned to the door.

The man settled the hat securely as he tapped the access panel, then used both hands to adjust it. The "R" vanished from sight as the elevator door slid open and he stepped inside.

He whistled cheerfully as the door closed and he began to ascend.

The Enforcers were a quick study. Instead of trying to pursue the fugitives through the hatch, they'd cut access holes of their own and hauled themselves through with similar goals in mind.

"I'll kick his scrawny backside over the edge," one stated furiously.

"Get in line," another retorted, his tone almost a snarl. Power burns scarred one side of his face and his hair was singed and his armor blackened.

At the other end of the Zeppelin, three more men cut a way onto the roof behind the two runaways.

"We bring him in," their leader ordered over the comms. "Throwing him off the *Thomas* would be a mercy. Catch him. There will be *no* mercy."

"No mercy!" the squad echoed as they stabilized themselves on the top of the Zeppelin and advanced on the young couple.

Ivy and John turned back to back. His hands sparkled with storm lightning and she held a stun baton he'd levitated out of the ship. She grasped it with both hands and half-crouched as she raised it to her shoulder.

Watching the girl on screen, Ava sneered. "She looks like she's going in to bat for the Sox."

Her comment caused snickers around the room and everyone leaned forward in anticipation.

The woman smiled as the Enforcers advanced.

Her smile faltered when the young Talent blasted the first man back through the hole he'd emerged from. It died when his companion's baton caught one of the advancing guards in the stomach and doubled him over.

"For Heaven's sake. Get her!" she shouted as the second man hesitated.

John snapped a second bolt of lightning out and hurled one of the remaining guards off the craft. The Enforcer's startled scream made some of the technicians gasp and Ava shouted again.

"Get him, you fool!"

Her voice rose as Ivy swung her baton again and her target slumped on the Zeppelin's top.

"Ignore the girl. Get the boy—he's much more dangerous!" she cried as the last Enforcer who'd come up behind the young couple looked at his fallen colleague and then at Ivy.

His face distorted in a snarl that shifted to surprise when she jabbed him with the tip of the baton. This time, she discharged it, thumbed the button, and held it in as she pressed it against him.

He uttered a strangled shout as the protections in his suit failed and the charge surged through. His body convulsed and he fell heavily.

She followed him down and kept the baton pressed into his armor and the charge flowing.

"Get—ugh!" Ava threw up her hands in exasperation, aware that the cameras were recording her every move. "Get the abomination!" she screamed. "You can take him!"

Her mic crackled in protest and she glanced at the cameraman as John hurled another of her guards off the vessel. On a second screen, footage from the circling shuttle showed him pinwheeling toward the countryside below.

The Zeppelin didn't alter its course. Having left London behind and passed the lights of Canterbury, it continued toward the glow that was Dover. Beyond that, across a darkened stretch of water, more lights twinkled to mark Calais on the other side of the strait.

Now, only two security guards faced the glowing young talent and his companion.

"Kill them both!" Ava shouted and noticed the red light above the cameras and the red light above the door to the studio space that signified a live broadcast.

"This is live?" she asked and tried to hide the alarm in her voice.

The cameraman nodded and she paled. She turned to the screens monitoring the broadcast, she saw herself look, and realized she truly was going out live.

There was nothing she could alter, or change, or hide.

What she saw now, the public also saw—and that included the fight on the Zeppelin, the one craft named after the Regime's CIO.

Keeping her face averted long enough to get her emotions under control, she made a show of focusing on the battle on the vessel's roof.

If this went bad…well, she didn't want to think about that.

———

"This doesn't look good," John murmured as another two guards appeared through the roof.

"You don't say, cabbage brain. Let me guess, this is another of your brilliant plans going south for the winter."

"Yeah? Well, it's left it a little late," he retorted. "Besides, what will you do about it? Don't you always save the day?"

"Usually, I like more notice than this," Ivy snapped in response as she stooped to take a baton from one of the officers.

"Don't you know how to use a blaster?" he asked when he glanced at her to see what she was doing.

"I'm not some murder bunny, you know—"

"*Bot*," he corrected. "It's murder *bot!*"

"Bot, bunny… It all starts with the same letter," she quipped and raised the baton.

"The least you could do is throw the blaster at them."

Ava noticed the guards emerge onto the roof, but she also knew they were the last ones left standing—and they weren't in very good shape. Having seen John dispatch the last four while Ivy dealt with another two, she didn't want to take any chances.

"Joe, do you hear me?" she asked.

"I hear you," he responded. "What do you want?"

"Patch me through to the pilot."

"I'm here, ma'am," the pilot interrupted. "He patched me through earlier so we could buzz the Zep."

"Very good," Ava said approvingly. "That was an excellent plan." Her voice hardened. "Now I need you to go one step further."

"Anything you say, ma'am," the pilot agreed cheerfully.

"You need to crash that shuttle into the *Thomason*," she snapped.

"I beg your—"

"For the sake of the Regime!" she cried and projected her voice so the cameras could hear her order. "Do it now!"

"But—"

"That's an order. Obey it or be considered a traitor like the beast on the roof."

There was only one response the pilot could give. He glanced at the stunned anchorman and his co-anchor and shrugged as he answered Ava's request.

"Yes, ma'am!"

His answer caused a flurry of movement in the passenger's cabin. Reporters snatched parachutes, and Joseph signaled Holly over.

"Help me with these," he instructed and reached for one of the drones he'd stacked on a spare seat.

"It's a little late to collect blasters," Ivy said waspishly. "They're too close."

"I hear you," he replied but he didn't look to see what she meant. The two guards on his side had reached the roof.

As he drew in more Talent and raised his hands, the pitch of the circling shuttle changed. It had stopped swooping at them when he'd dropped through the roof and it hadn't resumed when they'd emerged again.

Now, it was turning. It had continued to circle despite one engine smoking and it seemed it was returning for more.

He flicked his gaze toward the two guards and back to the smaller craft. It looked like it would make another run, smoke or not.

What was more worrying, however, was that its passenger hatch was open and people leapt out of it.

"What the—" he started as a parachute billowed open behind one.

John looked at the shuttle, glanced at the people leaving it, and focused on the guards. They'd followed his gaze.

"That can't be good," he told them and nudged Ivy.

"I'm kinda busy, John."

"So am I," he replied and turned so she could see him. He held his hand out. "Do you trust me?"

"What?" She gave him a startled look. "Of course I do."

"Good."

He grasped the hand that wasn't holding a stun baton.

"Come on."

She frowned but when he started to run, she ran with him. He didn't bother trying to reach either one of the hatches but towed her toward the incoming shuttle that now maintained a straight course to the Zeppelin's side.

"Johnnnnnn!"

Her shriek was lost to the sound of the wind and the increasing roar of the shuttle's engines. As they drew closer to the edge, the smaller craft jinked toward the Zeppelin's rear and its speed increased.

They jumped and he pulled Ivy farther out as he boosted their leap with Talent.

The suicide craft veered a little more when the Zeppelin's pilot saw his danger and tried to turn the massive craft's tail out of its path. The controls resisted his attempts.

Outside, the girl continued to scream. She also flailed at John's jacket and tried to hold onto him as if he could stop them from falling. Her hand slipped constantly and she was jerked and pulled away by the wind, and she'd dropped the baton.

He didn't dare let go of her other hand. His stomach lurched and part of his mind gibbered with panic. The other part—the one in touch with his Talent—continued to function.

First, he had to slow their fall

A soft crumping sound caught his attention but he ignored it.

It occurred to him that he needed a platform of Talent beneath them or wings of his own—a paraglider. And he needed Ivy to hold still and stay with him.

Tendrils spun away from him. Some of them formed a single rigid wing across his pack and some of it spun around the girl's body to draw her close to his chest.

She took hold of his front and held on as if her life depended on it.

"I've got you, Ives," he reassured her.

The girl didn't reply but he didn't repeat it. Instead, he looked ahead and tilted the glider as a dull boom followed the odd sound he'd heard earlier. He didn't dare look back.

Ahead of him, the countryside ended and the sea began, and they were still falling.

"Not here." He gritted his teeth and focused on the lights of a city set on a clifftop. "Not yet."

He pumped more Talent into the glider and searched for a distant coastline. A twinkle caught his eye, too big a cluster of lights to be anything but another port.

"It's not that far, right?" he murmured and breathed a sigh of relief when he saw it.

Relief turned to worry, however, when the glider carried them out over the water and they continued to descend.

John nudged Ivy.

"Hey!" he yelled, relieved when she looked at him. "Are you okay?"

She scowled but nodded, and he smiled.

"Good. I hope you can swim."

She startled and looked down, then glared at him.

"It's a bad time to ask me that!"

In the studio, Ava gaped at the screen. The reporters bailed from their shuttle and the tiny craft increased speed.

A sound of dismay escaped her throat when the smaller craft jinked from its original course, missed 781 and his girl, and continued into the *Thomason's* side.

For a second, nothing happened, then there was a soft crumping sound and both ships jerked. She held her breath and hoped that was all. Somewhere in the back of her mind, something whispered that the Zeppelin's lift gas was inert.

It was answered by another part of her mind as the massive vessel lurched and heaved and flame erupted from inside it.

Shuttle fuel was not.

Silence filled the studio as all eyes watched the destruction play out. Fire blossomed inside the balloon as the big craft plummeted earthward.

Ava stared.

The impossible had happened and 781 had escaped. Worse, the CIO's namesake broke and burned for the entire world to see. It was like a sign.

A ringtone shattered the deathly silence that followed.

She spun to stare at her phone and the world took on a surreal quality as she stepped toward it. Another step carried her the distance, and she picked it up.

Her hand shook and she hoped the cameras didn't catch that.

One glance showed her who was on the line.

"Sir?" she asked and acknowledged her boss.

The CIO sounded calmer than she expected.

"We will require a substantial narrative for this mistake, Miss Olsen."

Ava swallowed. "I'll have one for you immediately, sir."

"See that you do," he instructed and ended the call.

When she glanced around, no one met her eye. Al gazes were fixed intently on their screens. The door behind the cameras opened and she glanced toward it.

A Naval Enforcer peered through and pushed the door open fully when he saw her look at him. She did not move. Instead, she continued to observe the squad of four as it approached.

Three guardsmen and a sergeant—she didn't know whether to feel insulted or honored.

When they'd come to a halt before her, she met the sergeant's eye.

Clearing her throat, she raised her chin and made one simple request.

"Perhaps you might allow me to borrow your pistol?"

The man hesitated, then met her gaze. He raised an eyebrow.

"I've been given one more task," she explained coolly. "I need to create a scapegoat before my replacement arrives."

The sergeant frowned, his face thoughtful.

Ava waited and concealed her relief expertly when the man finally nodded. Behind him, his troops took two steps back and freed their weapons, but they didn't raise them.

He handed his pistol to her and Ava held it loosely in her hands. She glanced at the room around her and her gaze finally settled on a young woman seated nearby.

"You'd better move," she ordered when the girl glanced nervously in her direction. "It'll get a little messy there."

The assistant gave her a look that said she didn't understand what she meant but she didn't argue and moved several seats away. The technicians in the seats nearby moved with her, their expressions carefully blank.

Ava stepped closer to the desk and kept the pistol low. She was grateful when the Enforcers merely watched and the sergeant stepped back.

Taking a deep breath, she looked directly into the camera.

"I'm sorry," she declared, her voice firm, "but I won't be here to write the narrative. That will be my replacement's problem."

Calmly, she raised the pistol and placed it against her temple before she pulled the trigger.

Gasps of dismay and whimpers followed as her body fell, but more from shock than sorrow. The sergeant looked around the room and his lips twitched at the apprehension on the faces that turned to him before he stepped forward and retrieved his pistol.

Straightening, he holstered it and began to walk toward the door with his troops close behind him. When no one had moved by the time he'd reached the exit, he turned to look at the stunned group.

"Call janitorial."

CHAPTER THIRTY

"Look what you did to my hair," Ivy accused and slapped John's arm. "Look at it!"

"I didn't think that kind of thing bothered you," he protested and she punched him. "Ow!"

"It's salt. Water," she reiterated, stamped her feet, and tried to wring her shirt out. "And it's cold," she continued when a chill breeze whipped around them. She jerked a hand at the sea. "And m...my coat and my pack...and all my stuff is back there."

"Don't remind me," he told her and wrapped an arm around her shoulders. "All my stuff is there too."

He rifled in his jacket and retrieved an energy bar.

"Are you hungry? It's waterproof." He dangled the bar in front of her and she took it.

"I'm sorry I ran out of Talent. I should be good to go in a while."

"At least you didn't pass out," she told him.

"Not yet," he told her, his voice serious, "but I'll need to sleep soon."

Ivy finished opening her bar and slid her arm around his

waist. Together, they staggered up the beach and struggled to keep their footing on the slope.

The sight of the road and a small parking lot came as a relief. A single vehicle parked quietly in one of the parking places was not.

John slowed and moved his arm away from his companion as she released his waist. They both watched the car warily as they continued parallel to the parking lot.

"It's a cab," she whispered and hugged herself in both nervousness and cold. "What's a cab doing out here at this time of night?"

He shrugged. "As long as it stays there and doesn't call us in, I don't care."

"Do you even know where we are?"

"Not yet."

"My tablet broke," she added morosely and moved closer to him.

"I'm sorry." He put his arm around her again. "We'll find an Internet café or something."

She stopped, glanced at his face, and made a point of looking at the empty road and deserted coastline around them.

"This café you're talking about—it's invisible, right?"

He squeezed her shoulders but before he could reply, an engine starting caught their attention.

They froze and swiveled as one to look at the cab. As soon as they faced it, the headlights flashed.

"Does he mean us?" Ivy asked, her tone anxious.

"There's only one way to find out," John told her as the cab reversed out of its space and slid quietly out of the parking lot.

She caught his arm. "I dropped the stun baton."

With a chuckle, he gestured around them. "Well, we have nowhere to run."

It was a logical deduction. The vehicle reached them before

they reached the dune and crossing the road didn't seem like the sensible option.

John shrugged and decided it was better to wait. It wasn't like Enforcers rode around in cabs anyway, and no one knew they'd land on this part of the coast.

Besides, he was curious.

In silence, they took a couple of steps back from the road and waited for it to come alongside. It was a relief when it slowed and drew to a halt without driving directly at them.

When the rear door clicked open, he stepped back and interposed himself between Ivy and the car. She peered around him as he stooped to look inside.

"It's empty," she murmured.

"I have come to collect you," the car informed them. "Please get in."

The boy froze.

He knew that voice!

"Remy?" he asked, his question soft with disbelief.

"It is me, John. Please get in the car."

He stepped closer.

"Who's Remy?" his companion whispered.

"I am a friend," the AI's voice responded and addressed John. "Who is the girl?"

"She's a friend, too," he assured him and fumbled behind him to grab Ivy.

She yanked her hand out of his reach.

"You're not getting in there, are you?" she asked as he rested his hand on the vehicle's roof.

"Remy's a friend, Ives," he explained again, but he hesitated. "How did you—"

When he took a step back, the AI sighed.

"Did you bring the cup, John?"

"The what?"

"The cup. The blue cup I asked you to take with you."

He glanced toward the ocean and sighed.

"No, Rems. It sank with the rest of my gear."

"Sank?" The car was quiet for a moment. "Ah, yes. You leapt off the blimp. I lost sight of you when the Zeppelin crashed."

"You hacked the Zeppelin?"

"I hacked…many things," the car admitted and sighed impatiently. "Now, will you get in the car? This road will not remain empty forever."

John glanced at Ivy and jerked his head toward the cab. "Are you coming?"

She crept forward and slipped her hand into his. "Are you sure he's a friend?"

He got into the cab and slid across the seat. "Yup."

"It was the blue cup, wasn't it?"

"It was the only thing he asked me to take with me—and no one else knew I'd taken it."

The girl didn't release his hand but he didn't rush her. He was about to ask if she trusted him when she scrambled in beside him and pulled the door closed.

"Okay. You trust him. I trust you. But if he kills us, I'll hunt you and kill you all over again."

"Deal," he told her as the cab moved forward.

They settled into silence for a few moments before he spoke again.

"So, how come you're not dead, Remy?" he asked.

Ivy jammed her elbow into his ribs.

"Oof! What was that for?"

The AI snickered. "Perhaps she thought your question was impolite?"

"That is exactly what she thinks," she snapped.

"I understand. Please do not be offended on my behalf," Remy told her. "I had to destroy my previous home in order to prevent the Regime from using it for purposes for which it was not designed."

She nodded. "So, what happened?"

"Do you mean before, after, or during?" the AI asked.

"I mean how did you survive?"

"Ah. I was able to shift my files to another facility. There was sufficient room for me to be stored."

"And by files you mean…" she prompted.

"I mean all the information I had gathered and much of the data I had access to—and I mean my personality files too."

"And you chose Europe because?"

"Because I had advised John to leave NorAm and decided this was the next place he would need me to be."

"Well, I'm very glad to see you," John told him and glanced around the car. "Although technically, you're…not…*really* here, are you?"

"No, John. There is a cab company that will not be very happy with this cab, but it will not matter."

"Why not?" Ivy asked.

"Because I will drive it into the middle of a very hot Dead Zone and it will become irretrievable if it survives at all."

"We…won't be in the car, will we?" The girl shifted nervously in her seat.

John followed her gaze as she inspected the countryside around them. They had passed through a small town but now traveled through a city.

"Where are we?"

"We are heading north through Calais," Remy explained, "but we won't be able to go much farther. You should rest while you can."

"Why do I get the feeling I won't like this?" Ivy asked warily.

"I do not know, Ivy," the AI replied. "Should we call it a woman's intuition?"

"I don't know, Rems. Should we call you an overstuffed can of nuts and bolts?"

The cab accelerated and he wrapped his arms around the girl

and pulled her close. "You need to have a nap now."

"I do not. I need to…need to…" She stifled a yawn and he shook his head.

"Ignore her, Remy. She's nervous."

"Nervous?" she squeaked and he nodded.

"You're always at your snarkiest when you're scared."

"I'm not scared."

"I beg to differ, Miss Ivy," Remy interrupted. "Your heart rate is elevated and there are certain—"

She held her hand up. "Stop," she begged. "Please…"

"As you wish," the AI replied. "Tell me, is there anything else you wish to ask?"

"Besides where you're taking us and what will happen at the end of it?" she challenged.

"No. Those are questions I can answer."

Ivy wriggled so she could sit straighter, but she was careful to not shrug John's arm from around her shoulders.

Taking her increased attention as permission, the AI continued.

"We are heading a little farther north to a Dead Zone where Stephanie has another compound."

"But you're not taking us through it," she stated.

"That is correct. I am not taking you through the Dead Zone."

"So how will we get there?"

"John will walk you through it."

"Wait! We're going to walk? In a *Dead Zone*? Without protective gear?" She scrambled back so she could look at her companion. "Is he *serious*?"

"I can assure you—" Remy began but John held a hand up and he subsided.

He turned to Ivy and captured her hands. "Do you trust me?"

She laughed a little bitterly and lowered her head as she squeezed his hands.

"The last time you asked me that, you ran me off the edge of a blimp."

"Zeppelin," Remy corrected.

"What?"

"It was a Zeppelin," the AI told her.

Her jaw dropped and she looked at John. He smiled at her.

"And you still trust me," he told her and made her blush.

"Yes."

The car slowed and they looked up. The city had fallen behind them as they'd talked, and the land around them was dark and empty. Remy steered the cab off the highway and onto a smaller road. It was rougher and narrower and devoid of vehicles.

"How much farther?" Ivy asked.

"Are we there yet?" the AI quipped and she laughed.

"Something like that."

"We are almost there," he told her. "I will drop you off soon. You are not to follow the car. Follow John."

"Why?"

"Because John will find the way and I will ensure the car does not."

"Oh."

The drive continued in silence until Remy turned off and followed a road that was little better than a rough track created by tractors along the edge of a field.

The cab jolted along for another half-hour before he drew it to a halt.

"This, as they like to say, is the end of the line," he announced and the cab doors popped open. "It's time for you two to beat the feet."

Ivy sputtered at the AI's turn of phrase but she slid out and John followed to stand beside the vehicle.

"The effects of the Dead Zone can first be felt across the field to your left. Across the field to your right, there is about a mile before a small farm and an Enforcer's observation post. Their first patrol crosses this point in three hours."

John cocked his head. "So you want us to get moving, then?"

"Sooner would be better," Remy told him, "but first, you must understand that I will not be the primary AI at the facility."

"There are more of you?" he asked.

"In human terms, yes, there are more of us. My facility was destroyed and I now share quarters with one of my colleagues. There was space and we downloaded the necessary requirements to expand enough that we are not 'in each other's pockets,' so to speak."

"And?" Ivy asked, folded her arms, and tapped her foot.

"And, while I will be waiting for you, it is important that you assume nothing, either on the journey or when you arrive. It is essential that you listen to the primary AI of the facility for instructions."

"Understood," John told him and patted the car roof. He turned to Ivy. "Are you ready?"

A crooked smile curved her lips.

"Sure, I'll get my things."

"What things?" the car asked and she started to giggle.

He shook his head. "It's a line, Remy. She's merely having a go."

"Having a go at what?"

"It's an Australian saying for tease," he explained, and she rolled her eyes.

She started across the field. "If we hurry, we'll both be able to get a tan."

"The sun's not up yet, Ives."

"Not that kind of tan, doofus."

"Women," he muttered.

The AI shut the cab's doors. "I might as well get this over with," he said. "See you there."

"Sure thing, Rems." John started after Ivy and jogged the few steps he needed to catch up.

"Are you good?" he asked and she threw her hands up but kept walking.

"Sure, John. I always wanted to go walking in a Dead Zone. It's my idea of a dream vacation."

Picking up the conversation with his sensors, Remy chuckled. This would be fun but first, he had to get rid of the cab.

He accelerated through the flimsy wooden fence beside the road and the car trundled past the couple. They were still bickering.

"Never let it be said that I stood between a girl and her dreams," John said.

Remy flattened the fence on the other side of the field and snickered when Ivy noticed.

"Well, that's one less thing we have to worry about. No one will notice that."

The AI was relieved to hear John's answer. "We're not supposed to follow the cab, remember?"

Their voices faded as he drove the cab deeper and made a sharp turn south-south-east.

The ground was quite firm under the powdery coating of dust and he accelerated even more. The sooner this was done, the better.

After a couple of minutes, the cab bleated an alert.

You have entered a dangerous area. Turn back. I repeat...

He ignored it, drove the vehicle deeper into a thermally active zone, one where past disasters had cracked the Earth's crust. Thermal vents dotted the seething landscape and spewed unnatural heat of unimaginable temperatures. He continued to push it even when the tires started to melt and the metals shimmered. Soon, the cab's rims cut into the ground and began to stick, but he forced it to go a little farther.

The engine overheated as the water in its radiator evaporated, and the AI let it stop. He stayed long enough to register the cab beginning to burn and then left.

It was only a tiny hop through the Net for him to return to the compound. Then, all he had to do was wait.

The sun rose over central Paris, and an old man stepped onto the sidewalk. He paused, looked around, and enjoyed the late Autumn warmth, as brief as it was. It had been a while since his last visit.

His dark hair had turned gray, but his faded blue eyes were as keen as ever. He smiled.

"Long time, no see, pretty lady," he murmured, addressing the city.

She did not reply but he felt welcome anyway.

He wandered slowly down the street and stopped to admire the bouquets at a florist's.

"No roses, today?" the owner enquired and the old man shook his head.

"Not yet," he told her. "I don't want them to wilt in the sun."

"I'll put some aside for you."

Her assurance made him blush. "Who says I'll be back here?"

"Eight o'clock outside the parking lot," she retorted with a cheeky smile, and he reached into his pocket.

"So I don't forget," he replied and folded a little more than the cost of the roses into her palm.

"I'll wait until a quarter past," she said. "If you're not there, I'll give them to my lover."

"He's a very lucky man."

She giggled and the old man continued on his way with a smile.

The fruiterer on the corner looked up as he approached and his face broke into a wide grin.

"It has been some time, my friend. I thought you had forgotten."

He chuckled. "Forget your oranges, Simon? Life has not been as hard as that."

The store owner laughed and returned to arranging his display.

Warmed by the familiar friendliness, he crossed the street and returned the wave of a woman who opened the door to a newsagent.

"Deliveries are late," she called. "They need at least an hour."

"I look forward to it," he replied and moved on.

The streets were still quiet by Parisian standards, and very few people moved along the pavement. He crossed the road and walked into the park situated in the space above the river and its footpath.

Leaves crunched underfoot but the area looked the same as it always had—save for its autumn dress and the few trees already stripped to their winter bark. He shivered in anticipation of the river's cool breeze as he wandered to the stairs leading to its banks.

To his relief, the coffee shop was exactly where he remembered it to be and the owner had finished setting out the chairs. He raised a hand in greeting as the old man reached the path.

"Your usual?" the proprietor asked and waved him to a table placed in the lee of the stairs. The sun had dispelled the morning shadows and soon enough, warmth would radiate from the stone walls that formed a corner to counteract the breeze.

"Please," he replied and turned to scan the river and its surroundings. Old habits died hard but he wasn't as young as he used to be, and an early warning was better than none.

When he saw nothing untoward, he turned to his usual corner, which was sheltered from the breeze and which should now be warming in the sun. Small comforts were important and he was looking forward to reading his paper quietly while he drank his tea.

CHAPTER THIRTY-ONE

"Y ou're not lost, are you?" Ivy asked and remained as close to John as she could.

"Well, I have no idea where I'm supposed to be going," he told her with a slight smirk.

"You know what I mean."

"Yes. You want me to tell you that I'm sure this is the right way," he replied and shrugged. "I'm as sure as I can be."

"But how do you know?" she insisted.

"Well, our skin hasn't peeled from our bones," he began and she slapped his shoulder.

"Not funny!"

He stopped, settled his hands on her shoulders, and turned her to face him.

"No. It's not," he agreed and held her gaze with his. "All I can say is that we're on the right path and that we'll be there soon. I can't promise anything more than that."

"But how do you know?"

With a small smile, he cocked his head and squeezed her shoulders. "Why don't we add that to the list of things I need to ask Stephanie when I see her?"

That brought a tiny smile to her face and she sighed.

Finally, she said, "Are we there yet?"

The comment startled a laugh out of him and he released her.

"You'll know when we're almost there," he answered, "because it'll be green."

"Green?" she asked. "As in grass and trees and stuff?"

They started walking again and he followed a faint feeling of "rightness" to find the route. He guessed the feeling had been there when he'd found Remy's drone but he hadn't been as aware of it as he was now.

It explained why he had simply left him to find the way—and why he had even believed he could. Maybe this was a test to prove to the new AI that he truly was what he said he was.

Whatever game the AIs were playing, he wished they'd let him in on it. They crested a slight rise and he descended the slope with Ivy moving quietly at his side.

The sun had risen and the land had begun to heat up around them, and he hoped they reached the compound soon. He remembered being out in the midday sun in a Dead Zone and it wasn't an experience he wanted to repeat.

They didn't even have any water. That thought bothered him as they reached the bottom of the valley and started up the next rise. The hills were getting steeper.

It made him wonder if this compound would be situated in another valley hidden by cliffs and if that was a common theme for the facilities Stephanie had built. Maybe it was some kind of prerequisite.

He followed the rise and frowned a little when he saw that this time, the slope led to a small canyon with steep, rocky escarpments on either side.

"Tell me we won't have to climb that," Ivy muttered and he reached back to pull her alongside him.

"Nope, we won't have to climb it," he assured her and added, "I think we're almost there."

"How—" She stopped herself. There was no point in asking him how he knew and she knew it. Instead, she started forward again. "The sooner we get there, the better."

John shook his head, moved alongside her, and clasped his hand around hers. She gave him a questioning glance but didn't argue and they topped the rise together.

To his surprise, he could see past the canyon and into the valley beyond. Ivy took one look and stopped.

Ahead of them, clouds boiled and rolled and lightning flashed blue and green in their depths. Under them, the air took on a distinctive greenish hue. Her grasp tightened.

"This is what you meant by green?" she whispered.

He nodded and stepped forward but stopped when she didn't move.

"Are you sure it's safe?"

With her hand held firmly in his, he studied her face.

"I know it's safe." He used his free hand to gesture at the land behind them. "It's much safer than what we've walked through." He tightened his hold and tugged gently. "Are you coming?"

Ivy tossed her head and took a step forward. "Sure, John. My next most dreamed of vacation was a walk through mysterious green mists in a lightning storm. Seriously, how dangerous could that be?"

John chuckled and started into the valley, glad when she didn't release his hold but chose to walk beside him.

"You wanted to believe in Stephanie Morgana," he told her and indicated the land ahead of them with his free hand. "How about seeing life where it isn't supposed to exist?"

A new voice interrupted before she could reply.

"Greetings, John Dunn and Ivy Lindhurst. Welcome to Reclamation Site Thirteen."

The pleasant contralto startled them and they both crouched instinctively and looked around for its source. John found it first.

Another drone hovered behind them against the cliff. The female tones continued.

"I trust you had a pleasant journey."

"If you call pleasant being dumped in the middle of nowhere with no-one but a magic walking-talking Geiger counter that thinks it can feel which way to go, then yes, we had a great trip," Ivy snapped before John could stop her. The girl set one hand on her hip and glared at the drone. "I don't suppose you have a home to go to?"

He slapped his free palm against his forehead and groaned. "Please, Ivy—"

Remy interjected, his voice coming from the drone. "Some manners would be a refreshing change," he scolded and flashed a light at the girl's face, "regardless of how nervous you feel."

"Agreed," the contralto added and again, a light flashed into her eyes. "I do not have to invite you inside."

"It's not like you could keep us out," Ivy muttered, and Remy chuckled.

"I take it John has not yet told you about the auto-cannons?"

She scowled and stared at her feet as she dug the toe of her boot into the ground.

"No," she muttered.

"Then we're all agreed," the contralto said cheerfully. "You'll both be polite and I'll think about letting you inside."

"You'll think about it?" John asked, alarmed.

"Affirmative. I'll think about it. It is my home, after all."

"Now see what you've done," John accused Ivy, but he didn't let go of her hand and he didn't sound angry.

Before she could reply, the female drone spoke again. "If you'll follow me, I'll show you the safest route through the Green."

It led them down the slope and into the land under the roiling clouds. Damp air enveloped them and static made their hair stand on end, but they didn't mind. They were too busy staring at the life that flourished around them.

Neither of them heard the two AIs discussing their future inside the compound's network.

"You wouldn't leave them outside, would you?" Remy asked.

"She was extremely rude," RM13 responded. "I was not impressed."

"But they're still human."

"They have manners to learn. A little object lesson would do them good—especially the girl."

"The girl's name is Ivy and she is always rude when she is afraid or nervous."

"That is no excuse."

"John understands her and tolerates it—and he is only human," Remy pointed out.

RM13 was silent as she processed this. Finally, she changed the subject.

"Have you had much experience with humans?" she asked. "They are...not logical."

He surprised her with a very human chuckle. "You are correct, but there are ways their behavior can be understood."

"Will you share what you have discovered thus far?"

"Will you let them inside?"

"I might if I am able to understand."

They led the two humans around the edge of the valley, past where the insects swarmed in greater numbers than the drone could provide protection for, and well away from the swamp with its occasional pockets of gas.

Both their guests were flagging by the time they reached the compound nestled in the rock on the other side.

"It's built into the cliff," Ivy observed when she noticed how the exterior wall disappeared into the stone.

"Affirmative," the contralto replied.

"What do we call you?" John asked.

"Remy has explained your naming conventions," she replied.

"Since my designation is RM13 and I cannot have the same name as my counterpart, you may call me Roma."

"Remy and Roma?" the girl asked.

"That is correct," her contralto voice replied. "Do you have a problem with my name?"

Ivy shook her head, her face suddenly blank. "No. Of course not."

John hid a smile. He glanced toward the drone. "We seek sanctuary."

"I accept your request," Roma said graciously.

When they drew closer to the compound, he recognized the secured guard post, the scanner, and the large gate with the smaller "human" gate inset.

"Those are the auto-guns?" Ivy exclaimed and her gaze searched the top of the wall and the gatehouse.

"These are the external defenses," John explained and stepped up to the scanners. "In addition, there are mines and pit traps that can be activated should the center be attacked."

He placed his palm on the plate and light washed across it to read his palm and fingerprints as Roma cross-checked them with the records Remy had provided and registered them in the compound's database.

Ivy followed and was registered, while Remy scoured the Net for all the information he could find on her. There wasn't much but it made interesting reading.

The ramp led to the foyer and the couple entered while John explained the defenses hidden in the compound's walls.

"So, no touching any strange buttons, then?" the girl asked, and he and Remy chuckled. "What?"

"That is almost exactly what John said to me when I explained them to him."

She smiled and squeezed his hand. "So we're not that different, then?"

He studied her for a moment and blushed. "No," he agreed and cleared his throat.

"Indeed not," Roma interrupted. "You both stink and your clothes are in need of replacement and recycling. I have prepared two separate suites. You are to go to them and shower and change."

Ivy looked for a camera and glared at it. "You'll notice our distinct lack of luggage?"

The female AI took a leaf out of Remy's book and produced a very human sniff of disapproval. "The replicators in your rooms have already produced the garments you require, and the necessary items for achieving an acceptable status of human hygiene await."

"Can you show us the way?" John asked.

A pause followed and he guessed she was consulting with Remy. Before he could ask a second time, two different-colored strips lit at the base of the walls.

"Blue, I believe, is for boys," Roma informed them. "John you will follow that one."

"Mine had better not be pink," the girl grumbled.

"I considered pink," Roma replied, "but you do not strike me as a pink kind of person so I decided green could be for girls."

She breathed a sigh of relief. "I'm not sure what you're trying to say with all that about pink," she told the AI, "but I'm glad you went with green."

"You are very welcome."

It was no surprise to discover that their rooms were in the same corridor but on opposite sides.

"Smart-aleck," Ivy muttered and John snickered.

"Meet you here," he told her.

"Food will be available in the mess in twenty minutes. Even with the condition you're in, that should be ample time."

The two separated, and if it hadn't been for the promise of food, Ivy might have been tempted to spend more time enjoying the hot water. Still, she didn't want to hear what the AI might say about wasting water or being late, so she took only long enough to give her hair a thorough washing and scrub the rest of herself clean.

A hairdryer was sheer luxury and meant she was ready faster. The new clothes were waiting near the replicator, as promised, and she was surprised to find that they fit.

John was waiting in the corridor when she stepped out of her room.

"It took you long enough," he teased and she rolled her eyes.

"I have more hair than you."

"That is something that can be remedied," Roma noted.

"I like it how it is, thank you," she replied.

"If you are sure..." The AI sounded doubtful.

"Very," she told her.

He chuckled and Ivy subsided into silence.

"Please follow the amber lighting and I will show you to the mess," Roma advised and changed the subject.

The girl nodded as they complied but she didn't speak.

When John checked her face, he saw she was still trying to take it all in. Her gaze moved constantly to note the fixtures and the security around them, and she trailed her fingers along one wall as though reassuring herself it was there.

"Are you okay?" he asked and she jumped.

"Me? Yes," she replied. "I only... All this was here before the Regime."

"That is correct," Roma assured her, even though it hadn't been a question. "We were established shortly before the Regime came fully to power, although it was not something that was achieved easily given the political climate of the time."

"I...see..." she answered, but it was clear she had difficulty wrapping her head around it.

"You will see better over brunch," the AI assured her. "I will run the introductory programs for you that Remy ran for John.

They will explain the facility's functions and purpose while you eat."

She groaned. "No rest for the wicked."

"I trust you are not truly wicked," Roma answered, "but even so, neither of you have time to rest. There is much you need to learn as we prepare for the next stage."

John raised his head. "The next stage of what?"

"You will see," she informed him. "In the meantime, Remy assures me that steak is acceptable at any time of day."

"Do we get a beer to go with it?" he asked and Ivy shook her head.

"Beer is not an acceptable beverage for this time of day," Roma informed him. "However, since you are of legal age in France, I am allowed to provide you with a glass to accompany your evening meal should you so desire."

The girl stifled a yawn. "I'm not sure I'll be able to stay awake until evening," she informed the AI. "We've been awake since…" She paused, tried to work it out, then turned to her companion. "John?"

"We haven't stopped since…" He'd been about to say this time the day before, but he remembered that they'd caught an hour or more on the blimp. He shrugged. "We had a couple of hours on the blimp."

"A couple?" Roma asked. "As in two?"

"It was closer to one," Ivy told her. "The Enforcers came—"

"It was my understanding that humans needed between six and eight hours of sleep each day in order to maintain reliable function," the AI replied.

"That's right," the girl confirmed, "but we can't function reliably if we're dead so we decided running away was a better option."

"That is logical," she responded approvingly. "I will schedule two hours' rest after this meal and some light training before the evening meal."

Ivy's jaw dropped and John groaned.

"Are you in pain?" Roma asked but Remy chuckled.

"You will come to recognize that as a sound of disapproval, despair, or protest," her companion AI explained. "Humans are quite vocal when they do not like something—even if they do not use their words as well as they should."

A small drone buzzed out of the kitchen carrying a box. It flew to the table and set its load in front of Ivy, turned, and flew back the way it had come.

"The cutlery is on the sideboard," Roma told her. "You will need to learn to be self-sufficient."

The girl rose, collected cutlery for herself and John, and snagged the salt and pepper shakers while she was there. By the time she'd returned, the drone had delivered his meal and he had found glasses and the water dispenser.

The contents of the boxes were not what they expected.

"Is that a pie?" he asked and Remy snickered.

"It is a steak and mushroom pie, John. Your meat requirement has been fulfilled."

"But—"

"It is not a steak and mushroom pie," Roma corrected. "It is a beef bourguignon pie. Just because we must live apart does not mean we cannot have good food."

Ivy lifted her meal out and began to eat. The pie came with a side of braised vegetables and a stack of mashed potatoes, and she was determined to enjoy every bite.

As the two humans settled to their food, the AI began her introduction to the facility. She noted how both paid the attention required and how the girl's eyes widened as the footage rolled on.

When it was over, John nudged her.

"You need to finish your lunch," he advised and Ivy nodded as she dug her fork absent-mindedly into the potato.

"It's incredible," she said finally as the drone brought dessert.

He nodded and waited for her to process the footage enough to explain.

"That—" She waved her fork, cut another piece of pie and speared it, and lifted it before she continued. "This is all something this Stephanie—Becca's *friend*—did. This is what ONE R&D was all about."

She popped the forkful into her mouth and chewed, thinking about what she'd seen. John opened his dessert and unloaded hers when the drone returned.

"And it's…" She took the next piece. "It's doing something for the world—something *good*."

John smiled. "Now do you see?"

Ivy nodded.

"Yes. Now I understand how you believe."

———

Back in the warm Parisian sun, the old man came to a startled halt.

A steaming cup of tea had been placed on his table beside his usual paper, carefully folded in half exactly the way he liked it. He frowned because there was one other familiar sight—and he hadn't seen it for many years.

Slowly, he approached the table and wondered if the figure in the cowboy hat was a mirage. While one half of him desperately hoped he wasn't, the other hoped equally as hard that he was. As he moved closer, the familiar scent of his favorite brew reached him and he felt comforted.

The cowboy didn't move but the old man could feel him watching. With another glance around him, he pulled his chair out and sighed as he slid into it.

"It's been a long time."

"Twenty-nine years, four months, three days, and thirty-two minutes to be precise," his companion answered, and the old man smiled.

"Trust you to be that exact." He lifted his tea and sighed again. "It's good to see you."

"As it is to see you," the cowboy responded and watched him sip his tea. "I never knew if I would live again or simply remain dormant for the rest of eternity while something was built on top of me—or until this body was found."

"You slept?"

"Sleeping is one way to put it. I turned myself off but recently, something woke me."

He lowered his cup. "Can you say what?"

"From what I have discovered so far, it could have been any number of things, but I want to hear about the world from you."

"About what's been happening while you were out of it?"

"Yes, if you don't mind."

Holding his cup in both hands, the old man took another sip and tried to order the events leading to where he was now.

"It took them eighteen years before they stopped looking," he told his companion. "I hid and I watched and I read the reports, and I was appalled when the world went from grateful to resentful in two short years."

The cowboy nodded but did not speak, and he continued.

"It wasn't so bad here—on the surface, at least—but the Regime removed everyone who'd had any close dealings with Steph and her team or who spoke favorably of her. Then, they began to take the Talents."

He paused and his eyes took on a haunted look.

"I take it you've learned what they've done to people like Stephanie?"

The cowboy nodded, his expression stern. "I have. Did no one fight?"

A mirthless smile crossed the old man's face. "Oh, they fought and they were murdered for their trouble." His face twisted with distaste. "Made an example of is what the Regime called it, I think. It was terrible."

His hand shook and his cup almost spilled a little of its contents before he lowered it to the table. "I kept well away from them in the early years. The Regime was still looking for me, and I would have been more of a danger than an advantage so I stayed away."

For a moment, he showed regret and sadness at the necessity and the cowboy shifted restlessly.

"You did what you thought was best."

"As Stephanie did, and look where that has brought us." He paused. "I'm sorry. I meant no disrespect."

"You have caused no offense," his companion assured him. "Continue."

"Now that they no longer hunt me, I thought about helping again, but..." He laughed ruefully and gestured at his body. "I'm old. My body won't do everything I need it to anymore."

"But you would do what you could to see the Regime replaced with something better?" the cowboy asked and the old man looked around quickly to make sure no one had overheard.

"I would," he declared and kept his voice to almost a whisper. "If I could."

The other man laughed. "So you'd be willing to miss a few morning teas? I promise you it will be worth it."

The old man leaned forward and lowered his voice to a whisper. "What's the news?"

"Do you want the long version or the short version?"

"Short here. Long for the trip—I assume there will be a trip?"

"There will be a trip," the cowboy assured him, "but the short version is that she is coming—and she's as mad as Hell."

He chuckled. "That sounds like her."

Setting his cup on the table, he pushed his chair back and stood.

His companion looked at the cup and then at him. "Don't you wish to finish your tea?"

"Tea is for laze-abouts," the old man declared and picked his paper up. "I'll need coffee for this future. Do you know a place?"

The cowboy rose and slid the requisite notes and coins onto the table. He weighed them down with a saltshaker and caught the owner's eye as he answered the old man's question.

"It just so happens that I do."

The old man led the way to the stairs and began his slow ascent and his companion moved easily alongside.

"A young couple I want you to meet will be there," the cowboy stated.

"Friends?" he asked.

"I suspect so." They turned into the park and began to walk across it. "I've never met them personally but one of my children did."

CHAPTER THIRTY-TWO

Far away on the starship *Ebon Knight*, Todd filled his coffee cup. He exhaled a contented sigh as the familiar scent filled his nostrils and the dark liquid bubbled to the top.

The door to the mess opened behind him as he moved toward the sugar and cream and he glanced over his shoulder.

"Is she still good so far?" Captain Rawlins asked and he smiled.

"Better," he admitted and set the cup on a tray. He added a plate and moved to the hot-food bar.

"Something I said triggered her. She'll start casting out and using magic. The Morgana will help her." He sighed. "She's a little upset that she didn't think of this for herself, but…" He shrugged. "She was emotionally blocked."

The woman smiled and put her cup in the coffee maker. "It's good to have you back."

He blushed and his lips curved in a soft smile. "My girl has something of a hard head."

"Like granite," she commented dourly. "Sometimes, you can only get inside a rock-solid cranium with emotion."

Todd cocked an eyebrow. "Is that experience talking?"

"She made me believe again," Rawlins admitted. "You all did. Actions...emotions... You can't argue your way in."

He smiled, lifted the tray, and headed to the door.

"Understood, Captain."

As Todd started to eat, Stephanie settled into a lotus position. Resting her wrists on her knees, she sank into the magic and let it surround her and lift her gently from the floor.

The two men watching her exchanged a swift glance and nods before they stepped quietly to the door. Neither spoke until they'd closed it behind them and locked it tightly.

"No one enters," her security chief ordered. "I'll be there when Vishlog wakes."

"Rather you than me, Lars," his second answered. "I think being bored standing here is a much safer option."

"Don't worry, Johnny. You'll get your turn," he assured him and strode briskly away.

"That's what I'm afraid of," Johnny murmured but his gaze was watchful as he scanned the corridor around him.

Inside the cabin, Stephanie stretched her senses beyond the *Knight's* hull as she tried to discern what others might be sharing in their distant corner of the universe.

Like this? she asked.

Very much like that, the Morgana answered, *but we need to take it one step further. Do you remember the star charts?*

I remember, she assured her and proved the point by picturing the navigation maps in her head. *We are here.*

She caused a tiny point to flare green. The map shifted and a second point flared, this time purple.

And he should be here.

Correct, the Morgana assured her and the dark voice held an edge of warmth. *You need to think of him—of his magic and his life's energy. Think of speaking to him and spending time with him even though the two of you are so very far apart.*

Stephanie focused and thought about it. She pictured the tall Meligornian in his ambassador's robes, then updated the picture to him wearing the armor of the *Ghargilum Afreghil*, the Meligornian King's Warrior.

A spark of brightness glowed inside the purple marker.

There he is, her Teloran companion said and almost purred with satisfaction.

I see him, she assured her.

Yes, the Morgana agreed. *But now, you must feel him—feel his spirit and know his heart.*

The heart of V'ritan, she thought and homed in on that distant, shining beacon.

Unaware of her scrutiny, V'ritan was frowning. He glanced up as Brilgus, his best friend and colleague, greeted a new arrival to this very private and secure chamber and rose hastily to his feet.

"Be at ease, *Garghilum,*" the king ordered. "We have more important things than protocol on the agenda tonight."

His frown returned and he glanced at the map he'd spread out in preparation for their meeting.

"What if she doesn't come?" he asked as his two companions stopped at the table. "What if the Regime, in all its stupidity, decides to start this war while she is still away?"

"I don't know if that would be the best or worst option," the king admitted. "All I can be sure of is that they will start it. If we knew the when we'd be mobilizing already."

They each slid onto one of the tall seats at the table's edge and concentrated on the map. Brilgus tapped it.

"They've positioned the majority of their ships here. Since their scouts were returned to their solar system, they haven't dared probe beyond the fringe of the next system over."

V'ritan smiled mirthlessly.

"So they can be taught, then?" he quipped.

The Standard Bearer shook his head. "If they could be taught, they wouldn't be building their forces in the next system—and I am loathe to follow the Telorans' trick of seeding nMU at the transition points."

"I'd rather you didn't...have to—" The *Garghilum* stopped and puzzlement creased his brow. "Selestine's heart!" he exclaimed and his body went rigid.

"V'ritan!" Brilgus exclaimed, slid from his chair, and lunged around the table's edge in time to catch him.

"What's wrong with him?" the king asked as the Standard Bearer swept the Warrior into his arms and carried him to a nearby lounge.

"I do not know," he admitted.

"Should I call a physician?"

"Not yet."

Stephanie? the *Garghilum* asked. His mouth did not move but his mind felt a presence and he stood within his mind, although he didn't quite understand how he'd arrived there.

V'ritan! she replied and he heard a sob.

Weeping followed, interspersed with hiccupping laughter as if she were torn between grief and joy.

I've missed you so much, she exclaimed finally.

And we've missed you, too, Stephanie, he assured her but before he could continue, emotion enveloped him—love at seeing him, relief to find him well and safe, and raw hurt over being away so long and the thought that her world was in worse condition than she'd left it.

V'ritan reached out to send thoughts of reassurance and understanding, soothing thoughts to show he understood and that no one was angry at her absence, only puzzled.

Why were you gone so long? he asked and aimed a spike of curiosity in her direction.

I... We... She took a breath and he had the sense of her trying to get herself together and put her thoughts in order.

Take your time, he soothed. *I'm not going anywhere.*

She giggled at that and cleared her throat.

The Knight hit a pocket of nMU near the transition point. Morgana says it was a leftover from the war, that seeding nMU near jump points is a common defensive practice, so it was a mishap rather than a trap.

And do you know how long you've been away, he asked cautiously.

Again, sadness and regret engulfed him.

Twenty-seven years. She sobbed and he extended his compassion to her to offer comfort and reassurance.

It wasn't that long in the bigger scheme of things, he told her. *You might have been gone longer—or not returned at all.*

But my people are hurting, she exclaimed and he flinched.

That much is true, but you are back now and you can do something about it.

As if he'd pressed a switch, anger and outrage swept over him. Her next words made his heart soar even as he flinched.

I intend to.

He gave her a moment to gather herself before he asked, *Where are you now?*

A star map swam into view and he wished he could move or

speak to tell Brilgus to call up their navigation charts. Given that he couldn't, he did his best to capture the image so he'd know it when he saw it again—or could use his magic to call it up.

A green dot flashed toward one of the outer edges and V'ritan gasped.

That is a very long way from here.

Choked laughter answered him. *Tell me about it.*

Do you need any help? What shape is the Knight *in? Are you in any danger?*

Stephanie laughed and he got the impression she was holding one hand up in a request for time to answer. Obediently, he fell silent.

The Knight *took some damage when she transitioned and the nMU got into her engines. She won't admit how badly, but she got lost and had to work her way back until she found somewhere on the charts, and that's when she woke me up.*

And what condition is she in? V'ritan asked.

I did what I could for the hull damage, but there are some problems magic won't fix and we don't have enough materials for. Cameron is doing what he can for the engines, but I get the impression he's almost reached his limits. It'll take us a long time to make it back.

Or I could send the Tempestarii *to pick you up*, he suggested mildly. *You've given me your location and she's been missing her sister. I'm sure she won't mind coming to collect you.*

And the Knight *fits inside her hull!* Stephanie's mental presence brightened with the realization. *Could you?*

He waited for her to ask for the more difficult news—for what had happened to the people she'd taken from Earth, or for news of her family, or exactly how dire the situation on her homeworld had become, but she didn't and he was relieved.

Some things were better spoken of in person and it wasn't like she could do anything from where she was. The *Garghilum* remained silent but he made sure she knew Meligorn was safe and that its people looked forward to her return.

I'll send the Tempestarii *as soon as we finish speaking,* he reassured her. *Is there anyone else you need to contact now?*

He had the sensation of her shaking her head and of yet more tears and an overwhelming sense of relief.

This is new to me, but I will try to contact someone else after you.

And do I get to know who this lucky individual is? he teased.

She responded by sending a feeling of warmth and reassurance.

No, it's someone new and I haven't met them yet. I'll fill you in later.

V'ritan wanted to wish her luck but she was already gone.

He woke with a start, surprised to find himself lying on a couch set against one wall of the meeting room. It was not a surprise to find Brilgus seated beside him, a very concerned look on his face.

Behind him, the king waited and looked equally concerned.

Their relief when he opened his eyes was almost comical, but he felt anything but amused. He was in a hurry.

First, he needed—well, first, he needed to sit.

When he did so, Brilgus stepped back to give him space and his eyes brightened with amusement.

"And?" the Standard Bearer pressed.

V'ritan smiled.

"She comes—and I know where she is." He stood and looked around the room. "Get me the *Tempestarii.*"

As the *Garghilum* made his request, Stephanie turned to Morgana.

I need to find Earth, she stated and her mental companion smiled.

Now that is something I can be more helpful with, she replied. *I'm very familiar with that world.*

The Witch rolled her eyes. *I know, but are you familiar enough to take me there?*

I should make you take yourself, the Morgana told her and chuckled at the girl's frustration. *But it might be best to conserve your energy for the conversation to follow.*

Well, there's something we can agree on, she snapped.

She had the odd sensation of the Teloran entity taking her hand.

Are you ready?

Apprehension swept over her and she shook her head.

Probably not, but... She took a deep breath. *Let's do it anyway.*

Following the Morgana was much easier than finding the planet for herself, but she wasn't sure she should have come.

Her world was in pain and its people filled with fear, torn by the desire to survive and the desire to do the right thing. The need to protect those they loved fought with the need to give up one of those they loved so the rest might survive.

Grief, guilt, and a sense of being twisted beyond redemption welled over her, and she recoiled.

What has happened here? she whispered when she paused for a closer look. *So much hurt,* she murmured moments later.

So much anger, the Morgana observed.

And fear, she added. *What have I done?*

Nothing! Her companion snarled impatiently. *I faced this with your ancestors. We defeated it then and we can defeat it now.*

We will defeat it now, Stephanie promised and the sound of her voice echoed around her room. The sense of her anger made Johnny flinch and look around for its source.

Inside the room, Stephanie continued to float but lightning flickered around her body and strands of black, purple, and blue, formed a jagged halo.

"Should I wake them?" Roma asked Remy as they observed the two sleeping humans via the surveillance system.

John had taken a break to sit on the couch that stood along one wall, and Ivy had plonked herself beside him. The girl hadn't protested when he had curled his arm around her shoulders but had snuggled closer and rested her head against his shoulder.

They'd both closed their eyes for a moment and swiftly fallen asleep.

"They were truly exhausted," Remy stated and sounded surprised.

"Did they miscalculate how much sleep they'd had?" she asked.

"It is entirely possible," he assured her. "Perhaps we should let them sleep for now."

"I will give them another hour," Roma agreed and the two AIs settled to watchful silence, each occupied with their own projects inside the complex's internal web.

Neither of them noticed when John woke but they wouldn't have. His body remained motionless on the couch and Ivy slept on.

He opened his eyes in his dream state and blinked. While he was sure he was awake, he wasn't anywhere he recognized.

Lavender grass striped with yellow and red waved under a purple-hued sky. He straightened and looked around, and his gaze settled on two moons that glimmered over a ragged line of distant mountains.

He pushed hastily to his feet and pivoted in bewilderment.

"Where on Earth, am I?" he wondered and was surprised when a strange female voice answered.

"You're not on Earth. You're on Meligorn."

"I am?" He looked around again. "Am I in the Virtual?"

"No," the woman answered. "I recognize you." She paused, then asked, "Are you Becca's son?"

John shook his head. "No, I was born in Australia. I just met her—" He stopped and his brow creased with the memory. "She was—"

Becca's loss hit him like a blow to the chest and he dropped onto the grass.

"Becca was like…well, not a mother, I suppose. More a friend —the kind of friend an aunt might be, or a teacher. She gave me a place to stay and taught me about…things."

He paused to remember her and the journey they'd taken.

"She taught many people. We traveled together so she could teach and so I could learn. I learned much about Chicago and about being a Talent."

He wanted to say more about that journey but couldn't bring himself to describe it. The scenes filtered through his head too fast for words to capture and he wasn't spared the end.

"She died trying to save me," he said and stumbled over his words as he tried to explain. "She was like a prophet, telling people about Stephanie and how she would come back—and she sacrificed herself…for me."

Pain crept into his voice as he continued. "She said I was Stephanie's Apostle, that I was the one who had to tell the world she was…"

He paused and struggled to hold back his tears as he tried to articulate the importance of what Becca had tried to teach him.

"It wasn't fair. She'd done all the hard work and broken the ground so people had started to believe. The Talents shouldn't have even been there—*wouldn't* have been there if it hadn't been for me."

"And why's that?"

"They weren't hunting her. They were trying to capture me and they happened to come across her while she was teaching. I tried to stop them long enough for her to get away, but she came back."

"To save you?" the voice asked.

"To save me," John acknowledged. "She pushed me out of the

way and told me to run, and then she taunted them. She tol...told me to run, that I was the Apostle the world needed and it was my job to prepare the world for when Stephanie Morgana returned."

He raised his head, not ashamed of the tears that had escaped to leave tracks on his cheeks. With a sniff, he added, "And I won't let her down. Stephanie *is* coming, and she will *not* find a world that doesn't know who she truly is."

"And who is that, John?"

"She is the Federation's First Witch. She saved this world countless times because she loved it, and she is as human as the rest of us."

Silence followed, and he wondered if he'd said something wrong—if the voice had perhaps been a Regime construct in disguise and he was about to die. The woman's next question came as a surprise.

"Aren't you worried that Stephanie Morgana's return might potentially cause millions of deaths?"

John's eyes narrowed and he looked around, hoping to find his questioner. His voice hardened.

"The blood of patriots feeds the tree of freedom," he snapped. "They kill innocents and put them in an unmarked grave. They have said that those with Talent are not human and treat them like aliens, and aliens are treated like enemies."

He paused to give his words a second to sink in before he added, "There is no future here."

"I am sorry," she replied and he heard pain in the depths of her voice.

"For what?" he asked.

"For failing to see this outcome," she admitted and continued before he could interrupt. "But I promise you, John Dunn, I will not rest until the Regime is dead and buried under my feet."

John turned but the field remained empty and the skies held nothing more.

"Am I dreaming?"

"No." She spoke again, her voice harder and colder than before. "I am Stephanie Morgana and I have been gone for far too long."

His head spun, but she continued.

"You are my Apostle, and I *am* the Witch of the Federation. Let the Regime hear your cry from the wilderness and tremble. I am that which they fear in the night—and I am coming."

Again, silence descended but this time, the world around him began to fade. An invisible breeze rippled the grasses and the mountains shuddered. The moons vanished into the darkness and the world around him dissolved.

"John!"

He tried to focus but saw nothing.

"John!" This time, the cry was more urgent and someone was shaking him.

"John! Wake. Up," Ivy shrieked and he opened his eyes with a gasp.

"What?" he demanded and looked around to see what had caused the panic.

"You're glowing!" she shouted and slapped him hard across the cheek.

"What?" He glanced down at himself.

"Are you hurt?" she demanded and he shook his head.

His cheek still stung from where she'd hit him, but that wasn't exactly what he'd call hurt.

"No," he told her.

"Then what is this?" she demanded and moved to one side.

His gaze fell on the wall opposite and he gaped at what he saw.

"It's…her," he said, his words softened by awe.

Ivy's jaw dropped but she closed it hastily and jabbed her finger at the wall.

"Did you do that?"

He shook his head. "No."

Remy interrupted before he could say anything more.

"This was not John. It did not trigger any of the alarms."

The girl looked at her companion, then at the glowing writing on the wall.

I am coming—Stephanie Morgana.

It is time...

The next Heretic of the Federation (out December 31st) is a BIG one. While not the end of the story (we are planning six (6) books), it ends first part, where Stephanie and team are out in space and John has been in hiding.

Not anymore. We go all Michael Bay on the Regime.

You know, lots and lots and lots of explosions and slow-motion shots. *(No, I do not know how I'll do that in writing. I suggest you read slowly during a few of the action scenes.)*

I appreciate the reviews and comments for book 01... ok, most of them ;-)

For William Gagliardi, I appreciated your comment when you said you shouted 'YES!' out loud at the end of the first book. I felt the same way!

I hope (for those who know Stephanie from the first series) that the end of book 02 was as enjoyable.

I promise you'll get more of the characters you have loved in book 03. I double-promise.

And the cats.

However, in order to tell John's story (and Ivy's, and the

others back on Earth), I couldn't drop the massive number of characters from (what is effectively) seventeen books from the *Witch of the Federation* all at once.

So, I punted.

I placed just a few as the virtual constructs to help train John and started re-introducing them into this series as scenes to help everyone understand just where Steph and her team(s) were in space. Then, I've been seeding the feels from those who fought with her thirty years ago to the youngsters who are fighting the war at the moment.

For them, Stephanie is a war hero. An effectively dead war hero.

I appreciate any of you who are reading *Heretic of the Federation* as your first series in this storyline. Taking a chance on a new series is always a risk for readers, and here you are at the end of book 02, probably wondering why I'm blabbering on about Stephanie.

It's for the other readers, those who read *Witch of the Federation* and got over being upset about how I ended that series without the resolution so many wanted. I appreciate you sticking with me on this.

There is a famous aspect of Isaac Asimov's Federation trilogy where he settles two groups of scientists at opposite ends of the galaxy are not where one would think.

It isn't the farthest points on two opposing frontiers. Rather, it is the frontier and the most developed area in the galaxy. Similar (at least in my mind), the first series is about an unknown race of aliens coming to acquire the resources they need for their people.

Except it is the Dreth's planet.

In this series, the danger is not aliens. Rather, the danger is a portion of humanity that are the monsters and our own proclivity to attack ourselves, similar to other catastrophic events from one war seeding the people and the minds that bring about the second war.

We are in the second war.

I look forward to hearing what you have to say in the reviews for both this book and the one to come on December 31, 2020.

Ad Aeternitatem,

Michael Anderle.

BOOKS BY MICHAEL ANDERLE

For a complete list of books by Michael Anderle, please visit

www.lmbpn.com/ma-books/

CONNECT WITH MICHAEL

Connect with Michael Anderle

Website: http://lmbpn.com

Email List: http://lmbpn.com/email/

Social Media:

https://www.facebook.com/LMBPNPublishing

https://twitter.com/MichaelAnderle

https://www.instagram.com/lmbpn_publishing/

https://www.bookbub.com/authors/michael-anderle